THE QUEEN & THE KING

**BOOK THREE
IN THE
LOVE & FATE
SERIES
BY
JEANETTE ROSE & ALEXIS RUNE**

ROSE & STAR PUBLISHING

Cover Design by Fae Lane
Editing by Aisling Mackay

*To Every Reader Who Ever Felt Forced
To Hide Their Lethal Thorns
Underneath Pretty Petals*

This book is significantly different than the previous two and explores some potentially triggering themes.

A list of content warnings can be found on the Rose & Star website and listed on both Alexis[1] & Jeanette's[2] instagrams.

1   @authalexisrune
2   @fatedloves

Chapter One

Hades

MY HANDS. *MY USELESS FUCKING HANDS.* I close and open my fists repeatedly. Useless. My power is rising in me, a flood of darkness, and I don't have the will to beat it back. Why bother? I could have all the power of the Underworld, and it would change nothing. My completely healed wings are lying useless on either side of me. The chill slides over me as icy despondency creeps in, detaching me from my emotions and body. I shiver and stare at the unmarred, leathery webbing of my wings, hating the sight of them. They're the reason she's gone. Was it worth it? No. I would have rather died, but since I didn't, Persephone is now in the hands of her wicked mother. With that thought, a new emotion starts to eclipse the never-ending void growing inside me.

Wrath.

I slam my fist against the marble floor, watching as it cracks beneath me. Once isn't enough, and my fist slams into it over and over. My knuckles split and heal, the palace fixing the floor between each assault. The slight bite of pain keeps me focused, the anger brewing and growing until it consumes me.

She made a mistake leaving me alive, and she would pay dearly for it.

The darkness hums inside me, and I welcome it. It wraps around me, stoking my fury into an inferno, and the Underworld responds to its king's will. Black clouds billow across the realm, heading toward the palace. I stand, my body coiled tight with anger. The darkness sweeps closer, and its proximity resonates inside me, feeding on the black rage boiling through me.

She wants a war? I'll fucking give her one. I am the King of the fucking Underworld, and she thought to cross me? Me?!

"Morpheus!" I roar, all the rage vibrating inside me, reverberating off the walls.

The God of Dreams forms next to me, bowing slightly, his inky hair falling into his fathomless eyes.

"Your Majesty," he whispers, the echoes of a forgotten dream lingering in his voice.

"The queen has been taken."

My queen.

My Persephone.

Morpheus straightens, his expression unchanged. No visible signs of shock at the news or even dismay. Not that I expected either from him. There is little that elicits a reaction from this particular son of Nyx.

"Melinoë!" I shout.

The Goddess of Nightmares appears with a frown, her arms crossed. I doubt she's happy that I summoned her in such a way. All gods who call the Underworld home can be forced into my presence if I so choose. In the past, I rarely used that power unless I had no choice. But that was before.

"Persephone's been taken," I repeat, watching as the scars on one side of Melinoë's face darken with her anger. Her mismatched eyes spark, and any anger aimed at me by my summoning is immediately redirected.

Morpheus shifts away from Mellie, undoubtedly his skin crawling at her presence. She feels *wrong* to him. She should be under his dominion as the Lord of Dreams, yet she exists apart—something the younger goddess loves to remind the oldest of the Oneiroi of.

"I understand your distress, my king. What I do not understand is why you need me," Morpheus adds, his tone flat.

The darkness surrounds the palace, pressing over the windows and blotting out the light. Mellie looks out, her brows drawing slightly in concern.

I roll my shoulders. "She's been taken to Olympus."

The palace responds to the darkness, lights flickering to life inside, attempting to combat my abilities.

Mellie hisses, her one black eye flashing.

"And you cannot follow," Morpheus provides. Even if it wasn't almost time for my six months in the Underworld, he knows that Olympus is not a place I can tread easily.

The darkness presses in on me, eager to take control. I push it back but allow it to build. When the time is right, I will unleash the death blow. Until then, I'm going to savor this power coiling inside me like a viper. I will sink my fangs into the throat of my enemy and drown myself in their blood.

"Her mother has taken the power of Gaia and used it to snap our bond," I snarl, barely leashing the anger inside me.

"That's not possible," Melinoë growls harshly, sounding more animalistic than a moment before. The careful tightrope she walks between lucidity and insanity is being affected by my power. I'm not merely pushing her balance one way. I'm cutting the rope she stands on. Normally, I'd be horrified at this, but right now, I want more. I want her unleashed. I need the Mellie ready to rip out throats—the unstable one.

"I need to speak with her, and there is only one way I can," I continue.

Morpheus's fathomless eyes blink, and he takes a short breath as he realizes what I mean. "You want to dreamwalk."

I nod, my jaw tight.

Mellie takes a step back, her head moving side to side slightly, almost out of sync. The voices in her head are no doubt shouting.

"You could never wake up," she hisses, moving farther away with each word.

I lock eyes with her. "I am aware."

It is worth the risk to see her, to talk to her.

"There must be another way," she insists, still backing away from me.

I look between the two gods. "I need someone to put me under and another to pull me out."

Dreamwalking is not like speaking to Persephone through her dreams, like when I was trapped. Not only were we in the same physical realm, but our bond made it easy to connect. The bond Demeter snapped. My stomach rolls when I reach out for her familiar warmth, but instead, I find nothing but cold, aching loneliness.

"I'll need time to prepare," Morpheus states.

Mellie backs almost into the wall. "No. We're not doing this. The risk is too great."

I close the distance, grabbing Mellie's shoulders. "Please." I press my forehead to hers. "I have never asked you for anything, but I need her."

She frowns. "I understand that, Hades. But this realm needs you. We need to exhaust other avenues before we jump into something so... dangerous."

I pull back, grinding my teeth. "What other avenues?"

"We find out what's happening on Olympus."

Morpheus scoffs. Again, the only emotion he ever shows is when it involves Melinoë. "You think they'll open their golden gates to you?"

Mellie snarls at him, "Do not condescend to me, Morpheus. Take your bitch ass insecurities and back the fuck up."

Morpheus just blinks at her in shock, his mouth slightly open. He clearly wasn't expecting that from the Goddess of Nightmares.

I growl, "You want to send your boyfriend to Olympus?"

Mellie growls back at me, "Not my boyfriend. But yes. Helios could go on a little scouting mission."

I look between the two of them. "You have one day."

Both gods vanish from my sight, leaving me achingly alone. Alone with nothing else to do but feed this growing anger, this growing darkness, until it could reach through to the tallest part of Olympus and rip the Goddess of Harvest in two.

Chapter Two
Hades

ALONE THE DARKNESS STARTS TO PRESS IN ON *ME.* I look at the bed with its sheets still tossed from our bodies hours before. I take a small step closer and reach for her pillow. Lifting it to my nose, I bury my face in it.

With my eyes squeezed shut, I can erase the last hour and forget everything. I can believe that when I open my eyes, she'll be here, and I will see her dark hair with that hidden fire lurking between the strands. She will look up at me with those eyes, the sun shining on a blue sky, twinkling with a laugh or exasperated with me. Yet when I open my eyes, I can no longer pretend.

The darkness inside me trembles, trying to shield me from reality. A world where my fated queen slipped through my fingers because I was not strong enough to fight my enemy, where I wasn't smart enough to predict her movements so I could prepare for the coming conflict. I cling to anger, putting the pillow down on the bed and turning away.

My eyes catch on Persephone's discarded negligee draped over the back of the chair. Her brush sits on the vanity, several strands of her hair wrapped in the bristles. The marks of the life we had together, only a few precious moments. It is a glimpse of the life we should have had for the rest of eternity.

The rage flickers again, close to being eclipsed by heartbreaking despair. My breath is sharp, each one painful, coming faster and faster. She's gone. I can't get her back. I'm too weak.

I stumble to the wall, catching myself in time to slide down and pull my knees into my chest. I cover my face with my hands, trying to regain control, but it's like trying to stop a flood with a single towel. The more I fight it, the faster it comes.

My breath only comes faster and more painfully. The darkness cloaks me, trying to shield and comfort me. But there is no comfort in shadows. They're cold and hollow. They're not her.

Cerberus paws at the shadows cloaking me, and I want to lower the shield. Yet I don't have control over it. Every time I reach out to force the shadows down, they only become thicker, more impenetrable.

"Get your shit together, pussy!" a familiar voice pierces through my haze of panic.

Zeus.

I look up, trying to find my youngest brother through the shadows. My eyes, so accustomed to darkness, refuse to see through to the light. I am trapped within the tornado of pain surrounding me.

A tremble of static makes the hair on my arms raise, and I roll away from the bolt of lightning Zeus hurls through my shadows. The blinding light cuts through my shield with brute force.

"The fuck?!" I shout.

My shadows tremble and drop, revealing Zeus dressed in an offensively bright Hawaiian shirt and cargo shorts. I could strangle him. My breath is still short, but my annoyance with my brother gives me enough focus to slice through the darkness, just like his bolt. *Fucking dick.*

"I heard," Zeus says, tucking his hands into his shorts.

I pant, wiping the sweat off my brow. "You heard, and so you decide to throw a fucking bolt at me?"

Zeus smirks. "What do you expect from me? A tearful hug? An 'everything will be alright' pat?"

I struggle to my feet. Zeus stands there watching me

with a smirk, his teeth flashing in his tanned face. I really want to punch him. He makes it so easy to hate him. It's no wonder most of the pantheon does. Most of the world hates him, yet he couldn't care less. Sometimes, I envy him that ability. But not right now. Right now, I want to turn his stupid shirt into a noose.

"Why are you here?" I growl.

Zeus looks me up and down. "You got what? A few days left before you can't leave, right?"

I narrow my eyes at him. "Yes, what does that—"

Zeus grabs my arm and, in a blinding flash of lightning, teleports us to another place. I groan when we land, stumbling slightly. I hadn't braced for the impact. Zeus's method of traveling was just like him: abrasive, abrupt, and leaves you short-fused. I rip my arm from his grasp and snarl, "You couldn't warn me—"

A fist slams into me with the force of a meteor, throwing me across the landscape. I hit the ground and bounce, the breath leaving my body. I snap my wings out to stop myself from flying any further.

I shake the dirt out of my hair, taking catalog of what the fuck Zeus has gotten me into now. It is night, and the stars above us are dazzling. A giant white observatory sits to our right, and it's enough for me to place our exact location.

The Griffith Observatory. Los Angeles.

A shadow lunges at Zeus, their powers colliding and exploding. One a blinding, searing bluishwhite, the other the color of glittering stars, shifting and moving.

Fuck.

Krios.

The Titan of Constellation glows, the stars descending from the sky and forming an astral shield over him. Zeus shatters the shield before it fully forms and throws the Titan, sending him tumbling.

"Witnesses!" my brother shouts to me.

I curse, my gaze snapping to the observatory deck. Some of the mortals are in the process of fleeing, but others are filming the fight on their phones.

I throw my hand out, hurling a net of power. It catches on each of the mortals, anchoring to their internal darkness. I grab their minds, yanking the shadows over their eyes and blotting out their memory. One by one, the mortals crumple to the ground. I could only turn their memory dark for a short period after it formed. Zeus was lucky to have brought me. Though I doubt *luck* had anything to do with it.

The Treaty of All Pantheons prevented us from exposing ourselves to mortals, signed into effect before we were even born. It kept all pantheons to a strict code, even forcing the Primordials of all pantheons to sit out wars. Zeus is pushing his luck by doing this in the open. The last fucking thing I need right now is a Great Tribunal.

I release the mortals as they find unconsciousness. My shadows collect their devices and wipe them. Shockingly, I'm forced to clean up after other gods.

Zeus's next bolt explodes the carefully groomed ground, sending debris soaring into the air. My shadows prevent any of it from landing on the unconscious mortals.

Krios roars as he struggles to his feet, a formation of stars glittering over him with the force of the cosmos. He shifts the constellations above us, forming an astral ram to hurl at my brother. It nails Zeus in the stomach, sending him soaring.

I do not have fucking time for this.

The shadows return to me, drawing Krios's attention. The darkness forms a cloak around my shoulders, armor scaling down my chest.

"Coward," Krios snarls, charging up for his next attack.

The steel of my old friend, the bident, forms in my hand. I can do this. I can fight rather than crumple into a ball. I want fury instead of desolation. My knuckles turn white with the grip on the bident. This is a welcome distraction. I will fall into violence to stop thinking about sorrow, embracing the darkness that lurks inside me. It waits to consume me, feeding on my blackest thoughts and my most turbulent emotions.

What good did sealing that part of me away do? I'd

locked it inside an obsidian box in my mind, acting like it didn't exist. It didn't help me when Persephone was taken. I was fighting with one hand behind my back. What happens when I finally let go? What happens when I shatter that obsidian box in my mind?

My armor breaks, the shadows becoming more chaotic, more out of control, reflecting my own emotions and release.

Why hold back?

I hear Zeus shout, but I can't understand what he says. The darkness surrounds me, whispering to me, calling to me, beckoning me. It slides along my body like silk, a midnight wave of power.

Krios is about to hit me, and I unleash it. A torrent of darkness, despair, and agony slams into him, and the Titan buries his feet into the ground, trying to hold out against it. That obsidian box flies open, and two thousand years of dark emotions come flying out.

I've never unleashed like this.

I can't stop.

I don't want to stop.

It feels good.

Krios's feet slide back against my power, his eyes completely white. He is screaming something. I don't care. I keep unleashing the darkness. Krios leans into the onslaught, trying to hold his ground against shadows from every part of me, from the depths of my soul.

A hand grabs mine, breaking my focus and releasing Krios. The box slams shut on the darkness, and the Titan vanishes in a flash of starlight.

I snarl and turn on Zeus. "Why did you stop me?"

Zeus looks at me, his eyes filled with something I've never seen in him. *Fear*. He doesn't speak, which is also unusual. He holds up the hand he grabbed, showing me what made him intervene. The tips of my fingers are black like they're stained with ink. My brows furrow as I try to control the darkness and remove it from my fingers. The box is supposed to be closed. Nothing happens, and I shake my hand again, panic gripping me.

Zeus stops me, grabbing my hands again. "This will hurt."

Before I can say I'm ready or even ask what he means, he uses his lightning on my fingers. I shout from the sudden pain, trying to pull away, but Zeus holds me firm. I grind my teeth, watching as the darkness starts to flake and fall away from my fingers. Once it's gone, Zeus releases me.

I pant, my hands on my knees. "How...How did you know that would work?"

Zeus shrugs. "I didn't."

I glare at him. "Dick."

I flex my fingers again, thankful that the darkness doesn't reappear.

Chapter Three

Persephone

MY EYELIDS STRUGGLE TO SHIELD ME FROM THE BRIGHT SUN, MAKING ME WINCE IN DISCOMFORT. I shift in bed, trying to hide from it, clinging to unconsciousness in an effort to stay in the bliss of sleep for a few more moments.

The movement is futile. Sunlight fills the room like this is the only place in the realm it longs to be. I slowly blink my eyes open, my head throbbing in pain. At first, I pass it off as the light in the room causing the ache, the gleam that even in sleep I couldn't seem to escape, but my brain seems to throb as if it's been hit with a hammer over and over. Maybe I am just dehydrated.

I stretch, my white cotton nightdress restricting my movements somewhat. Gods, I hate this thing. It feels like a straightjacket. I look up at the ceiling, the white paint practically shining, reflecting the sunshine. I shove my sheets off and sit up at the edge of the bed, pushing my feet into my slippers. The fluffy lining tickles my arches until I press my soles into them.

They are always in the same position, always ready for me.

I walk to my vanity and sit in front of it, looking at my reflection. My eyes are bloodshot, and there's some redness at my temples. I frown, tilting my head slightly to see it better. Both sides of my head have matching bruises. They're small and sit just over my temples.

My bedroom door opens, and Margaritte enters, pulling my gaze.

"Good morning, Lady Persephone! It is so nice to see you!" she chirps happily.

"To see me?" I ask, blinking.

Margaritte's smile falters, her eyes going a little wide. "I'll… draw you a bath." Margaritte corrects her face and disappears into the bathroom. After a moment, I hear her start to hum the same tune she has hummed since she first started here over one hundred years ago.

I shake my head and look back at the redness, brushing my fingers over the areas.

"Margaritte?" I ask, still looking in the mirror.

"Yes, my lady?" she calls from the bathroom.

"Do you have any idea what this might be from?" I ask.

Margaritte has never been someone I fully trusted, being under the employ of my mother, but she is a constant in my life. I once thought about befriending her. It quickly became clear that we had little in common, and she had no interest in becoming friends with the daughter of her boss. Which is fair, I suppose. I don't imagine it would ever be a good idea to mix business with pleasure, especially when it comes to my mother.

Margaritte comes through from the bathroom and stops beside me. I tilt my head so she can better see the areas in question. Something I can't identify passes over her face, something that came and went too quickly for me to even try to figure out.

"Perhaps my lady is allergic to something?" Margaritte says, her voice giving nothing away. "I changed your sheets yesterday. Perhaps a new detergent? I shall ask, my lady." Margaritte hurries back to the bathroom to continue readying it for my soak.

I look back in the mirror, my brows drawing. Something is different. I know it is, but… what?

I sigh, pushing my chair back and standing from the ornate vanity. Everything in my bedroom has been custom-made for me. There is not one piece of furniture that doesn't sport a flower or a bouquet. I look around my bedroom, a wash of pastels and softness. Like I've done hundreds of times, I cast an eye over it, trying to pick out one thing I would have chosen for myself. I hope that maybe one day I'll find something that I can say, "That is me. That is Persephone Prosperina." With that, I might start to fit into the mold my mother so desperately wants to shove me into. But alas, all I see is the perfect little princess my mother hoped for. It's imbued into every pastel pink and baby blue, into every vase and trinket. So much so that when I look at my room, all I feel is my mother's disappointment pressing down on me, so heavy that I swear one day it will smother me.

"Lady Persephone, your bath is ready!" Margaritte calls from the bathroom.

"Thank you, Margaritte. You're dismissed."

Margaritte leaves the bathroom and curtsies to me. "Your mother wishes you have breakfast with her in one hour."

I nod, moving over to sit on the edge of my bed. Margaritte hovers for a moment, like she wants to say something, but when I glance at her expectantly, she simply curtsies again and leaves.

The second I'm alone, I open the drawer of my bedside table and pull out my pink journal, placing it on the bed next to me. I roll my eyes at it, and I know my mother reads it. I'm unsure what she expects to find in it, but if she's looking for my true thoughts and feelings, she'll be disappointed. Instead, I fill it with wistful ramblings, only ever allowing my positive thoughts to be written down.

The truth is, I've always been afraid of my mother and what she would do to me if she ever found out half of what went through my mind. To her, I am the Goddess of Spring, the perfect little princess who she's kept hidden for centuries. She has never known the other side I keep under lock and key. I have repressed that side so completely, but I still sometimes feel the darkness rage beneath my skin.

I look back in my drawer, emptying it of the pens and books. I glance at the door once, straining to hear. Ensuring no one is outside, I press a spot on the plywood about three inches from the bottom left-hand corner. There is a soft click, and the board pops up enough for me to get my fingers around. I lift it out and smile down at my true secret treasure.

A single rose.

The petals are vibrantly red, the color of love and passion. The stem is the deep green of healthy growth. But that's not what makes this rose special. What makes this rose special is the single, elegant thorn that sits about halfway up the stem. The tip is sharp, but the sides are smooth and solid gold.

I have always loved roses. My mother allowed me to have a patch in her garden, and I filled it with roses. Her one rule was that they were not to have thorns. Any thorn that grew was to be removed immediately, and if I failed to prune them properly, there would be consequences.

"Why would you want those hideous thorns on your beautiful roses, Persephone? They are only beautiful if they are pure."

My mother finds beauty only in that which she understands, and she doesn't understand imperfection.

When I found this rose with its gold thorn, I was compelled to keep it. I'm not sure why, but I've never found thorns ugly. They add to the whole picture. In some ways, I actually find roses more beautiful when their thorns are still intact, maybe because I find beauty in complexity.

I lift the rose and stroke the petals before bringing it to my nose and inhaling the sweet floral scent. I look over the flower, gliding my finger over the stem and the thorn, letting it slice into the pad of my finger. The bite of pain reminds me I'm alive.

I tuck the rose back in the drawer before replacing the board and all of my items. I shut it again, and with it, I lock away the other side of me. The one I'm desperate to explore.[3]

Chapter Four

Persephone

IT'S STILL STRANGE TO BE ABLE TO MOVE FREELY AROUND OLYMPUS. For so many years, I knew only my house. I've walked the halls so often that I could don a blindfold and still easily make my way from one end of the house to the other without colliding with anything.

My mother says that this was always the plan, that this is the appropriate age for me to make my entrance into society with a chaperone, but I'm still an outsider. People are looking at me, perceiving me, regarding me. I don't blame them for their questioning stares. I imagine it must be strange to see Demeter's best-kept secret. Most of them acknowledge me with interest. Some have more somber expressions, but the worst is when I can see fear in their eyes. Do I look like I should be someone to fear?

I've seen Olympus in books, and through the pictures, I could appreciate the beauty of it, but there was always an undercurrent of resentment. I longed to walk the streets as I'm doing now, to see something different.

I take in the gardens of the other dwellers, appreciating their beauty. These plots aren't all carefully landscaped like my mother's garden, and it amuses me to consider what my mother's reaction would be to see gardenias and pansies in the same patch. I move closer with my chaperone trailing me. I hear someone calling to someone. The affectionate nickname makes me smile, but I don't look up, not wanting to intrude on a private moment between friends or lovers.

I study one of the flowers closely, enjoying how the colors blend, turning from deeper orange into yellow. A warm hand wraps around mine, and I tense, my head snapping around. I'm never casually touched by anyone. Mother would remove their hand permanently.

"Petal?" I meet the gaze of a tall male with tanned skin and caramel-brown eyes, boring into mine. I yank my hand free and move away from him. His gaze is kind, and while there's definitely something familiar about him, his brazenness has me on alert.

"Persephone?" His blond eyebrows knit together, and his gaze becomes cautious. He doesn't wear the same mask of fear as the other Olympians, but there is definitely a glimmer of unease. His power feels... different. I blink, racking my brain for context or a clue as to why this person would know my name and why he would act so familiar with me.

"Yes?" I ask, keeping my voice docile.

"Persephone, we really must get back," Florence, my chaperone, says. Her voice is kind, and I know she's given me as much allowance as she possibly could. My time outside of our home is still restricted, but my mother has assured me that over time, I will be allowed more 'exposure', as she calls it.

I return to Florence's side, and we walk in silence, the same question buzzing around my brain over and over. When we approach the last turn, I can't hold it back any longer. I'm too intrigued. "Who was that man from earlier?" I ask her.

Florence glances at me, regarding me carefully. "Which man, Lady Persephone?"

"The one who appeared to know who I am," I reply, trying to decipher her micro-expressions.

"Perhaps he confused you with someone else, Lady Persephone," she replies after a moment.

My brows draw. "He called me by name."

"Perhaps he is someone who has heard of your entrance

into society and wished to introduce himself to you." Her words are a little more clipped, and I sense there is more to this.

I know I should drop this, but… "But you are unfamiliar with him?" I push, needing a sliver of information about him.

Florence looks as if she's about to answer when we turn the corner, and the house comes into sight. My mother stands at the gate, waiting for me. Her arms are crossed, and she's regarding me with disappointment.

No change there.

Florence both tenses at seeing my mother and seems to exhale in relief that my questioning has ceased.

For now.

I smile at my mother as we approach. The smile she taught me. "Hello, Mother."

My mother completely ignores me, turning her furious gaze to Florence. "This is unacceptable, Florence. I told you to be back ten—"

"It was my fault, Mother. I apologize. I was completely distracted looking at the gardens of the people of Olympus," I interrupt.

My mother's gaze snaps to me, her eyes narrowing.

Fuck… I don't think I've ever interrupted her before.

She lifts her chin, regarding me, and I try to avoid nervously pulling on my fingers. Fidgeting would only make her more furious with me. She scrutinizes me for what feels like an eternity before she says, "The *gardens?*"

I nod. "I was looking at one in particular. It had gardenias and pansies in the same patch. Scandalous, isn't it?"

My mother keeps her inscrutable gaze on mine for another moment before her fury melts away, and her lips twitch. "The people of Olympus have no taste, Persephone." She looks at Florence, whose gaze I feel plastered to the side of my face. I'm not sure if she's breathed since we got here. "You are excused."

"Thank you, Your Greatness," Florence mutters, curtsying and scurrying off.

Your Greatness. My stomach turns at the title my mother insists upon.

Mother links her arm through mine and leads me into the house. "I had lunch prepared for us, sweetling."

"Thank you, Mother," I reply, taking care to straighten my back and lift my chin, walking as she taught me. I'm not sure why, but it is harder to maintain walking like this now. It's like the muscles in my back have weakened.

"I had them prepare your favorite meal. Roasted vegetables and rice," she states, like it's a kindness.

"Thank you, Mother," I reply, keeping my voice light. Roasted vegetables have never been my favorite, but apparently, it is proper, and what am I if not the perfect little proper princess? I need to stay in her good graces if I want to retain what little freedom I have.

When we arrive in the dining room, we take our usual seats. My mother sits at the top of the table, and I sit to her right. The long table only has four chairs, so I sit about halfway down, by no means close to my mother.

Mother gestures for the servants to serve the meal, and she lifts her goblet of wine. "How was your outing today?" she asks. She sounds nonchalant, even bored, but I can sense the slightest hint of interest. Something that I probably wouldn't catch if I didn't know her so well. But why?

Never has she been interested in anything I do. She only cares about things I do wrong. She only cares about punishing me for not being perfect.

"It was lovely," I reply. "Olympus is beautiful, just like in the books."

My mother looks at me, her gaze full of cold, calculated intrigue. "Did you talk to anyone while on your adventure?"

It is an odd question. Am I not supposed to? I decide it would be unwise to tell her of the mysterious man who approached me. He should be a secret until I know more about him.

"Only Florence and the tailor."

My mother nods, seemingly pacified, and cuts into her vegetables. "You are permitted another outing. Next week."

I glance at her, my eyes wide and my heart soaring. It is another taste of freedom, another moment out of my—

"There is one small caveat, Persephone," my mother adds, her voice growing cold. My stomach plummets as I see the change in her eyes.

"Oh?"

"It is that time again," she says, tilting her head.

My brows furrow, but then it hits me. "N-no. I just had them done not two months ago."

My mother smiles at me, but it's not kind. There is something cruel about it that sends a shiver down my spine. "What are they?" she asks, her voice like ice. She waits for the reply she has drilled into me, and I know she will punish me if I don't say it.

I know what she wants me to say. I can already feel the acid of my words against my tongue.

I look away, tears welling in my eyes. "H-hideous…"

"And what do we have to do to them?"

A tear slides down my cheek. "Remove them…"[4]

Chapter Five

Hades

ZEUS AND I SPEND THE NEXT TWENTY HOURS *TRYING TO TRACK KRIOS DOWN TO NO AVAIL.* We scour every possible hiding place across Olympus and into the Underworld. It is impossible to catch someone who can literally summon the stars from the sky to cloak them. Zeus wants to continue the search, and I know he will continue until he drops dead from exhaustion. A part of me is tempted to do the same, but I have duties to tend to in the Underworld.

I collapse into my desk chair in my study, the leather creaking under my body. Thankfully, Zeus went back to Olympus. I can only tolerate him for so many hours, and I am well past my threshold.

The only person I can stand to be around is *gone*, and I am alone again. I am alone in a cold, dark palace with no one but souls to speak to. For a moment, I see a different future for myself.

The shadows around me flicker and swirl around the room, climbing up the walls and shattering several lamps. The castle immediately replaces them. I swallow roughly, rubbing my temples, pushing that darkness back into the box I kept it in, but it won't remain there. I broke the box. The lock box of control in my mind is fractured. Each time I use my abilities, the cracks in it grow bigger and more of those repressed abilities and memories leak out.

I drop my hands, glaring at my fingers. My power no

longer stained them, but I could still feel that darkness lingering like an oil along my skin.

Every dark thought or emotion I've ever had waits to burst forth as a violent power. How long had I repressed my darkest instincts, too afraid to unleash that side of me, too afraid to face that side of me?

Before I think better of it, I pick up the phone and dial.

"Dr. Pathenos's office, how can I help you?" the receptionist answers smoothly.

I open my mouth to speak but end up slamming the phone back into the cradle before I can say anything. Fuck. What could I gain from therapy? Especially from Athena, who is *still* not a licensed therapist. I need another way to find another outlet for these brewing feelings.

I jump up and stride from my office, heading for the library. I reach out to touch the spines of the books, greeting old friends. The well-worn leather beneath my fingers and the scent of old parchment invoke reminders of the words scrawled on those pages. Stories that once took me away from my reality to another world, another quest, another crown. Each one was another escape. Yet there is no familiar feeling of serenity.

I pace along the shelves, trying to calm my racing mind. All the previous avenues to release my stress are gone, and that tornado of dark emotions continues to swirl inside me.

My eyes snap up when the Underworld fluctuates. A new presence has arrived, and this one has an invitation.

"You took your sweet time," I growl at her, whirling to face her.

"You gave me a day," Mellie hisses back. "Don't allow time you're not willing to give, Hades."

My eyes narrow, closing the distance between us. Mellie's mismatched eyes slide over me, and the hardness in her gaze softens as she takes me in.

"You look like shit."

I'm sure I look awful. I can't remember the last time I ate anything or slept. But Mellie doesn't need to point it out. I'm very aware of how I'm unraveling at the seams. Yet I can't think of a way to stop it, much less figure out a way to stitch myself back together.

I glare at her, waiting for her to speak.

"Helios saw Persephone," she says, crossing her arms over her chest.

My foolish heart leaps at her name. I don't know what I expected her to tell me, but just hearing that she's out there gives me the slightest bit of comfort. She's not with me, but she's somewhere.

"And?" I ask, trying to read Mellie's face, searching for a sign of how Persephone is.

"She's okay. Demeter is allowing her out of the house."

Bitch. Just the sound of that woman's name makes the shadows flicker around the room. It's enough of a change that Mellie notes the way my powers are whirling.

"She's not hurt?" I ask hoarsely. "He's sure?"

Mellie sidles closer like I'm a skittish horse on the verge of bolting. "Helios said she was fine. I'll ask him to keep an eye on her if you want. But for now, we should wait it out."

I mimic her stance, crossing my arms. "Wait it out?"

Time is the very thing I don't have. With each passing second, I draw closer to the deadline for when I can no longer leave the Underworld. With our bond snapped, I would be here alone. Again. The shadows swirl on the walls.

"You think Persephone dove into this without a plan?" Mellie asks, her eyes narrowed, and I can see her watching the way my power is fluctuating.

"Her mother took her from my arms. There wasn't time to plan."

Mellie hisses at my tone. "Then it's time for you to make a plan. A smart one."

A plan. Right. I'm known for planning, observing, and carefully executing strikes. And where exactly had that ability gotten me?

Nowhere.

"I have a plan," I growl at her, narrowing my eyes.

"Not dreamwalking. It's too dangerous, Hades."

I close the distance, grabbing her arms. "Mellie... I need

her."

She softens slightly, no doubt seeing the desperation etched into my face. "I know you do, but you're not thinking rationally."

I laugh shakily. "Of course I'm not! I just lost the love of my life!"

The entire Underworld shakes, feeding off my turbulent emotions.

"We will get her back," she states. "But we shouldn't take unnecessary risks."

I close my eyes and exhale. "Just let me see her."

Mellie tenses, and I drop my hands. "You'll need to give me time to prepare."

My eyes open, the slightest bit of hope filtering in. I nod before moving to the old chair I've spent hours reading in. I slouch in it, laughing sadly. "We just made up… finally… and now this."

Mellie watches me, her eyes sad. "She will return, Hades. You are fated."

I cover my eyes with my hand, rubbing my face wearily. "This doesn't feel fated. It feels doomed."

She touches my shoulder. "You don't believe that."

I shrug, keeping my eyes closed. Mellie squeezes my shoulder. "I'll see you in three days."

I nod.

Chapter Six

Persephone

THE PAIN IS STILL PRESENT. IT WILL BE FOR AT LEAST A FEW DAYS, BUT IT WILL FADE EVENTU-ALLY."

The shame is still present. It never fades. It is the constant.

I look down at my latest diary entry. The room is lit only by the small lamp on my bedside table. A soft breeze blows through the white gossamer curtains, revealing the expanse of Olympus illuminated by the silvery glow of the moonlight.

I close the journal, storing it back in the secret compartment in my bedside table. Never do I feel quite so alone than when she takes my horns. It took hours to remove them this time, and I have no idea why. She had them shaved down not two months ago. I thought that once I mastered my glamor, the removal surgery would cease. I am now at the stage where my glamor feels natural, and I feel wrong when it is down. But is that my truth? Or is it my mother's?

It hurt more this time. It didn't matter how many times I asked, begged, or cried for them to stop, to give me a break. They wouldn't.

My mother asked for the horns. Usually, she would have them incinerated, but this time, she demanded they be placed in a bag and put in her office.

I slip from the bed and move to the open balcony doors, taking a deep breath of the fresh Olympus air. My lungs feel underwhelmed. The scent is not the one I'm craving. I usually love the smell of flowers, and I still do, but it's not what I need right now.

Citrus… Oh, how I would love to smell something citrusy. I make a mental note to ask my mother about planting an orange tree tomorrow. Maybe if I keep the conversation light and about gardening, she won't punish me.

I climb back into my bed, the soft cotton sheets caressing my skin and the fluffy pillow immediately molding to my head. The dull ache from the exposed roots of my horns makes it a little more difficult to relax. A twinge of unease rolls deep in my stomach, and I rack my brain, searching for the source but finding no answers. My head pounds with a raging tension headache. I close my eyes, willing myself to sleep, praying that tomorrow will be a day full of joy, hope, and happiness. For now, I'll return to my dream meadow of serenity.

"Good morning, sweetling," my mother chirps as I enter the dining room, her eyes sweeping over a copy of Olympus Today.

"Good morning, Mother." I sit in my usual seat, and Margaritte flits around me, filling my cup with coffee and serving my breakfast.

The paper rustles as my mother peers over it. "Fruit only for Persephone this morning, Margaritte." Her tone is demanding and cold.

Margaritte bows her head, removing the plate filled with eggs and toast she had set before me.

"From now on, we eat only what we can grow. Understand?" Her cool stare pierces me, and there's an undertone of suspicion in her words.

"Of course, Mother. Is there any reason for this?" I ask carefully.

"I can only trust the produce that comes from our garden," she replies, going back to her paper and ending the conversation.

I glance at Margaritte. She has brought me another plate and is filling it with fruits.

"There is an article in the paper today, and it's all about you. It seems your entrance into society has the realm abuzz." My mother looks at me again, her head tilted.

"Oh?" I spear a strawberry.

"I have asked Hermes to set up a meeting with one of the journalists. If they are going to write about you, it will be an official, approved interview. And we will need to take some photographs."

I tilt my head, eating the fruit.

"It's better we get on top of this, Persephone. Besides, it's time you were properly introduced into society."

"Yes, Mother."

"Good. I will schedule it for the end of the week. I want the interview and the photographs set up here." She nods, looking pleased with my submission.

It's mid-morning before I make it to the garden. My mother seemed to want to take her time with breakfast, and I did my best not to seem impatient, but from the moment the sun rose, I longed to be outside.

I kneel in my patch, looking over my roses. I notice that they're not quite uniform, and I frown. It's not something I ever cared about, but my mother has poisoned my entire patch for less. I wave my hand over the flower, calling upon the roots to shift back a little. The soil roils as the flower moves until it's perfectly lined up with the others.

I cup the head of a rose that looks a little sickly. I stroke the inside of a petal, nurturing it. It begins to look healthier immediately, but my brows furrow when I notice dark veins trailing up from the base. I lean in for a closer look. That creeping darkness looks bad, and I expect the rose to feel weak and sick, but it has never felt stronger. I release it, sitting back on my heels. The veins are barely noticeable from the outside, and yet, the rose seems to glow with a new strength.

"Persephone." My mother's cold voice snaps me from my thoughts, and I push down the instinct to hide the rose from her, knowing that if she sees it, she will destroy it.

"Yes, Mother?" I ask, tilting to look at her.

"Leave that useless patch alone and come help me," she says from the other side of the garden.

I glance back at my small collection of roses and smile almost apologetically before I stand and join my mother.

Chapter Seven
Hades

I **SPEND ALL THREE DAYS WAITING FOR MELINOË** **TO RETURN, HUNTING TITANS.** I don't sleep. I barely eat. I hunt. I rarely feel the injuries I gather, the Underworld healing me almost immediately upon my return. I miss the pain of them, even postponing my return to the palace so I can feel it longer. I need that little bit of sensation to remind myself that this is real, that I'm alone, and she's not coming back.

The darkness becomes my constant companion. The moment I stop moving, those feelings of isolation, despair, and hopelessness take hold. In those moments, I depart even more from myself, detaching emotionally. Any image I hold of myself seems to be tied inextricably to Persephone. Compassion leaks away from me, and I lack any form of empathy. The few Titans I've detained, I interrogate in the most brutal and vicious ways possible. I am done pretending to be someone who holds any kind of moral compass. Where had maintaining a code of honor gotten me? It didn't stop Persephone from being taken away. It didn't stop the Titans from escaping.

I start to… enjoy it. I enjoy their screams as I tear into them, my shadows making the pain never-ending. Each moment feels like an eternity to them until they confess everything to me. I'm the God of the Dead, which grants me the ability to understand how to extend pain to bring them close to death but not push them over.

Yet, no matter what I did, they wouldn't tell me where to find my father. There was no torture I could imagine, no agony I could create that made them break. Zeus had snapped at me, insisting I wasn't pushing them hard enough. I volunteered him to experience it himself if he doubted me. He unsurprisingly declined my very generous offer. Yet, none broke and confessed where my father was or his plan.

Only when I break Perses, Titan of Destruction, do I finally find out why.

Perses smirks at me, even though his teeth are mostly missing and his tongue has barely grown back. "Poor son of Kronos. You don't understand, and you never will. He swallowed you, but you never lived under his rule. Anything you can conjure is nothing compared to his tyranny."

I took his tongue again for that.

They think he is crueler than I? Challenge fucking accepted. My interrogation only turns more harsh, shifting to psychological warfare from physical torture. Several fall for the idea that I am hesitating about the war, considering turning against my brother in favor of my father. A couple think I will do anything to get my wife back, even killing Zeus and taking his place. Those who fall for that don't understand how she was taken. Misinformation is rampant among them. Most are surprised I have a wife, while others believe Kronos took her.

Most have no idea about Demeter's involvement and are astounded when I ask about her. She hid her tracks so well it is like she doesn't exist. She thrives on being dismissed as a minor goddess. How long has she planned this? Since the Fates first revealed my wife would be the Goddess of Life? Since Persephone's birth? Even before?

The most deadly enemy is always the one you never see coming. I was supposed to be the one who outmaneuvered, who watched and listened. I was supposed to be the unexpected enemy. Yet, I found myself completely outwitted by the Goddess of the fucking *Harvest*.

When it's time for Melinoë to return, I head to a guest bedroom. It is opulently appointed, with silver silk sheets and a buttery soft duvet. I haven't stepped foot in our bedroom since she was ripped from my arms. Not that I sleep much, saving all my dreams for time with Persephone. Dreamwalking is dangerous, even more so for a god bound to a realm. Unlike Melinoë and Morpheus, I am bound to a physical realm, which means my dreams are rooted in the Underworld. Even when I dream in the mortal world, the Underworld always plays a part, though sometimes it is only the presence of my queen. To cross from my realm into the dream and from there into Olympus is something even weaker dream gods struggle with. Each layer of a dream is blocked by our innate ability to keep our dreams to ourselves. Those who are connected by a fated bond are able to call to each other, but without it, I need the help of a dream god. To cross from the Underworld to Olympus, I need to break through thousands of wards that keep other dreamwalkers out. I will have to wear my consciousness thin, along with my power, to step into Persephone's mind.

"Melinoë," I murmur, greeting her. My tone is flat and emotionless.

She looks over my face, her dual-colored eyes no doubt recognizing my fatigue. "I'm still not sure about this."

I nod, moving to sit on the bed. Morpheus appears, silently standing at the side of the bed, his fathomless eyes completely dull.

"It's why I asked for some help. I need someone who has successfully dreamwalked across realms before."

Mellie frowns as Helios swans into the room. The Titan had informed me that, unlike other gods, he is tied to a celestial object that appears in all three realms: the Underworld, the Dream World, and Olympus—even if the sun in the Underworld is only a mirror of the one in the mortal realm. Mellie snarls at him before dismissing the Titan and focusing on me. Hmm, I thought they were in a relationship. Perhaps they broke up.

"I would like to say that while Morpheus is more than willing to plunge you into this dream, and while Helios claims to have used the sun shining out of his ass to do this before, I am the one with the power that will bring you back safely. You are putting my life in danger along with yours. The second I say we need to leave, we leave."

I nod again. Fuck, I'm exhausted. How long is this without sleep? Ninety hours? "You know that we're not getting answers lurking around Olympus."

Helios rolls his eyes at me. Melinoë had attempted to convince me not to do this, claiming that Helios could get us more information. He had failed.

I have no energy to even admonish him with anything other than a dark stare.

"I mean it, Hades," Mellie reminds me. "The second I say we're leaving, there will be not even a moment of hesitation from you."

I nod at Morpheus as I lie down on the bed.

Mellie rolls her shoulders and then her neck. "You know how to signal me."

I squirm to get more comfortable and close my eyes. Morpheus sprinkles his sand over my eyelids, and I'm asleep before the last grain falls.

Chapter Eight

Persephone

THE GRASS IS SO SOFT BENEATH MY KNEES, softer than I've ever felt anywhere in Olympus. It tickles the pads of my fingers as I brush over it again and again. I hear the faintest sound of a brook babbling in the distance. This is true peace.

I've never been here before. It's not somewhere I recognize, and yet… it's so familiar to me that my heart aches. Every night I have slept over the last week, I have come to this exact meadow. Nothing ever changes. It's warm but not uncomfortable. The sky is blue with a tinge of light gray, but in a way that makes it look like the most glorious of springs. The sun always shines brightly across the plane, but it doesn't sting my eyes.

I've been looking forward to sleeping every day for this very reason. I'm not sure I've ever felt so relaxed than when I'm here. This place is my own personal heaven.

My clothes are different here, too. No longer am I wearing that tight cotton nightdress but a short sundress. It's light pink and covered in daisies, the straps are thin, and the bust has a ruched effect. In this place, my hair is always down. There is no place for the tight buns or plaits in this place. This is *my* place.

"My spring." The deep voice makes a shiver run down my spine, and I tense as a large hand cups my shoulder.

My skin tingles beneath his touch, and I slowly turn my head, looking up at the latest addition to the dream. My eyes meet his, and my heart races at the sight of them.

Sapphire blue.

I study his face. He is so handsome, but who is he, and why is he here? And why is he looking at me like that?

He drops to his knees beside me, his hand shaking as he gazes at me with something close to desperation. My whole body is on high alert, and I feel like I should be running, but something is keeping me here. My instincts are battling it out.

I just watch him, tilting my head a little as I take the time to fully appreciate him. I'm not sure I've ever seen a man this handsome, and he's looking at me like—

Suddenly, he pulls me into a hug, burying his face against my neck. My entire body goes tense, and I freeze.

"Fuck," he practically groans against my neck.

I blink, my arms held out at my side, not touching him.

He kisses along my neck. Each touch of his lips feels like a jolt of electricity going right to my core, but there is also a strange barrier between us. "Fuck, I was so worried." He moans, continuing to kiss me.

Why is my body reacting to this... mad stranger?

I push him away and scoot back. "What are you doing?"

He blinks and tilts his head. "What do you mean?" he asks, his body tensing with unease.

"Do you always go around kissing strangers?" I ask, unsure why I've not run away from this psycho yet. All I know is that something is keeping me here. I push to my feet, watching him warily as I put space between us.

"Strangers?" he asks, standing slowly but making no move to get closer to me. "Persephone, don't you know who I am?"

My eyes narrow. "How do you know my name?"

His face falls, something like horror flashing through his eyes. "What has she done to you?" he whispers. He steps forward, lifting his hand to... caress me, maybe?

I step back. "I should go…"

The man grabs my hand. "Persephone, what is my name?"

I tense, my body once again reacting to the contact, but something in my brain is telling me I need to wake up now. I tug my hand from his grasp. "What am I? A mind reader?"

His lips tilt up at the corners at my retort, and he moves in closer, cupping my cheeks. I look up into his sapphire blue eyes and nearly lose myself in their depths. "My name is Hades, and I am your husband." Hades presses his lips to mine, and while my body melts into him, my heart urging me to kiss him back, my mind pulls me back, and I slap him.

I'm not married. How absurd.

"I am *not* married," I growl.

Hades grabs my left hand and shows me the ring. I frown down at it. The band fits snugly around my ring finger. At the center, sparkling rubies and diamonds surround the most stunning rose. It is the most perfect ring and obviously tailored to me.

That's new…

"What's this then, hm?" he asks, his thumb rubbing over the band absentmindedly.

"You're insane. Absolutely insane." I yank my hand free and pull back.

"You can't explain it, can you?" he growls, "Just like you can't explain why you feel hollow. Like an empty shell."

Hollow? How does he know? I take another step back, needing to put distance, not just between him and me, but also with the harsh truths he's throwing at me. Truths I was barely aware of until he mentioned and named them.

"She took you from me. From our home." His gaze seems to pierce my soul as he searches mine, looking for something.

There is a flash of an image in my mind, large dark bricks with dark green ivy climbing—

I scream. There is pain… so much pain. It is like a red-hot poker piercing my brain. I cradle my head, the image dissolving to nothing but the pain lingering.

"The dream is unstable. We need to go." I hear a woman's voice echo through the dream, but all I feel is the pain.

Tears slide down my cheeks, and I whimper.

"A moment longer." I feel Hades gather me close. He buries his nose in my hair and inhales deeply. "I love you. I will come for you."

I cry out in pain once more before the warmth of Hades is gone, and everything goes black.

Chapter Nine
Hades

SEND ME BACK," I DEMAND, the second I'm out of the dream. The three gods look at me like I'm insane. They didn't see her face, they don't understand. I doubt I can explain it in any way that will make sense to them at the moment. How do I explain something I can barely cope with myself?

Helios has an arm wrapped around Mellie. Her nose is bleeding. Clearly, it took a lot out of her to pull me out, especially as I fought her. I should feel guilty about that, but all of my emotions are tied up in replaying the dream with Persephone, every millisecond and minute expression that occurred.

Do you always go around kissing strangers?

She didn't know me. She looked at me, and not even a shadow of recognition flickered in her eyes. It isn't enough that the bitch took her memories of me. She took more. I didn't recognize the Persephone I just saw. That wasn't the Persephone I knew or the self-assured goddess who started at Plutus. She is a shell of the woman I fell in love with. It is as if Demeter took everything that made Persephone special and hollowed her out until the only thing left was what she approved.

My fingertips begin to darken, swirling tattoos crawling up them as I think of all the ways I'm going to make that bitch pay for this. My new experience with torture is going to be useful once I get my hands on that fucking goddess.

Mellie snarls at Morpheus, shoving away from Helios. "The dream was unstable. What the fuck was that?"

Even the Prime of Dreams looks worn from the dream-walk. It took a lot out of them to send me across realms. However, he is rebounding much faster than Melinoë.

"It was not the dream," Morpheus growls back. "She was unstable."

Helios still stands at her side, glaring at Morpheus while the goddess flays him with her words. "And you couldn't feel that before you plunged him into it? Take some fucking responsibility."

I wave my hand, putting it against my head. "Please, my head is pounding."

She doesn't know who I am. I thought the memories and torture were bad, but Demeter found something worse for me to endure. I have to look into Persephone's eyes and see nothing. No sparkle. No life. Hollow. It is a unique and devastating pain.

"She was fine until confronted with the truth," Morpheus snaps.

Mellie shoots daggers at all three of us with her eyes. "We are not doing that again, ever." She sends me a withering look before storming out of the bedroom.

Helios sighs before following after her. I nod dismissively at Morpheus, who vanishes in a swirl of shimmering sand. And I'm alone again.

I lift my hands from where I'd hidden them, seeing the way the darkness is climbing up my fingers. It's even farther up than it was in the fight with Krios. I turn my hand over, studying how the intricate patternless black markings swirl over my skin. [5]

"You're embracing the darkness," a new voice intones, and I almost jump out of my skin in surprise. For a moment, I'm prepared to fight, but I relax when I see who is sitting in the room with me. Her midnight hair is braided into a crown around her head, and her glowing, starry eyes are

5   The Nightmare & The Daydream Chapter 4

focused intently on me.

"Nyx," I gasp. "What are you doing here?"

The Primordial of Night smiles, making herself at home on the settee. "Your manners leave much to be desired."

I clear my throat. "My apologies. I was surprised by your presence."

There are few gods I would apologize to, but Nyx will always be among them. The old gods that came before us, before the Titans, deserve a modicum of respect. Even though they handed over control of our realms, they still maintain a level of power that I've never completely understood.

"I heard what happened," Nyx whispers into the silence. "Your queen and my sister."

I wince. How had I forgotten about the tie between Gaia and Nyx? Though *sisters* is a very loose term since they were spawned from Khaos, with no true mother and father. Regardless, Nyx and Gaia were close.

"My sympathies for your loss," I whisper, scanning the Primordial's starry eyes. As I watch, a star shoots across them, windows to the night sky contained within her.

Nyx stands and turns to the window, looking out over the sweeping gardens. Does she notice my poor attempts at gardening in Persephone's absence? The work I've put in trying to keep that single red rose alive?

"You've begun to embrace the power you were born with," she muses.

I grind my teeth and curl my fingers, trying to hide that the tips are still black.How could she possibly know that?

"There was a shift," Nyx says, still staring out the window. "Stars going out."

I stand, moving to stand next to her, looking out over the gardens. "How do I stop it?"

"Why would you do that?"

My brows furrow, and I turn to stare at her profile. "It's darkness." It's fueled by consuming dark emotions, it fed on them, twisting my soul around it.

"You're suffering from a common misconception."

I bristle. "A misconception?"

Nyx looks at me, cupping my cheek, making me recoil. "Darkness is not inherently evil, just as light is not inherently good."

I step back from her, stopping myself from rubbing my cheek. She would take it as an insult. It is an insult. The only person allowed to touch me without warning is Persephone.

Nyx looks back out. "There was something sent for you."

She holds out the small long box to me, and I frown before taking it. It's wrapped in green paper and a yellow bow.

I glance at the primordial as I rip off the green wrapping. I open it, and I take a moment to understand what I'm seeing. There are two long, twisted pieces of bone nestled almost lovingly in the yellow box. The scent of roses in a dense fog hits me, and realization follows. These are Persephone's horns.

When I explode this time, I take half the palace with me.

Chapter Ten

Persephone

THE SOOTHING BREEZE AGAINST MY NECK IS THE ONLY UPSIDE in having my hair pulled back into this tight bun.

Don't complain, Persephone. Or she'll only make it tighter.

I look down at my small patch of daisies. They are a reward for my good behavior during my outing this morning. Mother came with me this time, and I stayed by her side, looking at the ground the whole time. Her threatening gaze darted around, bouncing off everyone we passed, her body tightly coiled with tension. I kept my cool, and I did what I used to do as a child when I was trying to behave like her little perfect princess. I keep my eyes down but angle my chin in a way that is flattering and feminine. My posture is perfect, shoulders back and spine straight. It's an effort to stop myself from swaying my hips as I walk, and I wonder when I started doing so. I have no memory of ever doing that as I walked before. To keep my eyes from straying, I identified flower breeds silently in my head in both English and Latin. I recalled one interesting fact about each, the exercise centering me.

On our return, my mother pointed to a pitiful patch of withered flowers. It is my patch. She poisoned it as a punishment for what she deemed as my misbehavior, forcing me to watch them all die. This time will be different. I will behave. I will protect them.

With my powers, I transformed the debris of the wilted flowers into mulch for the new and began planting a bed of daisies. It took only a moment for them to grow into seedlings and another minute to become small-budded flowers. Soon, they will be strong and proud. The petals are a brilliant white with sunshine yellow at **their** centers. There is such joy radiating from them.

"Persephone?" I lift my head to look at the approaching man. I've seen him before, on my last outing.

I smile up at him kindly, still feeling the remnants of happiness from planting such a beautiful patch of daisies.

"Yes?" I say, standing.

"I didn't get a chance to introduce myself the other day. I'm Helios."

I tilt my head, studying him. His bronzed skin glows so brilliantly. I pull off my gardening gloves, holding out my hand. "Oh, lovely to meet you, Helios. I'm…" I pause. "I suppose you already know my name."

Helios chuckles. **It's** melodic and infectious, but I'm too curious to join in.

"How do you know my name exactly?" I ask.

Helios takes my hand between both of his and squeezes. "Well, you're all the talk on Olympus."

I feel my cheeks heat. "Oh, I am?"

Helios nods. "Well, of course. Your mother finally letting you out has drawn a lot of attention."

Those words seem to wound me, but I'm not sure why. They are my truth and the truth of all of Olympus. Of course, they are going to be curious about Demeter's shut-in. I look down at my flower bed, worried that my face might give away too many of my thoughts to the man who seems to miss nothing. I pull my hand free of his.

"What?" Helios asks, stepping in closer.

"I think I want to move these here," I say, needing to change the subject. I point to a bed of sunflowers and then to an empty patch of soil. "And these here." I point to my roses and then to the patch where the sunflowers are growing.

A yellow light appears from Helios's direction, and I look at him, seeing the bright, fiery orb he is holding in his palm. It looks like a miniature sun.

"I could help," he says. "Sunshine for the flowers."

Something about his kind offer makes me bristle. Without thinking about it, I quirk a brow and wave my hand over the daisies. Instantly, they grow to their full size, beautiful and thriving.

Helios's lips pull into a smirk, and my stomach twists at my outward show of defiance. A trait my mother has been working hard to quell.

"Persephone! Lunch!" My mother's harassed voice comes from somewhere within the house, and I look in that direction. My heart races that maybe she has caught me with this stranger, but she is nowhere to be seen. I look down at my daisies. While they are basking in the sunlight, still healthy and strong, they have sagged a little. It's as if my emotions are tied to their well-being.

"Coming, Mother!" I call back, looking at Helios.

Something passes over Helios's face that I can't identify, and he places his hand on my arm, squeezing lightly before turning and leaving. I watch after him for a moment and then go inside to have lunch with mother.[6]

Chapter Eleven
Hades

MELLIE PACES ACROSS MY OFFICE RUG, SPIN-NING ON HER HEEL sharply with each turn. One direction shows the face she wears around Plutus Industries. In the other direction, the burn scars mar the perfection of her profile. On one side, she is the Goddess of Nightmares, on the other, the Goddess of Ghosts.

I flex my fingers, still not used to the leather gloves on my hands, but they conceal the swirling tattoos I can't seem to get rid of. Every moment I look away, it crawls higher as if my distraction feeds it. The only warning I receive is a slight shiver as it moves higher up my hand. The designs covered my palm now, stopping just shy of my wrists. For some reason, this darkness refuses to obey me. I am its master, yet it continues to mark me without my consent. I'd even tried to expel all of my power, purging until I dropped from exhaustion, hoping it would take the tattoos with it. Nothing worked, and I will not ask Zeus for help. I would never hear the end of it.

So gloves it is. Hopefully, it never rises higher. Gloves were already strange enough for me. Covering my hands felt unnatural and drew attention to them. Though, the only person who would notice the slight change has no idea who I am. My chest aches slightly, but I force myself not to rub at the phantom pain.

"You want to go back there?" Mellie shrieks, never stopping her pacing. Back and forth. Back and forth. A relaxing metronome of black and white. Scars and no scars.

"Yes," I answer resolutely.

She snarls. "No. You said you'd listen to me last time. You said you'd leave with no hesitation. And what did you do? You fucking hesitated! And then I spiraled and ended up with that fucking asshole's head between my legs! Which is your motherfucking fault!"

She's lost me. I open my mouth, about to explain, but my mouth closes again. I can't connect the points of her statement, no matter how I try.

"W-what?"

Mellie keeps pacing, and my brows furrow, trying to follow her train of thought. "Then he told me he's falling for me! Again, it's your fault because I spiraled! So no. We will not be dreamwalking again."

I rub my brow, trying to figure out what she is talking about. "Helios said he's falling for you?"

She spins on her heel, planting her feet to face me fully. "I cannot fuck Helios again. And I fucking hate this because my friend is gone, which leaves you as the only person I have to talk to about this shit. And you are the reason I keep fucking him!"

My lips twitch as I look into her dual-covered eyes. I'm normally good at reading people, and Melinoë's emotions are plain as day on her face at the moment. "You're falling for him, too."

She snarls at me again, and for a moment, I'm pretty sure she is thinking about lunging at me, no doubt to claw my eyes out. She has a thing about eyes. The moments when she's completely unleashed her abilities, her victims almost always enucleate themselves.

She slams her hands on my desk, leaning forward. "You will not be dreamwalking again."

To most, her stance would sponsor some kind of retreat. Not only am I not like most people, but I also have absolutely nothing to lose. She could take my eyes if she wanted. They'd grow right back.

"I will." My eyes narrow on her. The truth won't change even if she did attack me. "And you'll still be in love with him. Even if I didn't dreamwalk."

Mellie fumes, about to turn and storm out. Her buns are quivering with her anger. She had no right to be angry. I stand, calling to her, my voice whipping across the space. "Do you enjoy that she's in Olympus? That she's trapped there?"

She whirls on me. "How fucking dare you!"

"Then present me with solutions!"

Mellie snarls. "What does dreamwalking do?"

I pause, my shoulders slumping slightly. "I get to see her."

She doesn't know who I am. I look into her eyes and see nothing. No recognition. As much as I need the contact, the situation feels doomed. How many times must we give all of ourselves to appease fate? How much do I have left?

I glance at my wrists, frowning when I see the darkness crawl up the edge of my gloves. Fuck. So it's not just rage that makes it grow, but despair as well.

"One more shot," Mellie sighs, drawing my attention. "And don't invite Helios."

I relax slightly and move around my desk, doing something I can't recall ever doing. I hug Mellie. She stands completely still, arms at her sides. She goes completely rigid, not hugging me back.

"Whatever, dude. This isn't necessary."

Yet she doesn't push me away, just standing in my arms. I know this is taking a toll on her, but I squeeze her for a second longer. "I know. I hate it, too."

She pauses, still not pulling away. "So I'll come back tonight?"

I nod and pull back, dropping my arms from around her. "Thank you."

She steps back, looking over my face before leaving my office.[7]

---

[7]   The Nightmare & The Daydream Chapters 6-8

Chapter Twelve

Persephone

A FLASH OF BRIGHT LIGHT TEMPORARILY **BLINDS ME**, and I work to keep the smile painted on my face. Another follows almost immediately after, and the second it disappears, dark spots mask my vision for long moments.

"Tilt your head a little more to the left, Lady Persephone?" the photographer asks, shifting his position to capture me at yet another angle. My mother looks on from behind him, making her oppressive presence known. She is in control. She may allow me out into society, and she may allow Olympus Today to write an op-ed about me, but she sure is letting them know she will be breathing down their necks about it. Nothing will go forward without her meticulously combing through every photo, every opinion, and every word.

I lift my chin slightly, allowing myself to enjoy my hair being down. Mother said it should be down for the photographs, and I'm eternally grateful for the break from the tight bun or braid.

The outfit she insisted I wear took me by surprise. It is not the sort of thing she usually allows me to wear. The dress is pale pink with a boned corset, the material flaring at the hips and flowing to the floor. Dainty embroidered petals on the skirt give the effect that they're falling. The straps of the dress are thin, leaving my shoulders and arms uncovered. She even allowed Margaritte to apply some makeup to my face!

A man materializes in the room behind the photographer. The newcomer is tall and broad, wearing an immaculate suit, his dark hair styled perfectly away from his face. My brows furrow as I try to place this man. He is so familiar, yet not familiar at all. I am sure I have never seen him before.

My mind travels back to my dream from a few nights ago and to the handsome intruder who kissed me and took my breath away. Is this… him? No, it can't be. The man from my dream had the bluest of eyes, blue like sapphires, but this man's eyes are green.

My mother's whole body goes tense when she feels his presence. Her face contorts in rage, and she whirls around to face him. "Kronos," she hisses, her voice low. "You're not supposed to be here."

He smirks. "Now, now, Demeter. You might have all of Olympus trembling at your feet…" He moves in closer, his movements graceful. He leans into her, and I strain to hear his words. His voice is too low for me to hear what he says, but the blood seems to drain from my mother's face.

Kronos's gaze meets mine, and his smirk deepens. My mother glances at me and then ushers Kronos to the other room. I lift my chin, trying to follow them with my gaze, but it's futile.

"Lady Persephone? Would you be able to angle your chin down a little and look at the camera?" the photographer asks, a little more relaxed now that Mother's intimidating presence is absent from the room.

I do as he asks, and we're finishing the photo shoot when my mother reenters the living room, looking flustered and pale.

"Are we ready to conduct the interview?" the reporter asks.

My mother nods once and gestures for the maids to start setting up the seating area. I sit on the couch, my mother beside me, and the reporter across from us in the armchair.

"Hello, Persephone. My name is Eduardo. I will conduct the interview today. It is a pleasure to meet you."

I smile at him, nodding.

"And as you know, Eduardo, everything is off the record until I review the transcripts," my mother says, clasping her hands together and setting them on her lap.

Eduardo glances at my mother, and I swear I can see fear shimmer behind his glasses. "O-of course, Lady Demeter."

My mother nudges me slightly, prompting me to straighten my posture, and I can feel her disappointed gaze on me.

"So, Persephone. Tell me about yourself," Eduardo starts, nervously crossing one leg over the other.

I lift my chin slightly. "Well, I'm an avid gardener. I love to read. I love anything pink. My mother has said she will teach me how to bake this summer, which I am very excited about."

"I saw your gardening on my way into the manor. It's stunning," Eduardo adds.

I smile. "Well, most of that is thanks to my mother. She is wonderful at landscaping. I only have a couple of patches within the garden."

Eduardo nods, jotting down some notes while my mother scrutinizes him. "Well, Lady Demeter, you are extremely skilled."

"How one designs their garden tells you a lot about them," my mother replies, something about her tone vaguely threatening.

"Do you have a favorite flower, Persephone?" Eduardo asks me. I can tell he is feeling intimidated by my mother.

I nod. "Roses. I love them. Pink, red, purple, black—"

"A black rose?" my mother interrupts. "How hideous. Where have you seen such a monstrosity?"

I blink, my brows furrowing as I try to remember when I had seen a black rose before. Suddenly, an image flashes through my mind of a patch of all black roses with one red rose in the middle. A sharp pain shoots through my head, and I whimper.

"Stupid girl," my mother hisses. "Eduardo, give us a moment alone, please."

I squeeze my eyes, cradling my head in my hands, the pain radiating through me. I faintly hear Eduardo's hasty steps as he leaves the room and then feel my mother yank my hands away from my head before slapping me hard across the face. My ears ring, my cheek stings, and the headache throbs, but it's not like a hot poker anymore. It's as if that has been removed, and now there is just the throbbing void.

"You have never seen a black rose. You hate black roses. They are hideous," she hisses, grabbing my face and forcing me to meet her stare. I can hear the words she does not say as loud as the ones she does.

"Hideous, just like the darkness inside you."

My cheek still stings, and my mother glares at me for another long moment, pouring her fury and disappointment into me. She roughly releases my face and then shifts away from me. She lifts a small bell from the coffee table and rings it to alert the staff that she requires attention.

I try to hold back the tears and humiliation as the bell chimes, and I hear the light footsteps of Margaritte entering the room.

"Tell Eduardo we are ready to continue, Margaritte," my mother says, resuming her position of intimidating grace. Margaritte gives me a sympathetic look before flitting away to retrieve Eduardo.

Chapter Thirteen

Hades

POSEIDON CALLS ME TO THE BANKS OF THE *STYX*, and I stroll out to meet him. He's looking out at the river, watching as the latching beasts try to drag the souls to the depths. They will feed on them, suck them dry. Over the years, I developed a form of defense against them. I would need to teach it to Persephone if I ever got the chance. In the deep recesses of my mind, a voice demands I not be so negative. I squash that voice ruthlessly.

I stop on the banks next to my older brother. Normally, I look out over my realm with a sense of pride at all I had built. Now, exhaustion weighs my shoulders down like a cloak. Every time I try to sleep, I wake up a moment later to find that the darkness engulfing my hands has crept a bit higher.

I had caved and asked Zeus about it. He didn't know what it was, but he had attempted to burn off the darkness with lightning again. It had no effect.

"He told you," I state baldly, staring out over the river.

"He did," Poseidon says grimly.

I sigh and wordlessly pull my hand from the glove, showing it to him.

Poseidon tilts his head, studying the darkness staining my skin. "I've seen it like this before."

I turn my head to him in surprise. Poseidon is just staring at my hand.

"When you first summoned your powers," Poseidon says. "It's when you give in to the dark emotions you pretend you're better than."

I grind my teeth, my temper already short. "I supposed you never cared about anything enough to fear losing it forever."

I expect a laugh or a snicker. When nothing comes, I glance at Poseidon, blinking in surprise at his forlorn expression.

"You're not the only one of us who's fallen in love," Poseidon whispers, looking at the river again. For a moment, his eyes, which normally resemble a turbulent sea, look lifeless.

"You never said..." I whisper, trying to understand his expression. Poseidon always seemed so carefree. I never thought he felt much of anything.

Poseidon tucks his hands into his pockets. "When I took the crown, he didn't just step down."

"I remember. You had to marry one of his daughters." I am confused. None of this explains what Poseidon meant about falling in love.

Poseidon's lips twitch. "An arranged marriage to one of his daughters. Too bad I was in love with one of his sons."

My brain stops working. We Greeks aren't really tied to any preference when it comes to sexuality, so Poseidon's statement shouldn't surprise me, but it does.

Poseidon in love.

"You were in love," I sputter out, trying to reconcile this information.

Poseidon looks over my shoulder, back toward the castle. "You have to go."

I follow his gaze but find nothing. When I turn back to speak to him, there's nothing but a damp spot of ground left on the banks of the River Styx.

Dick.

I huff in annoyance. Fucking Poseidon. I head back toward the palace and see Morpheus waiting at the front doors. He has his hands folded in front of him, watching me approach with his eerie, fathomless eyes.

I tuck my hands into my pockets, following the path cut

through the garden. I reach out to touch the black roses, closing my eyes and pretending it's not the flowers but her scent perfuming the air.

I don't even care that Morpheus sees me taking the slow stroll through the garden, reminiscing about a life I only got a glimpse of, a handful of days with Persephone when we weren't at odds or war. My steps falter at the single red rose, the one I've done everything to keep alive. I brush one of the wilting petals with my gloved finger.

"I'll find you, my spring. I'll bring you home," I whisper to it as if she is listening through the rose.

I move away, heading toward the patient Morpheus. He nods at me solemnly, wordlessly following me upstairs to the guest room.

He's never been a talker, and sometimes, like now, I find his silence reassuring. But the silence ends the moment Melinoë arrives. Her very presence sets Morpheus on edge.

She glares at me. "Remember the rules, Hades?"

I nod, moving to lie down on the bed.

Melinoë moves to the other side of the bed, keeping the furniture between her and the leader of the Oneiroi.

"Try not to fuck it up this time, Morphie," she hisses.

The God of Dreams' lip curls back slightly from his teeth. He pulls the iridescent sand from his pouch and sprinkles it over my eyes.

Falling into the dream is like sliding into a perfectly heated bath. When my eyes open in the dream, my breath hisses softly past my lips. Persephone is looking up at the apple tree. Fuck, she's beautiful. My arms tingle, and without looking, I know that the creeping darkness that had climbed up to my forearm has retreated slightly. Her hair is loose, tumbling down her back in big curls, and her dress clings to her curves, showcasing every luscious inch of her.

I glide closer, speaking softly, even though I want to grab her and shout to the world. "If you touch them, they will turn to gold."

She tenses slightly, glancing at me over her shoulder. "Why would I want to change them when they're perfect the way they are?"

"Making them gold does not change their nature." I reach above her head, brushing her hair slightly. I touch the leaf, and the green turns to gold immediately. "It only reveals what was hiding beneath its surface."

She turns towards me slightly, reaching up to touch the same leaf, our fingers brushing. At her touch, the leaf turns into a ripe apple, responding to her power.

I pull my hand back, whispering, "Take it."

Persephone plucks the golden apple, rolling it in her palm. Her lips pull back into a bright smile. "What kind of tree is this?"

I love you. Smile for me. Remember me.

"It's a normal apple tree, but with special attendants." I strive to keep my tone neutral and unaffected, even though my heart feels like it is about to crack my chest. "Three nymphs spend their lives tending to these trees."

Her lips twitch, looking at me. "Hm. I didn't think you'd be back."

Nothing could keep me away, my spring.

I lean against the tree. "Why?"

"I was surprised to see you at my house yesterday," she murmurs, holding up the golden apple. "Why are your eyes blue here and not in reality?"

A cold finger of unease shoots down my spine. I straighten, closing the distance. "Persephone, where did you see me?"

She searches my eyes. "At my house."

No. No. No.

My body is tight even inside the dream, preparing to ward off a blow. "I need you to listen to me very carefully. What was I doing there?" I grab her arms, needing to reassure myself that she escaped this encounter intact.

She looks down at my hold on her, frowning. "You spoke with my mother. Don't you remember?"

I want to hurl. I should have protected her. He got so close.

"I don't have green eyes," I growl. "My father does. What

did he say to your mother?"

She lifts her hand, brushing her fingers against my cheeks, right below my eyes. I close my eyes in comfort at that tiny touch.

"He's a very dangerous man," I add, not opening my eyes or moving away from her touch.

She keeps stroking her fingers against my face, tracing my features. "Are you?"

"Yes," I answer without thinking. "But not to you."

Her fingers drop, and my eyes open, regretting my quick words. "Do I frighten you?"

Persephone tilts her head to the side, her eyes scanning my face, analyzing me. "No."

I let out a soft exhale of relief. "Did you hear anything else he said? My father?"

"He said something about Olympus trembling at her feet. Then she left the room with him."

Her eyes are curious, full of questions she isn't sure she can ask. Or if she should ask them.

"There's a war," I explain. "My father and I are on opposite sides."

She studies my face for a moment before sliding past me to sit on the blanket in the grass. "What are you fighting for?"

My lips twitch. Women fight for a cause. Men fight to prove who has the bigger stick.

I follow her, sitting next to her on the blanket. "Survival."

Chapter Fourteen

Hades

SHE TAKES A BITE OF THE APPLE, TUCKING HER LEGS UNDER HER.

"He wants to kill me and my brothers." He wants to wipe us from every existence, in every timeline, even parallel ones.

"Why?" She scans my face, for a moment looking so sincere, so like the woman I love that it breaks my heart. "Because you fight for survival?"

I glance up at the sky in this dream, smiling when I see how she's recreated the sky of our home. The swirling vortex of the night sky dances across the realm, every single constellation sliding over the darkness. It is an old gift from Nyx.

"Because we defeated him. We trapped him in a cell made from the bones of a Primordial for thousands of years." And I became his eternal jailor, alone in the Underworld.

"So… a mutually difficult relationship, then?" Persephone comments, pulling me from my thoughts.

I let out a surprised laugh. "Hard parental relationships seem to be a popular divine trait," I quip back.

She smiles but looks away, back up at the stars. I follow her gaze, whispering to them, "She wants you to be something you're not. Your mother."

I hear her slight intake of breath. "What makes you say that?"

"You don't dream of your home," I answer. "You escape."

Before dreams were my prison, they were once an escape. Now they're the only bridge to the woman I love, and she doesn't know who I am.

"Doesn't everyone dream of something else? Something more?"

My lips twitch. "Only those hoping to see more, to do more. To be more."

She focuses on me, tilting her head, her dark hair laced with flame sliding over her shoulder.

"And what do you dream of? When you're not loitering in mine?"

My eyes remain locked on hers. "My queen."

I dream of *you.*

She tilts her head, and for a moment, I remember how her crown glittered as she said her vows as the Queen of the Underworld.

"You have a queen?"

I shake my head. The hope of seeing some glimmer of recognition in her eyes vanishes. "*Had* a queen. I'm trying to get her back."

Her lips twitch, and the movement is so *Persephone* it breaks me a little.

"Can I make a suggestion?" she asks, smirking a bit more. "Maybe don't go around kissing strangers and hanging out in their dreams. She'll probably get jealous."

I toss my head back, laughing deeply. No one can ever make me laugh like Persephone. She laughs with me, taking another bite of her apple.

I smile as I look up at the sky. "Again, you're assuming you're not her."

She shoots me a look as I turn to smirk at her.

You're still in there, my spring, still sassing me even now.

Mellie's voice echoes through the dream, "Hades."

I sigh heavily.

"What was that?" Persephone frowns, looking around.

I lean closer, pressing my forehead to hers. "I have to go," I whisper. "Be careful. If you see my father again, do not mention me."

She searches my eyes. "I won't."

I keep my voice low, hoping she can sense the importance of my words. "You can be anything you wish, Persephone. Do anything. Spring is so much more than just growing pretty flowers."

She glances at my lips, and I lick them, luring her to me. *Kiss me, my spring. Remember me.*

The ground shakes, and I'm yanked from the dream. I snarl as I sit up in bed in the palace. "We were getting somewhere!"

Melinoë hits the wall, sinking to the floor. She mutters to herself madly, her dual-colored hair plastered to her head from the sweat.

I lunge out of bed and kneel in front of her, grabbing her arms. "Melinoë!"

Melinoë doesn't even hear me, her body twitching violently as she laughs maniacally. I shake her, but it does nothing. She disappears from my arms, vanishing in a puff of smoke, that eerie laughter remaining.

I curse as I hit the wall, slamming it with my fist. When did I become so fucking selfish? I threw Melinoë to the madness inside her for a moment longer with Persephone.

8

Chapter Fifteen

Persephone

MOTHER, I'M NOT SURE I UNDERSTAND. Why am I to dress in my best for this afternoon tea?" I ask. Margaritte pulls the corset ribbon tight, forcing me to exhale all the air from my lungs.

Mother walks over and smooths out my skirt before looking me over. "This is an important day, Persephone. Our efforts have reaped rewards." Her voice is light, almost… happy.

She steps back, taking me in fully, as Margaritte puts the finishing touches on my hair and makeup.

"You look pleasing, Persephone," my mother says, and if I didn't know her, I would say I could hear some affection in her voice. But my mother isn't able to show affection or love. She sometimes shows pride, but never regarding me.

The doorbell rings, and my mother smiles. "Hurry, Margaritte. Our guest is here, and he will be eager to meet Persephone."

Margaritte nods, moving faster. "Yes, Your Greatness."

Mother leaves, I assume to greet our mystery guest. My mind keeps going to my dream mystery man.

Hades.

Even thinking his name makes my cheeks heat. Is he real? He feels real. When I sleep regularly, I can very much tell I am dreaming, but when he is present, it all feels more real, and I wake up not as rested as usual.

I replay the last dream from the start. How it felt when our fingers almost touched, how his laugh sent a shiver from my spine right to my core in the best way. His words... *"Spring is so much more than just growing pretty flowers."* How I have longed to hear those words from another, for someone to see that I have so much more potential than just Demeter's shut-in daughter. Then I can't help but think about how my gaze slowly drifted over his criminally handsome face, landing on his perfect, full lips.

Were we about to kiss before the ground shook? Who was that woman's voice who called to him? His queen?

How would his lips have felt against mine?

"Lady Persephone!" Margaritte exclaims, flustered. "We really must go."

I flush, meeting her gaze. "Right, sorry. I'm ready."

As we walk down the stairs, I hear the muffled voices of my mother and the visitor. His voice is deeper than my mother's, but the pitch does not hit my ear with anything other than disinterest.

My mother spies me through the slight crack in the door and opens it, gesturing me inside. "Ah, Persephone! There you are! This is Adonis," she chirps, her voice almost unrecognizable. "Adonis, this is Persephone."

I turn slightly, looking at him. He's tallish, probably a few inches taller than me. His body is wrapped in muscle, but it almost looks unnatural, unlike my dream man. No, Hades' muscles make him look large and strong... *and I want to lick every inch.* I blush at my inappropriate thoughts, pushing them to the back of my mind.

I can tell that Adonis believes the blush is for him by the way his lips twist into an arrogant smirk. I allow myself to continue scrutinizing him, knowing that he believes I like what I'm seeing. His hair is longer on top and shaved much shorter at the sides. There is nothing kind about his eyes, and nothing about him draws me in. In fact, I want to run in the other direction, fast.

Straight into the bed of the mysterious Hades...

I blush deeply again, the heat spreading down my neck.

The more I blush, the more I seem to have a bad taste in my mouth. I recognize it as a reaction to someone trying to force their magic on me. It has happened a couple of times in my life.

Adonis narrows his eyes at me, and the foul taste worsens. I feel a weight wrap around my left ring finger, leaving it throbbing. I glance down at my hand to see nothing there, and I force myself not to react.

I hear the floorboards shift and look up, watching Adonis as he slowly circles me like a vulture. I keep my eyes on him until he is behind me, watching him, learning him. Something deep down makes me feel like it's vital that I get to know his weak spots. He's not divine. I can definitely tell that, but he's not quite human, either. There is something about his stance, his arrogance, that makes me think he isn't happy about his lack of a god title and power.

I glance at my mother, but I'm not sure why. She looks on passively, her face set in a biddable smile.

"Strip," Adonis demands from behind me. I feel him tug on the ribbon of my corset, loosening it.

My heart seems to stop and speed up all at once. I look at my mother again, praying to every deity that she will stop this. Every shapeless dress and every dull hairstyle has convinced me she will do almost anything to protect my modesty. At this moment, I would kill for her overbearingness to force me into a shapeless, unappealing box without womanly wiles.

My mother's cheeks go pink as she steps back. "I will leave you two to become better acquainted." My mother spins on her heel and glides from the room, closing the doors as she leaves.

I am frozen, my eyes wide as I stare at the closed door. My chest is tight, and though my corset has been loosened, breathing has never been more challenging. I stumble a step toward the door.

This must be a mistake. A dream. A nightmare.

"I said strip," Adonis growls, moving to stand in front of me again, his mud-brown eyes now almost completely black.

I back away from him, deeper into the living room. "No." The word is stronger than I expected, and I am surprised by the unrelenting rage that seems to simmer under my skin.

Adonis takes a step forward and lifts his arm, slamming the back of his hand against my cheek hard, forcing me back onto the couch. His gold ring slices my cheek. "You are mine. You will follow my orders."

I bring my hand to my cheek, protecting it. Thick gold ichor coats my palm. My eyes sting with tears, but I will not let them fall. I will not show him any weakness.

Adonis moves to me and grabs the front of my corset, yanking it hard and ripping the stitches. "I want to see if you are worth the price."

The fury bubbles more to the surface, roaring within me, and I shove him back hard, making him stumble over the rug.

"Do. Not. Touch. Me," I snarl, standing and covering myself with the ruined material.

"You will learn to respect me, Persephone." He narrows his eyes, practically spitting my name like a curse. Adonis looks me over again, and the blood in my veins feels like fire. Beneath my skin, I feel sharp spines, spurred by his words, his leering gaze, and the ichor trickling down my cheek from his hit. Their purpose is not to harm me but to protect me and do harm to others.

"I will be sure you are worth the trouble," Adonis growls. "I will not get on the wrong side of Hades for just anyone. Your mother better be right about you."

The anger dissipates a little at the sound of his name, and my face relaxes a little, my body humming for him.

Hades. Hades. Hades...

"Hades?" I ask, frowning.

Adonis snarls, "Demeter! I'm leaving!" Adonis storms out of the room, slamming the front door as he leaves. I flop down on the couch, thinking.

"I will not get on the wrong side of Hades for just anyone."

What could that possibly mean? Well, one thing is for sure: Hades is real, and he has been visiting my dreams. That simple thought makes everything a little lighter.

"What did you do?" my mother hisses, stomping into the room. The serene Goddess of the Harvest is long gone, replaced by the one I'm more familiar with.

I don't look at her, I can't. I choose to stay in the daydream of my meadow. Of Hades. My dream man.

"You'll be lucky if he's still considering you."

Considering me?

My brows furrow. "Considering me?" I slowly look up at my mother, unsure of what my expression reveals. "Mother, are you selling me?" I worry that my voice will waver, that she'll hear some emotion that she will disapprove of, but it doesn't. It is strong and fierce.

"Selling is such a cheap term, Persephone. I am finding you a match," she replies, but her furious gaze locks on me.

"Match?"

"Don't you want to get married? Have a family of your own?" she asks. Her voice changes, going softer. It is a manipulation tactic that I have more than learned to identify quickly.

"Who is Hades?" I ask, and I can tell it takes everything within my mother not to physically recoil.

She grabs my face roughly, her nails digging into the slowly healing cut on my face, making it bleed again. "Where did you hear that despicable name?" she hisses.

I feel that rage again, that fury, and I clench my fists, trying to push it down. "Adonis."

Mother digs her nails in harder, gold ichor streaming down my face once more. "You will *never* say that name again, won't even think it," she snarls. "He is a monster, the worst kind of evil."

I study her face, looking for any deception, but there is none.

Mother slowly relaxes her grasp on my face and steps back, wiping her hand free of my blood. "Go clean yourself up. We won't speak more of this."

I stand from the couch and wordlessly leave the living room, blood dripping down my neck.[9]

---

9   The Nightmare & The Daydream Chapters 16-26

Chapter Sixteen
Hades

SEVEN DAYS WITHOUT DREAMWALKING. Without sleep. Without Persephone. I rub my hand down my face, trying to focus on the newspapers. My father is leaving a trail across the mortal world, but it is microscopic, something only I would see or even know to look for. A man who dies a withered husk at age thirty. Mortals who turned to dust in a freak storm, time stolen over and over until nothing was left.

I reach for the phone as it rings, already knowing who it is. "He's in Budapest," I murmur, looking over the news.

"Not anymore," Zeus snaps, his voice like a thunderclap in my ear. "I have a Titan pickup."

I sigh and close my eyes, reaching out to Zeus to collect the Titan. My brows shoot up. "Epimetheus?"

Zeus hisses, "Yeah, his powers of afterthought were underwhelming, to say the least."

I direct my shadows to deposit Epimetheus into one of the restructured cells and rub a hand down my face. "The Primes are maintaining neutrality. The treaty of the Old Gods of All Pantheons stands."

"Fuck the treaty!" Zeus snaps.

I growl back. If only it were so easy. The Old Gods agreed long ago to maintain an oath of non-interference, even when it comes to skirmishes within their own pantheon. It is too easy for Primordials to wipe the world clean with their abilities. It is better looking at the big picture, but a giant fucking pain in the ass at the moment.

"They won't move on it. We can't force them."

Zeus hangs up, and I slam the phone back into the cradle.

The darkness climbs further up my arm, well past my elbow. It's like an insidious spill of oil I can't wash away. My gaze snaps up as someone walks into my office, and I blink in surprise when I see a disheveled Melinoë. One of her space buns is partially unraveled, and her mismatched eyes are sunken in. Is this what happens when she goes too far?

"I'm sorry," I blurt out.

She doesn't acknowledge me, instead slapping a newspaper on my desk. "We're dreamwalking tonight."

I blink in surprise and look down at the copy of *Olympus Today* Melinoë slammed on my desk. Persephone stares up at me, her eyes so cold, guarded, and lifeless.

"Read it," she hisses.

Persephone, the Goddess of Spring, has officially announced her acceptance of potential suitors and hopes to be married before the coming winter.

"The fuck?!" I shout.

She *is* married.

"If she's aware of this, the Persephone locked deep inside her will fight back hard. It will make her dreams more open and easier to enter and exit. But I... I think Helios should be here."

Helios... a Titan. I've been shielding Melinoë from the way Zeus was asking about her boyfriend and his allegiances, but I don't know how long that could last. But Zeus and the war can wait.

"He has an invitation now," I announce, and a moment later, the Titan of the Sun appears next to Melinoë. She doesn't even react.

Her eyes are focused on me. "Forget everything I told you. Don't go easy. Make her fall in love with you."

I note the way Melinoë's eyes are far away. "She won't forgive me if she returns and finds you past the point of no return."

"I don't care," she says.

Helios takes her hand. "If she goes, she won't be alone."

Melinoë yanks her hand from his, a flicker of her usual self coming through.

"Morpheus," I command.

The God of Dreams appears at my side a moment later and bows his head. "My king."

I step around my desk and head out the door. They follow me to the guest room and stand beside the bed as I lie down.

"Once Hades is in, lock the dream," Mellie orders Morpheus, then focuses on me. "No external forces will be able to wake either of you. You'll be trapped there until I unlock it."

I scan her eyes again, hesitating.

Helios grabs her hand. "She's got this."

"It's extremely dangerous," she continues as if Helios hadn't spoken. "But you need time with her. You think I haven't noticed your arms?"

I tense, forcing myself not to glance at them.

Mellie's eyes flash, and she yanks her hand from Helios's again. "Touch me one more time, sunboy, and I will remove your fingers and shove them up your ass."

Helios smirks. "There's my hellcat."

I lay back on the bed, and Morpheus steps forward.

Mellie glares at Helios. "I don't care what you have to do to me. Get them out of the dream before I spiral."

Helios nods, winking. "Fuck, you're hot when you're threatening me."

Mellie rolls her eyes and nods at Morpheus. The God of Dreams picks up some sand and sprinkles it on me, sending me into the dream before locking it behind me.

Chapter Seventeen

Hades

SLIDING INTO THE DREAM IS EASIER, AS *MELINOË SAID IT WOULD BE.* There's little resistance as I arrive in the meadow. I raise a brow when I see her pacing furiously back and forth. The flowers reach for her as she walks past them but retreat once she's too far away.

I breathe in the sight of her. Fuck, it has been seven days. An eternity.

"Persephone," I call softly.

Her head snaps up, and I snarl at the sight of her face. Bruises mar the side of her face. I close the distance, my rage making the dream shake.

"Who did this to you?" I demand, gently lifting her chin.

Persephone holds my gaze, looking for something. "My mother says you're the worst kind of evil. A monster."

The bruises tell a story. Someone struck her with the back of their hand. Hands that would decorate my office, a warning for all who would dare even look at my queen with the intent of harming her.

"And what do you say?"

Her eyes drop to my lips. "You're gentle."

"The worst kind of monsters never look like them. Instead, they wrap themselves in innocence and lull you into a false sense of security." I keep my eyes on her. "Trust your instincts. What do they say?"

Her eyes sear me, seeing me stripped to the bone. The sun around her pupil glows as if shining through the darkness clouding my mind, crowding against my soul.

She smiles softly before turning and walking away. I chase after her. "I missed you."

She glances at me over her shoulder, smiling coyly. "It's been a while."

Six hundred four thousand, eight hundred minutes, actually.

I take her hand. "This dream is beautiful."

Her eyes dart to our hands, and I pretend not to notice. "Where are we?"

The Underworld. Say the Underworld, Persephone.

"I'm not sure. It's perfect, though," she murmurs, looking around.

I mask my flinch. Persephone doesn't remember our home. Perhaps we didn't have enough time together for her to feel the tie to this place.

"It could use more color," I say. The gardens around the palace are shrouded in black. Only other areas of the Underworld display fantastical color.

She shrugs. "It's a nice change from pastels, though."

"You don't strike me as a pastels person." I laugh. "You need colors that speak to the passion inside."

When Persephone worked at Plutus, all of her outfits were full of statement colors with maddening pencil skirts that made me fantasize of the sounds she'd make when I ripped the threads that held it together.

Her eyes sparkle, and for a moment, she's that same woman who flaunted her body down the halls of Plutus. "And what do you know of the passion inside me?"

Everything. I know the sound you make when you want to play with me. The face you make when you provoke me so I can throw you over my knee. The taste of your kiss, of your cunt.

I lift my hand slowly, brushing my fingers slowly across her cheek. "I know it's lurking under your skin, screaming to get out."

Do you remember all the ways I've made you scream, my spring?

I step closer, breathing her in, hating that I can't fill my lungs with her scent. "You think you must choose one or the other: the Goddess of Spring or the darkness inside. But you don't. You can be both, no matter what anyone tells you."

Her lips part slightly, her breath hitching. "Darkness?"

"Do you feel it?" I whisper softly. "A coiled power, like a serpent sleeping inside you. Are you scared to wake it?"

Am I telling her or myself?

Her breaths become shallower. "I-I don't know."

I shift even closer until our bodies brush against each other. "Close your eyes and feel."

Her eyes close, and her trust in me is a balm to my bruised soul.

"You feel your power," I whisper softly. "You can feel the trees and the grass, the flowers..."

Even in a dream, she'll feel the echo of them.

She inhales deeply, no doubt feeling the flora around her. "Yes."

I never saw this side of Persephone, the one who is just learning to embrace her power. From the moment I met her, Persephone used her abilities as easily as breathing.

"Feel what lurks beneath the flowers, into the soil, the very earth," I cajole.

Her vines sprout from the ground, and I glance down, smiling as I see they're not green, not purple, but black as night, with gilded leaves. They wrap around my ankles, stroking me. I close my eyes, luxuriating in the familiar feeling of their touch.

My shadows greet them, dancing with them. I watch Persephone's face, whispering, "You've only scratched the surface. Break away from what you've been told you are. Become who you're meant to be."

The vines continue to dance with my shadows. It is an eternal dance of life and death.

Of a Queen and a King.

Chapter Eighteen

Persephone

WHAT DO YOU FEEL, PERSEPHONE?" Hades' deep voice vibrates through me, mingling with my powers like a caress. But that's not all I feel. My fingers tingle with the power I feel from the flora surrounding me. It's not a daunting power, not a dangerous one, and not a power to be used against. It's a power from within, and its only purpose is to enrich and nourish.

A soft moan escapes me, and my cheeks heat a little in embarrassment. The feeling of all the living things around me is so intoxicating that the discomfort quickly dissolves, and once again, I lose myself to the way the power brushes against my skin.

"I feel," I whisper, "everything…"

"Describe it," Hades commands. There's a strain in his voice that I can't quite identify.

The phantom feeling of denim grazes my fingers, and I have to bite back another moan.

I dive deeper into my connection with the greenery, permitting myself to get lost in it for a moment. The darkness within me swirls, as desperate for freedom as I am. It swells as I dive deeper, greeting me like an old friend, swirling around the light power like a long-lost lover.

I find myself slightly distracted by the feeling of the strange brush of denim against my fingers, and they twitch in response.

"This… whole other part of me that I didn't—"

My words are muted as I feel the brush of a hand over mine, pushing the pads of my fingers more into the material, but when I flex my fingers, there is nothing there. I snap my eyes open. To my horror, black vines with rich golden leaves have sprouted from the ground and are wrapped around Hades' legs, caressing him.

Please tell me those are not my vines...

Hades tilts his head at me and glides his fingertips gently along the upper epidermis. I shiver at the feeling. I can feel everything my vines feel, and his touch may as well be against my cheek. My whole body feels like it is aching and yearning, but how is it possible that I could feel this way about someone who may as well be a stranger?

My vines tighten, and I flush. "Oh! I'm so sorry. Fuck…"

My cheeks heat even more as the curse word passes my lips, and I push my flat palm downward, trying to pull the vines away, but they don't budge.

Hades furrows his brow. "Sorry? For what?"

I yank at the obsidian vines, trying to pull them away from him. "The… um, black vines."

Hades chuckles softly. "Leave them. I like them," he replies, and his eyes seem to sparkle a little before dark smoke appears. No, it's not smoke… they are shadows. They flow from Hades and coil around my vines, almost nuzzling them. Again, I feel his touch through my vines, and they seem to vibrate slightly in excitement at being wrapped in the darkness.

I tilt my head and lower my hands, withdrawing whatever poor control over my vines I was pretending to have. They release Hades' legs enough to coil around the shadows. I can't suppress the shiver that travels through my body at the feeling of his shadows playing with my vines.

I meet Hades' gaze, noticing that his pupils have nearly swallowed the sapphire of his irises, turning them almost black. The ache between my thighs intensifies, my core throbbing and pulsing.

My cheeks heat, and I clear my throat, yanking the vines

away and forcing them to disappear. "We shouldn't be doing this."

Hades tilts his head. "Why?"

"It's inappropriate. I can... feel what they feel." I'm certain my face must be as red as the tomatoes in my mother's garden. My cheeks feel as though they are on fire. I look away from him, trying to hide my embarrassment.

When he doesn't reply after a few moments, I look up at him. His lips are pulled into a wicked smirk, dirty and panty-dropping. "And?"

Panty-dropping? Where did that come from?

"Well, I..."

Gods, P. Stop blushing!

In my peripheral vision, I notice Hades' shadows sliding toward me, but I don't move my gaze from his. My breath hitches when what feels like large, strong hands graze my ankles and slowly move up my calves.

"I can feel what they feel," Hades says, his eyes dark with an emotion that makes my core tighten. Something about his expression is primal. I feel like I should run away, but all I want to do is get closer to him. The urge is extremely difficult to resist.

The shadow hands brush the back of my knees, and it's an effort to stop them from buckling. I pull my bottom lip between my teeth to stop my moan as his shadows creep up my thighs torturously slowly.

"Tell me to stop," Hades says. There is an edge to his voice like he doesn't want to ask the question outright, but he wants to give me the power to stop this. If I let it continue, what will happen?

My breaths are shallow. I can't seem to take in any air at all, and my head spins. "We should..." I begin.

"We should..." Hades' voice is lower, and I think I can hear something in it... desire, maybe. His shadow hands slide slightly higher up my thigh, and though everything feels duller in the dream as if there is an invisible barrier, it does not stop the electricity that seems to pass between us.

"Stop. We should stop." I manage to force out the words, my voice shaking only slightly.

77

"Oh?" Hades says. He tilts his head, his dark eyes glinting with amusement. "Then what are you doing with those wicked vines, Persephone?"

I blink, glancing down to see his legs wrapped in vines again. I try to remember at what point I started to feel the hard muscles of his calves and thighs against my fingers again. At what point did the soft brush of denim start to feel like I was pressing my fingers into him, needing to feel more?

I try to yank them away, trying to control them, but they don't budge. They continue to caress Hades like they need to be touching him. My head swims from the feel of his touch slowly drifting up my thighs, and controlling my powers becomes even more difficult. The whisper of his calloused hands tracks farther up, closer to where I need them to be.

"They are just giving you what you desire, Persephone," Hades says, his voice as alluring as the feeling of his shadow hands.

I need to stop this. I tunnel into my power, which only seems to add to my pleasure, but I mentally yank my vines hard. They retreat suddenly, so suddenly that I fall forward into Hades. Hades catches me, wrapping his arms around me, the shadows disappearing suddenly.

"Why did you stop?" Hades asks, looking down at me, his eyes still nearly completely black.

I pant as I look up at him. There is not one part of my body that isn't aching. "I…"

Hades leans in closer. "You didn't have to."

I find my gaze slowly wandering over his face to his lips, his full, perfect lips.

"Kiss me," Hades whispers, his warm breath tickling my lips.

My gaze snaps back to his, "I—"

Before I can continue, Hades silences me by brushing his lips over mine. The kiss is gentle. In a way that is showing me I am in control of this. I can either pull away or kiss him back.

The feel of his lips against mine, even though it is only

a phantom feeling, is enough to stoke the fire sitting low in my tummy. My skin feels as though it is on fire, and I deepen the kiss, softly sliding my tongue along the seam of his lips.

Hades' groan sends a jolt of awareness through my body, and in a flash, his hand is digging into my hair. He pulls me close, opening for me, his tongue playing with mine. I slowly glide my fingers up his arms, moaning when I get to his biceps. He is so strong.

Hades' hands wander down my body and over my back to cup my ass, squeezing it. I'm too lost in him to feel anything but desperation, and I moan as he digs his fingers deeper into my flesh.

"Fuck, Persephone," he groans into my mouth.

Hades bends slightly and cups my thighs, yanking me up. Eagerly, I wrap my legs around his waist and my arms over his shoulder, running my fingers through his hair.

"Missed you so much," he growls into my mouth before sliding his lips to my jaw, the soft kisses and sharp bites making me tremble in his arms.

I smile, tilting my head as he continues his exploration down my neck, leaving a trail of pleasure in his wake. "You hardly know me."

Hades pulls back, a flicker of something that resembles sadness in his eyes before he masks it with a flirtatious smirk. "Doesn't mean I can't miss you."

He leans in to kiss me again, but I pull back a little. "I can barely feel you."

Hades nods solemnly. "It's the dream realm."

"I want to feel you," I whisper, looking away.

Hades pinches my chin, tilting it so I look back at him. This time, his eyes look… hopeful.

"There is a way." He searches my eyes with his penetrating gaze. "For us to meet in person."

I tilt my head, intrigued.

"The announcement," Hades clears his throat, clearly bothered by my mother's quest to marry me off, "said you are accepting suitors."

I sigh. "So I've heard."

"Would you accept me as one?" he asks, and there is

something so endearing about his uncertainty.

"My mother would never allow it," I reply, my heart sinking.

Hades' lips twitch, and his eyes sparkle. "She wouldn't have a choice. Your mother made a mistake when she announced it in the paper."

Chapter Nineteen
Hades

I AM ASKING FOR PERMISSION TO DATE MY WIFE. It is ironic, **though** the true twist is that besides a single dinner in my penthouse, I've never taken Persephone on an actual date. Maybe this is my chance to make things right. To have the romance we should have had. The one she deserved.

"I worry she will just speed along with the current front runner."

I frown. "The current front runner?"

"Adonis."

"Adonis?" I snarl.

Fucking immortal dick. He is stuck in the past. He stole lust dust from Aphrodite. Then the prick turned around and used it on Hera until he convinced her to give him ambrosia, making him immortal. **Hera's** pride and **stubbornness** refused to allow her to admit that she had fallen for such a ploy. So she pretended it was all planned and even shielded the prick from **Zeus's** wrath. This only emboldened him, and he enjoyed feeling immune to consequences even gods faced. No one ever crossed the Queen of the Gods.

"You know him?" Persephone asks, her eyes wide and vulnerable.

This version of Persephone is so different from who I know her to be. Demeter had stripped her down to the barest studs, and it made my stomach roll to see it. Even if this is the time I never got with Persephone, the side I never got to see.

"He stole something from an acquaintance of mine." I grind my teeth. "Did he… did he touch you?"

Lust dust **didn't** just affect the person wearing it. **Even** gods **fall** to its potent pull. It took away consent from everyone in proximity.

She shakes her head. "Not really."

I search her eyes. "You **didn't** feel compelled?" Also, what does 'not **really**' mean?

Persephone scoffs, and my lips twitch. "I felt compelled to get away from him."

"You did?" My smile widens. I don't know why I had expected anything else from my queen.

"Yeah. **He's** the worst."

I laugh deeply. "I should have known **you'd** be immune." This is Persephone, after all.

"That must have been why he was so angry."

My laughter dies. I reach out to touch the bruise on her cheek. "This is from him."

She pulls away from my touch, the sparkle in her eyes dimming. I don't know where it comes from, but I suddenly know what marred her. I know that prick backhanded her. Even inside the dream, I can sense the swirling darkness **crawling** higher up my arms.

"It's nothing," she whispers.

"It's everything," I whisper back.

She presses her lips to mine in a frantic bid to change the subject. It **won't** matter. He crossed the God of the Dead, and no protection, no matter how powerful, will stop me from exacting retribution. I need to be smart about how to strike. I need to be cold and calculating. Two things I was once famous for, yet now they feel like butterflies caught in a net with gaping holes.

"Hades. It's time," Melinoë calls, breaking through the haze of desire and my plans for revenge.

"I'll be back, my spring," I promise her before pulling back and stepping out of the dream.

My eyelids rise, and all my senses, which were dulled inside the dream, spring to life again. The scents of those around me are almost overpowering, the sounds blaring, and even the sensation of my fingers against the bed beneath me seems overwhelming. It all feels wrong. Even more so because there is no scent of roses in a fog, only sunshine, darkness, and a taste of sand on my tongue.

A second later, the sand vanishes, and **Melinoë** stumbles back. She hits the wall, blood dripping from her nose. Helios is at her side in an instant, pressing his forehead to hers. For a moment, so fast I almost miss it, her eyes soften, and she leans into him. Then she shoves him away, moving back to my side as I sit up, her eyes surprisingly clear. She rubs her sleeve under her nose, wiping the blood away.

"**She's** still in there," I murmur to the Goddess of Nightmares.

Melinoë nods sagely. "It was easier this time. She wanted you there."

I slouch. "I need to arrange a date in Olympus with her."

"I thought you **couldn't** leave the Underworld," Helios says, wordlessly wrapping an arm around **Melinoë**. I wait for her to shove him away again, but instead, he lifts his hand to her temple, his palm glowing with light. The Goddess of Nightmare and Ghosts completely **relaxes** against the Titan of the Sun.

I shift from the bed and head for my office. I don't look back to see if they are following me but say, "**There's** a tenet from the Primordial of Love. It can circumvent the rules keeping me here, at least temporarily."

Five Primordials sprung from Khaos: Nyx, Erebus, Gaia, Tartarus, and Eros. The last died almost two thousand years ago, on the very night Eros, the younger god, was born. From the **Primordial's** golden bones came **Eros's** bow and arrows, giving the young god the ability to fell the strongest in our pantheon with a single knick. Before he passed, Eros the Prime instilled a rule of order so powerful that even the other Primes bowed to it.

Love among our kind is free to flourish and bows to no dictates, immortal or otherwise.

"Demeter will never allow it." **Melinoë** frowns, still in

Helios's arms.

I nod and pull a dusty book from a shelf, slamming it open on my desk. "She **won't** find out, but I'll need help from the one person **who's** more clever than my brother at sneaking around."

"You **can't** trust Hera," Mellie snaps, straightening away from Helios.

I flip through the pages. "I am aware. I'm the god known for plans, remember?"

Melinoë flops into one of the armchairs. "So **what's** your plan, demon daddy?"

Helios sits on the arm of her chair, glancing at her fondly. "You know I hate when you call me that."

Melinoë swats at Helios. "Stop mothering me." The Titan **doesn't** move. "How are you going to fly under her radar? According to Helios, Demeter knows **Persephone's** every move, and Persephone is never without a chaperone."

I smirk at her. "By giving her a bigger problem to deal with. Kronos has been spotted on Olympus. I have yet to inform Zeus about it."

Mellie's eyes slowly widen, her smirk growing. "This is a chaotic mess. I love it. How do I help?"

"Help me plan a date to win my queen?"

Melinoë jumps to her feet. "Okay, we need chains, whips, a butt plug, and some sort of suspension apparatus."

I choke in surprise, clearing my throat. "It will need to be… demure? This **isn't** the Persephone we remember."

She sighs dramatically. "Helios will be more help then. He's a mushy dickhead."

Helios only glows happily, slipping his fingers into **Mellie's**. "We can save that date for us, hellcat."

"Never," she hisses.

Helios grins at her before **providing** me with all the details of the Persephone he met many years ago.[10]

Chapter Twenty

Persephone

I **RUN THE BRISTLES OF MY SILVER HAIRBRUSH THROUGH MY HAIR AND LOOK AT MYSELF IN THE MIRROR.** The bruises from Adonis and my mother are no longer marring my cheek, but the memory remains, throbbing dully when I focus on it. Hades' kiss no longer lingers on my lips, but I will never forget how it felt within the dream. The passion stains my lips like the most luxurious of lipsticks, and though it was within a dream, he took my breath away with his kiss, leaving me feeling worshiped. I swear my lips look swollen.

My mother has permitted me to leave my hair down, and I am taking full advantage of the allowance. My hair curls softly down my back, the red highlights glinting in the sun, streaming warmly into the room.

"Ah, sweetling. You look lovely today," my mother says, breezing into my room graceful steps **convey** complete ease, but there is something about her eyes that shows inner strain.

I blink, glancing at her in the mirror, unsure how to react appropriately to the compliment. "Thank you, mother."

She walks closer and runs her fingers through my hair. "You do look much prettier with your hair up, but Adonis likes it better this way."

I don't even flinch, already anticipating her usual harsher

words.

"When your hair is up, you look much less… plump," she continues.

I just keep my eyes fixed on myself in the mirror, trying to tune her out. The insult flows off of me as usual. I am always ready for them.

"Well… he likes it this way, and he is the one who will be marrying you." She looks me over again in the mirror before moving away from me. I run my fingers through my hair as if her insults have wrapped in the strands, and I can remove them with my loving touch.

My mother waits at the door. "Come, Persephone. We can't keep your suitor waiting." Her voice is more clipped now. Whether she gets a reaction from me or not, it's never what she wants. Her myriad of insults always end up with her being angry with me.

I stand and smooth out the perfect pink dress Margaritte has practically tied me into before walking toward her. She roughly pulls my arm, linking it with hers, and we go downstairs to see Adonis.

"Shoulders back. Why do you constantly slouch?" my mother chastises. I straighten myself, wincing slightly in discomfort, still unsure why this feels so foreign to me now.

My mother hurries us out of the house, but when we reach the front garden gate, she slows her footsteps and lifts her chin. I can practically feel her amping up her intimidation. As we walk down the cobbled streets, I notice how the dwellers of Mount Olympus find anything else to look at other than my mother and I.

I meet the gaze of a goddess, and from the deep recesses of my mind, the name Artemis appears, along with a textbook entry. Although, I have no memory of ever reading about her. She trips over the curb as she quickly averts her gaze, and I can practically feel satisfaction rolling off my mother at her blatant submission. The sun is setting, casting a warm orange glow that artfully brushes against the brick of the houses, leaving a warm autumnal hue in its wake.

This is the kind of evening most would consider perfect. The air is still warm but not uncomfortable, and peace seems to cover the mountain like a blanket, yet it **doesn't** even touch the blissfulness of my meadow. I **can't** help but **wonder** if I would have more appreciation for the flawless evening if I were on Hades' arm instead of my **mother's**. If his warm body was walking beside mine, if his lips brushed my temple casually as we walked the stony streets of my home, I imagine it wouldn't matter where I was. I would find joy.

While I **can** appreciate the evening for what it is, it's as if I am watching from behind a screen, not living it. My attention is constantly pulled by the not-so-new-but-definitely-worse feeling of my inner darkness churning inside me. It feels more awake than before.

Did I truly use it within the dream?

The barrier between my light power and my dark power has been divided once again by the impenetrable layer that I constructed to keep them separate. I am used to them caressing the wall every so often, displaying an aching longing for the other, but now they are clawing, both desperate to be reunited once again. Along with the restlessness of my powers, I have felt as though there is a heavy pit in my stomach, an acute awareness that something is very wrong, and it all began the night Hades and I shared that kiss.

My mother lifts her hand to wave, and in the distance, I see Adonis waiting outside the restaurant, leaning against the wall. I can already feel the self-important arrogance slithering off him.

My mother tightens her hold on my arm to the point of pain, and I hold back my whimper. "Do not mess this up again, Persephone," she warns, her voice low and dangerous. We continue to walk, and I keep my gaze on the ground, not particularly wanting to anger either of them.

"Adonis!" my mother exclaims, releasing me and moving to kiss Adonis's cheek. "I cannot tell you how much Persephone has been looking forward to seeing you. You clearly made an impression on her. She has scarcely stopped speaking of you!"

I force my face into a polite smile and eventually lift my gaze to meet his. That leering twinkle in his eye is back, and

I am surprised by the fury I feel toward him. I make sure to hold the smile on my face, but I don't let it reach my eyes, wanting to keep them as cold and passive as possible. His predatory gaze sweeps over me, and I once again curse the fact my mother has allowed me to wear something more form-fitting.

Mother lifts my hand and places it in the crook of Adonis's elbow when he offers it, and he leads me inside. My stomach rolls when I notice the restaurant is completely empty, save for us and one server. I resist the urge to yank my hand away, to run and not stop until I am far away from everyone who will hurt me. I want to run until I get to Hades.

Adonis leads me to a table, and the server pulls out my chair. The table is for two, and I glance over my shoulder, watching as my mother sits at a table on the other side of the restaurant, completely out of earshot of us.

"You know," Adonis begins, his voice low and oily. I feel like it slicks my skin, making me crave a scorching shower to remove any trace of it. "There are many that would kill for my attention."

I lift the menu. "And yet, I am the unlucky one," I reply, quickly masking my surprise at my blatant rudeness. *Where did that come from?*

I pretend to look over the menu, considering my words. Something about them felt so right, like a piece of the puzzle has finally clicked into place.

I can feel his enraged gaze on me, but it does nothing but fuel my anger. There is no fear or doubt, only a deep surge of incandescent fury.

"I'll enjoy curbing your tongue," he growls.

I lower the menu slightly and quirk an eyebrow, allowing myself to lean into this new instinct that seems to have sprouted. "You don't have anything other than threats in your arsenal?"

Adonis narrows his eyes, and his hand shoots out, grabbing my thigh hard. His fingers bruise me, his nails digging into my flesh. I hold back the groan of pain, not wanting to give him the satisfaction.

"Do you want me to prove it to you, Persephone?" he

snarls. "You spread your legs for him easily enough, but he cannot help you here." His lips pull into a horrible, evil smile. "Even the king cannot save you."

The pain dulls at his words, and I frown.

Spread my legs? He cannot help me here?

"What are you talking about?" I ask, but deep down, I feel like I already know the answer. It's as if my heart beats to the rhythm ofHades, Hades, Hades, Hades.

My skin tingles with the anticipation of hearing his name, of acknowledging him in real life.

Adonis smirks. "I see you really have nothing but flowers in there. Your mother did well." He releases my thigh, the blood rushing back into my leg nearly as painful as his grip. "It doesn't matter. You will give me what I need. You will fulfill your purpose. The only thing you are good for."

"Purpose?" I ask, my stomach once again knotting and twisting.

"Heirs. You will give me as many as I want."

I snarl quietly. "You will *never* have me in that way."

Adonis laughs, throwing his head back. The sound makes my skin crawl. "Your mother has all but guaranteed it. Even offered me the chance to sample the goods *before* the wedding."

My heart stops in my chest, and my lips part. I am in complete disbelief, and yet this is also completely believable.

"She-she wouldn't…" I stutter.

Adonis sneers, leaning in. "She is desperate to get rid of you. Your mother understands that your only use is producing grandchildren for her. She hopes they aren't as disappointing as you."

I can't stop my flinch, though the words are not new or surprising to me. But hearing them from someone other than my mother adds another layer of humiliation that I have yet to experience.

He pulls back, the pride clear on his face. Oh, how he loves using his words to wound me. The wrath within me churns, the shame adding a new level to it. I don't just want to run from Adonis. I want to destroy him. Adonis focuses on the waiter, ordering for both of us, but all I can hear is the sound of my rage rushing through me.

I hear nothing for the rest of the meal, and I barely touch my food. Of course, it consists of nothing but vegetables grown in our garden. My mother had them delivered for tonight. I force myself to become completely numb to stop myself from smashing a wine glass and using the shards to slash Adonis's throat. Never have I felt anger like this. I didn't even know I had it in me. I'm the woman who cries when a flower dies, and here I am, going through different scenarios for how I could obliterate Adonis, and I don't feel a drop of guilt.

In a fury-filled daze, Adonis pulls me to my feet and slams his lips to mine. My whole body recoils. I pull back, just managing to refrain from wiping the taste and feel of him from my lips. I will not make a scene.

He winks at me, spanking me hard on the ass before leaving. My mother hurries over, beaming. I swear she has never looked so proud of me.

"Well, that went well!" she chirps, looking me over, but there's a wariness in her eyes that I identify easily.

I look at her, locking my gaze with hers, watching for every emotion, every micro-expression. "Did you tell Adonis he could *sample* me before the wedding?" I ask, my voice surprisingly even.

My mother narrows her eyes, lifting her chin as if about to challenge me. "Does that sound like something I would say, sweetling?" she asks, her voice light but with an undercurrent of a warning.

Her face is once again fixed in that faux smile, but she is too slow. I see the deception.

Chapter Twenty-One

Persephone

THE **PREVIOUSLY PERFECT EVENING ON OLYMPUS** now feels thick with tension as my mother and I look at one another. She scrutinizes my face, trying to identify what I am desperately trying to hide. I look away, breaking eye contact, feigning submission. I already know that's what she wants. It's what she's waiting for, what she's always waiting for, but I can't pretend I didn't see what she tried so hard to mask. I saw the deception. I saw the lie.

My mother, mollified by my looking away, brushes her hands down the sides of her brown dress. "We must hurry home. You have an important meeting."

She roughly links her arm through mine and walks briskly, practically pulling me along. I glance at her out of the corner of my eye. Her chin is lifted, and she once again seems to stare down the whole of the mountain. Everyone seems to quiver under her influence.

Who could I be meeting with now? Could Hades have been successful in arranging a date? No… Mother looks far too at ease for that.

"Mother?" I ask, ensuring my shoulders are back, but my eyes are glued to the ground.

"Yes?"

"Who am I meeting with?"

"The God of Love, sweetling," she replies. Her voice is even, but there is an undertone that dissuades me from asking any more questions until we are no longer in public. Although the cobblestone streets of Olympus are almost empty, the street lights illuminate the pathway home. The sun is long gone, and the moon sits proudly in the sky. The warm glow of the golden hour has morphed into the eerie silvery light of twilight.

The second we walk through the gates, my mother releases my arm and enters the house.

"Mother? The God of Love?" I ask, following behind.

My mother huffs, clearly frustrated. "Some silly formality. A god of love has to approve the match," she says, disappearing into the living room, and I slowly follow behind. "And the flighty goddess is off somewhere, no doubt sleeping her way through the mortal world." My mother pauses as she pours three cups of tea. "So, we are stuck with her son. That whole family is an embarrassment."

I tilt my head, watching her. She rarely gives so much information so freely. She's obviously stressed about this. Will the God of Love not be willing to bless the match? Could this be my way out? And who is this Goddess of Love?

My brow furrows as I begin to formulate a plan, but it all depends on who this God of Love is and how amenable he will be to listening to me. It is vital I find a way to get him alone.

I taste his magic before I see him. The second I sense his presence in the house, the ring finger on my left hand starts to throb, aching as if I'm missing something. That feeling has been so much more prevalent recently, something feels just barely out of reach. My mother tenses when he arrives. She feels it, too.

My head snaps up when he appears in the doorway. He leans nonchalantly against the mahogany surround, a devilish smirk pulling at his lips. He meets my gaze, and I am immediately taken by him. There is something about him that draws me in. Whether it be his golden hair, his sky-blue eyes, or his sharp jaw, or maybe it's the effortless way he easily spins an arrow on the tip of his middle finger. He

92

is dressed in a pristine dark -red tailored suit made from what looks like the softest material. The crisp white shirt below is a stark contrast to the suit and perfectly matches his paper-white teeth. My mother places her hand on my shoulder and squeezes hard, pulling me from my stupor.

"If you wouldn't mind turning your dazzle down slightly, Eros. My daughter is not used to it," she says with authority and more than a bit of unease.

Suddenly, he no longer draws me in as much. I can see how handsome he is, but it isn't as maddeningly consuming as before. His sky-blue eyes flash, and he meets my mother's gaze. I feel her hand tighten on my shoulder, her nails digging in.

"Unwise to keep a God of Love waiting. We are very fickle," Eros says, his voice like honey.

I feel my mother tense behind me. "You only just arrived."

Eros's lips pull into a wicked smile, showing those perfect teeth once again. "Did I? Or did you only feel me arrive when I wanted you to?"

I can practically hear my mother's jaw tense. The ground beneath my feet shakes slightly, almost as if my mother's anger is directly responsible. The chandelier tinkles musically as the ground continues to tremble. I glance at my mother. She is wearing the rage on her face proudly as if to scare and intimidate. Eros is the picture of complete ease, continuing to spin that arrow on the tip of his finger. The smirk hasn't left his lips, and his eyes twinkle with mischief.

I clear my throat, drawing attention to myself, and the second his gaze flits away from my mother's, the ground ceases trembling.

"I'm Persephone," I say, tilting my head at him.

Eros quirks a brow as if something has caught his interest. The golden arrow stops, the pointed head turning toward me. He throws it in the air and catches it with impressive ease before it disappears in a puff of red smoke. He bows, keeping his eyes on me. "Eros. At your service."

I smile brightly, about to respond, when my mother interrupts, "Do we have your approval?"

Eros straightens, slowly looking back at Mother. "We?

93

Are you planning to get married too, Demeter?"

My mother growls. In a flash, Eros summons a new arrow and throws it at my mother. It hits her in the arm before dissipating into a puff of smoke again. With wide eyes, I watch my mother look at her arm, fury blazing in her eyes. She looks up, and all the rage drains from her face. Her body completely relaxes, and she looks almost wistful. She sighs softly and links her arm through mine before gently laying her head on my shoulder, staring dreamily into the distance.

Eros smiles at her. "Be a dear and fetch us some more tea and biscuits? I need to speak to Persephone."

I blink at my mother, then at Eros, waiting for my mother to throw her full wrath at him. To my surprise, Mother nods and practically glides out of the room, closing the door behind her.

I blink at the closed door.

"It won't last long on a Primordial power but long enough for us to talk," Eros says, walking to the tea trolley and picking up one of the dainty pre-filled cups.

"Talk?" I ask, blinking at him.

Eros's lips twitch. "You have questions. I have answers."

I glance back at the door. "What answers do you have?"

"What questions do you have?" he retorts, smirking.

"I–I'm not sure."

Eros takes a sip of the tea and turns to look at me. The sight of the tiny pink and orange china teacup in his large hand would be comical if my brain wasn't such a mess of questions.

"We're a lot alike, you know?" he says, putting the cup down.

I tilt my head. *He knows nothing about me.*

He smiles softly and moves closer. "Everyone tells us we're one thing, yet deep down, we know we're something else."

"What am I?" I ask as if this stranger holds all the answers to such huge questions.

"You are," he pauses, looking into the distance, thinking, "duality," he finishes.

94

My brows furrow more. Something about that statement makes perfect sense.

"One part, the Goddess of Spring. The other is something else entirely. Such a dichotomy would tear apart most gods." He smirks. "But not you." He turns on his heel and walks toward the large French doors, walking out into the midnight black of the night. I follow behind, desperate for answers.

Eros walks into the garden, looking up at the stars, twirling his arrow again. I stand next to him, looking up at the same cluster of stars as he.

"What is the other part?" I ask, desperately needing one truth.

Eros looks at me, his smile dazzling. "Well. What is the opposite of life?"

I give him an exasperated look. "Do you always speak in riddles?"

He laughs, such a low and mischievous sound. "Occupational hazard as a trickster." He looks back up at the stars as if he is simply relaying the messages from them. "I'll give you a clue. I am the only child of the Goddess of Love and the God of War, one part lover and one part fighter." His face softens with affection when he mentions his mother, but he masks it just as quickly. "If you are one part spring and life. The other part must be the opposite."

I realize our time is running out, and this riddle will take some thought. I know I need to get to the crux of what I need from him at this moment and worry about this later.

"Please, don't approve of the match," I say, looking back up at the stars.

Eros glances at me before sitting at the small wrought iron garden table. "Why not?" he asks, and I glance at him.

I sit in the chair next to him, the cold iron spitting into the back of my thighs. "It's not right."

"And what is right, Persephone?" he asks, his gaze wandering around the garden cloaked in darkness. Only the brightest of the flowers are visible in the cool glow of the moonlight.

His question immediately pushes an image of Hades to

the forefront of my mind, and I feel my cheeks heat. "I—"

"I can buy you some time," Eros interrupts. "But only so much."

I feel myself relax a little. "My mother mentioned that your mother can also bless the match. Is there any chance she—"

"No." Eros's voice is hard and cold. When I look at him, I notice his face is devoid of all of that playfully smug arrogance. In its place is something fierce and protective.

I swallow, looking away. "All right."

"I can give you a week," he says, his voice slightly more relaxed, but I can still hear the strain.

I look back at him, his face more at ease but his eyes still hard.

"Thank you, Eros."

Eros meets my gaze, searching my eyes. "Did you figure it out?"

I sigh. "The opposite of life is death."

Eros nods slowly.

"But I have no idea what it means," I admit.

The smirk returns to his face. "I guess you have a week to figure it out. Tell your mother I'll be in touch." He winks and disappears in a puff of smoke. A single white feather gently falls from the sky, landing on the table.

I pick up the feather, gliding my finger along the edge. It softly tickles the pad.

"Did he leave already?" My mother's cold voice draws my attention, and I lift my gaze to look at her. It's obvious she's still fighting the effects of his spell, but it's rapidly diminishing.

"He says he will be in touch," I reply, smiling placidly.

Mother places the tea tray on the table and sits in the seat Eros recently vacated. There is a look of confusion on her face, and I do my best not to laugh.

"How did it go?" she asks, pouring some tea.

"He didn't say much. Just that he would return. He spoke a lot of riddles about love and marriage," I reply honestly. The best way to get around my mother is to give her just enough of the truth so she doesn't suspect.

96

My mother bristles, sipping her tea. "Flighty gods," she murmurs into her teacup. "Well, I suppose we will have to hold off until he returns."

"I suppose we will," I reply, sipping my tea to conceal my smile of relief.[11]

---

11   The Nightmare & The Daydream Chapter 29

Chapter Twenty-Two
Hades

THERE'S EVEN LESS RESISTANCE WHEN I DREAMWALK THIS TIME. Is this time. Is Persephone remembering me? Seeking me out? Or is that just a foolish fantasy, seeing things that aren't there? She's resting on a blanket, her eyes closed. Her hair is a dark wave around her, free and unbound, like I know she longs to be. I lay down on the blanket next to her.

She turns her head and opens her eyes. "I had a visitor today."

Adonis. My teeth grind, and I manage to hiss, "Oh?"

"You ever heard of Eros?"

I blink, tension leaving my shoulders. I was not expecting that, but I give a terse nod.

She laughs softly, the sound like wind filtering through sunflowers. "Not a fan?"

I sigh, shifting more toward her. "I'm not a fan of tricksters in general, but Eros, least of all."

Tricksters don't behave according to any form of logic and reason. They act on a *whim*. As someone who worships logic and reason, everything about them seems wrong to me. However, Eros is an enigma. He claims to be a trickster, and the way he acts certainly lends to that idea. Yet, I cannot shake the feeling that he is playing some larger game, that every seemingly innocuous *trick* is a part of another plan.

"Well, that trickster just bought me a week," Persephone says with a smirk.

"A week?" What the fuck does that mean?

"Mother asked for him to approve the match," she adds

98

as if that makes any sense.

I sit up suddenly with realization. In old times, they would summon Eros to approve betrothals. He even officiated at weddings.

My jaw ticks, and I grind my teeth. "Your mother moves fast."

She sighs, sitting up next to me. "I'm pretty sure… she's told Adonis that he can *try* before he *buys*."

Try before he buys? The fuck does that—

Realization settles in on me, and my entire body goes still. I'm not even sure I'm breathing. The shooting sensation of those swirling black tattoos climbing higher up my arms begins, and I know when I wake up they'll be even higher than before. The dream shakes with my rage, and I have to breathe deeply to rein in my temper. I roll my shoulders, moving my head from side to side to control myself again.

"Persephone," I say, my tone flat and uncompromising.

She looks at me, her eyes showing a glimmer of the fear she's hiding from me.

"I will *never* let that happen."

I don't give a fuck about any natural order, any realm, or any war. When it comes to my queen being harmed, I will show no mercy. I'll turn to the darkness I've suppressed for two millennia and wipe the fucking world clean. I'll rip the stars from the sky in a shroud of black until everyone is as lost in the void as I am.

She shifts closer to my side, moving onto her knees. I turn to face her, hoping to conceal the way my mind is imagining the world as nothing but a vacant void where I could start anew with her, with no one and nothing to interfere.

She brushes her lips against mine, her touch as soft as a butterfly, uncertain of her welcome. I deepen the kiss, needing her to ground me and remind me not to give in to the darkness, no matter how much it beckons me.

She pulls back after a moment. "Something's wrong. It feels like something is missing, and I—"

I gently touch my fingertips to her lips, stopping the deluge of thoughts. I know where this is going.

"Don't finish that sentence," I caution. Her eyes are filled with distress, but she doesn't speak. "Just listen."

She nods, and I lower my fingers from her lips, though I can't resist dragging them along the seam, giving her a hint of my skin's taste.

"Something has been taken from you, but if you push too hard, it fights back."

It flays your mind until you let out agonizing screams that echo in my head for days.

She frowns more, the lines around her mouth becoming severe, but she stays quiet.

"Remember how I told you about the war?" She nods shortly, that frown never dropping. "You've been a player in it since the beginning."

They think you're a useless pawn, Persephone. Let them until it's too late for them to flee. *Trap them in their arrogance and shatter them with your power.*

She swallows, her face flickering with fear.

"Does it frighten you?"

She exhales sharply, her eyes darting across my face, analyzing every minute expression. "Who am I?"

Goddess of Spring to many. Queen to some. Wife to one.

"Who do you want to be?"

She sighs and bristles, some of her old self shining through. "Never a straight answer."

Chapter Twenty-Three
Hades

I **LOOK UP AT THE SKY, MARVELING AT IT FOR A MOMENT.** "Do you remember how I said I had a queen and lost her?"

You. It's you.

She nods, disturbing the air with her scent. "Then you made out with me, so you can't be that committed to her."

I blink before letting out a stunned laugh, looking at her. Only Persephone could make a comment like that. Only she could make me laugh right now.

"I am very committed to her," I respond, taking a long look at her face. Her hair shines even here in the dream, and her eyes sparkle with mischief as she raises a brow.

"Then you're terrible at it."

I groan, falling back on the ground and throwing an arm over my face. "You're still such a menace."

This is an echo of her. It's as if I'm seeing a picture of someone I knew from long ago. She is the person I love, but I don't recognize the person in the photo. It is a snapshot of Persephone, and she has no idea who I am. She has never truly *lived*. She's only survived, and there's nothing I can do.

"Berry."

I tense. The word is spoken so softly I wonder if I imagined it. I slowly lower my arm from my face. Persephone's smile has died, her face solemn.

"What did you say?"

Remember.

My voice must break the fragile spell on her, and her

eyes clear. "Sorry, what did you say?" She smiles at me, but a tear slides down her cheek.

She knows. Somewhere inside her, Persephone knows what she's lost. I sit up, wiping the tear from her cheek. She touches my lips, noting the way I'm frowning at her. I try to smile for her, kissing her fingers.

"Just missing things... like you are."

Her eyes drop along with her hand. "Your queen?"

No, don't pull away. Please.

"The things we're missing, Persephone," I whisper desperately, "they're so similar, aren't they?"

She frowns and shrugs. "I guess."

Fuck, I want to tear my hair out. It's so close, I can see it just out of reach, but something is stopping her. The sound of her pain when I push the limits of her memory is devastating. I don't know how far I can go before she breaks.

"Would you like to go on a date with me?" I ask suddenly, scanning her face.

She blinks in surprise. "Yes."

I smile a bit wider and lean forward to kiss her softly. A brush of our lips, so fleeting in the dream. I don't feel any warmth or lingering taste of her tongue, only an echo, a memory, to remind me of what I've lost and what I'm fighting like hell to regain.

She smiles against my lips. "But... my mother."

Yes. Her mother. She made a mistake announcing the courtship in the paper. In the process, she triggered that ancient Primordial rule. *Sloppy, Demeter.* I doubt she realizes it. Not everyone enjoys looking into ancient laws and regulations. I'm pretty sure I might be the only one.

"I have a plan."

I barely get the words out before she slams her lips to mine, taking me down to the ground with force. I wrap my arm around her back, pulling her to straddle me. She looks down at me, her eyes dark with desire.

"I need you," I growl.

She bites my lip, her fingers tunneling into my hair.

"I want you," I whisper into her mouth.

"But, I can't feel you..."

102

The words shatter the small spell we're under, and she rolls off me. I sigh as I sit up, and she grazes her fingertips down my arm, the memory of her touch providing what I can't feel in the dream.

I watch her fingers. "It's like a memory."

Fuck, did I say that out loud?

Her eyes lock on mine. "What do you mean?"

I take her hand and flip it over, tracing my fingers along the lines. "You can almost feel my touch like you're remembering what it feels like."

"Remembering?"

I keep playing with her palm, willing the memories into her as if I can send them to her through my touch. "As if we've done this exact thing before."

Her eyes leave mine, focusing on my hand playing with hers.

Remember.

"We sat in a meadow just like this," I whisper, "holding hands."

She drags her eyes slowly up my arm, but I keep my focus on her palm, drawing a pattern. "Our problems are so similar, aren't they?"

We're both missing something we require to live. Figure it out, my spring. Figure it out! I want to scream and beg. I want to grab her face and force back the darkness that has taken her from me. Somehow, I need to unlock the memories in her mind. I refuse to believe they're completely gone. I *refuse* it. They're locked behind those eyes. I have to believe that.

"Hades?" she whispers, and my eyes snap to hers. "Why did you come to my dream that first night?"

"To see you," I blurt out.

"Why me?"

Fuck. Does she know how impossible this is for me? I long to just say the truth, spilling the reality that dances on the tip of my tongue. My love for her and our life together, the life we barely got to have.

I lean closer, brushing her lips with mine. "I would never be unfaithful to my queen."

She kisses me back, but she is frowning.

Melinoë's voice echoes through the dreamscape, "It's time."

I pull back, pressing my forehead to hers. "I have to go."

"Who is that?"

I push to my feet. "Her name is Melinoë." I catch the way Persephone's eyes narrow and add, "She's my adopted daughter."

"Hades!" Mellie snaps again. "I will beat your ass."

My lips twitch. "I really have to go. She will actually do it."

I kiss her one more time before leaving the dream.

Mellie's nose is bleeding slightly, and her eyes are slightly crazed as she hovers over me. Unsurprisingly, Morpheus has already left. He avoids time around Melinoë as much as possible. "So? How was it?"

"She remembered something," I announce softly.

Berry. It's something so small, but it was enough to tell me she is in there.

"She did?!" Mellie shrieks.

"Berry," I say. Cerberus lifts his heads at the sound of the nickname Persephone gave him, and the hope in his eyes makes my chest ache. He misses her, too. I've caught him rolling in her clothes more than once to get a whisper of her scent, and I can't even blame him for it. I keep one of her negligees in my pocket at all times.

"Did you hear that, Berry?!" Mellie squeals. "Mama remembers you!"

Cerberus stands from his bed, wagging his tail and barking. Mellie walks over to him, grabbing his middle head. "She remembers you!"

He wiggles in her hold and mentally shouts to me, *"MOMMY!"*

Helios crosses his ankle over his knee. "So we're going ahead with the date?"

Mellie's focus is still on Cerberus, but Helios straightens, walking over to her. For the first time, I can almost see the pull between them. It's as if she sends out a silent signal she needs him, and Helios is ready with an answer.

He presses his hand to the side of Melinoë's head, whispering, "Just to take the edge off."

I blink in surprise. Is he using his powers to cut through some of her insanity? I didn't know his powers had that capability.

She spins to him and slams her lips to his. I open my mouth in surprise at the sudden shift. Shock freezing me in place when he deepens the kiss, wrapping his arms around her and pulling her close. I expect Mellie to pull back and try to slap him, but instead, she pulls back and presses her forehead to his.

This is odd to witness.

Helios smiles. "Let's go home, hellcat."

"To our separate homes, yes." Mellie vanishes a second later from his arms.

Now, this makes more sense.

Helios smirks at his empty hands before disappearing in a flash of light. [12]

Chapter Twenty-Four

Persephone

REMEMBER HOW I TOLD YOU ABOUT THE WAR? YOU'VE BEEN A PLAYER IN IT SINCE THE BEGINNING."

I sit at my vanity, applying lipstick that I stole from Margaritte's purse. It's not quite my color, but my mother would never allow me to wear something so provocative. Well, she may be convinced if I mention *Adonis* likes it. Even thinking his name puts a bad taste in my mouth.

My head is still spinning. Hades' words echo through my mind, and though they are about war, there is a part of me that takes comfort in them. The part of me that feels like something is missing draws on the power of the words. It pushes at that part of my memory, trying to make me remember whatever it is I have forgotten.

I study my face, really trying to identify something different about me, something that wasn't there before. Maybe if I stare at myself long enough, it'll come to me, but no matter how long I look, the only thing I can identify is that my eyes are maybe a little harder than they used to be. My mother always used to commend me on my soft gaze. Now, the blue no longer looks like the stillness of the sky but a stormy sea, and the sunshine yellow around the pupil has receded a little.

Along with the frustration, my stomach twists with

nerves. I'm not sure when Hades will arrive or if he'll even show, and if he does, how does he plan to get past my mother? I briefly wonder if he has powers similar to Eros. My lips twitch at the memory of my mother's dazed expression as she floated off to follow Eros's instruction.

Suddenly, the night sky fills with bright light, and there is a loud crashing sound outside. Was that a lightning strike? It must have happened right outside. Thunder continues to roll, and the forks of lightning illuminate the room. I stand up and take a few steps to close the balcony doors when I notice black smoke and shadows collecting around my vanity. My brows furrow, and I tilt my head. Before I have time to react, they dissipate, and in their wake, a small folded piece of paper remains. I step closer and see my name written in a neat script across the top.

Hades.

I pick up the letter and open it. My heart races when I see more of his elegant writing on the page and then beats even faster when I read the words.

Sneak out. -H

The thunder continues to rumble outside, and I hear something smash downstairs, then the sounds of various staff running past my bedroom door. I purse my lips, considering my escape. My mother burned the trellises that used to line the walls outside my bedroom years ago. I silently curse her.

I put the note in the desk drawer and run to my wardrobe, grabbing my hooded cloak. It is the one item of dark clothing I own, made of brushed velvet in a deep purple. I pull it on over my purple dress, not caring that I'm covering it. My options for clothing are so limited that I simply picked the shortest sundress I could find for the date. At least this one is a wrap dress and gives me some semblance of shape. My mother bought it for picnic dates with Adonis. It falls just above my knees and can be concealed by the much longer cloak.

I move to my door and press my ear against it, waiting until the footsteps retreat downstairs. More items smash, and I can hear people shouting. I listen harder and catch

107

my mother's voice amidst the uproar.

I slowly open the door and peek my head out. The mostly dark corridors welcome me as I slip out, blending into the shadows. I make my way down the servant's stairs, hoping everyone will be where the trouble is happening.

My heart races, and I can barely hear anything over it. An orange glow leaks from beneath the door leading into the kitchen, and I sneak closer, pressing my ear to the wood before slowly pushing it open. I step inside and press my back against the stone wall. The room is empty, and I exhale heavily when my gaze meets the back door. The final hurdle is to get across this kitchen without being seen. I am halfway across the room when the main door for the kitchen opens, and I freeze.

"L-Lady Persephone?" Margaritte's voice is scared, hushed, and surprised.

I close my eyes, trying to plan my next move. There is another loud crash, this one much closer, and I hear my mother's furious voice as she yells at her assailant. I am running out of time, and I turn to look at Margaritte.

"Margaritte—"

Margaritte swallows, looking back at the door and then at me. "Go."

I glance at the door and then back to her. "But, I—"

"Go, Lady Persephone. I will cover for you," she says, hurrying to push me toward the door.

I pause at the door, searching her face. "But why?"

"I am so truly sorry," Margaritte says, her voice breaking. She nudges me again. "Go."

I nod, still confused about why she is sorry, but I hurry out the door into the soft greys of twilight.

The storm grows louder as I run through the gardens. No sooner am I past the perimeter of my mother's property when a hand grasps mine from the shadows. The touch sends a spark of electricity through me that has nothing to do with the raging storm. I gasp but make no move to pull away. On the contrary, my whole body begs me to move deeper into the shadows.

"It's me." His deep voice makes my stomach twist in such

108

a delicious way, and then he emerges from the darkness. His face is even more heartbreaking in real life. It seems the dream not only dulled the feeling of his touch but also the effect his presence has on me. My heart flutters, my knees feel weak, and I have a near -undeniable urge to be naked and beneath him.

I lift a shaky hand and brush my fingers over his cheek. His skin feels like the most luxurious of silk. "You're… real."

"You thought I was fake?" he quips, arching an eyebrow.

"Well, you…" My eyes roam over his face greedily, drinking in his presence. It is almost overwhelming. "You were a dream."

Another loud crash from the direction of the house pulls me from my trance, and my head snaps toward it.

"We have to run," Hades says. Heavy rain starts to fall, focused primarily over my mother's house and garden.

He pulls me away from the house into a large wooded area. The thunder grows louder and angrier the further away we get. I glance over my shoulder, the house almost completely out of view as we run deeper into the trees.

Hades' deep laugh rumbles in his chest, and the sound brushes over my skin seductively. He directs me, and we turn to the left, running to a cliff edge. Two glorious pegasi wait for us at the top of the cliff, huffing and stomping impatiently, longing to fly.

Hades and I come to a stop. He cups my cheeks and looks down at me. I look up at him, barely breathing, every part of my body anticipating his next move. My breaths are shallow as he stares hungrily at my lips, and I can't help but lick them, desperate for a taste of him.

He's going to kiss me. He's going to kiss me.

The storm above my mother's house feels like a spark compared to the electricity I feel right now. Slowly, Hades lowers his face as if giving me plenty of time to back out, but how could I? How could I deny him this? How could I deny myself this?

The second his lips brush mine, I can't stop myself from deepening the kiss. Feeling this fully for the first time is not something I could have prepared for. His lips are soft but firm, his tongue teasing mine with small flicks. The second I get that small taste of him, a wave of desire washes through me, and I moan into the kiss. The ache deep in my core now permeates every nerve and cell.

Hades pulls back way before I am ready. He presses his forehead to mine, his breathing fast, and I can nearly hear his heart pounding. I place my hands on his arms and close my eyes, the ache nearly unbearable.

"I missed you." Hades' words are breathless and filled with desire. He grazes my cheeks with his thumbs before pulling back, his piercing sapphire eyes searching my face. "Are you ready for our date, Persephone?"

I nod, unable to form any sort of coherent words.

Hades slowly drops his hands, his fingertips gliding down my arms. He slides his hand into mine and leads me to the pegasi. Gripping my waist, he lifts me easily onto the back of one of the beasts. He glances at the other pegasus before climbing onto the back of mine. He loops his arms around my waist and pulls me close. My breath hitches when my ass presses against his groin, his strong thighs pressing against mine. There is no doubt this man wants me. The evidence of his desire is undeniable.

Hades tuts at the other pegusus. It whinnies in answer and nuzzles the one we are on before launching himself off the cliff. He spreads his wings and soars into the distance. I feel Hades' legs flex as he squeezes the pegasus' sides. The pegasus moves forward, smoothly shifting into a trot. Each step pushes me back into Hades, my ass rubbing against him. He tightens his arms on me, and I feel his lips against my ear.

"Ready?" he growls in my ear, a shiver running down my spine. I nod, and I can practically feel Hades' smug smirk as the pegasus leaps off the cliff's edge. My stomach drops as it always does when I do a dive like this, and fuck, have I missed it. I lean my head back, rolling it against Hades' shoulder. I savor the exhilaration of plummeting, the exhilaration of feeling his arms around me. The only thing better is the feeling of him hard against me. When was the last time I felt this alive?

110

We continue to fall, and at the last moment, the pegasus throws open her wings, shifting into a glide. Her hoof drags through the salty sea water, spraying Hades and me with the mist. I laugh and throw my arms out, feeling the air slide over me as we soar. The pegasus ascends, and I lean heavily against Hades, trusting him to keep us both safe.

"Open your eyes, my spring. Let go," Hades whispers in my ear.

I open my eyes, gasping at the surge of emotion I feel at being in the air. How long has it been since I last flew? Since I last spread my wings?

Hades presses a soft kiss to my neck, and I tilt my head, opening for him.

I am soaring through the clouds on a pegasus with Hades behind me.

Alive! I am alive.

Chapter Twenty-Five

Persephone

I HOLD MY HAND OUT, THE CLOUDS FILTERING THROUGH MY FINGERS, and can't help but laugh in delight as the cotton-like pillowy fluff slips through my fingers.

Hades' lips pull into a smile against my neck, and he places another small kiss over my pulse before he loosens his hold on me. I glance over my shoulder at him when he removes his hands from me completely. He gives me a devilish smile and winks before sliding off the pegasus, plummeting toward the earth. My heart leaps in fear, and I search the clouds for him.

"Hades!" I shout, trying to catch sight of him. I try to redirect the pegasus, but she huffs in irritation and continues on her path.

A moment later, I see him in the distance, shooting through the clouds. Large leathery wings spread regally from his back, pushing against the air in powerful strokes as he ascends. His blue eyes pierce mine even from this distance. I feel that throbbing ache low in my body clench as I take in the glory of this man. His horns protrude proudly from his head, curling in such a pleasing way, and his forked tail curls behind him.

Hades effortlessly flies alongside us and looks at me expectantly. I feel my back twitch where my wings long to burst free, but I can't. My mother would... At that thought, I land on my decision. She does not rule me anymore.

I carefully swing my leg over the pegasus and drop. The feeling of falling again brings me such euphoria that I almost lose myself in it. I fall toward the earth like a floral comet until my instincts kick in. My wings break free of the firmly placed glamor, and I groan at the feeling of freedom.

I stretch them, and my descent slows, the white feathers bright against the midnight -black sky. With the first flap of them, I feel the muscles in my back ache, though not as much as they should, given the decades of disuse. I slowly ascend into the sky. The wind against my skin feels even better when I'm the one doing the flying.

I see Hades' shadow through the clouds, but I need another moment of this to myself. I want to enjoy this. The sea sparkles beneath me, the clouds float above, and I bask in the inbetween. It is a silent apology to my true form for keeping it hidden for so long, an apology for the vicious words from my mother.

I can only bear to be away from Hades for another few long moments before I move up through the clouds. He looks at me, his eyes glinting with what looks like affection. He holds out his hand for mine, and I slide my hand into his, my wings ruffling as I shiver at the contact. The top of my head throbs with a dull ache, the remnants of my horns reminding me they are no longer whole.My heart breaks that they are not.

Hades stops flying forward and hovers in place. I follow, taking his other hand, and we begin to spin. He pulls me away from the devastation I feel at the loss of my horns, and our laughter fills this perfect void.

Hades releases me, and I soar. I spin away, barely able to control my flight, but I've never felt more mastery over myself. Hades follows and grabs me, wrapping his arms around my waist. We hover there in the clouds, completely alone. He leans in, rubbing my nose with his and closing his eyes, his lips pulled into one of the most earnest smiles I've ever seen.

We slowly descend through the clouds. Hades' shadows surround us, cloaking us from view. They feel like I am completely wrapped in him, and I've never felt anything more perfect. Eventually, our feet hit the ground, and my shoes sink into the soft gold sand beneath us.

Hades pulls back slightly, but he keeps his arms around me. "Welcome to the mortal world, Persephone."

My eyes go wide as I look around. The beach is almost completely dark, but the sand reflects the moonlight, and a bonfire illuminates the night.

There are no signs of this being the mortal realm apart from the fact that this place *feels* human and a sign a few feet away that reads, "No shirt, no shoes, no problem." There is no overwhelming feeling of the power of the gods that usually surrounds me. I can see small imperfections on the beach. The areas of grass that line the beach. The shells aren't all bright colors, and some are even black. This place is nothing like the beaches of Olympus.

"The mortal world?" I ask, disbelieving.

Hades pulls back and takes my hand. He kicks his shoes off and leads me down to the water. He drops my hand and crouches down, splashing seawater. The area where he disrupted the waves glow, illuminating his face in the electric blue light. I squeal and kick my shoes off before eagerly stepping into the water. I gasp a little, not only at the phosphorescent glow but at the temperature. It's not freezing, but it's definitely not warm.

Hades straightens, tilting his head at me. "Would you like to swim, Persephone?" he asks. There is something in his voice that makes my skin tingle.

"I don't have my swimsuit," I reply, hoping the darkness masks my heating cheeks.

The corner of Hades' lips tug into a half smile. "I'll turn my back until you're in the water."

I swallow but nod. Hades kisses my hand before turning and walking a little further up the beach. My hands shake as I tug at the tie holding my dress together. I wish I had better underwear than this pink frilly set.

I can't even look back at Hades as I open my dress, exposing myself. My cheeks heat at the thought of his hands on my naked skin. I slip the dress off, throwing it to the beach, well out of reach of the gently rolling waves. I wade into the water, and I swear I hear a low groan from the beach. My stomach flutters in response, but I go deeper, covering myself beneath the surface. My skin breaks out in goosebumps, not only due to the temperature but the anticipation. When the water is almost up to my shoulders, I finally build up the courage to look at Hades, who is still dutifully looking away.

Did he peek?

"Can I look?" he asks, a similar anticipation making his voice tremble.

"Yes."

Hades turns to face me. Although he is far away, I can see the hunger in his expression. He unbuttons his shirt and slowly walks toward the water.

He reaches the middle button before I find the willpower to look away from him. The throbbing heat low in my stomach is so much worse now, and it has traveled to the ache between my thighs.

I hear the faint rush of the water as he walks through it, and half a moment later, his strong, calloused hands are on my waist. He squeezes slightly and turns me toward him. I can't stop the responding moan as my body comes into contact with his.

"You didn't have to look away," he growls.

I can't bring myself to look at him, knowing that his eyes will undoubtedly be as dark as mine. He slides his thumbs along my skin, and I moan again. The blush from my cheeks spreads down my neck, the feeling of his touch against my skin even more intense than I'd anticipated.

"You know," Hades leans in, his lips at my ear, "I snuck a peek, too."

My lips twitch. "Of course you did." I blink, the response coming before I'd even thought about it. It was as if the words had come from another part of me.

Hades pulls me in closer, my body flush with his. "Of course I did?" he asks, a hint of humor in his voice.

I move my hands to his shoulders and finally allow myself to look up at him. His pupils have almost completely swallowed the sapphire blue. "I thought you wanted to swim," I say, my breaths shallow, nerves and desire battling it out, waging an inner war.

His answering smirk makes the throbbing between my legs intensify. "I just wanted you naked."

Fuck, I'm in trouble.

I try to swallow my nerves, determined to be brave with this man. "I'm still wearing underwear," I reply, my gaze locked on his.

Hades' smirk deepens, and he lifts his hand, the moonlight reflecting off his claws. I feel my panties slide down my leg.

"There's some dangerous fish around here." His smile is menacing, devious, and fucking perfect.

My stomach flutters as I think about being bare against him. Hades lowers his hand and grabs my thighs, lifting me to wrap my legs around him. My pussy is pressed against him, and it takes everything in me to not rub against him, aching for some relief.

"Still… wearing my bra…" I manage to stammer out, wanting to be completely naked and pressed against him.

Hades' claws flash again, and I feel my bra release before he yanks it off, discarding it into the ocean. "Are you?" he asks playfully, but his need is so transparent. I feel his hardness against my ass, his shaft grazing my pussy very softly.

The ache. Gods. The ache. I need relief.

"Hades…"

Chapter Twenty-Six
Hades

THE PHOSPHORESCENCE THAT GLOWS as we wade deeper into the water is only a poor imitation of the limitless sky in the Underworld. It is the one Persephone continues to see every time she dreams. The one I stare at when I'm alone in the palace, gazing out the window. I pull her tighter to me, our bodies fitting together as if made for each other.

Her eyes are glowing, the blue making the phosphorescence pale in comparison. I drop my glamour again, letting my wings stretch out, feeling them slice through the water. The beauty of not having feathers is that my wings are just as suited for the water as they are for the air. However, my wings are far from my mind at the moment. Right now, my thoughts are consumed with how my body fits against my wife. Dreams are always a pale comparison to reality. With Persephone, there is no fucking comparison.

"Can I?" she asks, staring at my wings. The tremble in her voice reveals her emotions as much as the reaction of her body.

"You don't have to ask," I answer, moving my wings closer to her. "No part of me is off limits to you."

My eyes wander over her as I tense in anticipation of her touch. Her body is hidden beneath the dark water. Or it would be if darkness was not my calling. My eyes cut through the darkness as easily as I can summon shadows to my hand. Not that I will mention that to her. This version of Persephone would blush and hide with virginal modesty.

The Persephone I knew… well, she'd grab my cock and demand I fuck her as repayment.

I shiver as she reaches out and drags her fingers down the leathery surface of my wing. My eyelids flutter close as she continues to touch my wings. I remember when they first started to grow, how much I hated them. The Underworld was trying to turn me into a monstrous version of myself, a beast with wings, horns, fangs, and a tail. I didn't understand that the Underworld was finally accepting me as king, marking me as its ruler, and giving me weapons even when I'm unarmed. It was protecting me by making my form shift, preparing me for the war to come.

Persephone rakes her nails down my wing, and I groan, my eyes flashing open and connecting with hers. Her pupils have expanded and completely dwarfed any color left.

I should kiss her.

She slams her lips to mine before I can move. Oh gods, her taste. She tastes like pomegranates. How had I gone so long without it? The unfiltered, undiluted taste of my wife, my queen? Dreams were a pale imitation, but I'd forgotten how pale. I deepen the kiss, allowing her tongue to dance with mine. I sink my teeth into her lower lip, growling into her mouth. She moans and tunnels her fingers into my hair, gripping me tight and clinging to me like one of her vines.

I pull back and pant, trying to regain the breath she stole. "You keep kissing me like that, and I won't be responsible for my actions."

This isn't *my* Persephone. I need to remember that. I can't scare her off by going too fast or being too forward. She's *shy*. It's odd even to think of the word in relation to her.

"We're naked in the sea, demon," she whispers huskily. "You think you're currently responsible for your actions?"

Demon?

My muscles lock, and I scan her dark eyes. "What did you just call me?"

For a moment, there's a flicker of confidence in her eyes, a glimpse of my queen, but a breath later, it's gone. I can't let her answer. I can't hear her confusion about why she would call me demon. It hurts too much. So I slam my lips back to hers, losing myself in her mouth. Shifting, I rub my cock against her pussy, the heat of her a welcoming beacon. Fuck, I miss being inside her. I crave the clarity I feel when our bodies are joined as one.

Clarity. I don't suppose that could help her memory return, could it?

"Fuck..." she moans into the kiss, rocking her hips against me.

That sounds more like my Persephone.

I press my cock against her entrance. "My spring..." *Tell me to stop.*

Instead, she rolls her hips against mine, and I thrust inside her, unable to hold back. She digs her nails into my shoulders as I seat myself to the hilt inside her.

Clarity.

Fuck, I forgot how incredible her cunt feels wrapped around my cock. The sense of belonging shoots through me as I thrust. Every movement is frantic, and the space between our bodies feels wrong, even as minuscule as it is. I need every part of her pressed against me. I need to taste every moan she whispers against my lips, and I need every squeeze of her cunt seared into my cock.

My fangs descend, and I sink them into her neck. My claws dig into her ass, keeping her still as I thrust frantically inside her. Every time I withdraw from her pussy, I slam back inside, hating the sensation of not having her wrapped around me.

The anxiety. The despair. The hopelessness. I need to fuck it all out of me and into her. I need to give her fucking everything inside me.

She digs her nails into my back, breaking the skin. "Fuck, demon! Don't stop!"

Demon.

Maybe my hunch is correct, and I can fuck her into remembering me and the life we shared. She grabs my horns, pulling my lips to hers. The movement is so familiar, so *Persephone.* I dig my fangs into her lip, needing her to feel me even when we're apart.

You're mine. Memory or not. Wife or not. The end is always

119

you and me.

I swallow her cries and mumble into her lips, "I love you."

Come back, my queen. Look into my eyes and remember.

"I'll give you new to replace the old," I growl, thrusting even harder, and for a moment, fear and desire flicker in her eyes. "No matter how many times I have to."

I will win her in every way as many times as I have to.

"Hades…" she moans.

The base of my spine tingles, and I can feel myself getting closer. "It's you. My queen."

She winces, and blood trickles from her nose. The sight makes me want to roar with rage. She's not back.

"Come for me," I command, already too close to stop myself.

She screams my name as she comes, and I roar, rage and desire twined as one. We pant into each other as we descend from our bliss, our breaths mingling. I struggle to shore my emotional barriers back up. I can't feel the sorrow right now. It didn't work. She doesn't remember.

"Still with me?" I whisper, nuzzling her nose.

"Fuck, demon," she whimpers, kissing along my face, ears, and cheeks. "I missed you…"

I don't know which is worse: her remembering nothing or these aching glimpses of her remembering me. It is brutal to be teased with the woman I love.

"I missed you, too," I say, kissing her deeply.

I'm going to get you back, my spring.

I keep my hold on her, heading back up the beach, not putting her down or pulling out of her. If I can remain in this small sliver of memory a while longer, I can remain with Persephone.

Chapter Twenty-Seven

Persephone

MY BODY FEELS COMPLETELY BONELESS AS HE CARRIES ME FARTHER UP THE BEACH, holding me as if I weigh nothing, his steps light and graceful. His legs are obviously not feeling like jelly. Mine wouldn't hold me if I tried to stand on them.

I briefly feel offended that he clearly is not as affected by what just happened as I am. But one look at his expression corrects my assumption. His eyes are still dark, the barest glimmer of the deep blue rimming the obsidian black of his pupils, and his gaze is filled with such desire, affection, need, longing, and perhaps… No. It can't be.

I search his handsome face for what feels like the millionth time since he emerged from the shadows. Every time I take a moment to appreciate his features, I find something completely new to fawn over. This time, it's the perfect line of his jaw. I can't help but imagine running my tongue along his skin, tasting him.

My core aches again, not only from his size and the ferocity with which he fucked me but also with a deep craving for more. I feel my cheeks heat with the realization of what we have just done. I have had sex before. Once. It was with a servant, and while I don't regret it, there was none of the passion I had just experienced with Hades. What if he thinks less of me because of what happened?

Shit.

"I'm…" I pause. "I'm not usually a sex -on -the -first-date kinda girl." My voice shakes, and I silently curse. I'm not sure why because I'm not feeling any shame. I feel empowered and sated, with an overwhelming desire to do it again.

Hades smirks. "Is it really our first date?"

My lips twitch, and I quirk a brow at him. "You consider the dreams dates?"

Hades drops to his knees and lays me down on the sand, his already hardening cock brushing against my swollen pussy. My body weeps, eager for him to stretch me again.

"Yes," he growls, hovering over me, his fingers drawing maddening circles on the underside of my thigh, leaving a trail of goosebumps in his wake.

My heart flutters when I look up at him, my whole body tingling for him. "I've never felt like this before," I blurt out. It feels as if something within me is trying to break through a barrier, eager to be free and return to me something lost and precious.

"Like what, my spring?" Hades asks. His smile makes my breath catch in my throat. He is so fucking beautiful. He leans down, brushing his lips over mine, my mind fogging with my desire for him.

"I'm…" I pause and pull back slightly, needing the distance to obtain the clarity to say something of this magnitude without being blindsided by lust. This isn't me. It isn't in my nature to make big declarations, but a voice deep within me screams to admit this to him. It feels like if I don't vocalize this right now, my heart will implode, an internal Armageddon.

I cup his cheek, locking my gaze with his. "I'm falling for you." My voice is surprisingly steady, even as I make my admission. There is something so freeing about speaking my truth when my life consists of so many lies. This is a truth I can hold on to because it is not only mine. It belongs to him as well.

Hades' eyes sparkle with emotion, and he closes them after a moment, turning his head to kiss my palm. Even that small affectionate action sends a jolt of need through me.

122

"And I for you," he replies. His voice shakes ever so slightly, but I catch it.

It's not that I don't believe him. Even though his voice trembles on the words, it is not in a way that makes me think there is any hint of deception. After years of living with my mother, deception is something I have become an expert in deciphering. No, his voice shook with... sorrow and maybe desperation.

"You are?" I ask.

Hades opens his eyes and meets my gaze once more. He nods. "Does that surprise you?"

"We hardly know each other." Those words feel like a lie when they leave my mouth. It is true that we hardly know each other, but at the same time, it feels like no one has ever known me as well as Hades does. No one has ever understood me like he does. "But I'm drawn to you. Does that sound crazy?" I continue. "It feels like I've known you forever."

Hades kisses my palm again. "It doesn't sound crazy. Ask me something. Get to know me."

I think for a moment. "Okay. Well, you're obviously a god. What of?" I ask.

Hades smiles. "The God of the Dead, amongst other things. I'm also king of my realm."

I lift my eyebrows in surprise, but they furrow a moment later as Eros's voice echoes in my head, a memory of our conversation.

"God of the Dead," I repeat, looking away as I think back to the meeting with Eros. *What is the opposite of life if not death?* I whisper, repeating his words.

He can't have meant Hades. But...

"Two halves of existence," Hades replies, his eyes searching mine. "Life is special because it ends."

My gaze snaps back to his. "Okay. Don't freak out."

Hades raises a brow, shifting to support himself on his elbows. "No promises."

"Remember how I told you that Eros visited?"

Hades nods, and I catch the flicker of annoyance at the mention of the trickster.

"He may have hinted that you and I are…"

"Are…?" Hades prompts, watching me carefully.

"Meant to be together." My words are barely a whisper, and my cheeks flush at the statement. Did I scare him off?

Hades' only reaction to my words is a slight twitch of his lips, and his eyes glint with amusement. "Why would I freak out about that?"

"Well, it's kind of… a lot." I feel my cheeks heating more.

Hades laughs and leans in, kissing me softly. It's enough to stoke the fire deep in my tummy. "Is it?" Hades asks, amused.

"What about your queen?"

His smirk deepens. "Again, you are assuming you're not her."

Suddenly, an image shoots to the front of my mind. I tilt my head, seeing myself looking into a mirror in a large, darkly decorated room, a black crown perched on my head. I whimper as a sharp pain sears my mind. It feels like I'm being stabbed in the skull by a hot poker.

Hades slams his lips to mine, and the pain, the image, everything disappears but him. Once again, it is just him and me, alone, naked on a beach. I deepen the kiss, allowing myself to get lost in him. Instinctively, I lift my hips, a thrill traveling through me when his hard length grazes my pussy again.

Hades shifts between my thighs, pressing his cock against my opening, teasing me. I tunnel my fingers into his hair and try to lift my hips, needing him to stretch and fill me. He matches my movements, allowing no movement of his cock, keeping it so it barely breaches me.

"Need more?" he growls against my lips.

"Please, demon," I moan into his lips, completely losing myself to him. The second the words leave my lips, they are forgotten. Everything is forgotten except his lips against mine and his cock pressed against me.

Hades practically snarls, finally surrendering to his desire. He slams his cock into me. His girth stretches me, the bite of pain quickly morphing into pleasure. My head swims in euphoria at the feeling of him, and I cry out,

124

wrapping my legs around his hips and arching against him. I need to be closer to him, to have more of him. I need everything.

Hades digs his fingers into my hair and yanks it hard in his fist. "Eyes on me," he growls, the sound low and guttural.

I keep my gaze locked on his, moaning as he thrusts into me hard and fast. His other hand grasps my thigh so hard that I think I'll bruise, and I hope I do. I need proof that this happened. I need to hold on to the memory of this, the fantasy of him.

Hades snarls above me, and I catch sight of his fangs. My pussy clenches around his cock at the sight of him. Every form of him is as delicious as the last, and I am so wildly attracted to every single one.

"I need you." Hades' voice no longer sounds like his own. It's deeper, rougher, and deadlier, but I've never felt safer.

"Don't stop. Please," I beg, lifting my hips in time with Hades' thrusts.

"Never. I will never stop, Persephone," Hades says, slipping his hand to my calf. He lifts my leg and drapes it over his shoulder, opening me and allowing him even deeper.

I feel my arousal spilling out of me, every part of my body completely desperate for this god, for this king. My king.

Hades' black gaze seems to penetrate my soul, and he growls deeply, "Give it all to me, my spring."

I moan at his words, at the way he's looking at me, at the feeling of him fucking me. My breath catches when he leans down, stretching me more and slamming his lips to mine, kissing me frantically, passionately.

He moans into my mouth, "Come with me, Persephone."

Almost as if my body was waiting, it eagerly submits to his command, my orgasm ripping through me. Pleasure completely overwhelms me, and I arch beneath him, every muscle contracting. I scream his name, completely at his mercy.

I want to worship him. I need to worship him. He is my god.

Hades roars, and I feel his release fill me, sending another

125

wave of pleasure through me. I deepen the kiss as his thrusts slow, and he pants into me, spent.

Hades. My Hades. My husband.

I tense with a moment of clarity, and without thinking, whispered words fall from my lips directly into his. "I'm still here, baby." Before the last word has completely left my lips, my mind fogs.

"I know. I'll find you. I'll always find you," Hades says, pressing desperate kisses along my cheeks and jaw.

Find me? What does that mean? I frown. "Hm?"

Hades pulls back, a smile on his lips, but there's sadness in his eyes.

"Nothing," he says, kissing my nose and cheeks.

I moan softly at the small sparks of electricity every time his lips meet my skin.

"We have to go back," he says, nuzzling my cheek and sighing.

My stomach knots at his words. No, we shouldn't be apart. We belong together.

"No," I protest, tightening my fingers in his hair.

Hades slams his lips to mine and slowly pulls out of me. I shiver at the feeling of emptiness. I feel his release trickle out of me, and I moan at the idea that I'm full of him.

"Wait…"

Hades kisses me again before shifting to his knees. He stands and offers me his hand. "As much as I'm desperate to stay with you, we can't."

"But…" I try to come up with some excuse that we need to stay on the beach for a little longer. Five minutes, maybe. An hour. Eternity?

Hades' lips twitch, and he waves his hand, dressing us instantly. He takes my hand and pulls me to him, leaning in for a kiss. I close my eyes, anticipating the feeling of his lips against mine, but it never comes.

A furious snarl has my eyes snapping open. Hades' hand is yanked from mine, and he is thrown across the beach.

Chapter Twenty-Eight
Hades

MY FINGERS ARE TORN FROM HERS, THE BLOW THROWING ME ACROSS THE BEACH. Something is always tearing us apart, always pulling us out of reach, too far to touch. My breath leaves me in a pained whoosh as my back hits a tree. My sight blurs as I try to focus through the pain. That fucker definitely broke my shoulder when I hit the tree.

Persephone.

My vision clears immediately at the thought of her in danger, and I focus on the being that had emerged from the ocean. His body is a million different cascading shades of blue, his eyes completely black. He is hulking and monstrous. *Titan.* Oceanus, Titan of the River that encircles the world.

He strides toward Persephone. Adrenaline floods my bloodstream, and I throw my hand out, hurling my power at him. "Run!" I order Persephone, closing the distance between us. He's too close to her, far too close.

My power harmlessly bounces off him as he turns his body to water, becoming the very embodiment of his calling. He summons a wave, hitting me in the chest and pinning me to the ground. It's so easy for him to corral me. He is darkness and the ocean. He's seen the very depths of the watery abyss, making him practically immune to my abilities.

I slash with my claws at the watery fist holding me, pinning me, but it glances off harmlessly. My rib cracks under the force of the tsunami, pummeling me into the sand. I cry out in pain, blood staining my lips as bone punctures one of my lungs.

Persephone, run! I want to scream the warning, but I can't breathe. The air is turning to blood in my throat.

Oceanus storms toward me, his body still ever-shifting water, every color of the ocean painted on his skin. He smirks at me, his teeth made of dark coral, and I know his breath smells like salty brine.

My vision flickers, the edges turning black. Did she get away? Is she safe?

Black vines shoot through Oceanus's chest from behind, lessening his hold on me. I gulp at the air greedily, making up for what I lost during the hit. It won't be long before he recovers from Persephone's attack. I need to figure out how to take advantage of this.

Oceanus and I stare at the vines protruding from his chest as they begin to rip the Titan apart.

"Release him," Persephone hisses, her voice deadly as poison.

Oceanus sneers at her, and Persephone splits him in two, right down the middle. I gasp as the hold he has on me disappears, blood filling my mouth as I cough violently.

Hurry up and fucking heal.

Instead of dying, Oceanus merely separates into two identical beings, shorter and smaller than the original Titan. I wonder if each of them is less powerful now.

"Little Goddess of Spring, so far from home," Oceanus mocks, sounding like a crashing wave.

Persephone shifts slightly on her feet, putting one foot back. Her eyes, I know those eyes. I saw them on the battlefield after Tartarus was torn open. My queen is not fragile. She's iron.

The Iron Queen.

I cough up more blood, shuddering as my healing kicks in, my ribs cracking as they repair themselves. *Hurry up. Hurry up, heal faster.*

She smirks at the Titan. It is too late, but Oceanus finally notices the seaweed that has crawled up his body, wrapping like two nooses around his neck. The Titan struggles against the hold, but seaweed is made from the same components as him, so he is essentially battling himself. My fucking clever wife.

I spit blood onto the sand and stand, healed just enough to walk to her. I touch her shoulder. "Hold him tight. If even a drop of water escapes, so will he."

She nods, and I summon my powers, preparing the cell for him in Tartarus, one with no moisture and no escape. That swirling darkness crawls up more of my skin. The small amount that vanished in Persephone's presence reappears with force.

Persephone silently slides her hand into mine as I plunge the Titan into his prison, sealing the gate shut. I exhale, turning to look at her, gazing at her profile.

She turns toward me, and I lean down to press a gentle kiss to her lips. "We have to go."

I pull back, and she keeps her eyes on mine as I wipe my blood from her lower lip. I whistle sharply, and the pegasus responds to my call. When it lands, I put her on his back before swinging up behind her. I kick him, holding her close as he launches into the sky. Persephone is tense against me, silent as the grave as we soar through the night.

My unease ratchets higher. "What is it?"

Instead of answering, she holds up her palm, and I hold my breath, watching her. The flower that grows in her palm is black, with golden veins. The petals are sharp but appear soft, luring you in with beauty only to find a snake poised beneath. Persephone slides her other finger over the edge of the flower, blood welling from the cut.

I don't speak, not wanting to disturb this moment. Instead, I hover my hand above hers, letting my shadows drip from my fingers. They wind around her flower, almost dancing around it. The flower arches into my shadows as if seeking the darkness.

"Life and Death in an eternal dance," I whisper.

She leans back against me, closing her palm as we approach Olympus. I curse under my breath when I see the clear sky. "No clouds. Not a good sign."

I might have sent my younger brother to get his ass

kicked in order to take my wife on a date. I suppose I should feel remorseful about that. Yet it is *Zeus.*

"Land in the woods. I can sneak back in," Persephone says as I steer the pegasus to the woods, landing without a misstep.

I dismount first and grip her waist, lifting her down.

"I'll... see you later?" she asks, her eyelids lowered coquettishly.

"Yes." I smirk. "The more you wish for me in your dreams, the easier it is for me to be there."

She glances up at me, and I kiss her hard, unable to hold back. I pull away to stop myself from getting carried away. "Hurry."

She nods before sprinting back to her mother's house, leaving me alone in the forest.

Chapter Twenty-Nine

Persephone

SOMETHING TUGS AT MY CHEST, URGING ME *TO GO BACK TO HIM,* but I force my feet forward, back to my prison. My fingers tingle with the phantom feeling of the Titan's blood. I expect to feel guilt or remorse that I so brutally hurt another being, but all I feel is relief that I was able to use my power to save Hades. I shake my head, unable to think about this right now, needing to concentrate on getting home.

The skies above are inky black but clear of any clouds, yet there is still the sound of thunder. It's much more muted, and I notice the closer I get to my house, the louder it is. No longer is the storm above the house, but it is raging from within. Bright white light flashes through the windows, accompanied by a deep rumble of angry thunder.

I grimace when the gate squeaks as I open it. It is an irrational fear. No one will have heard it over the racket that is currently going on inside the house. I quickly close the gate and keep my back against the hedge surrounding the garden's perimeter, staying in the warm embrace of the shadows.

A loud crash sounds from inside the house, and I still. Everything goes eerily quiet,and my instincts flare. I know I only have another few moments before the window to get back inside and up to my room closes.

My heart races when I see the door, everything in me urging me to go back to Hades, to run away with him, and never look back. But what would my mother do if I went missing? If she found out I was with him?

I force my legs forward, sprinting to the nondescript door and opening it slowly. Suddenly, the door is yanked open, and my heart leaps.

Fuck... She's caught me.

Margaritte grabs me, her eyes wide with panic as she pulls me inside and into the back stairwell.

"You're cutting it very fine, Lady Persephone," she whispers urgently. She pulls the cloak off me and produces one of the dreaded white cotton nightdresses seemingly out of thin air.

"I'm sorry. I was—"

Margaritte looks at me, something I can't quite identify in her eyes. "I know." She pauses for a moment, assisting me in changing. I feel like she is trying to tell me something with her eyes, but I can't read the message. She sighs heavily, continuing to pull the nightdress over my head. The cotton scratches me in ways I've never noticed, feeling so wrong against my skin.

Margaritte offers me a wipe to remove the makeup, and as I'm cleansing my face, she's hurrying me up the stairs. The sounds within the house have quieted, but people are still running around, probably dealing with the chaos.

Margaritte pokes her head out the door, checking that the coast is clear before nodding at me and gently pushing me out the door. I run to my bedroom, trying to keep my footsteps as quiet as possible. My heart stops when I hear my mother's quick steps ascending the stairs, no doubt to check on me. I run faster and manage to just sneak into my room. As I quietly close the door, I see her shadow on the wall at the bend of the staircase.

I step back into the room, my heart racing from the adrenaline. I glance at the mirror and swear silently under my breath. The lipstick may be gone, but my lips are swollen from Hades' kisses. My skin seems to have a soft glow, which I can only assume is thanks to the earth-shattering

132

orgasms, and something else looks different. Something I can't quite put my finger on. *Do I look stronger?*

A knock vibrates the wood of my door. "Sweetling?" My mother's voice sounds a little panicked, and she knocks again.

"Come in, Mother," I call, noticing it's more difficult to force my voice into the placid tones she trained into me.

My mother opens the door and rushes over to me, cupping my cheeks. "Are you all right?"

I nod, but now that she's this close, I can see that while I might be all right, better than ever, actually. She is not. Her skin is pale and sheened with sweat, making it look like aged porcelain, but that's not what keeps drawing my eyes. She looks like a china doll that has been dropped. I lift my hand and slide my finger along one of the cracks, my brows drawn. "Are *you* all right, Mother?"

She turns away from my touch, her eyes flashing with fury. She masks it quickly, brushing it off and looking back at me. "You must have been so scared, sweetling."

I try to pull my expression into a look of fear, unconvinced if I've succeeded. My mother pulls me into a tight hug, tighter than would be comfortable, and I briefly wonder if she can scent victory on me, pride in myself.

"It's all right, Persephone. I will always protect you." She holds me tighter, almost hurting me. "You're safe."

If she senses any change in me, she doesn't show it. I exhale when she releases me and pulls back.

"You must have been so scared. You're a mess," she says.

I feel something like anger churning in my gut because, truthfully, I have never felt more beautiful. But I nod, not letting anything show on my face. "I was hiding under the sheets." The lie tastes like acid on my tongue. No longer am I content to be the helpless damsel, quivering and afraid.

My mother nods, something similar to affection in her eyes. "Why don't you get yourself cleaned up, and I'll have the servants prepare some food for us."

Eating with my mother right now is just about the last thing I want to do. "Actually, Mother, I'm not feeling too well. If you don't mind, I'm just going to retire for the evening."

My mother nods, cupping my cheek again. "Get some rest. You need your beauty sleep. You have a date tomorrow."

"Date?" I ask, but the way my stomach churns, I know exactly who will be joining me for dinner. I was wrong. I'd take a million meals with my mother over one with Adonis.

"Yes. With Adonis. I was going to tell you when I was so rudely interrupted." My mother glares. "Oh, and do be careful in the living room. There is currently a god-shaped hole in the floor."

I blink, but I know better than to question my mother about things she doesn't want to discuss.

"Mother?" I ask, knowing that this next question is also not something she'll want to answer but needing to ask it anyway, regardless of the punishment. "Are you sure Adonis is the right fit for me?"

My mother's gaze snaps to mine, and I can see the instant anger there. "Of course he is." She forces her expression to soften. "You have to trust me, sweetling. I always know what's best for you."

I nod, looking down at the floor. "Goodnight, Mother."

"Goodnight, Persephone." My mother spins on her heel and leaves my room.

The click of the door closing is all the permission I need to collapse on the bed. I bury my face in the pillow, and it all hits me at once. The memories of the night seem to wrap around my bones, sinking into them, and I bask in the feeling. Not only did I use my powers for more than gardening tonight, I used them to *save* someone, to save *my* someone. My powers ebb and flow within me, stretching after being used for what feels like their true purpose. They have been muted and underused for too long, and I already know they will no longer be satisfied to simply push flowers two inches back or forth. I shift slightly and moan at the ache between my thighs, distracting me from any thoughts other than Hades. The ache that he caused, the ache that already makes me crave *more.* Exhaustion wraps around me like the coziest of blankets, and I allow myself to succumb to it, falling back

134

into my dreams of Hades.

Chapter Thirty

Persephone

THE FIELD WELCOMES ME AS USUAL, AND I TAKE A DEEP BREATH, enjoying the peace. Hades will be here tonight. I know he will. I feel it in every fiber of my being. We will have to deal with the phantom caress and dulled senses, but I still crave his touch, and it's definitely better than nothing.

The energy shifts. A moment later, Hades materializes, standing in the middle of the meadow. My feet are moving before I've fully registered his presence. I launch myself into his arms, trusting that he'll catch me. It's funny that I've known this man for so little time, yet I've never felt more comfortable putting my trust in someone.

He wraps his arms around me, cocooning me in his strength and warmth. His chest rumbles with a groan or a growl. I'm not sure, but everything about this moment is almost perfect.

"Did you miss me?" he asks, his voice full of amusement.

Did I miss him? What a stupid question. I missed him the second we landed back on the cliff and started running home.

Instead of replying, I slam my lips to his, kissing him deeply. The fact that I can barely feel him is even more frustrating now that I know what his touch feels like, now that I know what his lips feel like, now that I know his taste, his smell, his aura, and his heart. Now that I know what I'm missing.

Hades moans into my mouth as I deepen the kiss, my tongue playing with his. I plunge my fingers into his hair, wishing I could feel the silky strands. He playfully nips at my tongue, but his growl tells me he's not being as playful as he's letting on. He is burning as hot for me.

I savor the taste of his need before pulling back and gazing greedily up at him, only one thought circling through my mind over and over.

Mine.

"You got home safe?" I ask. It's a ridiculous question, given he is currently here with me, but one I need to hear the answer to. I need to hear that he is safe.

Hades nods, pressing his forehead to mine, panting a little from our passionate kiss. His fingers dig into my ass, and I moan at the feeling.

"Did she suspect anything?"

Any mention of my mother is like a bucket of ice water over me, but we probably do have things to talk about.

"No, I had an accomplice on the inside," I say, my lips twitching. I need to think of a way to thank Margaritte for her kindness.

"Accomplice?" Hades asks, pulling back.

I nod. "One of the servants. I'm not sure why she's helping me, but she often has a look about her." I pause, trying to think how to describe Margaritte's almost pained expressions when she looks at me. "Like she's apologetic about something."

Hades' brows draw for a moment before he brushes whatever he is thinking away. He exhales heavily and presses kisses all over my face, obviously as relieved to see me as I am to see him.

"Was my brother still there?" he asks, nuzzling my cheek.

"I didn't see him, but I think so."

Hades tilts his head, waiting for an explanation.

"My mother said something about a god-shaped hole in the living room," I continue. "But I'm not sure who else was there."

137

Hades nods thoughtfully. "I didn't receive a progress report. Then again, he is a dick."

I blink and then burst out laughing.

Hades watches me, his expression almost awed. "Fuck I missed you…"

I smile, nuzzling him. I will take a lifetime of this if it means I am with him.

Hades grins, and the sight of it makes my heart ache for him. He looks so unburdened, so free, and I want to be the one to make him feel like this. He kisses me again, harder this time. My whole body shivers in response, but he pulls away much too quickly. I pout as he lowers me to the ground, but his perfect grin remains firmly in place.

"I have a surprise for you," he says, excited about whatever he's planned. I tilt my head, watching him.

What could he surprise me within the Dreamworld?

Hades trails the tips of his fingers down my forearms, and even the phantom touch makes my skin zing with need. He slides his fingers between mine and whistles sharply, the noise making me wince. Less than a second later, the ground trembles. Hades turns his head and smiles brightly. I follow the direction of his gaze, and my eyes widen as I see a huge beast barrelling toward us. Its dark, shiny coat reflects the sunlight, and I blink when my brain finally catches up to my fear. Three heads, it has three fucking heads. Its six eyes are trained on me, and its tongues are lolling out of its mouths. Its size is intimidating, but its expression surprises me, goofy and excited.

Maybe it's excited that it's approaching its next meal. Can I even be eaten in a dream? I back away as the beast comes closer. I look up at Hades, who still holds my hand, keeping me in place. He is completely at ease.

I yank my hand from Hades', who is obviously having some sort of psychotic break, and I move quicker, squealing as the dog gets closer. Hades grabs my hand before I get out of reach and pulls me into him, holding his other hand out. Shadows form and wrap around the animal, holding him back. He whines and pulls, trying to get to us.

"He won't hurt you," Hades says, wrapping a comforting

arm around my back. "This is Cerberus."

I blink at Hades, then at the huge beast still trying to get to me.

"He guards ou—" He stops, and a flash of pain crosses his face before he continues. "My home."

"Oh," I say, shuffling nervously, my whole body shaking in fear.

"He'll calm down if you pet him," Hades says, a note of humor caught in his voice.

"Pet him?" I ask, my gaze snapping to Hades. "He's trying to eat me!"

Hades laughs, nudging me forward. "Trust me, my spring."

I glare at Hades, and then I look at the beast, struggling in Hades' powers, the goofy expression still fixed on his faces. I slowly reach forward, my hand trembling as I move it closer to him.

Hades wraps a hand around my wrist, steadying me as I place my fingertips against the top of Cerberus's middle nose.

I don't move, frozen in fear.

"Tell him to sit," Hades says, still holding me. "He'll listen."

I look at the dog, swallowing thickly. "S-sit."

The ground shakes a little as he plants his butt down, his tail wagging so much that grass is flying all around us.

I blink, tilting my head at him. Should I be afraid of him?

"Well, tell him he's a good boy," Hades says, smiling at me.

"Good boy?" I say, but it sounds more like a question due to my uncertainty. Cerberus barks, and the noise is so joyous and happy that I can't help but smile.

Hades bends, whispering in my ear, "Watch out." He releases Cerberus from his power, and the dog lunges at me, tackling me to the ground. His huge, heavy body covers mine, and his wet tongue drags over my face.

Ugh. I'm partially grossed out, but I surprise myself by laughing. Cerberus's tail thuds against my leg as he continues to give me wet, sloppy kisses.

"Berry!" I exclaim as a phenomenon I'm becoming increasingly aware of occurs again. The words come before I've thought about them, and then they are lost to the ether.

I glance up at Hades, still laughing, hoping to get some assistance. Hades watches fondly as his huge dog pins me to the ground, nuzzling and kissing me. Even trapped beneath this three-headed monster, my body is completely relaxed, and I am at ease.

"He's a big marshmallow," Hades says, laughing with me.

Cerberus pulls back and looks down at me as if waiting for something.

"Are you a marshmallow?" I ask, smiling up at his goofy faces.

Cerberus barks happily again, and it feels like he collapses his full body weight on top of me. All the air leaves my lungs on a groan.

Hades laughs again and finally comes to my rescue. He grabs one of Cerberus's leather collars and tries to pull him off me. Cerberus is reluctant to move, and he whimpers sadly, looking down at me. Hades' shadows wrap around him, and he lifts the dog easily, setting him down beside him.

"You are a menace," he says, his voice full of such affection it makes my heart ache.

I sit up on my elbows and look at Cerberus. I have no idea what I was so terrified of. He truly seems like the gooiest of marshmallows. I can't help but smile at his silly, happy faces, the way his tail wags constantly, and the sweet red leather collars fixed around each of his necks. Each collar has a tag in the shape of a heart with "Berry" written on it. This dog is clearly very loved and clearly very loving in return.

Hades offers me his hand and then helps me up, kissing my temple once I'm standing.

Cerberus barks and shuffles his butt excitedly on the ground. I smile at Berry and move out of Hades' arms. "You are a big marshmallow, aren't you?" Cerberus jumps on the spot, clearly happy to be getting attention. I glance at Hades. "Is he always this excitable?" I ask, scratching behind one of

140

his many ears.

Hades smiles knowingly and shakes his head. "No. Only with... special people."

Chapter Thirty-One

Hades

IT MAKES MY CHEST ACHE TO SEE THEM TO-GETHER. Cerberus nuzzles his heads against her, trying to imprint his scent on her. He doesn't understand that all the scents are muted inside the dream, and he can't mark her as one of his family as he clearly wants to. Like I want to.

"What a mush!" Persephone exclaims, her bright smile almost splitting her cheeks.

Only with those he loves.

"He loves me already?" she asks, glancing at me.

Fuck, I must have said that out loud. "He can tell you're a good person." You're his mother.

Even in the short time we had in the Underworld, she took to him as if they were the ones bonded thousands of years ago. Cerberus doesn't understand why she's gone, and I can't even explain it in terms he'd understand. He's certainly smarter than a normal dog, much larger than one too, but he can't communicate like a person. He can project his thoughts, but it's more impressions of what's happening.

He plops down and rolls over for her to scratch his stomach, stretching wide for her. Persephone laughs in delight and drops to her knees, obliging him.

"Mommy!" Cerberus mentally shouts to me, wiggling for Persephone.

"You're spoiling him." My throat clogs with emotion. This exact moment occurred once before when I thought Persephone and I had an eternity to figure things out. How quickly things changed.

"He's a good boy!" she insists, kissing his stomach. "Aren't you? Are you a good boy?"

"Found Mommy! Mommy!"

I hold my hand out to her. "May I show you something else?"

My emotions are already trying to make a fool of me. If Persephone keeps playing with Cerberus like this, I'll start imagining foolish things like *children*.

She takes my hand and stands. The moment she touches my palm, I can sense the swirling darkness that's been crawling closer to my neck descending a little. *Curious.*

Persephone is clearly the key to whatever is affecting my powers. I pull her with me, heading deeper into her dream, striding through the fog. The garden around the palace slowly appears, the black roses dotting the landscape, the single red one struggling to survive. Nothing I've tried has helped the plant. The petals began falling yesterday, and with each one lost, a piece of my hope dies. How much longer can we keep this up?

Persephone pulls her hand from mine, heading directly for the red rose, drawn to it. Can she possibly sense the connection to it?

"I can't seem to keep it thriving," I admit, following her.

She kneels and cups the flower, and my breath catches. This is just like with Cerberus, a memory brought to life, an event only one of us remembers. Cerberus pauses at my side, watching her, too. Does he know how important this moment is?

Persephone's brows furrow as she focuses on the flower. Slowly, the rose flourishes under her touch, the thorn under her hand turning to solid gold. A tear slides down my cheek. She's still in there.

How many times can I use those words as comfort? How long until I realize that broken parts are all that's left?

The slight bit of skin that the darkness had retreated from is stained again. I rubbed the side of my neck, the feeling of the darkness strangling me even inside the dream.

I depended on my glamor to conceal what was happening to me when I was on my date with Persephone, but

143

I'm not sure how much longer I can hide what's going on. Melinoë is already suspicious.

"You truly are a Goddess of Life," I whisper solemnly.

Life and death. Perhaps I should have realized it in the beginning. Life and death are opposites. They are never on the same side. Is it a sign that I would never have my Goddess of Life completely? My stomach churns.

She stands and reaches up to wipe the tear off my cheek. I lean into her touch, closing my eyes.

"I missed you," I whisper.

Her other hand rests on my chest. Does she feel my heart slamming against it?

"You dream of my home," I add, slowly opening my eyes, trying to gauge what she remembers.

It's our home.

I gesture to the garden. "This is outside my palace."

She looks around, her eyes flashing. "But... I've never been to your home."

The words shouldn't hurt me. I am not expecting her to remember, yet I wish she did. I kiss her softly, covering the way my heart is breaking. "Yet you dream of it." Because you belong there with me.

"It's beautiful," she whispers against my lips.

"Would you like to see more?" Maybe something will break through the wall in her mind without ripping it apart.

She nods, and I take her hand, leading her through the roses. The black petals brush against us, seeming to bow before their queen. Cerberus stays at Persephone's side, his heads level with her shoulder.Each time he glances at her with one head, she places a kiss on his nose.

Please remember, my spring. We need you.

I lead us toward Asphodel, the golden fields and orchards appearing from the dream. She remembers them all so clearly, every reaching flower, every piece of golden wheat. It's so clear in her memory and reflected in the dreamscape she creates every time she sleeps. She mirrors the reality perfectly.

"This is Asphodel," I whisper. "The meadows of the after-life... a paradise."

"This is truly stunning." She looks around, her eyes wide with awe.

I pause next to one of the trees, touching it. "Look familiar?"

"Why would it?" she asks, and again my heart sinks. "But… maybe…"

My hope foolishly soars again, the constant ascent and descent of this foolish heart. "Touch it."

Persephone reaches up and touches a leaf. It turns gold, and an apple on the same branch ripens before dropping into her hand. She smiles fondly, offering the apple to me.

Instead of taking it from her, I bite into it, my eyes locked on hers.

Her eyes darken in response. She lifts the apple and takes a bite from the exact location I had.

There you are.

I wipe a drop of juice off her lip, but before I can lick it off, she sucks my thumb into her mouth.

What. A. Menace.

Chapter Thirty-Two

Persephone

SOMETHING ABOUT THIS PLACE IS SO FAMIL-*IAR.* The same as every place I have visited in these dreams, yet being here with Hades like this, I have the strongest sense of déjà vu. But how could I? I've never left Olympus. That feeling in my stomach twists again. I feel like I'm missing something, but I can't zero in on it now. Not while I'm looking up at Hades, sucking on his thumb, and feeling more desire than I maybe ever have.

"Menace," Hades growls, his nearly black eyes trained on me.

The term makes me feel warm and comforted, but it also makes me want to be mischievous, to misbehave in a way I've never dared before. I want him to call me that. I want him to growl it in my ear after I've just done something bratty.

Fuck.

I lightly bite the pad of his thumb, needing more reactions from him.

Hunger flares in his eyes. "When can you get away next?" he asks, his voice betraying him, allowing me to hear just how deep his need runs.

I suck on his thumb again and slowly release it with a popping sound. "Maybe next week. I think my mother has an engagement."

"With whom?" Hades asks, his body tensing.

"I'm not sure."

Hades scans my eyes and cups my cheek, towering over me. "Can I ask you something completely unfair?"

I will do anything for you, demon.

I lean my head into his hand, looking up at him.

"This war. You and your mother are at the center of it," he begins, and my brows draw. "Soon you won't be able to escape it." He pauses, his penetrating gaze looking directly into my soul. "Which side will you choose, Persephone?"

"Side?" I ask, looking up at him. Is he asking me if I will choose him?

Hades nods. "Your mother remains," Hades pauses again, struggling to find his words, "somewhat neutral at the moment. But she is tied to my father—"

"I'm on your side," I interrupt. Never has there been an easier decision, in my opinion.

Hades strokes my cheek with his thumb. "Are you sure? She's still your mother." Hades sighs. "I won't force you to my side. The choice is yours."

I nod and take a few moments to consider what he is saying. I am not worried about the choice to choose him, not even about the repercussions of the choice I'm making. What I am unsure of is how this will all come about. Will there be a battle? Will I be strong enough to fight for what I want? For what I love?

I pull back from Hades and start walking through the grove of the most beautiful, thriving trees I have ever seen in my life.

I feel Hades' eyes on my back. "Choice is not something you've had very much of."

I tense and reach out, brushing my fingers over the bark of one of the trunks.

"When I was born, my choice was stripped from me, too," Hades continues. "I was given titles I had no say in donning. Prisoner, Warrior, King."

An image flashes through my head of a painting on a dark wall filled with pain and uncertainty.

"Falling…" I whisper, the word disappearing from my mind a moment later.

"I want you to have what I didn't," Hades says, his voice closer now.

I nod, looking up at the leaves of the tree and the now-ripe apples.

"Don't choose now, but know that you will have to soon."

I turn to face him. The heartbreakingly sad smile that graces his lips makes my stomach knot.

"I wish I could take you from this. That war would not be the choice you need to make." He strokes my cheek with the back of his knuckles, and if I concentrate hard enough, I swear I can feel him more than usual in the dream.

"Hades," the words wrap around my heart and travel up my throat like a caress, "I-I know it's soon. I have no explanation for any of it, but there's something within me that…" My voice shakes a little. "Craves you." I swallow, my eyes misting a little. "I love y—"

Hades covers my lips with a finger, moving in closer to me. My heart sinks at the thought that maybe I have gotten this so wrong. Maybe I've misread things and involved my heart in a situation that will only lead to it being trampled. Have I just given my heart to someone who doesn't want it?

"I want these words, Persephone. Fuck, believe me, I do. But I want them when I don't have to leave. When I can kiss you, and you can feel it."

I feel my cheeks heat, embarrassment prickling my skin like an itchy sweater. Though, I'm not sure why. Hades wants the words, just not when we're limited to half a touch, which I can understand.

Hades leans down, resting his forehead against mine and closing his eyes. "Because I feel it, too."

My heart lurches at that and starts racing so fast I swear it's going to give out.

"Y-you do?" I whisper.

Hades nods and smiles. "So much." He laughs softly. "Everything is so fucked."

I sigh, pulling away. "I know."

Hades gently tucks a strand of hair behind my ear. "It seems being fated also means to be doomed."

"Having the mother I do makes me doomed," I reply, my

148

lips twitching.

"Then having the father I do makes us twice doomed."

I would rather be with you and doomed than blessed with anyone else, Hades.

Chapter Thirty-Three

Hades

TOGETHER, WE SIT DOWN AGAINST THE TREE **TRUNK, SHOULDER TO SHOULDER.** Cerberus puts a head into each of our laps, his third head resting on Persephone's legs. I think he is hoping to keep her here. There's comfort in the familiarity of us together, with Cerberus between us.

"I have a date with Adonis tomorrow."

Any comfort I was experiencing vanishes in an instant. "Men who've never struggled for anything are dangerous," I warn. "They believe they are entitled to things they are not."

She rolls her eyes in exasperation. "Oh, he thinks he's entitled to things all right."

Darkness swirls up my neck, and the sun darkens even inside the dream. Control. I need to regain control of this, or I'll shatter the dream. Persephone places her hand on my thigh, attempting to reassure me, but it does nothing to temper my rage.

"If something happens," I hiss, my voice barely audible, even to my ears. "You call for me. I will hear you."

She nods, her hand still resting on my thigh. "I want to touch you and kiss you."

Fuck. Persephone knows how to soothe me so easily, distracting me from the way I need to destroy.

"You will."

She moves her hand to cup my cheek, stroking her thumb under one of my eyes. My eyes flutter closed, so comforted. The darkness slides off me in a wave and soaks into the ground.

150

"How do you do that?"

Persephone brushes Cerberus off us and shifts to straddle my lap. "Do what?"

"Make the shadows run away."

She leans closer, hovering her lips over mine. Persephone doesn't answer, and I doubt she knows how she has that power over me.

"I love you, my spring," I whisper, brushing our lips against each other.

Persephone pulls back slightly, a pout flirting with her beautiful lips. "So you're allowed to say it, but I'm not allowed to say it back?"

She doesn't know everything yet, and it's unfair of me to want those words from her when she's only a shadow of herself.

"Kiss me," I order instead of answering.

She crosses her arms, full -on pouting now. "No."

I kiss her hard, biting her pouting lip. "I love when you pout."

She's such a fucking brat. Even now.

Persephone kisses me back, but she presses harder into me, trying to make up for the lack of feeling in the dream. She's had a taste of what it's like to kiss me in reality, and she is no longer satisfied with the lack in the dreams.

"I know," I soothe.

"Next week?" she confirms, no doubt feeling the need to have the kisses we shared on our date again. Nothing can take the place of reality.

I sigh. "Feels like years."

Her brows furrow, her hands digging into my shoulder. "Oh… I think I'm waking up…"

I frown, kissing her again. This is longer than we've ever spent together in a dream, yet it still is not enough. It will never be enough.

"Call for me if you need me." I touch her forehead. "Here."

She nods, leaning over to kiss all of Cerberus's noses before we both leave the dream.

151

Chapter Thirty-Four

Hades

MY EYES OPEN IN REALITY. I BLINK, TRYING TO EASE THE GRIP OF THE LINGERING DREAM.

Melinoë leans over me. She is slightly sweaty, but she looks to be in control. "How'd it go?"

I gently push her away and sit up. "She said she loved me."

"She remembers?" Mellie squeals excitedly.

"She doesn't, but she knows. There was something in her eyes when she almost said she loves me," I say, dashing her hopes.

I wipe my brow with the cloth I'd left on the bedside table. That is the thing about dreamwalking every time I sleep. I never truly *rest*. I tense when I glimpse myself in the mirror. The swirling black tattoos are just under my chin now. I can't hide them from Melinoë.

"Well, shit, you made her fall for you again?" She whistles. "Impressive, my dude. I think you're boring as fuck."

I use my glamor to cover the creeping darkness and shoot her a droll look. It doesn't phase her.

"Do you even stab her?" Mellie continues.

My eyes lock with hers. "Stab her?! Who does that?"

Helios whistles from the corner, drawing my attention. "No one here, obviously."

Mellie flips off the Titan. "You can go. Literally, no one wants you here, sunboy."

I toss the cloth to the side.

"Tell that to your nipples about to cut a hole through

your shirt," Helios volleys back.

I freeze, wincing. "Please. I cannot hear this."

I already miss the days when Helios maintained a healthy fear of me.

Mellie crosses her arms over her chest. "I'm cold, asshole."

"You're so not."

I groan and walk into the small closet to change my clothes. Every time I leave the dream, there is lingering sweat and sleep dust on me. I almost always change immediately upon waking. It's not like the clothes even smelled like her.

"How was it having Berry there?" Mellie asks as I come out of the closet.

Cerberus barks, mentally projecting to me, *"Saw Mommy!"*

I smile, petting his heads. "Yes, you did. You saw mommy, didn't you?" I glance at Melinoë. "She was scared at first, but she adjusted quickly. I don't know if it's better that she remembers anything when it's only for a moment."

Fuck, I shouldn't have said that.

"What do you mean?" Melinoë moves to Cerberus's bed, leaning back against the dog as he stretches out.

I pause, not wanting to relive the pain of having the moments of hope crushed. "For a single moment, she's back. She's the Persephone we know. Then, a second later, it's gone. It only reminds me of what I've lost. She cries but doesn't know why."

How I want to provide pain for each tear and revenge for each time her memory rescinds, but I can do nothing but dreamwalk. There are no plans I can put in place against this enemy, so I have to remain idle.

Beneath the glamor, the tattoos move over my jaw.

"I am going to tear that crop-loving bitch to pieces," Mellie hisses, giving voice to my silent resolutions.

I nod and reach for my phone, dialing Aphrodite. She answers on the third ring. "Hades. How is she?"

Of course, she knows. Did everyone know my wife was taken and the details?

"Fine. I need to ask you about Adonis."

I'm not going to discuss my dreams with Aphrodite. We don't have that kind of relationship.

"I've spoken to Eros." I hear Aphrodite's clothes rustle through the phone as she stands.

My lips twitch downward. "I heard he visited Persephone. Interference is not normally his style."

Carefully executed chaos is closer to his style. *Eros is the type to laugh during torture and then give the torturers advice on how to perform better.*

"Demeter summoned him," Aphrodite says. "You know my son, he is not forthcoming with information, even with me. But the scent of lust dust lingered in the house."

Fucking Adonis may exude lust and force those around him to lose inhibition, but to *scent* lust dust means he's trying hard to break through Persephone's natural defenses.

The tattoos cover my ears, and my jaw clicks. "He mentioned something about *sampling* her. I will not allow that to happen."

The tattoos continue to ascend, my glamor shattering beneath the power of my protective and possessive rage. My wings, horns, claws, and tail are all exposed, preparing me for battle and the execution of the man who would dare seek to claim my wife. Shadows slide from around my feet, the darkness I've struggled to contain, slipping from the leash.

"Chill out, rage issues," Mellie admonishes, but her eyes are dull. Again, my darkness is pulling out her own. I'm pulling her off the cliff and into the abyss with me.

"If there was the scent lingering in the house, he must have used a large enough amount to turn Persephone into a rabid sexual animal," Aphrodite continues. She has no idea how the darkness is swirling around the room and climbing the walls. "She must have immunity somehow."

My jaw clenches, and the swirling black tattoos climb up my face, not stopping until they're right below my eyes. I'm drowning in darkness and about to lose sight of everything. I am about to sink into the abyss and never resurface.

Aphrodite speaks into my ear, her words barely penetrating my mind. I hang up without saying anything, cutting her off mid-sentence.

"That was a dick move, demon daddy. Right, Berry?" Melinoë adds.

Cerberus barks in agreement.

I snarl, and that fragile leash I keep on myself, the one that keeps slipping out of my hand, vanishes completely. Darkness consumes the room, my powers unleashed.

Helios moves in front of Melinoë, throwing up his hands. His palms emit sunlight to keep the shadows back, but there is too much darkness spilling out of me. It eats away at the light he's attempting to project. Even as a Titan, he's in my realm and his powers are no match to the ones that come with being king.

Mellie's departure from sanity is potent. Her maniacal laugh alerts both of us to her descent into madness. "Let's torture some assholes," she says, vanishing from the room.

Good. Let's feed the darkness, the never-ending abyss. What good has it done Melinoë or me to deny this part of us? It didn't stop us from losing Persephone.

I shadow to the cells, my feet hitting the stone beneath me so hard it cracks. Melinoë lands at my side, her eyes glazed. The recaptured Titans sneer and call out, mocking and provoking us. They grow silent when the dust of my landing settles, and they see me clearly. The darkness clouds around my feet, the swirling tattoos surrounding my eyes. There's a shift of realization, but it's too late. I'm not the Hades they know. The one they taunt and call a coward. The darkness I pretend doesn't fester inside me is completely unleashed.

I shadow into one of the cells and wave my hand to merge them all. The Titans occupying them now have nowhere to go but toward me.

The first lunges at me, then another and another, hoping for a chance against their jailor. The person who defeated them not just once but twice. They mob toward me, and I keep my hands at my sides, allowing them to attempt to overwhelm me.

Their bodies block my view of Melinoë, but her voice still rings out. "Hello, handsome, want to play?" The question is followed by the sound of bone shattering.

Perses throws a punch, and I lean slightly to the side, causing it to go wide. The kick from another Titan hits another as it passes through me. I glance down at myself and raise my hand, looking at my fingers. I'm not just controlling the shadows. I am a shadow.

I grab the closest Titan, my shadow hand moving through his chest, grabbing his spine, and yanking it from his body. He opens his mouth to scream, but nothing comes out. I look at the spinal column in my hand. My lips curve in a grin. I've never had this ability before. I moved *through* the shadows and darkness inside the Titan's body.

Perses slams into me, but he passes through my body harmlessly.

With this new power, there is a whole new range of possibilities.

I slide into the shadows, my body now incorporeal as I wail on the Titans. My strikes are methodical and cruel, purposefully causing the most damage possible and inflicting the most pain I can at once.

Mellie's laugh echoes off the walls as she continues down the path of destruction. I catch sight of her holding a spiked baseball bat that she's using to break the knees of Titans. She's not even avoiding their blows. She's almost leaning into the hits, hoping to get hurt.

Titans fall one by one, the darkness inside me in complete control. Some blows might land, but I don't even feel them.

A solar flare erupts in the middle of the cells, the surprise forcing me out of my shadow form. Fucking Titan.

Helios flashes to Mellie. A Titan has sunk his teeth into her thigh, but she's only laughing. Helios's face is hard, his entire body emitting penetrating beams of light, cutting the Titan in half to force them away from Mellie. Several curse at him and call him a traitor, reminding him of his loyalties, but his only focus is her. He lifts her into his arms and pauses to look at me, pinning me with a bright stare of condemnation.

"She would be so disappointed in you." [13]

Chapter Thirty-Five

Persephone

ONCE AGAIN, I HAVE BEEN DRESSED UP FOR *ADONIS*. This time, the deep wine-colored velvet hugs every curve, leaving absolutely nothing to the imagination. The hem falls just above my knees, and my feet have been pushed into high black pumps. I brush my fingers over the velvet, feeling it tickle the pads of my fingers.

"Persephone! Hurry!" My mother chastises me from downstairs.

I quickly do another turn in the mirror, looking at the outfit. While I absolutely hate that it is supposed to be for Adonis, I do love how my body looks in this dress. It feels right. I feel like *me* somehow. Strong. Confident. Empowered.

I decide that the best way to get through this date is to set it in my mind that I chose to wear this dress for myself—no one else. Then my traitorous mind wonders how Hades would react to seeing me in this, but I push that thought away.

I take a steadying breath, ready for my mother's snide comments, and then I leave my room to head into the belly of the beast.

It surprises me how well I am able to walk in such high heels. It seems I'm seasoned in wearing these stunning stilts, my steps not faltering once as I walk down the corridor to the stairs.

My mother gives me a cursory look, briefly taking in my garb. She tilts her head and gives me the smallest look of disapproval, which disappears as quickly as it came. She pulls her face into a smile and says, "Now, don't you look lovely?"

I blink, then blink again. Unease fills my whole body at her compliment.

She grabs a long black trench coat from the closet and hands it to me. "Let's hurry. It isn't proper to keep your future husband waiting," she chirps. When she is closer, I can still see the faint cracks on her cheeks. Obviously, she has worked hard to cover them.

"Mother?" I say, pulling on the trench coat. She brushes my hands away, wrapping it around me and tying it tight. "I'm not sure this is right…" I bite back a groan of pain as she pulls the straps tighter. "I've only met one man."

When did I become such a good liar? Why don't I feel any guilt? Maybe because I know she is also lying to me.

Mother laughs cruelly. "Did you expect an abundance of suitors?"

I wince. "What?" Even though I didn't take her compliment on board, even the ghost of it makes these words sting even more.

Mother takes my arm and practically yanks me out of the house and down the path. "Adonis is waiting, and you have little to work with. We must strike while the iron is hot and get a commitment from him," my mother practically hisses. "You will give him divine children, and everything will be fine."

With every word, my stomach churns more, and my heart sinks lower. I always knew this wouldn't be my choice, but to have it so brutally forced upon me is devastating. Yanking myself free of her, I make no effort to fix my face into anything other than disgust. I continue down the path, my mother hot on my heels.

I am so lost in my own head that I barely notice the streets. Usually, I distract myself by watching people go

159

about their day. I make up scenarios about where they are going, where they've been, and who they're going home to. But all I can do this evening is face forward, clench my fists, and try to stay calm.

I sense Adonis before I see him, and the feeling of his magic clogs my throat, the deception like a veil over him. The second I turn the corner, his smug, arrogant face comes into view, and my stomach rolls.

"Betrothed," Adonis greets, his words laced with his over-inflated ego.

I barely look at him, taking the seat opposite him. "Adonis," I reply eventually.

"I've had a visitor." He pauses, the moment impregnated with his smugness. "The God of Love."

My body tenses. Eros said he would give me a week. *Shit, shit, shit.*

"He informed me that his approval of our match is forth-coming."

Forthcoming doesn't mean approved. I need to breathe. I finally meet his gaze, his eyes full of conceit and a sick kind of joy.

"Oh?" I lift my menu to hide because I can feel myself pale. I will never give him the satisfaction or ownership of my reactions.

Adonis pours two glasses of wine, the color nearly matching my dress.

"Yes. Drink. This is a celebration."

I feel the color return to my face, mostly thanks to the simmering rage that is now building within me, but still. I lower the menu and look right at him, pulling my lips into a bored smile. "No thanks. There is nothing to celebrate." I never know where this side of me comes from, but I so enjoy it when she comes out to play.

"It wasn't a request, Persephone." Adonis's voice drops.

I can tell he's trying to intimidate me, but it only spurs on my inner badass. Oh, how I love her. I quirk a brow, allowing her to take the reins, trusting her completely.

"Wow. It must really bother you, huh?"

Adonis narrows his eyes. "What?"

160

My lips twitch. "My natural divinity."

"Why would that bother me?" Adonis asks, trying to keep his voice even, but I can see the way his jaw twitches, and I can hear the snarl he's pushing down.

"Because of your lack of it." I smirk. "It's obvious, you know? I could feel it from a mile off."

"And yet," Adonis growls, putting his wine glass down just a little too hard to pass off as being unaffected, "I managed to gain immortality and a divine whore."

The badass inside me practically cackles at that, and I can feel her invisible claws. I'm under his skin, and I fucking love it. I allow the laugh to slip free and finally pick up my glass. Cradling the precious crystal in my hand, I take a sip before looking him dead in the eye and saying, "But you will *never* be a god."

Adonis lurches to his feet. My head snaps to the side, the force of the blow sending me to the floor. My ear rings, and my cheek stings from the impact. He moves around the table to stand over me, looking down at me. His face is contorted into a look of such rage, his eyes flashing and dark. "And yet, spring slut, my children will be. I have a whore who will birth me gods, and I will be their god."

I feel thick, hot ichor slide down my cheek, and I can already feel the laceration from his ring burning on my cheek. The gilded blood trickles down my face and neck as I look up at him. I stand and glare at him, not backing down from his furious stare. The door to the empty restaurant looks so welcoming, beckoning me, and I turn to leave. I want to get as far away from this evil being as quickly as possible.

Adonis has other plans. He grabs my hair and yanks me back. I lose my footing and fall heavily to the ground. I groan at the impact, but he doesn't release my hair. He tightens his grip and twists, pulling strands free from my scalp.

He drags me across the floor toward the back of the restaurant. I struggle in his hold, reaching back, trying to grab onto him. My scalp aches, and the rough stone floor scrapes the skin on my thighs and calves. He heaves me along carelessly, my heels left behind as I kick and struggle.

"You think a high and mighty bitch can't be broken?" Adonis snarls. "I'll have fun showing you how fucking wrong you are."

I snarl back, still trying to get free. I will fight to the fucking death. He will not take what does not belong to him.

Adonis sneers, dragging me purposely over some broken glass. It pierces my skin through my dress. The pain is unbearable, but I don't even whimper. He will own none of my sounds.

"You didn't even notice, did you?" Adonis laughs darkly. "No plants anywhere. Nothing to help the poor Goddess of Spring."

I look around, noticing he is right, and I growl. Yes, I have powers without plants, but they boost and strengthen me. There is nothing here.

I thrash in his hold, but that only increases the pain. By struggling at the moment, I'm only hurting myself more. Adonis pulls me through a door and then slams it shut behind us before finally releasing my hair. He picks me up from the floor and tosses me onto a springy surface—a bed. Adonis moves like a viper, pinning me down.

No, no, no, no, no, no, no, no, no!

"Release me," I demand.

Adonis pulls back and snarls. He slaps me across the face again, harder this time. The room spins, and I blink to clear it, but to no avail.

I'm vaguely aware of him straddling one of my thighs and unbuttoning his pants, but there seems to be two of him.

Fuck. Think, P.

The thick ichor is now trickling from my nose and my cheek. I can taste the coppery tang against my lips.

Adonis looks down at the dress. "Not a queen now. Just a whore." He grabs the neckline of my dress and pulls, ripping it open. He smiles as he rakes his gaze over me greedily. It feels like acid slicking my skin.

I scream and slam my knee into his balls as hard as I can.

Adonis crumples and falls to the side, groaning and curling, trying to ease the pain. Even though the room is still spinning, I take the opportunity. I stumble off the bed and

162

fall to my knees, struggling to get back to my feet as quickly as possible. My stomach rolls with nausea, and I blink, trying to clear my vision. I manage to stand and stumble to the door, yanking it open.

Tears fill my eyes and spill over, trailing down my cheeks. I take a few steps forward, but I am tackled to the ground. This time, my head cracks against the stone floor. Pain explodes in my head, and I feel more thick ichor escape from my body. The whole room is not only spinning now but vibrating, too. I don't seem to be healing.

"Adonis! Stop!" I think I'm speaking, but I push all my energy into trying to wriggle free of him. Another surge of strength slams through me as I feel him shove my ruined dress up, the air hitting my ass.

"Shut up," Adonis snarls.

Through the adrenaline and fuzziness in my head, I hear Hades' voice. *"Call me if you need me."*

"Get the fuck off me!" I scream, but inside my mind, I scream Hades' name over and over.

Hades! Hades! Hades!

Suddenly, everything goes black, but not from my injuries. My inner strength completely overpowers me, and I feel something sharp beneath my skin, many small points, like spikes or thorns.

I scream once more, and then I unleash. My vision returns just in time to see large, sharp spines emerge from my skin and penetrate Adonis.

Chapter Thirty-Six

Hades

SHE WOULD BE SO DISAPPOINTED IN YOU.
Helios' condemnation rings in my ears hours later.
He was right. She would be so disappointed in me.
Alone in my bathroom, I inspect the swirling black tattoos that have encircled my eyes. I thought the darkness might have receded a bit more from my outburst, having allowed it to vent.

She would be so disappointed in you.

The swirls of black across my skin make my unglamored self appear even more demonic. It's even crawled across the membranes of my wings and around my horns. How much longer do I have before it completely consumes me?

"Hades."

I whirl in surprise at her voice. *"Persephone?"* I try to respond through our mental link, but I'm met with a solid wall of terror that keeps me out.

"Hades! Hades!"

My eyes lock on the mirror, realization settling in.

If you need me, call for me.

My power explodes from me. The mirror shatters, and all the lights in the palace go out. I slam my hand against the glass, cutting my palm. I let my blood pool before I draw the ancient summoning symbol on the counter.

When I lock eyes in the shattered mirror again, the reflection is no longer mine but a woman bearing a striking resemblance to Nyx. She has midnight hair and fine features, but her eyes are black as if filled with ink.

The woman smirks, tossing her head back with a haunting, echoing laugh. "Well, well, to be summoned by the king."

"Your queen is in danger. I cannot interfere."

My hands are useless, but those under my command are not.

"You know the price," she says, her face shattered in the broken mirror.

"I'll pay it."

She laughs again, that haunting, cursed laugh.

She begins to fade from the mirror, but I narrow my eyes.

"Nemesis. Bring me his hands."

She laughs one more time before disappearing from the mirror.

Chapter Thirty-Seven

Persephone

I **BLINK AGAIN, TRYING TO CLEAR MY VISION, BUT EVERYTHING IS SO BLURRY.** The only sounds are my heartbeat thundering in my ear, and I'm vaguely aware of Adonis screaming in pain. I'm not sure how I even do it, but I pull the spines back, needing to get out from under his weight.

My body shivers as I feel the power in the room shift again. The hair on the back of my neck stands. This is not the usual godly power I'm used to feeling. This power is almost malevolent. The ghostly sound of a haunting laugh seems to come from every direction, surrounding us.

A black orchid appears in front of me. It is just one plant, but it's enough life to jumpstart my quicker divine healing. My vision clears, and while I'm still bleeding from a myriad of wounds, I definitely feel stronger.

Adonis whimpers as he is slowly lifted off me. I roll over on the floor to face him. His body is bleeding from the multiple stab wounds my thorns created. A red-hued smoke wraps around him, suspending him in the air. Terror fills his eyes. My stomach rolls as I realize that I'm finding satisfaction in seeing him broken and scared. He is feeling exactly how he enjoyed making me feel. My guilt completely dissipates with that realization.

"W-what are you doing to me?" Adonis stutters, looking

at me, panicked.

I tilt my head, watching him, trying to work out if it truly is me that's doing this. My question is answered not a moment later when that sinister laugh echoes around us again, the red smoke tightening on him.

"You thought you could take a queen, little man."

The voice sends a shiver down my spine. I look around, trying to find the owner of it, but the restaurant is still empty, save for Adonis and me.

The smoke slowly creeps up, swallowing his neck, chin, mouth, and nose until it completely consumes him.

A woman appears next to Adonis's covered form. While the smoke seems to caress her form, sliding over her smoothly, it seems jagged and unsettled around Adonis as if trying to repel him.

She bows to me. "My queen."

I blink, and my chest heaves as I look at her. Queen? Me?

In a blink, they are both gone, and I look around the restaurant, needing someone else to have witnessed that apart from me. I struggle to my feet. Wincing, I hobble to the entrance of the restaurant. There is only so much a single flower can do.

I feel an overwhelming sense of relief that my mother isn't there to greet me. She obviously believed the night would be extended. She knew what she was pushing me into. How could she do that to me? At what point am I going to stop believing the best of her?

I think of my conversation with Hades when he asked me to take his side, when he said, "She's still your mother." While biologically that is true, she has never been a mom. For that reason, and so many others, I'm certain that choosing him is right. I will always choose Hades.

The events of the night start to hit me as I limp up the hill to my mother's house, and I feel the burden of them sitting heavy on my shoulders. The sight of the house is anything but welcoming, but it has my bed and my doorway to Hades, making it good enough for now. I open the door, not even glancing to check if my mother is in the living room. I make a beeline for the stairs, but my limp slows me down.

167

"Sweetling?" my mother chirps, and my whole body tenses.

I just want to go cry alone in my bed and then see Hades. I want her to leave me alone. My body and my mind are in a conflict. My body just wants to cocoon itself and take stock, but my mind wants to scream at my mother, raining down on her all the anger from the past two hundred years.

I turn on my heel and walk back to the living room. What a sight I must be, covered in ichor, dress ripped, and bruised face.

My mother gasps the second she lays her eyes on me, feigning concern. "What happened?"

I feel a tear roll uselessly down my cheek. While I know this is not real, even fake concern has me finally sinking into the reality of my evening. How much worse would it have been if not for my inner badass I didn't know existed?

"You know exactly what happened, Mother." My voice is low and even.

"Sweetling," I feel my mother's gaze slide over me, "you know better than to fight these things."

I look at her, dumbfounded, another tear tracking down my cheek. I clench my fists, feeling those spines sharpen beneath my skin. "You told him he could *sample* me by any means necessary," I snarl. "And now you stand there, blaming me?"

"These are things we must endure as women, Persephone." She lifts her hand to cup my cheek, but I slap it away.

"You should be ashamed of yourself. You are no mother," I hiss, turning from her and leaving the room.

The tears begin a steady trickle as I walk from her view and continue well after I've closed my bedroom door. I press my back against it and close my eyes, finally allowing myself to whimper.

"Persephone?"

My eyes snap open at the sound of Hades' voice, and I look around the room.

"Hades?" I whisper, moving to the balcony and peering over it, but there's no one there. Did I imagine his voice?

"Are you alright?"

My head snaps up, trying to find him.

"I'm in your mind, my spring," he replies, and I can hear the tension in his voice.

I frown, considering if I can send a message back.

"You can. Our mental link is—" He stops himself. *"Are you alright?"* he repeats.

I walk to the bedroom door and use my vines to make as strong a lock as possible. *"I'm fine."* It might be a lie, but I'm safe now, and I'm talking to Hades, so I'm as fine as I can be under the circumstances.

"Nemesis wasn't too late?" Hades asks, and my heart aches with the choked fear in his voice.

"No." I walk into the bathroom and lock that door as well. I am about to wash my face when I catch sight of my reflection and completely break down. The sight of my injuries is the final straw. My lip is swollen, and my face is covered in cuts and bruises. Scratches and Adonis's fingerprints mar the creamy skin of my arms.

I hear Hades inhale sharply in my mind, and I can tell he's pacing, probably wearing a trail into my perfect black rug with an accent of silver around the border. My brows furrow at the memory, but this time, it doesn't leave immediately. Another tear runs down my cheek, and then the memory is gone, and I'm left only with the repercussions of the night.

"Persephone, say you want to go on a date with me right now," Hades demands.

I sob softly. *"I can't. I look awful."*

Hades growls, *"Persephone. Say yes. I can't come to you otherwise."*

"Yes." I sob again, closing my eyes.

Less than a moment later, I feel the energy shift, and I'm wrapped in powerful arms. Long, strong fingers plunge into my hair and pull my face against a large, comforting chest. The scent of citrus and sandalwood surrounds me, making my heart skip a beat.

I thought I was crying before, but when Hades pulls me into his arms, and I feel the safety of him surround me, that's when the true tears begin. As I sob, it occurs to me

169

I've never had this before. I've never had someone who I could cry to, who I was confident would comfort me. Oh, to be loved by someone... no, to be loved by *him*.

Hades nuzzles my head, and his chest rises as he inhales deeply. The sobs don't ease, instead becoming harder, and I feel like I can't breathe, like I need to get all the tears out of me. I need to rid myself of Adonis, what he did to me, and what he almost did to me.

Hades strokes my back, kissing my head over and over, and I feel something wrap around me. It doesn't feel like his shadows, but it's something that is innately part of him wrapping around me, healing me.

"I'm here, my spring," Hades whispers into me, squeezing me, trying to calm me, and it's working. Though I continue to sob, I can breathe, if only to inhale more of his intoxicating scent.

Hades lifts me into his arms and carries me to the bathtub, climbing into it while still holding me as he sits down. I'm not sure when he filled it, but hot water surrounds us, and we sit there, both still fully clothed, his hands gently stroking my back. All I can do is stay curled into him, crying. His magic has healed me externally, but this, what he's doing right now, is healing me internally.

After what feels like hours, the tears finally dry up, and I nuzzle my cheek against Hades' shoulder as he strokes my hair. It suddenly occurs to me how I must look, covered in dried blood and probably dirt. I pull away from Hades slightly and turn so my back is to him.

"I don't want you to see me like this," I explain as I turn the water on and start to wash my face.

Hades grabs my chin with a growl and forces me to face him. "That is unacceptable." I meet his gaze after a moment, his eyes fierce but also so full of love and devotion. "You do not hide from me, Persephone." He moves his gaze down the length of my body as though cataloging every newly healed injury like he can still see them.

"Do you... find me *ugly* like this?" My voice trembles a little at the word.

"I find you beautiful always," Hades growls, meeting my

170

gaze again.

A small sob escapes me. "Is he dead?"

Hades nods once. "I would never let him live. He's lucky I was not able to attend."

Something about the way he talks, the words he's saying, makes me feel a slight thrill, and I find my gaze wandering to his lips.

"Kiss me," I demand.

Hades doesn't hesitate, easing my fear that he doesn't want me. He leans in, brushing his lips over mine. It is the barest of kisses before I pull back.

"Not like that," I say. That kiss made me feel delicate and broken, but I am not those things when I am with Hades. He makes me feel empowered, sexy, and strong.

Hades tips his head, studying my face. "What do you mean?"

I shift to face him more and lean in, pressing my lips to his and kissing him deeply, passionately. My tongue slides along the seam of his lips, practically begging for entry, which he allows eagerly, and my tongue brushes over his. I dig my fingers into his hair, softly moaning before I pull back.

"Like that."

Hades pulls my thigh over his lap. I straddle him, and he kisses me again, his fingers digging into my hips.

Oh, yes. This is what I need. I start to open his shirt. It is soaked, and my fingers fumble slightly in my rush. Hades catches my hands, stilling them. He pulls back, his gaze searching mine. "Are you sure?" he asks.

"I want you to fuck me. Here. In my bed. In my prison." I look over his face. He is my salvation. "You make me feel free."

Hades cups my cheek. "And you make me feel everything."

My breath catches at his words, and I kiss him again, working the buttons until the shirt is completely open. Hades stands in the bathtub, lifting me, and steps out, his lips never leaving mine. I yank his hair as we head to the bedroom, both of us dripping wet.

Chapter Thirty-Eight
Hades

IN MY PRISON.

My claws shred her gown, needing that last remnant of her night with the now very dead male gone. I knew the moment it was done. My hands withered and vanished from my wrists. The Underworld has already healed me, and that *cretin's* hands already hold space in a globe in my office.

Over the next couple of weeks, I'll lose my hands suddenly and without warning. The loss and pain of it is the price demanded from the Goddess of Revenge. A price to be paid. One I'd pay hundreds of times over. If she had demanded to lose my head or heart, I still wouldn't have hesitated. She called me for help.

She needs me now. It's written in her eyes and how she shoves my shirt off my shoulders, the franticness of her kiss.

I rip the offending fabric from my body, tunneling my fingers into her hair, my tongue flicking against hers. Her hands fly to my pants, tearing them open. I groan at her urgency. I can't get rid of the clothes fast enough for her.

I roll onto my back, making her straddle me. "Break free. With me." Don't leave me behind this time.

"I love you," she whispers again, her lips against mine. She shoves my pants off, positioning her cunt right above my cock. I arch, brushing the piercing in the tip against her pussy.

"I love you too," I growl softly against her lips, gripping her hips but not yanking her down onto me. I know she needs this control.

She locks her eyes on mine, barely a breath away from my face. Then she slams her hips down. My claws dig into her hips, but the control remains hers, riding me like she needs, like I need.

I sit up, kissing her hard, biting her lip, moving our bodies together rhythmically. She squeezes me, her cunt like a wet, warm vice on my cock.

"You're mine, Persephone," I groan. "You've always been mine." Just like I've always been yours.

She moans, running her fingers through my hair. I slide my hand up her back, cradling the back of her head, digging in, clinging to her. Everything is perfect at this moment. We're just a man and a woman searching for a connection and finding it in each other.

"Give it to me. Give me everything," I order her softly.

She presses tighter against me, her heartbeat syncing with mine, a single humming between two bodies bound by fate and love.

I flip us to put her beneath me, taking control. The thrusting turns frantic, and I lose myself in her. My glamor drops without conscious effort, and thankfully, the darkness moves to Persephone, continuing to heal her. My tail wraps around her thigh, lifting her leg to wrap higher around me so I can thrust deeper and harder. A rush of liquid heat fills her cunt, bathing my cock.

Her glamor drops, a silent response to mine. My heart lurches at seeing the short stubs of bone hiding in her hair. My shadows swirl around her head, sensing the hurt and replacing the horns, giving her shadow horns until her real ones grow back.

She yanks my head to hers, sealing her lips to mine, fusing them as if she needs to kiss me in order to live. I need her in order to live, too. Her pussy squeezes me tightly. She is so fucking perfect. She's close.

Come with me, my spring. Be free with me.

As if she hears my silent entreaty, she comes, squeezing my cock like a vice, robbing me of my orgasm, claiming my essence.

Panting above her, I press my forehead to hers. She reaches up, touching the horns I gave her.

"You... aren't repulsed by them?" she asks, vulnerability flashing in her eyes.

"Repulsed?" I blink, shocked by the question.

Repulsed by her horns? The ones that mark her as an Underworld Goddess from birth? The ones that gave me my *own* horns?

A tear slides down her cheek, and it all makes sense. I should have asked Nemesis to take Demeter's hands instead.

I kiss the tear. "The only thing repulsive to me is that they were removed."

She whimpers slightly, and I nuzzle her nose. I keep her close, wrapping her in acceptance, something she's clearly lacked in her life before me, before Plutus, before everything. I thought this Persephone was a shell, a shade of the woman I love, but I realize now this is Persephone. Her deepest insecurities, the trauma she overcame, and the mother she broke free from. It is at this moment that I realize I'm in love with this version of her, too.

This Persephone is so scared of affection, cautious, and shy, expecting denial at every turn. I set out to make her fall in love with me, hoping her memory would return. Yet, I fell in love with her as well. This is the Persephone I never got to meet, the one who was convinced her immortal goddess form was repulsive and should be hidden.

It seems no matter the timing, no matter the aspect, I am meant to fall in love with her in every way. Memory or not. God or not.

She is mine, and I am hers.

174

Chapter Thirty-Nine

Persephone

I SMILE DOWN AT HIM SO WIDELY THAT THE ALMOST HEALED CUT ON MY LIP OPENS SLIGHTLY. I barely wince at the pain, too caught up in this perfect moment with him, my Hades.

Hades' brows furrow when he sees the cut open. Seeing any injury on me is obviously something he finds unacceptable. He leans down, licking over the cut, and that action alone makes me moan softly, my whole body melting for him. I'm so acutely aware of my love for him. It runs so deep, so overwhelmingly. Almost like—

"Hades?" I whisper into his lips.

"Yes?" Hades pulls back slightly, looking down at me.

I swallow. "There's something I'm missing. Isn't there?"

I feel Hades tense above me, his gaze searching mine. He's reluctant to tell me. Why?

He nods, and his eyes flash with pain. He desperately wants to tell me but can't for some reason. I cup his cheek, sliding my thumb gently beneath his eye.

"And there's a reason you can't tell me. Right?" I ask, searching his face.

"It hurts you," he replies, his voice thick with despair and memories.

I nod, stroking his cheek.

"I'll replace it with new things," Hades says after another

moment, the pain in his expression easing a little. He leans down, brushing his lips over mine, and I smile into the kiss, my heart soaring for this man. I'm not sure what I've lost, but I am sure of what I've gained.

Hades pulls back too soon, his gaze traveling to my horns. It takes a lot not to pull away from him, to hide them. I'm not used to people seeing them, even less used to people seeing them as anything but hideous.

"Those can't grow back fast enough," Hades growls.

I sigh heavily. "She'll only cut them off again."

Hades' jaw clenches. "Bitch." I stroke his cheek again, just watching him, admiring him. My cheeks heat when his gaze meets mine again, knowing he caught me staring. "Your horns are beautiful, Persephone."

My vision blurs a little as my eyes fill with tears. "Really?"

Hades nods. "In the Underworld, everyone has horns."

"I've never seen anyone on Olympus with horns."

Hades smirks playfully, tilting his head so his horns are on show. "Well, technically, you have."

I smile, reaching up and wrapping a hand around his proud horn, enjoying how perfectly it curls away from his head.

Hades moans, his eyes shuttering. "Fuck."

My eyebrows lift at his reaction, and my stomach heats a little. I squeeze the horn, and Hades growls in response.

"Not fair when I can't do it back."

I stroke my hand up and down his horn. "I love them."

Hades smiles, his eyes still dark. "I didn't have any for a long time."

"You didn't?" I ask, squeezing his horn again.

"It's... uh, really hard to think when you do that." He moans.

I reach up with my other hand and squeeze his other horn. I'm rewarded with a low groan from Hades, his eyes rolling back a little in pleasure.

"Hades?" I kiss along his jaw, wanting to hide my face as I voice the question I'm about to ask him.

"Hm?" Hades moans, lost in pleasure.

"Can I..." I feel my face burn with a blush, "suck your

176

cock?"

Hades pulls back, looking down at me as if I've asked him the most ludicrous thing. "My spring. My cock is yours to do with what you will."

In a flash, I push him onto his back and straddle him, kissing down his neck. I don't know what has gotten into me, but I need to taste him.

Hades groans, and I can feel his eyes searing into me. His shadows caress my skin as I kiss down his chest, and I glance up at him. He is resting his head on his hands, the picture of male satisfaction, and I've never been more turned on.

Well, that's a lie. I'm always this turned on when I'm with Hades.

One of Hades' shadows palms my ass and then spanks it hard. I moan in response and continue placing my trail of kisses down his body until I'm kneeling between his thighs. The sight of his rock-hard cock takes my breath away, and all I can think about is how badly I want to choke on his length.

Hades' cock twitches under my gaze, and I lick my lips. He is so beautiful, from the thick shaft to the bead of pre-cum on the tip to the piercing glinting in the light of the lamp. I slowly bend, licking the tip of his cock, my eyes rolling at the taste of him. Fuck. He is so perfect.

"Suck it," Hades growls, looking down at me.

I close my lips around the head and slowly begin sucking on him. His shadows slide up my stomach and roll my nipples between what feels like his fingers. I press into his touch while taking his cock deeper into my mouth.

I take him deeper, moaning at how it fills my mouth and how badly I need more of it. Hades' shadows spank me again, and suddenly, I can't fucking wait. I drop my head on his cock, taking his length as deep as I can. My throat constricts, struggling around his size. I gag hard but don't stop trying to take more of him, needing more.

I feel Hades arch, and I meet his gaze. My eyes are stinging with tears, and I blink to clear them, needing to see how much he needs this, how much he needs me. The tears slide down my cheeks, but these are tears of desire, tears of pleasure.

I lift my mouth off him and then plunge back down again, choking on him. Hades covers his mouth, trying to muffle his shout, and I suck hard, bobbing my head faster, each time taking him a little deeper, each time gagging on him. I feel my slickness sliding down my thighs as I suck on him.

Hades thrusts his hips up at the same time as I drop my head, and I take him even deeper, needing everything he can give me. Hades snarls, biting his fist as he comes, filling my mouth with his seed. I swallow it, moaning at his taste, needing more of it. His body completely relaxes beneath me, and I pull back, licking his cock clean, needing every ounce of his release inside me.

"Come here." Hades pants as I crawl up his body, kissing him deeply.

My core throbs, desperate for him, but I know we don't have time.

"I'm here," Hades moans against my lips, deepening the kiss.

I pull back a little, cupping his cheek. "How much longer can you stay?"

My heart sinks, already knowing the answer, already anticipating him leaving.

"A few more minutes." Hades pulls me against him and presses kisses to the top of my head. It's as if he can't stop himself from kissing and touching me.

I sigh heavily and bury my face against his neck, inhaling him.

Hades nuzzles into my hair and says, "I wish I could hold you as I drift off." I pull back, looking up at him, and he brushes his lips over mine. "That you could wrap me in your vines so you'd know I couldn't leave."

"I don't want you to leave," I whisper. "Ever."

Hades kisses me again, his lips as soft as a feather against mine. "I know." He looks over my face. "Soon, things will change."

"Okay, demon. I trust you."

Demon?

"I love you," Hades says, smiling softly, but I see that pain

178

in his eyes again.

I kiss his chest. "I'll... see you soon?" I ask hopefully.

Hades nods, kissing my head. "Very soon."

I kiss his neck. "You should go."

"Just..." Hades' eyes fill with tears, and he keeps his gaze locked on mine. "Just a moment longer."

I press my lips to his and kiss him, pushing all of my love and devotion into it, needing him to feel it as much as I do.

Hades whispers into my lips. "Goodbye, Persephone."

"Goodbye, Hades."

His shadows wrap around him, and within the blink of an eye, he's gone.

"I miss you." His voice echoes in my mind, and I smile.

"I miss you too."

I shift in bed, laying my head on the pillow he was using, his scent still so potent. I quickly fall asleep, but I don't go back to our meadow.

Tonight, there is only darkness.

179

Chapter Forty

Persephone

I **STRETCH IN BED, HIS SANDALWOOD AND CIT-**
RUS SCENT SURROUNDING ME. *I reach for him, my*
hand only meets cool, untouched sheets. I frown, patting
at the mattress, *not ready* to open my eyes quite yet.

"Hades?" *My voice sounds groggy and sleep-filled.*

Could he have gone to work already? Surely not. It is too ear-
ly. *I hug* his pillow close *and quickly fall back to sleep.*

I nuzzle into my pillow, inhaling deeply of Hades' scent,
the scent of dreams. Last night was the first night I hadn't
dreamed of our meadow for a long time, and I missed it.
No matter how much I searched for it, all I could see was
darkness. I wasn't lonely or scared. It wasn't isolating or
eerie. It was just black, and there was something comforting
about it.

I stretch in my bed, the cotton brushing against my naked body, and slowly blink my eyes open. While meeting

Hades in the meadow every night is everything to me, it doesn't make for a very restful sleep.

I start to truly wake, peeking through my lashes. My eyes snap open, and I lurch up in bed, looking around. Black vines with gold leaves and thorns cover my entire bedroom. They line the walls and obscure every piece of furniture except for the bed.

My mother knocks on the bedroom door, and my eyes snap to it. "Persephone?"

Fuck. Shit. Fuck. Fuck.

I look around the room, my heart racing in my chest, thinking of what she'll do if she sees this. And even if she's somehow okay with the fucking jungle of vines, will she be able to scent Hades?

Reckless, Persephone.

"I'll be right down!" I call, trying to make my voice sound as even as possible. Somehow, I need to keep her out of my room until I can work out how to reverse whatever I did in my sleep.

"Hmm," my mother replies, but thankfully, I hear her footsteps retreat down the corridor after a moment.

I climb out of bed and grab my robe. I look around the room as I pull it on. The vines appear to be throbbing as if matching my heartbeat. I close my eyes and try to will them back, but when I open them again, there has been absolutely no movement.

Fuck.

A moment later, the door rattles as someone tries to open it, probably my mother. She often used this tactic, trying to catch me doing something I shouldn't be, like reading books about other gods.

The vines tense over the door, preventing anyone from entering, and I blink in fear. It will be horrible if my mother manages to get in. What if I have completely lost control over these powers I didn't know I had? My vines have just recently become black, and they have never been this strong or powerful before.

"I will be right down, Mother." I try to hold back my growl, but I'm not sure I'm successful.

181

Finally, I hear my mother go downstairs, truly leaving this time. No doubt I'll pay for that later.

I close my eyes again, trying to pull the vines back, needing to force them to do... something, but they continue to defy me. I sigh heavily and make my way through the bathroom to wash. The vines only move enough to let me enter and exit.

I dress in a simple sundress and leave my hair down. I don't care about my mother's rules anymore. She went too far yesterday.

My mother looks up when I enter, and her eyes trail over me. I can feel her distaste, but I don't even look at her. I can't. Even the thought of her face makes me want to destroy her house.

Her copy of *Olympus Today* rustles as she lifts it again, and the servants sporadically filter in and out, placing plates of vegetables down and filling our cups with water and tea. I keep my eyes on my plate, picking at my breakfast. I can't even face eating at the moment, especially when it continues to be the homegrown vegetables from my mother's garden. It wouldn't surprise me if she tried to poison me.

My mother clears her throat. "No contact from Adonis. You must have burned that bridge good."

"Oh, don't worry about that, Mother." I glance at her, finally meeting her gaze. "He got exactly the night he deserved."

My mother's jaw ticks as she watches me, her nostrils flaring slightly. "No matter. I will find another."

I laugh humorlessly. "Do you plan to let him *sample* me, also?"

My mother slams her newspaper down on the table. "Yes," she hisses.

I hold her gaze, refusing to back down.

"I will let a whole army do it if need be. Until *he* can no longer look at you," she snarls.

I quirk a brow at my mother's slip. "Who?"

Mother narrows her eyes at me, the paper crumpling in her tensing hands.

I don't look away, not for a moment, rage bubbling un-

182

der my skin. Say. His. Name. I dare you.

"You are my daughter. You will do what I order."

The cracks on my mother's skin become more pronounced with every second of our conversation, and I look back down at the table. "As I have been, Mother."

"And you will continue to do so." She stands from the table, her chair almost falling from the force. "I will be looking for a suitor who will accept you, tainted as you are."

My mother thinks she won that round, that I submitted. I want her to think that because what she doesn't know is that she gave me the biggest clue she could have. *She* took something from me, and it's something to do with Hades.

Check, Mother.[14]

---

14   The Nightmare & The Daydream Chapters 34 & 35

183

Chapter Forty-One

Hades

WHAT DO YOU MEAN YOU CAN'T FIND HER DREAM, MORPHY?" Melinoë demands. The two Gods of Dreams hover over my bed, prepared to drop me into Persephone's dreams.

"It's as if she... gone."

I snarl, the sound more feral and monstrous than ever. My shadows erupt from me, slamming into both of them. Mellie flies back, hitting the wall hard, denting it. Morpheus slams into a table, snapping his teeth and biting back his retort.

"Throw my girlfriend one more time, and we will have issues," Helios warns, narrowing his eyes on me. He moves to help her to her feet.

"I'm not your fucking girlfriend," Mellie hisses, slapping his hand away and standing on her own. "Hades. You need to calm the fuck down. We're doing all we can here."

I jump to my feet, my glamor failing to hide the darkness in my face. I'm too scattered to even manage it at the moment. "Yet it is not enough! We are at war, and my queen is trapped!"

For every Titan I help to collect, I remember how they escaped, how I lost her, and how the war seems to become more complicated. The traces of Kronus have vanished. Whatever my father is up to, it is not good. Soon, there will be nothing left, and I can't fight. I am fucking trapped in the Underworld, relying on others not only to fight but for access to my wife. I have to sit idle.

"Are you fucking kidding me?" Mellie snarls. "I have been

nearly killing myself to ensure you can see her as often as you want, and you have the fucking nerve to tell me it's not enough?"

I don't need a mirror to know the darkness spreading over my skin is staining my eyes now. The proof is in the way the rage, sorrow, and frustration are encroaching on my mind. "Is she here right now?"

"No, and neither am I!" She whirls, shouting, "Berry! Come!"

Cerberus trots to her side, and I can't stop my mouth. The boiling rage is too much. "You must not truly care about her."

My breath whistles out of me as Helios slams into me with the force of a comet. We hit the window, breaking the glass with my back. My wings snap out to stop myself from plummeting into the gardens below.

"You may be a king, but you don't have to be a dick," Helios growls, his eyes glowing like two solar flares. I can only imagine how this is affecting the actual sun.

Mellie doesn't look back, taking Cerberus on a walk with her, leaving Helios and me alone. Morpheus must have taken the opportunity to vanish.

"Question my loyalty all you want." Helios glares at me. "Yeah, I wasn't on your side last time."

That was understating it a bit. He was a fucking *general* in the last war, but he cut a deal with me to avoid him and his two sisters being locked up in Tartarus like the rest of the Titans.

"And this time?" I hiss, my eyes narrowing. Who is he truly siding with? Is this all an act? A long, drawn-out ploy?

Helios slowly rakes his eyes over me. "I'm not going to answer that because *my* loyalty isn't important."

My jaw ticks. *His* loyalty isn't important? Tell that to Zeus, who constantly tries to get me to imprison him.

"*Mellie's* loyalty? To question *that?*" My jaw audibly cracks, but Helios doesn't pause for a second. "P was my friend first, so yeah, I hate this. I hate that this cold bitch has a hold of her. But I know of all people, even without her memories, Persephone never needed saving. Anyone who crosses her is put into the ground or worse. So get your head out of your ass."

Helios spins on his heel, leaving me alone and robbing me of the response I would eventually have come up with. Instead, I'm alone, and this time, I fucking deserve to be.

I glare at the broken mirror in the bathroom. I don't know if it's because it's the same mirror I summoned Nemesis to, but the palace hadn't repaired the cracked glass. The tattoos had consumed the whites of my eyes, making the sapphire blue seem even more stark. My horns and wings are covered in the darkness. I glance at my tail, inspecting it. The dark swirls cover it as well.

Fuck. I've been consumed.

I thought releasing it once would be all right. I thought I could put it back into the obsidian box inside me and seal the lid tight. But the box is not just broken. It is fucking shattered.

Mellie leans in the doorway. "Pull yourself together."

I laugh sadly and move past her, using my glamor to hide my wings and horns. There is no hiding the swirling tattoos anymore. I've tried, but it's like they're inked onto my glamour too. Mellie walks to the small bar and pours two measures of scotch, handing one to me. I sit in one of the dark armchairs while Mellie curls up on another.

"I'm really... I'm losing control," I whisper.

Mellie takes a long sip. "Persephone is being so strong. So wherever your control is, I suggest you find it because she'll be pissed when she finally comes back to us, and you're batshit."

She would be furious. Not that I let the darkness get this far, but that I gave up on myself.

"Zeus wants Helios," I look at her, "in chains."

186

Mellie's glass shatters. "What?"

"He wants to bring in Helios's father and his two sisters by using him as bait," I admit, watching her. Zeus made it clear that any deal I had with Helios is off.

Mellie snarls, not even noticing as blood drips from her hand.

"Helios hasn't... mentioned anything?" I rub a hand wearily down my face. "About which side he's on?"

Her face contorts, her scars darkening. She snatches the drink from my hand, downing it. "I have to go."

Does that mean he has mentioned something or he hasn't?

"I'll be back tomorrow," she says just before she vanishes.

187

Chapter Forty-Two

Persephone

I **SIT UP IN BED, PANTING. MY ROOM IS STILL COVERED IN BLACK VINES.** It's lucky my mother hasn't seen them yet. I've managed to make excuses to the maids about why I don't want my room freshened up, and every time anyone tries to open my bedroom door, the vines tighten over it, declining entry.

The meadow continues to elude my dreams. There is nothing but the same blackness every night. Every so often, there is a flicker of a bright white light. Every night, it becomes a little more frequent. It has been eight nights since I last saw Hades. Even the temporary mental link seems unavailable to me, and it's driving me insane. I miss him. He consumes my every thought. I know he hasn't left me, but what if there's something wrong? I'm so fucking helpless here.

I climb out of bed, and following my new morning routine, I try to remove the vines. Sometimes, when I get very frustrated, there is slight movement, but mostly nothing changes. I take a deep breath and close my eyes, about to delve into my power, when my mother's raised voice from downstairs distracts me.

I open my eyes and glance at my bedroom door. The vines part for me, encouraging me to investigate. I glare at them before pulling on my robe and quietly leaving my room, heading down the corridor. My mother's furious voice carries down the halls.

"Do not try to force me into anything, Kronos," she snarls. I tense at the name, Hades' warnings flashing through my mind. I silently creep down the stairs, expertly missing the steps I know creak.

Kronos growls and the sound makes my hair on the back of my neck stand up. "If you will not join, I will take all you care about."

"You can try, *Titan*," my mother practically spits the word. "But you will find yourself back in the cell I released you from, your bastard son's prisoner once again."

"Careful, Demeter." Kronos's voice sounds different now. I can hear the danger. "It would be unwise to make an enemy of me."

I continue to move downstairs, trying to peek over the banister.

My mother's laugh is harsh. "How can you be my enemy when you are so far beneath my notice?"

My brows raise in surprise. How is she not scared of him?

I stretch more, trying to see, but I lose my footing and have to move down a step. The wood creaks loudly, and my breath catches, my whole body going tense.

I remain deathly still, hoping that they missed the noise and the conversation will continue, but Kronos suddenly appears in front of me. I thought he looked like Hades before, but now that I know Hades, now that I've spent hours looking at his face, memorizing him, it's clear that there's only the barest of similarities. Kronos's face isn't as handsome as Hades'. His green eyes are cruel, unlike the perfect blue sapphires of Hades'. Kronos has harsh lines etched into his face, aged from savageness or his time in prison.

Can't wait to fucking send him back. I blink at that thought, but quickly focus on Kronos.

His cruel eyes look me over, but I refuse to shrink from his gaze. I harden my stare and use my position on the stairs to my advantage.

I have the high ground, bitch.

My mother hurries up the stairs, and though the stare-

189

off feels like it's been going on for hours, it's only been seconds.

"Kronos." My mother gasps, and when I look at her, I finally see some fear in her eyes.

Kronos continues looking me over, a maddening smirk curving his lips. "Well, well, well, it's the little flower goddess that's causing all the fuss."

I look back at Kronos, trying to keep my gaze hard as a memory of a battlefield, a large crack splitting the ground, flits across my mind's eye.

Kronos moves in closer, pulling my attention away from the memory I want to explore. "Hm… I don't see it."

I lift an eyebrow and tilt my head. "Oh, no. How will I go on?" I say flatly, glaring at him.

In a flash, Kronos grabs my wrist, his eyes glowing. My mother screams, trying to move around him, to pull me away, but Kronos shoves her against the wall.

I expect something to happen, to feel pain. I'm not sure what Kronos is trying to do, but I blink and look down at my wrist when nothing happens. Kronos tightens his hand on my wrist, squeezing it painfully, but still nothing happens. I look back at him, my eyebrows raised.

He snarls and slams my back against the wall, my head smacking hard. There's a flash of bright light, and my head aches as my mind fills with… me. Memory after memory floods me like an internal movie reel. The human realm, Helios, Jackson, Mellie. Plutus Industries. The Underworld, Hekate, Thanatos, Berry, and… Hades.

I am Persephone Prosperina Plutus.
Wife of Hades.
Goddess of Dark Spring.
Queen of the Underworld.

I quickly school my face, though my rage is unbearable, no longer simmering or easily manageable. I want to destroy everything. I will destroy this whole fucking realm to get back to my own, to get back to my husband. My love. My king.

"What are you?" Kronos snarls in my face.

I'm about to react, knowing I'm about to blow my cov-

190

er, when Kronos is yanked away from me and plunged into the ground, the earth below the house swallowing him. My heart slams against my chest, and I feel the prickling of the spines beneath my skin, but now is not the time. I need to regroup and find out what I've missed. I need to know if Mother still has Gaia's power and the ability to hurt Hades.

The cracks along her cheeks are even more pronounced now. Fuck, how didn't I see it before? She still has Gaia's power, but she can't handle it. I look away, the building rage overwhelming. I can't even look at her. My whole body trembles with fury and a desperate longing for my husband.

"Well—" my mother starts.

I clench my fists. "Who was he? Another suitor?"

"Well, I hadn't thought of him as such, but…"

No, no, no, no, no, no, no. Think P.

My lips twitch, and I know how to dissuade my mother from Kronos. "He reminds me of someone…" I pretend to ponder as if I'm trying to remember something, allowing some of the true longing I feel for Hades to seep through.

"Perhaps it's meant to be. However, he did kill his last wife…"

"He really reminds me of someone," I push, furrowing my brow and rubbing my temples.

I feel my mother's gaze on me. "Don't think of him. I will find another suitor."

I internally exhale a breath of relief. Externally, I blink, letting my face fall back into the easy smile I usually force myself to wear.

"It's still early, sweetling. You should go back to sleep."

I nod, straightening from the wall. "Yes, Mother."

I hurry back to my room. Closing the door behind me, I start to pace. The memories hurt my head. She stole them from me. She ripped me from my home, from my husband, and then took everything that makes me *me.* How could she? She will pay for this. I continue to pace, the vines slowly retreating as if they're satisfied now that I remember.

Even my bones feel tired when I settle back into bed. Having years of memories flooding back into my mind has

191

taken it out of me. I collapse completely, burying my face into the pillow that Hades lies on. His scent is long gone, but the memory of him is imprinted into it. It doesn't take long until sleep takes me, dropping me right into... our meadow.[15]

Chapter Forty-Three

Hades

WE HAVEN'T MADE ANY PROGRESS WITH THE DREAMWALKING, AND WE'VE STOPPED TRYING TO PUSH IT. There is no point when we can't find Persephone's dream, no matter how much we search. She is gone, at least from dreams. Helios assures me she is still alive and well on Olympus. She is just missing from the dreamworld. What happened? Did she change her mind? Does she not love me anymore? Did she ban me from her dreams?

I've barely done anything but prepare for the war and try to track down my father. I've been scouring through social media, news articles, and even CCTV footage, hoping to come across even a trace of him. But I've found nothing, not of my father nor any of the Titans. It is like the world is suddenly wiped clean of them.

I collapse into bed, weariness tugging at my bones. Maybe tonight I'd truly sleep. I'd sparred with the heroes of old in the Isle of the Blessed, hoping to at least exhaust myself enough to allow me to sleep. My head hits the pillow, and I'm immediately in the meadow from her dreams, but clearly, it's my dream, not hers. The meadow itself is darker, the colors paler than they were in hers. Everything is significantly less vibrant. I sigh, looking around, but my heart stops when I see I'm not alone. She's here.

"I'm not dreamwalking," I blurt out. How can Persephone be in *my* dream? I want to run to her, but something keeps me rooted.

It takes a moment for me to realize why. It's her eyes. There's something different in her eyes, and it makes my heart leap in my chest.

"Demon?" she asks, and my heart slams again in response.

"My spring?" I whisper, not daring to hope.

Persephone springs into motion, sprinting toward me, and my feet move on their own. I meet her halfway, needing to see for myself if this is just another hope to be dashed. She jumps on me, wrapping her legs around my waist, clinging to me. She slams her lips to mine, and the second our lips connect, I know.

She remembers.

I dig my fingers into her hair, deepening the kiss.

She remembers.

The memory of her touch inside the dream is enough in this single moment because she remembers.

A tear slides down my cheek, and I don't even try to brush it away. She presses her forehead to mine and whispers against my lips, "Fuck. Are you okay? Is Berry okay? You healed, right?"

"You remember." I kiss her again, our lips salty.

She nods, tears sliding down her cheeks. "I remember. Gods… I missed you so fucking much."

"You remember," I repeat.. She brushes away my tears and cups my cheeks. "I swore I would find a way back to you."

I keep brushing my fingers over her face, hair, and shoulders, tracing her curves down to her hips. I need to make sure this dream is not… well, a dream.

"I love you." She kisses me again, sobbing. "I love you. I'm so sorry."

I shake my head, the small movement feeling arduous. "Berry misses you so much."

I try to wipe away her tears. "I miss him too."

"I have been so lost," I whisper, my voice hitching. Persephone kisses me again, closing her eyes, and the questions that burn inside me need answers. "How… How did you… What happened?"

My brain isn't working. *She remembers.*

194

"I think my powers were slowly trying to pry them back. I was having these strange dreams and waking up with my room covered in vines. But I would only get glimpses of memories before they vanished. Then Kronos slammed me into a wall, and they... clicked into place."

"He *what?*" I snarl.

"Hades." She shakes her head. "Later."

I ignore her, inspecting the back of her head for a bump or a bruise. "Did he take anything? Time?"

Did he steal days from her? The one thing I can't ever replace?

She shakes her head, and I exhale in relief.

"Mellie? Helios?" she asks. "What's happening with the war?"

She would be so disappointed in you.

I clear my throat before saying, "Mellie's been helping me dreamwalk. We've captured some Titans, but not all, and my father remains elusive."

Persephone steps back and paces. The action is so familiar that my chest aches. But she isn't just the Persephone I lost. She is also the Persephone I found. There are traces in her face of the young girl who was controlled by her mother, who thought she was unworthy of love and affection. The girl who thought her horns would repulse me. If possible, I love her even more now than I did before. I love her past as well as her present and future.

I look down at my hands, inhaling sharply. "There's more."

She stops and glances at me.

I brace myself and close my eyes, letting reality seep into the dream, showing her how the darkness now covers my body in black swirling tattoos. "I can't stop it."

I listen to her footsteps as she moves closer. "Oh, baby."

Persephone cups my jaw, gliding her thumb over my cheek. I slowly open my eyes, letting her see the way the darkness has intruded upon them. She traces her fingers along my cheeks and neck, following the lines of the swirling tattoos.

"This is a manifestation of your anger and grief. Only

195

you can make this better," Persephone says.

Shame burns me. "I can't do that without you. I need you home with me. Safe."

She grabs my face roughly, forcing me to look at her. "You are not without me. I need you to be strong. I need you to keep *you* safe. I can take care of me."

She'll take care of herself?

"You're coming home now," I hiss. "You can't think to stay."

"Being in Olympus gives us an advantage," she insists. "My mother can't handle Gaia's power."

No. No. No.

"You want to spy on her? Are you insane?"

She crosses her arms, her expression stubborn. "No. I'm not."

I grab her upper arms, hissing, "I can't have you in danger anymore."

The darkness starts to move on my skin, and she snarls at me, "Control. It."

I roll my neck, trying to get a handle on it, but there is no effect.

"Fight. It."

I grind my teeth and focus on her face, panting out, "For you."

She shakes her head, putting her hand on my chest. "No. Not for me. For you. For your realm."

I pant, sweat beading on my skin even inside the dream as I struggle against the darkness.

"You let this go too far, Hades." She watches me. "You gave up."

I flush and look away. "I didn't see a way through."

A tear slides down her cheek. "I have to go. Can you ask Helios to bring me a cell phone?"

I kiss her softly. "I'll fight it."

She keeps her eyes on me, her eyes flashing with challenge. "Prove it."

A moment later, I'm opening my eyes in bed, my face buried into the pillow. Nyx's words echo in my mind, *"Darkness is not inherently evil, just as light is not inherently good."*[16]

16   The Nightmare & The Daydream Chapters 37 & 38

Chapter Forty-Four

Hades

HELIOS NOTIFIES ME THAT HE MANAGED TO **SLIP PERSEPHONE A CELLPHONE.** After an exhausting day of sparring and torturing Titans for information, the only thing I want to do is talk to my wife. Instead, I'm sitting in my office, surrounded by other gods who are decidedly not Persephone.

My phone rings, and I answer, my heart leaping at her new number. The camera takes a second to connect, showing her sitting on her bed on the small screen. "My spring? Are you all right?"

She nods, scanning my face. "Are you?"

I nod. Since the dream, I've managed to pull the darkness from my eyes, and my glamor is covering them again. "I missed you."

Mellie grabs the phone from my hand. "We have so much to catch up on. Okay, so you know how Helios is a major asshole? Well, he's like basically stalking me and—"

Helios grabs her from behind, wrapping his arms around her. "And she said she loves me. We're also expecting triplets!"

She elbows him hard in the stomach. "Don't touch me, dick brain." Her dual-colored eyes are focused on Persephone. "None of that is true. I once told him I'd love it if he imploded and turned into a black hole."

Helios smirks. "It's all true. I have the ultrasound."

Cerberus barks, trying to get attention, and Mellie shoves away from Helios to show Cerberus sitting. I can hear the tears in Persephone's voice as she speaks to him. "Is that my

198

Berry boy? Hi, Berry! Mama misses you so much."

He barks loudly, running to his toy basket and returning to show her the toy he chose. I smother a smile when I see the toy he's holding is a stuffed version of Zeus.

"Look at that toy!" Persephone gasps. "I can't wait to play with it with you."

I stand and snatch the phone back from Melinoë, catching Persephone wiping the tears from her face.

"He misses you so much," I say.

So do I.

She nods, brushing away another tear. "I miss him too."

I sit back at my desk as Helios and Mellie continue to bicker. "Another Titan was captured, a minor one, Tethys, Titan of Fresh Water."

Persephone nods. "I'm going to hunt for some strays on Olympus."

My entire body goes tense, my muscles squeezing, locking on bone. "You don't have your tie to the Underworld anymore. This would be you alone."

She locks eyes with me and nods. "But the alternative is to give up. Which I refuse to do."

The way her mouth is pressed into a tight line, and her eyes flash, I know she won't be moved on this, despite the danger. They are between Persephone and her family, and they will pay the price.

"Zeus is missing, as well." I sigh. " No one has seen him since our first date."

I should feel bad for sending him to Demeter as a distraction, but I really don't.

"I doubt Hera is making any rescue efforts," Persephone adds tartly, and she is right about that. My darling and deadly sister-in-law thinks he's out creating more bastard children for her to ignore.

Those are her words.

"It is possible he's buried under your house after his fight with your mother." My lips twitch at the way Persephone shrugs at that. She is so nonchalant about the missing King of the Gods.

Fuck, I miss her.

199

"She can't hold Gaia's power for much longer," Persephone whispers. Mellie stops arguing with Helios at that, looking at the phone with a frown.

"Why do you say that?" I ask.

"Her face, it looks like it's cracking."

"Cracking?"

"Probably because she's a stone -cold bitch," Mellie retorts, crossing her arms over her chest.

I shoot a look at the goddess before I focus back on Persephone. "I don't know if there's ever been a god who couldn't hold on to the power they absorbed." No one was insane enough even to *attempt* it.

"She's got all of Olympus terrified of her. No one even looks at me," Persephone says.

I prop the phone on my desk and pace, trying to plan our next steps. It is less than ideal that Zeus is imprisoned. Once released, he will be furious and even more unpredictable.

"If she's losing that power," I murmur, "she won't be able to hold Zeus for much longer."

Zeus is king for a reason. Poseidon and I knew he deserved to be king after freeing us and winning the war, but there is more to it than that. Zeus's power is not limited to his first calling, like Poseidon and me. He has the ability to summon any Olympian's ability if he so wishes. Any of his subjects, the many gods who call Olympus their home, he can wield their abilities as natural as breathing. So holding him in any kind of prison, even for a goddess wielding Primordial power, would be taxing, to say the least.

"I should go if I want to make any headway on catching Titans," Persephone says. My head snaps toward the phone, and I grab it, cradling it in my hand.

"Be careful," I warn. I want to tell her not to go, that she doesn't have to fight. We've already lost so much, paid so much, endured so much. But I can't say any of that to her. "I'll send Cerberus to join you." I glance at the dog. "You want to go hunting with Mommy?"

He barks excitedly, spinning.

"No. He stays there," Persephone growls.

"He can help."

She grinds her teeth. "No."

My jaw twitches with annoyance, but I nod silently. She's won this round. She wouldn't be *Persephone* if she bowed to my every demand.

"I have to go. Love you guys." She holds my gaze.

I nod. "I love you too."

Be safe and come back to me, my queen.

Chapter Forty-Five

Persephone

MY PHONE PINGS WITH A MESSAGE, AND I GLANCE AT THE SCREEN, seeing an adorable photo of Cerberus wearing a different hat on each of his heads. He is wearing a baseball cap on the left, a cowboy hat on the middle, and a deerstalker on the right.

My lips twitch, and I reach for my phone but shake my head. I need to stay focused. My powers are strengthening, but they're nowhere near as strong as when I was in the Underworld. Plus, I'm still feeling a little mentally fatigued from the memory release. I remember everything now, but I still find myself getting flashes of smaller moments that most people wouldn't even think of again.

The feeling of the leather of my seat at Plutus Industries. A flash of walking past Hades' office and glancing at him through the glass walls.

My mother took everything, even things from the very back of my mind. Some of it's coming back in pieces, and it's tiring.

I look through my closet for something to wear that I can move in easily. I curse under my breath as I sift through pastel dress after pastel dress. Finally, I find one dark item in my wardrobe. My mother permitted me to buy one pair of old pants to garden in, then she'd never allowed me to wear them, but I kept them. I pull them on, and they fit snuggly. They're not the most comfortable things I've ever worn, but I can move in them easier than a dress. I find a deep blue long-sleeved t-shirt and pull the jeweled brooch off.

The only shoes that aren't shiny and loud are black leather boots I got for Christmas one year. Again, I was never allowed to wear them, but my mother loved to gift me the dream and then rip it away. The heels on the boots are high, and they're relatively silent when I walk, the leather going to just under my knee.

I decide to leave my hair free. It is a decision I will probably regret when I'm elbow -deep in Titan guts, but I can't bring myself to tie it up or braid it. I want it free.

Like I will be.

The house is completely silent as I sneak out of my room and down the servant's stairs, slipping out the back door without seeing a single soul. I run through the garden and jump over the fence before taking off into the woods to regroup.

I unlock the phone and find the handy app that Helios downloaded to help me locate Titan energy. It won't necessarily lead me to a Titan, but to a place they've been recently. The app opens to a map of Olympus, and four orbs of light immediately flash, one only around a mile away.

I stow the phone away and hold my hands up, practicing with my vines for a moment. My magic is so new to me, and because of my mother, I was forced to push it down just as I was learning to embrace it. I worry it will feel weird to use my vines again after weeks of repressing them. I was wrong. The darkness curls around the lightness within me, but I can feel something missing. It is probably my tie to the Underworld. The loss of it still aches, and I'm still so acutely aware of it. Even after my memory was stolen, I felt it. Some of my power must still be within the Underworld.

The now obsidian black vines protrude from the earth as if they're stretching and then move as I want them to. The golden leaves sway gently in the light breeze, the gilded thorns glinting dangerously.

I exhale and feel for my power. I realize it is weaker, but

it still comforts me. Even at reduced power, I'm still more powerful than a few errant Titans. I lower my hands, and the vines recede. They brush gently against my arm, caressing me and welcoming me back.

It doesn't take me long to get to the first location. The phone vibrates in my pocket when I near the last corner, and I press my back against the brick, tilting my head slightly, listening for any signs of life.

The clatter of a loose cobblestone is loud in the darkness. The following curse has me peering around the building, but the streetlights barely permeate the shadows in the alleyway.

I see a flicker of movement and a pair of red eyes as the being moves into the light. I turn, pressing my front against the bricks to get a better look before raising my hand, sending a vine out to wrap around his ankle. He falls hard, cursing again, louder this time.

"What the fuck was that?" he growls, shifting to see what tripped him up.

I smirk and push off the wall, slipping around the corner as he struggles to sit up and release his ankle.

"You're a long way from home, Titan," I say, sticking to the shadows.

He whips his head around, narrowing his eyes, trying to see me better in the darkness. "Who goes there?"

My smirk deepens. "Oh, come on. You know who I am." I step into the light. "Are you pleased to see me?"

He hisses, trying to lunge at me, but his foot is still trapped. He snarls and increases his efforts to get free. Knowing how dangerous Titans can be, I decide it's best not to play with him any longer. I lift my hand, pushing one of my long, sharp spikes from my palm, severing his head from his body.

I pull my phone from my pocket and open my conversation with Hades.

PERSEPHONE

Incoming.

204

I shove my phone back into my pocket and watch as the being disappears in front of me. It looks like he's melting, his head the last to go. I grimace a little at the gory sight.

One down, on to the next.

My next encounter is about two miles away, but this time, the Titans I come across are much less interested in being discreet. I roll my eyes from behind a tree, watching them. This time, I don't have the luxury of hiding in an alleyway. They're in public, blending poorly into a crowd of patrons outside a bar in Olympus. Luckily, they've not caused any harm yet.

It surprises me that no one has noticed them. They're so different from the divine beings in the bar. They are taller and more monstrous, but they've concealed their red eyes somehow. Then again, it's clear that everyone standing outside the bar is less than sober, and all seem to be distracted.

I need to figure out a way to draw them away. My idea is juvenile, but it will probably work. I pick up a stone from the ground and throw it at them, hitting the closest one on the head. His head snaps around, and I quickly duck behind the tree to avoid him seeing me.

His growl vibrates the air, and I hear his heavy footsteps as he moves closer. I dash to a tree deeper in the shadows, needing to move this fight further from the crowd.

I peek around the trunk, seeing that he is searching where I just was as his friend watches from their original spot. I throw another stone, hitting him right between the eyes, and then run to the field. This time, I let him see a flash of my back, wanting him to chase me. I climb up one of the trees and form a trap with my vines. Now that they're black, they're much harder to see. In the darkness, and without the thorns and leaves, they're practically invisible.

I pant, adrenaline coursing through my veins, and my stomach twists when I feel a heavy body collide with my vines, followed by a loud snarl. His friend appears a moment later. Growling, he rushes to assist his friend. I jump down from the tree, smiling at them.

"Hello, boys."

The look they give me is venomous. The one trapped in

205

the vines is struggling, and I can see my death in his eyes. I widen my stance as the other Titan starts toward me.

He lunges at me, and I quickly side -step him, lifting my hands to summon my vines. I push my hands out, and they pierce his chest, the thorns exploding inside him. He snarls and throws a dagger at me. It slices my arm, and I feel the gold ichor soaking my shirt. I snarl, pushing my hands apart, and the vines spread inside him, effectively cutting him in half.

A heavy weight hits my side, the other Titan taking me to the ground and pinning me. I groan in pain as he straddles my hips, holding me down.

He smirks. "Can't wait to tell Kronos that I am the one who did it. I killed the queen." He wraps one of his hands around my throat and squeezes. I struggle in his hold, his power stifling me a little. He lifts his other hand, brandishing a large serrated blade, his eyes flashing in delight at the kill he's about to bag and the energy he's about to consume.

I feel weakened beneath him, his Titan abilities stifling me, but I can't give up. This cannot be the end. Some stupid, inconsequential Titan will not defeat me. I tunnel down into my weakened powers, drawing on them, and I cry out as I unleash them. My spines burst free of my skin and penetrate him every place he's touching me.

The Titan screams, trying to move off me, but my spikes have him pinned. He drops his dagger, and I grab it, stabbing him in the stomach. He slumps forward on me, and I consider how I'm going to contact Hades to take them. Luckily, a moment later, they disappear into nothing.

I glance at my arm. It is already healing, even though the dagger was definitely lined with some kind of poison. From the intense pain, it would have killed most. But I am not most. I am the Queen of the Underworld.

Hours later, I glance at the sky, noticing the glow on the horizon. Sunrise.

Ten Titans are all safely back in the cells in my realm, and Olympus is ten Titans safer. I watch as the latest dead Titan dissolves into nothing before I head back toward my mother's house.

I hurry back, but my anxiety about her catching me has dissipated since my memory returned. She has always loved her hold on me, but it is now broken. I no longer fear her. It is useful for me to remain in Olympus just now to monitor Gaia's power. I need for her to remain in the dark about my memory coming back, or she may take it again. At least I know that my tie to Hades, my love for him, is so strong that she can never steal them permanently.

When the house comes into view, the sun is just beginning to breach the hills, and I see people bustling about inside, getting ready for the day. I walk to the side of the house and look up at my bedroom window.

"I wonder…" I ponder before lifting vines from the ground and wrapping them around my waist, directing them to lift me up the side of the house. They gently place me on my feet in my bedroom. I stroke one of the golden leaves before waving my hand and sending them back.

Exhaustion hits the second I sit on my bed to take my boots off. I hear my phone vibrate, and I pick it up. I get a new surge of energy when I see his name pop up on the screen.

HADES

Proving a point?

I smile, my bratty heart fluttering.

207

Yes.

I see the speech bubble appear, the three little dots jumping up and down as he types before they stop. I pout a little, but then the screen fills with a photo of his face along with the words: **Incoming call from Hades**

I make him wait for exactly three rings before I answer, my whole body tingling with awareness when I meet his sapphire gaze. He's laying in bed, and he looks devastatingly handsome, but also like he has not slept.

"Still upset with me?" he asks, his gaze holding mine. I'm sure he stayed awake to ensure the Titans I sent were firmly locked in their reinforced cells, and I know he was worried about me.

My sweet God of the Dead, I love him so much, but yes, I am still upset with him. I stand and move to my dresser, propping my phone up before pulling my shirt off, utterly comfortable knowing my husband is watching me undress. I want him to.

"Yes," I admit, pushing my pants off and walking in my underwear to grab a nightdress.

"Because I wanted to protect you?" he asks, and I can feel his gaze on my body. I unclasp my bra and pull the dreaded nightdress on, the cotton scratching my skin.

I turn to look at him. "Because you gave up, Hades."

His answering wince is a stab to the heart, but it needs to be said. I understand how hard it must have been to not only have physically lost me but mentally as well. I can see the toll it's taken on him, and I can see his struggle. It breaks my heart that he stopped believing in my promise to him, but at the same time, guilt claws at me. I chose this path for the right reasons, to protect him, to save him, but the cost is the obvious toll this has taken on the man I love more than life itself.

"Persephone…" he starts, but then pauses.

"What?" My tone is filled with false acid, fuelled by

frustration that I'm not there with him.

"I didn't…" He exhales heavily. "I didn't give up on you."

I search his face, moving closer to my phone. "You allowed yourself to lose control." Unfair. I'm being so incredibly unfair, but I can't help him in the way I know he needs, not from this realm. While I'm not saying anything untrue, I'm being cruel and harsh, but I need to be. This is the only way I can help him right now, pushing him to get control before he completely loses himself forever.

Hades looks away. "You're my strength."

I shake my head because that absolutely isn't true. "Hades, I am your wife. I am your queen. *You* are your strength."

"I don't know how I got so lost." Hades closes his eyes, rubbing a hand over his face and it's all I can do to look at him, to stay present with him. I ache to reach out and touch him, to provide him comfort, but all I have are brutal words of encouragement to ensure that when we are reunited, he is still the husband who captured my heart so completely.

I grab the phone and sit on the bed again. "When you were gone and trapped in the tree, I was lost, too. I understand, I really do, but you need to find yourself. Now." *For us. Be strong enough for us.*

"How?" Hades whispers. The desperation in his voice makes my heart ache for him.

"By trusting me." I search his eyes. "Trusting us."

Hades lifts his hand, probably touching the screen. "I miss you."

I lay down in bed, trying to stop my voice from breaking as I reply, "I miss you too."

Hades props the phone up on the bedside table and pulls his shirt off. I sigh, distracted by the perfection of his body. Fuck, he's so beautiful. Then I see what he's showing me. The swirling black tattoos are even lower on his chest now. He is getting a handle on his powers.

I smile, relaxing a little. There's my demon.

209

"I'm getting there," he says, smiling softly.

"I'm so proud of you," I reply, pride swelling in my chest.

"You know who else you should be proud of?" Hades asks before flipping to the back camera, showing me my sleeping Berry on his bed.

I smile, the burden still sitting heavily on my shoulders, but the tightness in my chest eases just enough that I can breathe again. "My sleepy boy."

Cerberus stirs a little, rolling his huge body onto his back, his front paw twitching.

I sigh heavily, homesickness sitting heavily on my shoulders. "I want to come home."

Cerberus lets out a small bark in his sleep, and my lips twitch.

"I think he agrees," Hades says, turning the camera back to his face.

"How many Titans are still at large?" I ask.

Hades grabs his laptop, pulling up a spreadsheet. "There are still seven. Eight, counting my father."

I nod. "I'll do what I can from here."

Hades growls, looking through the list of names on his computer.

"Why is everything so hard all the time?" I sigh. "It feels like fate bound us together and then threw every obstacle at us. We didn't even get a proper wedding."

Hades shifts, lying down again. "We will."

Suddenly, I feel overwhelmed with emotion, probably from exhaustion and seeing him but not being able to touch him. My eyes fill with tears, and the longing for him becomes almost too much.

"I miss you," I whimper.

"I miss you too, my spring," Hades whispers.

The tears fall down my cheeks, and I sob softly.

"Persephone?" Hades' voice pulls me from my despair. "Would you like a big wedding?" he asks.

"I don't care. I just want to come home." I sob again. "I'm sorry I just—" sob, "I love you, and I need you, and it just all feels too fucking much."

Hades' voice breaks a little. "And you will. You'll come

home to me."

The throb on the top of my head grabs my attention, and my sobs become louder and harder. "She took my horns."

Hades wipes a tear from his cheek. "I know."

"I'm sorry about everything. I'm sorry that I'm—"

Hades growls, interrupting me. "You have nothing to be sorry for."

I close my eyes, taking a deep breath, trying to center myself. "I'm here because she was going to kill you. You are alive. You are safe. Berry is safe. Mellie and Helios are safe." It is m*y mantra to maintain my sanity.*

"You're physically there because she's an evil bitch," Hades growls. "But you're mentally there because you are strong."

I look at him, and I can see the devastation I am feeling mirrored in his eyes.

"You went out and captured ten Titans because you are strong." Hades holds my gaze. "She thinks you are porcelain, Persephone. You are steel."

Another tear falls, but I'm not feeling as sad anymore. I feel strong and empowered again because my husband is not afraid of my strength. He encourages it.

"Once I am home, you and I are going to get married. I want a small ceremony, just us, Berry, Mellie, and Helios. And then we are going to go on a honeymoon, okay?" I look at him, my stomach fluttering.

"Whatever you want. We'll go away, and no one can contact us for weeks. Just you and I," Hades agrees, his eyes sparkling.

"The Underworld will be okay?"

Hades smirks and shrugs. "Let it burn."

"I would burn Olympus in a second if it meant I could return to you."

Hades' smirk deepens. "It would look so much better on fire."

I laugh softly. "Except I'd want to save the flowers."

"Which flowers, my spring? I will fill the garden with them."

"I have a really lovely patch of sunflowers here."

211

"Show them to me?" Hades asks.

I immediately climb out of bed and hurry to the window. I flip the camera and show him the small patch below, the bright yellow petals beginning to open as the sun rises.

"They're stunning, Persephone. But nothing compares to your beauty," he says.

I smile, swapping the camera back and climbing back into bed.

Hades yawns. I hear him pat the bed, and then there's a loud thump as Cerberus climbs in.

"You're letting him on the bed?" I ask, my heart so full of love for them.

Hades shushes me, smiling lovingly. "Don't let him think this is the norm."

I sigh, grabbing the pillow from the other side of the bed and hugging it before propping the phone up so he can see me.

"My boys," I whisper.

"He's too big for this bed." Hades flushes a little. "We're in the guest room."

"I noticed," I reply. "Why?"

Hades blushes more. "Because… that's *our* room."

I whimper again and start to cry.

"No, don't cry, my spring," Hades whispers comfortingly. "You are everything to me, demon."

"As you are to me." Hades' eyes glisten with unshed tears. "I'm sorry. I don't know what's wrong with me."

Hades shakes his head. "You have been taken from your home and stripped down to a version of yourself you don't recognize. She took you from me."

This man is perfect. He is my perfect husband, and I love him so much.

"Hades?"

"Yes?"

"I'm truly honored that fate chose me to be yours." My voice cracks, betraying all of my emotions.

"I will never deserve you," he says, his voice trembling.

"You already do, demon," I reply, and it's the truest thing I have ever uttered. "I love you."

"I love you so much more."
I smile and slowly drift off, knowing how cherished I am.

Chapter Forty-Six

Hades

I **JOLT AWAKE AT THE SOUND OF AN ECHOING THUNDEROUS CRASH.** I bounce to my feet, my bident already in my hand, prepared for the enemy. There's another crash, and I whirl, trying to find the source. The tattoos on my body tighten, and for the first time, it's not like a manifestation of my emotions. They almost feel like they are *protecting* me. I hear a voice raised in anger, and my eyes lock on the balcony. This time, the sound is almost familiar. Is someone yelling?

I open the balcony doors and have to cover my ears, the air nearly vibrating with the violence of the thunder. It is deafening. I blink and slowly lower my hands, tracking the sound across the landscape. My lips twitch as I head back inside, closing the doors to mute the noise. I pick up my phone to text Persephone.

HADES

Found Z.

Demeter must have used the same ability that Gaia used to imprison my father to end her battle with Zeus. Therefore, Zeus ended up in the same place Kronos had—the cell.

PERSEPHONE

Hope he enjoys a night of incarceration.

I smirk. There is no love lost between the two of them. I suppose she was right. Zeus could wait, and he'd be a wild-card the second we released him.

So, instead, I fall back asleep to the sound of an echoing storm.

The next morning, I dress carefully before shadowing to the Halls of Night. If I am going to bring Persephone home, we need to strip Gaia's power from Demeter. Not to mention, it would handicap my father's side of the war. If that means I go to the Primordials with my hat in hand and humbly ask for help, then I will do it. There is little I would not do to get her back.

"Nyx? Erebus?" I call quietly, walking into the hall.

The black marble beneath my feet turns to an image of space far from this planet, projecting constellations across the entire room. The stars illuminate the room better than most lights. Nyx glides through the double doors, her black dress trailing behind her. "Hades. Did you bring my son?"

"I did not, but I do have a question for you."

The stars dance around us, some flaring angrily. "Something the almighty God of the Underworld doesn't know? How intriguing."

I mask a wince at that. "If Gaia's power is returned to the earth… what happens?"

Nyx glances at me before tilting her head back. She stares at the dome above us, and the night sky reflected on its surface. "Have you ever pondered the stars, Hades?"

I follow her gaze, watching as the night sky turns to galaxies, universes, and things even I've never seen and will never understand.

"No," I answer honestly, watching the dome of infinite

215

realities and nights play above us.

"When a star dies, the power, the matter, doesn't die with it. It remains."

I tense, watching the dome light up as a star turns into a supernova, then slowly morphs into a black hole, consuming everything around it.

"An imploding star is a dangerous thing," Nyx continues. My eyes lock on the dome above us. "An imploding goddess, even more so. When Gaia was killed, her power was absorbed by another. However, it has since changed."

My head snaps toward her. "Changed?"

Nyx's gaze remains on the stars. "Gaia spent millennia with her power. She honed it, cared for it, and used it only to keep the balance. The power was like a gentle wave, ebbing and flowing with the natural order."

My brows furrow. What does she mean? What has happened to Gaia's ability?

"Demeter is not using the power with anything other than malice, so the wave crests and crashes. If you return the power like it is, that dying star will consume everything in its wake."

I don't have to look at the ceiling to know the black hole has devoured the entire universe above me. Persephone said her mother couldn't hold Gaia's power for much longer, and now, if we release it back into the world, we could destroy *everything* along with it. Demeter is an explosion about to go off. My mind whirls, trying to come up with a solution.

"Without her tie to the Underworld, Persephone could absorb a portion of it, lessen the impact," I murmur. It could buy us some time.

I rub my chin, feeling the growth of stubble under my hand. I continue thinking out loud, "But when she's bound to the Underworld again, she won't be able to hold even a fraction of it."

She's cracking.

I look down at my gloves, realization sliding down my spine with an icy finger. These tattoos are not a result of my power. It was never me. I tug off my gloves, letting them

216

drop to the ground. The darkness has reached my chest now, and I finally notice the swirling tattoos inked on my skin are no longer random, intricate designs of darkness. They are *vines*.

Persephone unlocked a part of the Underworld when she became queen, and when our bond broke, the power needed to go somewhere. I'm absorbing her tie to the Underworld, and it's overwhelming me.

"Perhaps it is time to give it back," Nyx whispers from my shoulder.

I stop myself from jumping in surprise. When had she moved?

"How?" I ask, watching the vines dotted with tiny black thorns and roses grow and tighten over my skin.

"Have you considered that the reason you cannot control the tie is that it does not wish to be held by you? That if you released it, not only would it not be lost forever, but it may find its way back to its rightful wielder, no matter the distance?"

Why do all the Primordials speak so vaguely and dreamily? Not everything needs to be a metaphor.

I flex my fingers. "Will you contain it?"

"Under one condition," Nyx says.

My brows furrow, locking eyes with her. What could she possibly want in exchange?

"Can you get my son to visit? I miss him terribly."

It is not what I expected her to ask. As the Reaper, Thanatos is constantly being summoned to ferry souls to the Underworld. I suppose that leaves little time for visits to his parents. I nod and say, "Thanatos, I summon you."

Thanatos appears, bowing his head, his face hidden by his cloak like always. "My king."

Nyx glides to him, and before he can squirm away, she tosses his hood back. Thanatos's tattoos move over his body, depicting various scenes of death. Normally they hover above his skin, a part of him but somehow independent. The most noticeable is the one transposed over his face. It is a detailed skull that looks like a transparent mask, the shadow of his handsome features visible beneath it—

217

the skeletal reaper.

At his mother's approach, they retreat, and she kisses her son's cheeks. The Reaper blushes all the way to the roots of his white hair. Even his short, sharp horns peeking through the silky strands glow pink. Nyx cups his face, and the black drains from his eyes, revealing the natural bright green of his irises. I don't think I've ever seen his real eyes. The green is so vibrant, so... young. It's not what I expected.

The Reaper looks wildly uncomfortable at his mother's affection.

"You promised you would visit more," Nyx admonishes him. "Yet your father and I have not seen you since your last visit with our queen."

My brows shoot up, *our queen.* It drops so easily from the Primordial's lips as if it belonged there.

"I've been busy. Katie and Nem have been to see you." Thanatos turns a deeper shade of red beneath his tan. Even covered beneath his cloak, he maintains the dark tan of the Mediterranean. It marks him as one of the Greek pantheon, the people who first thought us into existence.

"It would not do to neglect parents who love you," I speak softly. "There are far worse things."

Like being imprisoned by your father and having your memory erased by your mother.

Nyx cups her son's cheek, smiling. "Go in and see your father. I need to stop our king from blowing up half of the universe."

My brows shoot up, *our king.* It's odd to hear from Nyx. Thanatos pulls his hood up with a deep sigh before going deeper into the halls, leaving Nyx and me alone in the domed entrance.

"Are you sure about this?" I watch Nyx, her starry eyes focused on me, reflecting the painted night sky.

"Like Demeter, you are harboring powers that do not belong to you. They are destroying you both." I bristle slightly at the comparison. "Besides, they should be returned to their true owner. We do not have a choice."

218

Nyx glides across the marble, holding her slender hands out to me. I pause before taking them. Her hair blows back softly at first, but the wind soon picks up. A gale surrounds us, whipping and whirling faster and faster. I hunch my shoulders as the cyclone becomes impenetrable. Nyx's hands tighten on mine, and the wind yanks on me.

I close my eyes, blocking out everything and focusing on letting go.

I need to do this for myself, releasing everything. The vines tighten on my arms, thorns digging into me, not wanting to let me go.

The fall. The ascent. The war. Everything flashes through my mind: the past, present, and even the haziest memory of a dream filled with Gods of Fate. I grind my teeth, the vines still curling around me, sliding around my neck like a noose.

Let go.

The darkness is clinging to my emotions, my hidden impulses, repressed memories, and unmanaged trauma. It has dug deep into everything I hid inside that obsidian box and pretended didn't exist.

Do it for yourself.

Nyx's power surrounds me, the vines loosening their hold slightly, unable to fight the gale -force winds around me. Sweat beads and drips down my face, the effort to detach my emotions from the power all-consuming.

Darkness is not inherently evil. Just as light is not inherently good.

Nyx's words from weeks ago ring in my head. The wind tunnel tightens around us, my hair whipping with it. A single vine is ripped from me, thrown to the spinning wind. An overwhelming scent of roses in fog follows.

"Persephone," I whisper.

"Hades," the wind whispers back.

I need to do it for myself. Let go for myself. Tears mix with the sweat on my body, the dark emotions wanting to take control. My teeth grind. *F*ate needs the Dark Spring. The Destroyer of Worlds. The Iron Queen.

A couple more vines are ripped from my skin to be sucked into the cyclone.

219

I open my eyes, locking on Nyx's, which are completely black, her hair whipping around her face. "It won't leave completely!"

"You're still holding on!" Nyx shouts back. "The power is not your love for her! Trust in fate!"

"Fate has never been a friend! It put me in a prison, on a battlefield, on a throne!" Tears blur my eyes. The hold on her hands is the only thing that keeps me from being consumed by the cyclone.

Her nails dig into my hands. "Fate gave you Persephone. Fate is fighting for you both. Join. The. Fight."

I keep my eyes on hers, and my mouth slowly opens, letting out the broken roar coiled inside me. The darkness rips from my skin, consumed by the cyclone and vanishing into the world. My strength disappears, and my eyes roll up before I collapse. This time, the darkness is welcome.

I blink my eyes open and lift my hand, moving my fingers, seeing all the vines are still gone.

"It worked," I whisper.

"You no longer possess the power," Nyx says, and my eyes drift to her. She is staring up at the starry ceiling again.

I struggle to sit up, my strength completely sapped. "It's on its way back to Persephone?"

"It will find her," she confirms.

I stand slowly, forcing my body to work through sheer force of will. "You won't enter the war," I assure her. "The treaty will remain intact."

She nods slightly. "It is not our war."

"I had a dream where I was confronted by all pantheons' Gods of Fate," I say, watching the Primordial's face for any hint of her thoughts. "They warned me that something is coming. That this is merely a skirmish of little note."

Her face doesn't change, not even a flicker, nor does she pull her gaze from the stars. "Nothing is certain when it comes to the future. Only the past is written in stone."

I move closer to her, watching her. "Did you ever doubt your decision to hand over this realm?"

Did you ever doubt me?

"There is no place for doubt. The decision was easy."

I blink in surprise, studying her profile. "I wish I could live without doubt."

"Stop wishing for it, and simply do it."

My mouth gapes slightly at her answer. I can't even form an appropriate response before Nyx vanishes in a flash of starlight, leaving me alone.

Chapter Forty-Seven

Persephone

I **SIT BACK ON MY HEELS LOOKING AT MY ROS-
ES WITH ADMIRATION.** They are so vibrant and
strong. They would be fierce, too, if they were allowed to keep their thorns. I tilt my head and study them.
They're not any weaker without their thorns. They just
look more unassuming, just like me. When I was without
my memory and my tenacity, I didn't look strong, but I
was. It was still in there.

I reach out to brush my fingers over the petals when everything goes black, and my whole body tenses. The only
awareness I have is of the darkness within me vibrating excitedly. It feels like it's beckoning to something. My body
arches and my nerve endings spark. It's not pain. It feels
good and powerful. I feel the darkness fill me, but it doesn't
eclipse the light. Somehow, it makes it even brighter. For
the first time since I left the Underworld, I feel my full power, and my whole body sighs in relief.

"Persephone!" my mother calls. I can tell by her tone that
she is irritated. "Why are you bothering with those roses?"

I bristle. My vision clears, and I glance at her, the rage
bubbling, the spikes pinching beneath my skin. I take a
breath before saying, "What would you rather I tend, Mother?" I ask, hearing the slight edge in my voice. My mother
looks at me, and I can see the smallest glimmer of suspicion

in her eyes, but she pushes it away.

"While the vegetables need pruning, you could dedicate this time to accentuating your figure," she throws back at me.

"My figure?" I snap back, struggling to rein in my anger. "Perhaps, Mother, if you didn't insist on me wearing such frumpy, shapeless clothing, you would notice that my figure is, in fact, definitely not something you need to concern yourself with."

My mother's eyes blaze. "What was that?" I notice the crack on her face deepen a little, and realizing something, I tilt my head innocently.

"I asked which part of my figure you wanted me to work on," I say placidly and move toward her, feigning a look of concern. "Are you all right, Mother? You look pale."

My mother frowns and looks down, trying to understand, and I can see how much she's struggling with this. Has she been having hallucinations regularly? Gaia's power is destroying her.

My mother touches her head. "I think I should go lie down," she says weakly.

I nod. "I'll ask Margaritte to make you some tea."

My mother mutters to herself incoherently as she walks into the house, still cradling her head.

My lips twitch as I watch her, satisfaction filling me. I glance at her prized vegetable patch. While I would never harm a plant or flower, I can change them in a way that she will hate. I wave my hand over them, and every single vegetable grows prickly thorns.

I hear someone tsk from behind me, and I tense, dreading that someone caught me in the act.

My anxiety is short-lived when Helios says, "Now, now, what are you up to?" I hear the signature smirk in his voice.

I glance at him. "Do you know how long it has been since I ate anything that wasn't a homegrown vegetable?" I smile. "Plus, she's losing confidence in Gaia's power. Can't hurt to hurry it along."

Helios's eyes glimmer with mischief, and I know they reflect my own. "Well, good thing I came prepared." Helios holds up a paper bag with the logo from my favorite takeout place in the city. "With love from my girlfriend." Helios practically beams with pride when he uses that label for Mellie.

I am almost embarrassed for him. I grin at him, taking the bag and moving to a sheltered area where I can't be seen from any of the windows of the house. We sit next to each other on the grass. "Girlfriend, huh?"

Helios's smile grows even more, if possible. "Yep, girlfriend, but I'm working toward wife."

I roll my eyes. "You're playing with fire, Helios." I take a bite of the noodles and curse under my breath. "Fuck, this is incredible."

Helios shrugs. "I love the burn."

"Weirdo." I laugh, nudging him.

Helios snickers. "How are you and the big man?"

That feeling of longing comes back, and my chest aches. "I just want to go home."

Helios wraps his arm around my shoulders. "I know, Petal."

I lean my head on his shoulder, enjoying the comfort of a friend. Helios opens his hand, and in a flash of sunlight, a rumpled white shirt appears.

"It's Hades'. He wore it yesterday. For you."

I sit up, glancing at him, and then pick up the shirt. I bring it to my nose and inhale deeply, practically moaning at the scent of my mate.

"Home," I whisper.

"You're obsessed. It's embarrassing."

I rub my fingers over the soft cotton but force myself to pull back after a moment, looking at him with an eyebrow raised. "You're wearing Mellie's neon hair tie around your wrist. Fuck off."

"But the difference is, everyone already knows I'm obsessed with her already, sooo..." Helios looks wistfully down at the hair tie, brushing his fingers over it.

I nudge him. "Thanks for the food."

Helios chuckles. "I do have to admit, Mellie sent me. She's worried about you."

224

I don't miss how his face changes when he talks about her. He's got it bad.

I sigh. "I miss her. How is she?"

Helios groans, leaning his head back. "Hot as fuck. Insane. Perfect." Helios lifts his shirt, showing several healing stab wounds.

I blink, trying to find the words but coming up short.

"Told you. So fucking hot," Helios says, pushing his shirt down.

I just blink again. "Well, whatever works for you."

"Don't hate."

I hold my hands up, shrugging. "No hate. Whatever you guys are into."

I think of Hades, and my chest aches. I must not have hidden the pain well because Helios tilts his head and searches my face. "What's wrong?"

"Just missing Hades." I shrug, and Helios squeezes me.

"I know, Petal." Helios smirks. "Remember when I caught you two fucking in the club?"

"And you took a photo like a pervert," I growl, but the memory makes me smile. "And we were not fucking."

Helios lifts a brow. "Uh -huh."

I glare at him. "We weren't."

"I mean, it sure looked like it. His pants were suspiciously loose in the photo." Helios says, his voice stupidly smug. I glare more. " What? I mean, you guys are married now. Who cares if you were fucking in a club alcove like a pair of horny teenagers?"

I flip him off and finish the noodles he brought for me.

"I have absolutely no regrets since it got my Mellie's number from you," Helios reminisces.

I roll my eyes. "Damn, you got it so bad."

Helios sighs dreamily. "So bad. It's like Herpes. Permanent."

I blink. "You're comparing your feelings for Mellie to an... STD?" It strikes me at this moment just how similar Helios and Mellie are.

"She's... really fucking something," Helios says, obviously not listening to me at all.

"Is she?"

Helios centers his gaze on me again, looking more serious but still dreamy. "She said she loves me."

"Fuck, she did?!"

Helios nods proudly. "And I didn't even have to blackmail her!"

I laugh with him, just enjoying spending time with my friend.

"I have to head out. You'll be all right?"

I nod, handing him the empty takeout box. "You'll need to take this. Mother monitors the trash."

"She's so fucking unhinged," Helios says, shaking his head as if he has not just shown me multiple stab wounds that his girlfriend gave him during sex.

Helios looks at me more seriously than he ever has. "P? What will happen if you..." He hesitates, looking away, thinking how to word what he wants to say. "If you have to kill her?"

"What do you mean?"

Helios looks down at his hands. "I've been helping my sisters stay ahead of the Olympians. I know it makes me—" Helios exhales heavily. "But they're still my sisters."

I tilt my head, watching him.

"Will you be able to kill your mom?" he asks, finally meeting my gaze.

"She has never been a *mom*, Helios. She is my mother, but if it comes to that, yes." I search his face. "You and your sisters are safe, Helios."

He chuckles. "Not with Zeus. Not even I am safe with him."

"You are safe," I repeat.

"I might have to take Mellie on the run with me," Helios whispers, looking away again.

I stand, and Helios follows. I place my hand on his arm. "You always have a safe space in the Underworld."

Helios looks at me, searching my eyes for any hint of lies or deception. He won't find any. "Thanks, P."

I smile. "Give Mellie a hug for me? And keep looking after her."

226

Helios pulls me into a hug, nodding. "I'll see you later." He winks and vanishes in a flash of sunlight. I use my vines to deposit Hades' shirt safely in my bedroom before going into the house to find Margaritte.

Chapter Forty-Eight
Hades

THE SHRILL RING FROM MY PHONE IS ALMOST COMFORTING AS I FACETIME PERSEPHONE ONCE NIGHT FALLS. She answers the phone, wearing one of my shirts, curled in her bed. Her hand is tucked under her head, her eyes soft.

"Hi, demon," she purrs softly.

"Nice shirt." I smirk, and she buries her nose into the collar, inhaling my scent.

I smile at her and turn the camera to show Cerberus sitting obediently, a sign that says *HI, MOMMY* at his feet.

"Hi, baby boy! I miss you so much!" Persephone smiles wide at him, and Cerberus barks, wagging his tail aggressively. He knocks the sign over, trying to get to her inside the camera.

"You were supposed to stay still!" I admonish him, pushing his heads away.

I turn the camera back to face me, pushing the dog back until he heads back to his bed and flops down with a huff.

She smiles softly, cuddling her pillow tightly.

I touch the screen, imagining I could stroke her cheek. "How was she today?"

Persephone sighs again, her eyes slightly glazed. "She's losing it. Her hold on Gaia's power is slipping."

"I spoke with Nyx about that." I shift to sit up slightly, propping my head up. "It's more than her inability to hold on to the immense power. She is also upending the natural order. Whoever takes the power on has to put the world into balance before the earth can absorb it."

The way her eyes go dull sets me on edge.

"It has to be someone who can handle that amount of power," I add, trying to read her expressions and understand where her mind is. But there's nothing. She just keeps rhythmically stroking her pillow.

I watch her eyes, the vulnerability and loneliness shimmering in them. "Would you like to go on a date, my spring?"

Her eyes focus on mine, reading my face, but she looks present, not as lost.

"Very much," she whispers.

I smile at her, shadowing into bed with her. She lunges at me, wrapping her arms around my neck and inhaling me. I close my eyes, burying my face against her neck. I knew it. The way she holds me is different, familiar, but also new. It's both Persephones, the one I know, and the one I fell in love with all over again.

Persephone needed me but didn't want to ask it of me. Being here is risky, but I don't care. She is adrift, losing herself in the lie. I pull back slightly, pressing my forehead to hers. She slams her lips to mine, digging her fingers into my hair. Her kiss is both familiar and not. She still tastes like pomegranates and strawberries, but there's the slightest bit of something new. It is something that I can't identify but love all the same. The Persephone I never got the chance to meet and the Persephone who first stole my heart, bound together.

Fuck, I love her every side, even the ones I've yet to see, yet to understand. I'll love her all the same. I groan into her mouth, allowing her tongue entry, nipping at it. She straddles me, tugging at my shirt. I yank it off, pausing when I see the black vines that used to cover my entire body wrapped around her wrists, delicate tattoos marking the power that was always hers.

"Your bond to the Underworld is restored," I whisper.

But not her bond with *me.* That's where Demeter focused all of her power. Her goal was to sever our marriage, but the bond will reappear once that bitch is dead.

She drags her nails down my chest. "It is."

I arch into her touch. "I didn't give up."

229

"Good." She smirks, kissing me hard. I growl into her mouth and grab her hips, rocking her against my already aching cock.

She moans. "I miss my husband."

"And I miss my wife."

My glamor drops and my claws flash, shredding her panties. She pushes me down beneath her, keeping me there with a hand on my chest. She releases her wings, sitting up on me, a queen taking control of her king. It is a control I willingly surrender, something I will only do for her. I stroke my claws over her feathers, making her shiver.

She leans down, hovering her lips over mine. "Devour me?"

I smirk wickedly and cup her ass, guiding her up my body until she is sitting on my face. I moan into her cunt, finding it already soaked for me. Her clit is already swollen, and my fangs ache. I sink them into her, stiffening my tongue and vibrating it inside her. My shadows move around my tongue, pressing deep and filling her up, making the sensation even more intense. She covers her mouth to muffle her scream.

Good. Those sounds are only for me. When I get her home, I want my eardrums to shatter from them.

She rocks her hips over my mouth, and I suck on her clit, my fangs digging deeper. I move my tongue faster inside her. My shadows move up her body, mimicking my hands, cupping her breasts from behind.

"Hades... fuck," she whispers shakily from behind her hand. My wings reach out for hers, guiding them to spread wide along with mine. Her pussy squeezes the shadows and my tongue. She arches as she comes, wildly grinding her pussy against my face.

I pull my mouth away for only a second to order, "Again."

Her hips rock, her breath coming in muffled sobs, and her entire body shuddering with waves of pleasure. "But..."

"Again," I demand, my voice nearly demonic.

She moans, moving faster over me. This time, my shadows take over. They fill her completely, her pussy, ass, and mouth until every part of her is fucking consumed by me.

She cries out, the sound cut short by the shadows that slip into her throat, filling her mouth. Her eyes roll back, and she suckles deeply. Her body writhes, and I dig my fangs in deeper as a moment later, she comes again.

I moan softly, disappointed that she didn't last longer, but I suppose I've made her too sensitive. I pull my fangs from her slowly, letting the shadows disperse. She groans, sliding off me, completely boneless. I lick my lips, savoring her taste.

She grabs my face, pulling it to hers and kissing me hard, sucking on my tongue to taste herself.

Fuck, she has to know what that does to me.

I roll to pin her and grab her hands in one of mine, pinning them above her head. I slam inside her without warning, uncaring if she's too sensitive to come again. She is mine, and I want her. She will come for me again.

She looks up at me and wraps her legs around my waist, locking her ankles behind my back. I kiss her hard, biting her lip until it bleeds, my thrusts deep and punishing.

She moans into the kiss, arching her hips into me, trying to get more. "Mine. My demon."

I rotate my hips, hitting deeper inside her. "My spring."

My fangs throb, and I strike, sinking them into her neck. She cries out but tips her head to the side, surrendering herself to my will. "So close, baby... don't stop."

I don't. My fangs dig in even deeper, my hips bucking, her heels digging into my back, spurring me on. She tightens around me, robbing me of my cum as her orgasm rips through her. She moans softly, kissing the side of my face. I release her hands after a moment, and she slowly lowers them, running her fingers through my hair. I press my forehead to hers, our breath mingling.

231

Chapter Forty-Nine
Persephone

I **LOOK UP AT HIM. MY HUSBAND. MY KING. MY FATED.** Like the first time I saw him, I'm completely captivated. His skin practically glows from his orgasm as he looks down at me. The love in his gaze is so raw and real that my whole body aches for him.

"I missed you," I moan, continuing to run my fingers through his hair, the silky strands sliding through my fingers.

Hades smiles, satisfied. He dips his head, pressing perfect soft kisses over my cheeks. Fuck. He makes me so incandescently happy. Hades continues to press kisses over my face until he lands his lips back on mine. He kisses me deeply, breathlessly, hopelessly, completely shattering everything in me.

He smiles, capturing my bottom lip between his teeth. "I missed you too."

I graze my nails lightly down his back, clawing at him a little. "Tell me something."

Hades pulls back, growling at the sting but arching his back in pleasure. "Hm?"

I drag my nails down his sides to his fucking impeccable abs. "Was the sex better?" I ask, searching his face. "When I was scared, little naïve Persephone?"

Hades blinks, the haze of his orgasm clearing. "What?" he

232

asks, more seriously.

I lift my hips, pushing Hades over and shifting so I'm straddling him. I bend and kiss along his jaw, nipping at the skin with my teeth. Am I really jealous of my other self?

Hades places his hands on my hips, digging his fingers into my flesh. "Persephone," he growls, and I pull back to look down at him. I can practically feel the vulnerability seeping out of me. "You are my wife. Memory or not. Every time we are together, it shakes my whole universe."

I feel my cheeks heat, so I bend again, biting his ear. "So you didn't prefer it when I was like that?" I hate how uncertain I sound. I hate how insecure I feel. My fucking mother has a lot to answer for.

Hades digs his fingers harder into my sides. "No. It was just the side of you I never got to meet."

I rock my hips against him, feeling him harden beneath me. I kiss down his neck. The second my lips press against the sensitive skin, he tips his head for me, releasing a deep groan. Starved, I have been starved of him.

"To see another version of you," Hades begins, his voice deep and thick with need, "only deepened my love for you."

I rock my hips again, moving my lips to hover over his, our breath mingling as we pant. Both of us are desperate, like addicts craving their next hit.

Painfully slow, I move in closer, groaning when our mouths finally meet. I glide my tongue along the seam of his lips, needing for him to permit me entry to his taste, to him. He doesn't even hesitate, and his moan sends electric pulses along my skin. He deepens the kiss, tunneling his fingers into my hair and clenching them into a fist at the roots, holding me to him.

I place my hands on his chest, lifting my hips. His cock springs up, perfectly lined up with my pussy. Despite how sensitive I am, I can't help but to lower my hips and take him inside. It is bittersweet torture, and I feel like I'm going to die if he's not fully sheathed inside me this second, but I want to take my time, enjoy the agony, and bask in him.

A knock at the door makes my heart stop, along with the voice that follows it.

"Sweetling?" my mother says sweetly. I lurch up on Hades, his cock still half inside me, and we both look at the door, barely breathing. My door handle turns slightly, and I curse under my breath. I cover Hades' mouth and quickly decide to fake that she's just woken me. I put on my sleepiest voice and lift some vines behind the door, ready to hold it closed if necessary.

"Yes, Mother?" I say, then pretend to yawn loudly. I feel Hades laugh silently, his body shaking beneath me.

The door handle stops turning. "Oh, I didn't want to wake you. I'll speak to you in the morning," she says. I remain tense, watching the door, waiting for her to retreat, bearing in mind her trick where she comes back to ensure I am truly sleeping. After a few tortuously long moments, I'm confident she won't be back. I exhale heavily, uncovering Hades' mouth.

He lifts an eyebrow at me, his eyes gleaming with mischief. "Well, that was close."

I laugh, shaking my head before slamming my lips to his, kissing him hard, and dropping my hips, taking him the rest of the way. I don't want to waste another moment. This time we're having is so risky, but it is so necessary. I was losing myself. I needed time with Hades, time to touch him and feel him, time to be *myself* with someone who loves me so completely. It ruins me. Hades thrusts up, taking my breath away, his claws digging into me.

"It's not natural for us to be apart," I moan as I start to rock my hips on him, the pleasure almost blinding me.

Hades groans beneath me, "It's not. It's awful."

I lift my hips before slamming them back down again. He cock fills me so fucking exquisitely. Hades sits up and tangles his fingers in my hair, yanking my head down to kiss me desperately.

"I fucking love you, Persephone Plutus," Hades growls into my mouth.

Persephone Plutus. Fuck. My name sounds so good on his lips. I pick up the rhythm, chasing the orgasm I can feel building at the base of my spine. I kiss him fiercely, needing him to taste all the love, adoration, and need I feel for him.

234

There will never be strong enough words to convey how desperately I crave him.

Hades pulls back, looking up at me, his eyes black. He tightens his hold on my hair, forcing me to hold his gaze. "My queen."

I moan, summoning midnight black vines to form a crown on my head, with bright gold leaves woven within the intricate twists.

"My king," I reply, my pussy squeezing his cock as I ride him.

A moment later, a crown of shadow appears on top of his head. I slam myself down on him over and over, biting my lower lip to hold my orgasm back, waiting for him. I need to feel his release fill me at the same moment my pussy contracts around him.

"Come with me, my spring," Hades groans darkly, and that's all it takes. I press my lips to his, letting him swallow my scream of pleasure as our orgasms come hard.

Hades moans into my mouth and kisses me almost desperately, my hips still gently rocking on him, riding out the last of our pleasure. I pull back after a moment, pressing my slick forehead to his and closing my eyes, enjoying the closeness.

Too soon, Hades pulls back and growls, "Fuck. The Underworld is calling me."

I sigh heavily and kiss him again. "Duty calls."

Hades smiles against my lips. "I love you."

"I love you too, demon."

Hades stares at me for a long moment, grazing his knuckles over my cheek before shadowing away.

I sigh, falling heavily onto my side and looking up at the ceiling. The ghost of pleasure still throbbing through my body, the dull, satisfying ache somehow comforting me, reminding me it actually happened. He was here.

My phone pings, and I grab it, knowing exactly who it'll be.

HADES

It feels wrong to leave you there.

PERSEPHONE

One day you won't have to.

My response makes the ache worsen a little. I believe to my very core that the day is coming when I will be able to return home, but that doesn't help the yearning I am feeling now.

HADES

One day soon.

PERSEPHONE

It better be. Or I will tear the realms apart to return to you.

HADES

You're so sexy when you're bloodthirsty.

I roll my eyes at his message, but my lips tug into a wide smile.

PERSEPHONE

Just when I'm bloodthirsty?

HADES

Or you know...when you're breathing.

I laugh, shaking my head at him.

HADES

I love you. I want you home soon.

PERSEPHONE

I love you too. I need to be home soon.

HADES

What do you want to do first?

I think for a moment. There are so many things I want to do with Hades. We had such a short time together in our realm, and we spent a lot of it separated or fighting. Not anymore because we are a united front now. We have grown and adapted. We have the rest of the time to be together.

PERSEPHONE

Spend all day in bed with you.

HADES

We could do that...on our honeymoon?

I grin at my phone like a teenager in love for the first time. Ideas for our honeymoon flood my mind: where we'll go, what we'll see. I wonder if we could stretch an Underworld honeymoon and then a human realm one the next time we are there.

Definitely on our honeymoon. But I think I want to change my answer. The VERY first thing I want to do is go on a walk with you and Berry. Just the three of us walking through our realm.

The next message I receive is a selfie of Hades and Berry cuddling in bed. I laugh, thinking about how difficult it must have been to get all of Berry's heads in the frame. But on closer inspection, both of Hades' hands are tucked under his head, and there is a tendril of his shadows in the corner of the photo. I quickly make the photo my lock screen and curl up in a ball, trying to find comfort without Hades and Berry.

My eyes widen when I see a little ball of Hades' shadows collect at the foot of the bed. I sit up, tilting my head when the shadows morph into a form. It looks like... a puppy Cerberus!

The tiny marshmallow clumsily pads up the bed, his goofy faces the same as the real Berry's. He licks my cheek once before collapsing. He is surprisingly heavy, considering his small size. The precious little creature curls beside me and falls asleep in Cerberus's favorite position. I smile at how all six of his ears stick up, looking far too big for his tiny body. My heart aches thinking about my boy at home and how he would have grown into his ears and paws.

I shift in the bed, smiling, the warmth of the mini Berry comforting me. I pick up my phone again and send Hades a selfie of me and shadow Berry before passing out.

Chapter Fifty

Persephone

I **STRETCH IN BED THE NEXT MORNING, MY** **BODY ACHING IN THE BEST WAY,** sore from being wrapped around Hades last night. With every movement, I am reminded of our intimacy.

Shadow Cerberus snores softly beside me, and I scratch his middle head fondly before climbing out of bed. The sun is barely above the horizon, so it must be early, but I feel so awake and ready for the day. Every day brings me closer to going home, to being reunited with my true family.

I've barely made it to my dresser when there's a knock on my door. I glance at it and whisper to shadow Cerberus to hide. At the command, he begins to disperse like smoke.

"Persephone?" My mother knocks again and starts to open my door. I glance around, making sure there are no remnants of Hades from the night before. I'm vaguely concerned that she may scent him, but it seems my concerns are unfounded when I finally see her. Her skin is pale, almost gray, and the cracks have deepened. Her eyes look almost sunken in.

"Oh, you're awake. Shall we go for a stroll?" she asks, and I can hear the exhaustion in her voice.

I nod. "Yes, Mother." I tilt my head, looking at her closer, noticing that her eyes are bloodshot and she is much slimmer than usual.

Gaia's power will kill her.

"Mother, are you all right? You look terrible." My words are laced with concern, but it's a lie.

My mother's face hardens. "Is that any way to speak to the person who gave you life?" she hisses at me, her eyes blazing dully.

Unable to hold back my anger, I snap right back at her. "You've said much worse to me as a compliment."

Mother narrows her eyes at me. "The difference, Persephone, is that I am your mother. I can say whatever I want about you."

I quirk an eyebrow, not quite challenging her but also showing that I'm not completely bending to her venomous words.

The fury on my mother's face dies suddenly. Her complexion goes greyer, and she leans against the door frame. "Get ready. I will meet you downstairs in twenty minutes." She turns and shuffles away.

I walk back to my bed and grab my phone, opening my messages with Hades.

PERSEPHONE

> My mother isn't looking so good. I'm going to try and get some information out of her. Love you.

I tuck my phone into the hidden compartment of my bedside drawer, and then I get dressed, pulling on a basic summer dress and pumps.

When I get downstairs, Mother is already ready and waiting for me. She looks a little less gray, but I can tell it's because she's applied a lot of makeup. The crack on her face is still visible. It tracks down her neck, red and angry -looking.

I wait to see if she comments on the fact I've left my hair down, but she barely looks at me before turning toward the door and leaving the house. I follow after her, my guard up. She's never asked me to come on an early morning walk

240

before.

We walk in silence through the near -empty streets of Olympus as the sun climbs higher in the sky. I'm so on edge that it startles me when she begins to talk.

"No one used to fear the Goddess of the Harvest," she begins, looking ahead. I glance at her and notice she is limping with each step.

"Then I became something to fear," she continues. While her voice sounds weak, some pride shines through.

I stop walking and look at her. "And that's something to be proud of?"

She stops and looks at the ascending sun. "It got me what I wanted."

"Which was?"

She pauses, lifting her chin a little, the sunlight casting an eerie glow over her ruined face. "What I have always wanted." She turns to look at me. "To protect you."

"From what?" I ask, shaking my head a little, trying to rein in my anger.

"The world, Persephone."

I scoff, looking away and rolling my eyes.

I feel her eyes still on me. "No one protected me. So I protect you."

My brows draw, and I look back at her, trying to read her mind. This is maybe the most honest she has ever been with me, yet I still don't fucking trust her.

"You," her voice breaks a little, "are my greatest gift." She looks at the sky again as if it will provide an answer no one else can. "A gift I should never have shared with the world," she murmurs.

"You're wrong." The words slip out, the barest of whispers but the truest of truths, something I can not hold back. Because she allowed me that ounce of freedom, she gave me more than I could have ever possibly imagined.

My mother slowly turns her head, looking at me. "What?"

I'm at a crossroads. I can continue with the lie, pretend I didn't say anything, or I can take the risk, knowing that this could go very, very wrong. But looking at my severely weakened mother, I realize that there may never be a better

241

time for this.

I don't shrink under her scrutiny. Instead, I rise like a phoenix from the ashes. "You kept me hidden for too long."

She just looks at me and blinks, multiple emotions crossing her face—anger, resentment, sadness, and… fear. I can read each one easily.

"I should have *never* given you an inch," she snarls.

I snarl back, clenching my fists, "You are wrong, Mother. You say you wanted to protect me, but all you did was keep me captive. You abused me verbally and physically. No one has ever treated me worse than you."

I try to stop, but it keeps coming, a flow of millennia of anger and repression, all exploding from me.

"You stole me from my husband, ripped my memories from me, and took my horns. And for what? So you could have your perfect little Persephone?"

My mother's eyes widen when she realizes this isn't just an act of rebellion but that I have recovered what she took from me. But I don't stop. I can't.

"Well, I *am* perfect. Just as I am, and while you may have birthed me, you did *nothing* to shape me into the woman I have become. A woman I am proud of, my husband is proud of, my friends are proud of."

Mother's eyes glow a little, making her look possessed. She grabs my arm, digging her nails into me. "Mnemosyne will wipe that memory clean again and again and again. You will learn your place."

I shake my head, trying to pull my arm free, but my mother must be tapping into some of her overwhelming power to hold me there. Gold ichor spills from small crescent-shaped cuts where her nails dig into me.

"It won't matter," I snarl. "I will remember again and again. Because my love for Hades and my realm is bigger than everything."

My mother tugs my arm again, but suddenly, my shoulders are wrapped in the arms of another. "I'd love to test that little theory, daughter-in-law," Kronos's deep voice growls in my ear.

My mother's eyes go wide, and she lurches forward. Be-

242

tween one breath and the next, she is gone, and Kronos and I are surrounded by dark brick and the overwhelming smell of musty, damp sand and earth.

243

Chapter Fifty-One
Hades

I **INHALE DEEPLY, FILLING MY LUNGS WITH THE CRISP SEA AIR.** I close my eyes, absorbing the peace of being so far from responsibility.

The Isle of the Blessed, the Home of Heroes, is one of my favorite places in the Underworld. One part of the island is filled with perfect white sand, and those who call it home linger around the various domains they've created here. But the other half has been abandoned, the cliffs dropping off into the river below.

I smile and draw on my tie to the Underworld, creating a small stone cottage on the cliff. Each stone falls into place, and the windows form, looking out over the cliff. Inside, it is tiny compared to the palace, but it contains everything we might need, most especially the massive bed. There is even a dog bed big enough for Cerberus. This is a retreat for us when this is all over. We can have the honeymoon we never got to have.

I open my eyes and stare at the cottage, smiling as I think of Persephone seeing it for the first time.

"It's beautiful," a deep voice murmurs. I look up and see Odysseus lingering at the lower path.

"Thank you." My eyes narrow. "Illusions won't work on me here, Niece."

Odysseus smirks, his form rippling and changing, replaced by a goddess with grey eyes. Athena.

"I didn't think I was welcome," Athena says, striding up the path toward me.

You're not.

"Yet you came anyway," I say drolly, looking out at the rivers that flow toward the cliff. Zeus must have brought her here. She does *not* have an invitation. Zeus enjoys dropping his children off here or in Atlantis to harass Poseidon and me, using his standing invitation to slip them past the wards.

"You called my office," she says, stopping at my side and looking out at the view.

I wince. "A misdial."

Athena laughs, her all-knowing eyes pinning me. I force myself not to shift under her scrutiny. Fucking Goddess of Wisdom.

"Persephone trapped on Olympus can't be good for your mental health," Athena says, studying my reactions.

My eyes narrow on her, and my voice lowers to a dangerous softness. "It would be unwise to provoke me."

Those clear grey eyes flicker with uncertainty for a second before a flash of stubbornness chases it away. Fuck, she looks so much like her father with that light in her eyes. She's not going anywhere until she gets what she wants. I spin away from the cliff, going to inspect the cabin, my shoulders bunching as she follows after me.

"It would be understandable if you were feeling the strain with all the changes in your life recently," she continues.

"Changes?" I ask, grinding my teeth.

Fuck, why did I ask? I know it just enables her to pry even deeper.

"Yes." She steps inside the cabin, and I bite back a growl as she settles into an armchair in the corner. *My armchair*, the one with a wider seat where I imagined Persephone curled in my lap with her head resting on my shoulder, her eyes closed as I read to her, lost in my voice. It was not for a nosey, unwelcome Goddess of Wisdom with a questionable degree in therapy. "Not only in your personal life but in your abilities as well."

I sit down on the couch, crossing my arms over my chest. "That has cleared, and your father should learn not to gossip."

Athena laughs. "He is awful at keeping secrets, but I was

245

not talking about the markings."

I tense slightly, shifting under her gaze. "You weren't?"

"No." She smiles. Her every expression is designed to lure me into a sense of security. "The markings were simply a physical manifestation of what you were experiencing emotionally."

"They were a result of me attempting to absorb power that did not belong to me," I volley back. What is she getting at?

Athena tilts her head, her gray eyes seeing through me. "Yet the markings did not appear when your wife's bond to the Underworld was first broken."

I open my mouth to respond before closing it. She's right. The vines didn't start appearing until that fight with Krios.

"And if it was truly just you absorbing power that was not yours, why was my father able to burn it off the first time?" she asks, crossing one leg over the other.

My brow furrows, and my mind races as I work through what Athena is implying. Why was Zeus able to break it the first time? I lower my arm, shadows dancing around my fingers.

"You think there was more to it?" I whisper, watching the shadows slide around my hand.

"Do you think there was more to it?" Athena responds.

I watch the shadows playing. Could there be more to it? The first time the markings grew was when I stopped repressing everything and unleashed during a fight. It was when I allowed myself to feed my powers with the dark emotions inside me, the ones I've spent millennia pretending didn't exist.

"Perhaps your powers have been hampered by unhealthy coping mechanisms?" she jibes. My eyes snap to hers, and I growl.

The house shakes suddenly, and I jump to my feet, ignoring Athena as I race outside. Night has fallen... very, very early, and when I gaze up at the sky, the constellations whirl, mimicking the Primordial's emotions.

I glance at Athena as she joins me. "Looks like you're not the only member of our pantheon whose powers are tied too tightly to their emotions."

246

My jaw ticks, and I vanish back to the palace, leaving Athena behind. Something's changed, and I need to know what. Athena can attempt to psychoanalyze me another time... or never.

Chapter Fifty-Two

Persephone

I **LOOK AROUND THE DARK CAVE, TRYING TO ORIENTATE MYSELF.** Fuck, I could be in another realm as far as I know. Where would Kronos have taken me? What is he hoping to achieve?

Kronos unwraps his arms from around me and pushes me to the ground. I fall forward, trying to catch myself, but it doesn't help, and I feel the sharp sting as a stone slices my cheek. I growl. Why the fuck do these assholes keep cutting up my face? Dicks.

Kronos steps over me, moving deeper into the dank space. He kneels in front of a pit filled with driftwood and deftly lights a fire.

Light fills the space, and it becomes clear he's been living here. A fairly large pallet of rotting wood sits in the far corner, various furs strewn over it haphazardly. Dirty clothes litter the ground, along with various empty liquor bottles. I wrinkle my nose. He could at least clean up a little for a guest.

When Kronos is satisfied that his fire is substantial enough, he stands and leans against the cave wall, looking at his handiwork, his expression unreadable.

I shift, sitting up and watching him somewhat warily. I'm not stupid enough to underestimate Kronos, but I'm betting he's underestimating me.

Kronos's eyes reflect the fire, and he tilts his head, staring into the flames. "I don't know who will come for you first, your mother or my son." His voice is quiet, with an air of threat.

I stretch my leg out in front of me, inspecting another laceration from the jagged floor of the cave. "My husband is unable to leave the Underworld." I lift my gaze to look at Kronos, finding him looking back at me. "We both know that, but it's not him you're hoping for, is it?"

Kronos narrows his eyes at me. "You are supposed to be inconsequential," he says. "In the weaving of time, the Goddess of Spring should be nothing."

While his words are meant to knock me down, to wound me, they make me proud because he's right. If my mother had her way, that's exactly what I would be. Inconsequential. But I worked my ass off to become who I am. I am who I am because of me, because of Hades, and because of my family and friends.

My lips twitch. "Having people underestimate me and reduce my title and power will never get old."

"I said that's what you should be, yet you're not." Kronos tilts his head at me, trying to read me like I'm the best-kept secret, but I know I'm giving nothing away. "In every other timeline, you are simply part of a story, but in this one… you are different."

I try to stop myself from reacting, but I feel my brows draw a little.

"In every single timeline, the Goddess of Spring marries the God of the Dead," Kronos says, his voice curious. "But in this one, you are wrong. You are more."

I lift my chin, forcing my lips into a smirk. "I am exactly who I am meant to be."

He scoffs in answer, rolling his eyes. "I predict your mother shall arrive in less than an hour." He waves his hand, summoning an ornate chess table. The marble lands heavily on the sand, somehow not sinking. Two chairs follow, one on either side, perfectly matching the style of the table. "Fancy a game?" Kronos asks, picking up the black king.

249

"I don't play."

Kronos smirks and sits in one of the chairs, replacing the king in its starting spot. "Too bad. I was going to make the wager... interesting."

I lift an eyebrow at him. "Oh?"

He places the tip of his finger on one of the black pawns. "The war is here. Soon, I'll face my sons on the battlefield. If you beat me," Kronos glances at me again, "I'll spare him."

I laugh at the absurdness of his offer. "First of all, it's bold of you to think you will be in a position to spare anyone. Second of all," my laughter dies, "you think I trust a single word that comes out of that treacherous mouth?"

Kronos keeps that infuriating smirk etched on his face. "I would swear it on the River Styx."

I narrow my eyes at him. That would definitely make it a binding agreement, but I'm sure he would find a loophole.

"Like I said. I don't play."

Kronos looks back at the board, the pawn spinning under his finger. "The Primes are out of the game. Without them, there is no hope for your side."

I stand and sit opposite him, leveling my gaze with his, refusing to back down. "The Titans are mostly recaptured." I pick up the white queen piece. "You have nothing without Gaia's power."

Kronos's smile deepens. "You didn't think it was strange how easily they were captured?"

I tilt my head, waiting.

"Almost as if," Kronos picks up the pawn, rolling it between his thumb and forefinger, "lining up soldiers for battle. You have done the hard bit for me. You have rounded up my troops."

I lean in a little, smiling. "You know what I think?" I place the queen back down in her space. "I think you're bluffing. You have nothing."

"He used to visit me every year." Kronos shifts in his seat. "At the same time. For millennia. Except for this past year. He was two months late because of you."

I tense, watching him carefully, trying to keep my face neutral.

250

He tsks. "Such a reckless move on his part. I had only to mention you, and he lunged. He's usually so careful." Kronos clicks his fingers, the black pawn vanishing. "And just like that, I stole three days from him with a mere touch."

I lean back in my chair. "It's funny the accomplishments you're proud of."

"And you? What accomplishments are you proud of, Daughter-in-Law?"

"Many. None of which I will be sharing with you." I hold back my growl.

Kronos raises a brow. "Oh?" He studies me, making my skin crawl. He smirks as the pieces on the chessboard begin to change. Soon, they are no longer knights, rooks, and pawns. Now, one is a three-headed dog, the perfect little marble Cerberus. A piece changes to a girl with space buns, one half of her face scarred. Another becomes a man, and even against the black marble, his skin glows. I watch as one becomes a hooded man with a scythe.

In my anger, small but mighty vines wrap around his king. "Do not threaten me, Kronos." The marble king is crushed in my vines, the dust and debris spilling through the gaps.

Kronos simply tilts his head, looking at the ruined chess piece. "It's not a threat, my dear Persephone. It's a promise."

I meet his hateful gaze. "What is it you're asking for here, Kronos?"

He laughs. "You have nothing I want."

I scoff, crossing my arms over my chest.

"I wonder if he'll scream while I slowly end him," Kronos ponders, picking up the newest addition to the board, the most perfect marble Hades. "I hope so. Maybe I'll make him watch as I kill you first."

I watch as he looks over the piece, his eyes full of malice and hate, but his threat does nothing. I will protect Hades with everything I am and everything I have.

I roll my eyes. "We can just not talk, you know?"

Kronos's eyes snap to me, and I can see that he wants to tear me limb from limb, but then he would lose his leverage. Checkmate, bitch.

I tense when the ground rumbles, my gaze swinging to Kronos, whose eyes are narrowed on the mouth of the cave. He is furious but ready. He is not the source of the quake.

"Time's up," he growls, and a moment later, my mother storms into the cave. The earth rises to meet her feet as she strides in, her eyes glowing with Gaia's power. The cracks that started on her face are lengthening by the second, extending down her arms. "You think you can hide?" she snarls at Kronos.

Heavy, rusted chains snap around her, holding her in place. The glow in her eyes completely extinguishes. I sit up, looking at the chains, recognizing them from my research before the coronation. These are the very chains that once held Prometheus.

Kronos surges to his feet. "You always did think with your heart instead of your head, Demeter."

Demeter struggles in the chains, but they hold her tight. Her gaze locks on me, and if I didn't know better, I think I see a flicker of… regret, but it's gone as soon as it appears. She opens her mouth, about to say something to me, but Kronos summons a sword, swinging it fast and true, slicing her head clean off. I gasp, watching as it rolls away from her body. In a rush, deep green light escapes her and circles the cave like a maelstrom, looking for a vessel. Instinctively, I step toward my mother, but before I reach her, I'm wrapped in a cocoon of bright white light that lifts me off my feet.

"There should be balance." The voice sounds like it is shouted from miles away, the merest of echoes. It also feels like it's being whispered directly into my ear. It is nowhere and everywhere all at once. *"Always balance,"* it repeats. *"Your mother decimated the natural order. Should I make you pay for her crimes?"* Holy fuck. This is Gaia. *"Or give you a chance to fix what she broke?"* she asks.

I feel as if I'm floating in the bright void. There is nothing but light and power. "I am nothing like her. I long for the natural order to be restored, to be returned to the Underworld and my king." Saying the words makes me ache from how true they are. I long for home and Hades.

Gaia continues, *"You're not. You are much stronger than her*

252

and will be even more so when I reinstate your bond to your king and the Underworld."

My heart leaps.

"Alas, this means you will have even less time to restore balance before my power tears you apart. What will you do with it?"

I close my eyes, a tear sliding down my cheek. "All I want is my realm back. My king. Then, if you tell me how, I will restore the balance and release your power."

Something snaps inside me, like when the bond was broken, but this time, there is no pain. Instead, elation, power, and rightness fill me, and my whole body arches.

"With my power, you could be the queen of all realms with the snap of your fingers."

She's testing me. I know that, but I don't care about any of the other realms, just my own, mine and Hades'.

"I don't want that. I want my realm. My husband." The bond ebbs and flows through me. Fuck, how did I manage without this? How did I not know that the huge gaping feeling in my chest was this?

Gaia hums happily. *"Then, when you return, you repair the harm that has been done. Call for me, and the power will be released."*

I nod, basking in the warmth of the bond. I feel complete once again. The light vanishes, and I drop, landing delicately on my feet. I can feel Gaia's power within me, but I also feel my own, and it is raging beneath my skin, repressed for too fucking long.

Kronos looks at me with a smirk, his nostrils flaring. "I'm going to have fun breaking you, Goddess of Spring."

I grin and roll my shoulders, my tie to Hades and the Underworld once again strengthening me. Careful not to disturb Gaia's power, I send black vines toward him. They shoot at him like vipers, so fast he can't dodge them, golden poisonous spines piercing his skin on impact.

He wraps his hands around them, and they wilt under his power. His evil eyes glow in victory, but I continue to smirk, knowing the poison remains. He won't notice until it starts rotting him from the inside out.

Kronos charges at me, but I feel the bond yanking at me,

253

trying to pull me home. It looks like my time in this realm is up.

I summon my sword, the comforting weight boosting my confidence tenfold. I feel the intricate patterns of a trellis draped with vines and roses on the handle. I try to resist the pull, knowing that I can't let Kronos get away. I should end this now to protect my family. But the Underworld tugs at me again, and shadows surround me. The curse will not be denied.

I swing my sword as Kronos gets closer, but the blade merely cuts air as I'm deposited in the same spot I appeared when I was first brought to the Underworld. I look around the empty throne room. The fire still crackles cheerily in the corner, and our thrones still sit proudly on the dais, awaiting my return.

"My queen?" Thanatos's voice makes me whip around, and I see his hooded form watching me from the door. I can tell he's surprised to see me from the tone of his voice. Suddenly, any worries about Kronos and thoughts of my mother are gone. I have only one thought.

My sword clatters loudly to the floor. "Hades?" I take off, running past Thanatos and down the long halls of our palace. "Hades!" I call for him over and over as I run through our home, easily navigating the corridors. I come to a sudden halt when I see him walking through the door from the library. He stops, and his gaze meets mine, his jaw dropping. We silently stare at each other for a long moment, my eyes filling with tears.

Home. I'm home.[17]

Chapter Fifty-Three

Hades

I'M DREAMING. I HAVE TO BE. SHE'S NOT HERE, **SHE CAN'T BE.** I rub my thumb against my fingers, my brows furrowing. Wait, I can feel this…

The sound of her feet isn't muted as she runs to me, eating up the space between us. Even the colors of her cheeks, the light rose flush vivid, not dimmed. Her dark hair flashes with the fire twined through it. Her body is slightly slimmer, no doubt from that fucking bitch starving her, and what the fuck is she wearing? She has on a shapeless summer dress that's torn in places. It's an outfit that is very *not* Persephone, one I would never dream of her wearing.

This… isn't a dream.

She slams into me, throwing her hands around my neck, and her scent hits me like a freight train. It's not muted. It's completely familiar, and it makes my chest ache as it surrounds me, clouding my mind.

This isn't a dream.

My eyes mist, and I wrap my arms around her, burying my face against her neck. The heat of her skin, the softness of her hair sliding over my cheek. It's all real. She presses into me. My hands shake as I dig my fingers into her hair. I inhale her scent again, tears sliding down my face and hitting her neck.

She's home.

She whimpers slightly, her hands scrabbling at me, trying to pull me closer. I wrap my arms tighter around her, knowing I am crushing her, but I need to merge us into one person, breathe the air from her lungs, inhale the scent of

255

her soul.

"You're here," I sob brokenly into her neck.

She nods, her voice equally clogged. "I'm here. I'm home."

I kiss her neck, tasting my tears against her skin. Her perfect pomegranate taste. Fuck. It isn't muted by the dream or clouded by scents of Olympus or the sea. It is *her*. It is everything.

"It's you."

Persephone nods again, kissing along my jaw and over my face, taking her time to inspect me. She is just as desperate to assure herself this is real. I don't know how long we stand there, frozen in that moment, before the thud of enormous paws comes from down the hall. Cerberus must have come to investigate the commotion. I can't pull away from her, even as Cerberus barks and bites Persephone's dress, trying to gain her attention. She pulls one arm away from my neck. Her legs are still wrapped tightly around my waist, but she reaches out to hug one of Cerberus's heads. I rub my tears against her neck, though my voice is still filled with them.

"He missed you so much," I whisper.

She kisses his head and smiles, her eyes shining. He pushes against my hold, even biting my hand to get me to put Persephone on her feet. She laughs, wiping away her tears and untangling from me to focus on Cerberus.

"Hi, marshmallow! I missed you so much!" She kisses each of his heads, scratching between the ears of one. He sniffs her for a moment before lunging at her, flattening her.

"Cerberus!" I scold.

"Berry!" She laughs. Cerberus collapses on top of her and growls at me when I try to help her up. *At me!* He is like a protective mother hen with a new chick.

I wave my hand, my shadows lifting him, holding him suspended as I pull Persephone to her feet. "Behave, you menace."

She keeps her hand in mine and squeezes. For the first time, I truly look into her eyes, and dread, unlike any I've known, courses through me. Those clear summer eyes, the blue with the sun around her pupils, are marred. The bottom of her irises are turning a familiar, terrifying green.

She looks away. "My mother is dead."

"Persephone," I whisper. "We need to get it out of you."

Those terrifying green eyes belonged to Gaia. Persephone has absorbed the Primordial of the Earth's power, and it is already ripping her apart. She is far too powerful to take on anymore. How long does she have? Did returning to the Underworld, to me, give her back even more power?

She cups my cheek, stopping my inward spiral with a simple touch of her fingers. "I'm going to release it. Gaia is going to show me how. But we need to eliminate your father as soon as possible."

What did my father have to do with her mother? Was he the one who killed her? The green is growing in Persephone's eyes, overtaking it.

"He can wait, this can't. We need to get this power out of you."

With this Primordial power, we could win the war. Persephone could wave her hand and imprison my father without a second thought, but in that moment, she could die.

I will take losing the war, my crown, my kingdom, and my life. If it means she lives.

Chapter Fifty-Four

Persephone

HE'S RIGHT. AS USEFUL AS THIS POWER WOULD BE TO DESTROY Kronos, to obliterate him, I can feel Gaia's power writhing against my control. It surges through me like a stormy sea. The power is immense, terrifying, overwhelming, and eclipsing, yet no part of me wants to explore it. I relax into my own power, feeling it wind around me comfortingly. It's missed me as I have missed it.

Hades watches me, fear in his eyes. Doesn't he see that I have no interest in this power? All I have ever wanted is to return to him, to come home.

I cup his cheek and nod before stepping back from him. Removing my hands from him is almost painful. I don't ever want to stop touching him. Cerberus watches, all of his heads tilted. I know he can feel the other power within me, but he's too excited that I'm back to care.

I close my eyes, and I can see the power within me. No longer is there just darkness but angry wells of red and orange. My fingers tingle at the feeling of it coursing through me, the foreign power conflicting with my own. It's draining me. I'm not sure how my mother lasted as long as she did with it inside her. Though, I believe the more powerful you are, the more difficult it is not to succumb.

258

"How do I begin to restore the balance?"

"Just breathe and allow my power to move through you. Think only of love and joy." Gaia's voice echoes in my mind, reverberating in my skull.

I take a breath and think about all the love in my life. My reunion with Hades and how my heart leaped when I first collided with him. The way his scent surrounded me like the coziest of blankets. I think of Cerberus and how his tail wagged so fast when he first saw me that I thought he might take off.

The roiling colors begin to calm. They are still swelling angrily but a little more muted, no longer jagged and hard, now with a gentler curve. The crimson red deepens to a maroon.

"Keep going, Persephone," Gaia gently commands, her voice softer.

I think about Mellie and Helios and how I long to see them, catch up with my friends, and hug them. I remember the dream Mellie took me to before I was taken and how much peace it brought her. The only place of comfort to the Goddess of Nightmares. Until Helios.

It's not long before my mind goes to my mother, and I'm surprised to find pain there. How could I possibly be upset that she is dead after all she has done?

"Concentrate, Persephone," Gaia growls. Clearly, thoughts of my mother are doing nothing to fix what she broke. I feel my energy waning, putting everything into trying to correct the balance. My power surges within me, attempting to expel the foreign one trying to destroy me from the inside out.

I cling to thoughts of Hades. He is the key here. Hades is my joy and happiness. I remember the first time we flew together. I hold tight to the memory of the first time I showed him my true self and how he reacted to seeing me with wings and horns. The power calms more, morphing into a deep purple, placidly waving in front of me.

"You are almost there. Keep going."

I groan, feeling so weak, and I have no idea why. I'm barely doing anything, and yet things feel calmer. Her pow-

259

er isn't pushing against mine. It's gently weaving through me.

I need more memories.

Watching Pride and Prejudice on his couch, trying to resist him. Showing him the dress I had designed for my coronation. Seeing the look of pride on his face when I looked up at him while he crowned me.

Hades. Hades. Hades.

Something snaps gently within me, and along with it, complete understanding.

"It is done."

I open my eyes to find I am wrapped in a cocoon of light. A figure appears in front of me, and I have to squint to make out the features. It dims ever so slightly, and I can see her clearly. Her long red hair billows in an invisible wind, and her vibrant green eyes are shining. She hovers in front of me, wearing a loose white chiton cinched at the waist.

"Gaia," I whisper, my eyes wide.

She floats toward me and cups my cheek with a kind smile on her face. *"You weren't even tempted, were you?"*

"Well... I considered using your power to kill Kronos," I reply honestly.

Gaia laughs, the sound like wind chimes in a soft breeze. *"But you knew the cost, and you understood that you had to choose between one or the other. You were never tempted to keep the power, to try to harness it for your own gain. Even if you had used it to kill Kronos, the intention was to protect the greater good."*

I nod. *"I just wanted to be home."* A tear tracks its way down my cheek at my truth and how much I am still yearning for it, even though I *am* home.

Gaia gives me a soft smile, and I feel the power shift slightly, my mother appearing beside Gaia. Demeter no longer looks angry or weak. She looks stronger than she has in a long time. She looks at peace.

"Is there anything you wish to say before I release her spirit?" Gaia asks.

I look at my mother, and my heart breaks for what we could have had. She could have been a mom to me. We could have been friends, but she was so desperate to hold me close

260

and hide me from the world that I ended up resenting her.

I should hate her, and a major part of me does. But another part of me, that scared little girl who always yearned for a mother who loved her unconditionally, still exists, and now that I'm here, looking at her spirit, I don't have any words for her.

"I just wanted to keep you safe," she says after a moment, her eyes tortured and regretful.

I wait for the anger. I wait for the hate -filled words to come to me, but they never do because she lost. She lost me in more ways than one. Now, I'm home with the husband that she stole me from, and she died knowing that I would always choose this life over one with her. That is far more cutting than any words I could muster.

I lift my chin, finally affording her one truth from me. *"I forgive you,"* I say, and I do. She locked me away and stole centuries of my life. It ends now. She is dead, and so is my resentment toward her. I fucking won.

"You don't. Not really," she replies, searching my eyes.

"I do."

Her eyes fill with tears. *"I wanted you safe, and now you're not. You never will be again."*

"You're wrong." I tilt my head, watching her. *"I am with my husband, who loves me more than the realms themselves. I am not a naïve little girl. I am strong. I am powerful. I am enough."*

A tear slides down my mother's cheek, and she reaches out, sliding her hand into mine. *"I'm sorry."*

I feel my own eyes fill with tears, and I squeeze her hand. *"I know."*

She looks at me, smiling through the tears, and it's the first genuine smile I think I've ever seen from her.

"My powerful girl," she whispers, squeezing my hand again before she fades away.

Gaia places a gentle hand on my shoulder, smiling down at me. *"Now. Let go, Persephone."*

I close my eyes, and my head tilts back as I feel Gaia's power draining out of me and returning to the ground. My body tingles as it leaves, my own power filling all the gaps it's vacated.

"Be free, little dark flower," Gaia whispers.

I exhale as the last morsel of her power drains from me, and then everything goes black.

I wake moments later, my eyes fluttering open to see Hades' concerned gaze searching my face, his hand against my cheek as he cradles me in his lap.

Fuck, I love this man.

Hades searches my eyes and exhales, leaning in and burying his nose into my hair. "Fuck. You're back."

I cover his hand and lean my cheek against his palm, luxuriating in being surrounded by him. "Hi, demon."

Hades kisses my face, trying not to miss even an inch of skin. "You smell like you. Fuck."

I run my hands over his chest and arms, anywhere I can reach, needing to touch him everywhere. I want to merge with him and never be separated from him again.

"You're here," he repeats, nuzzling me, his tears wetting my cheek. My poor demon. I pull back, looking up at him and tunneling my fingers into his hair.

"Did you kill her?" Hades whispers, looking down at me, his face settled into an expression of complete awe.

I shake my head, staring at him. Will I ever get tired of just looking at him?

"Then how?" he asks, his hands roaming over me.

"Kronos."

I feel him tense beneath me, and his hands become more insistent as he checks me for injuries.

"He barely touched me, baby." I try to ease his concerns, but he simply pulls me into him, squeezing me so hard I can practically feel the relief radiating off him.

I hug him back, desperately trying to press even closer together.

262

"I'm not convinced you're really here," Hades whispers against my neck, and I tighten my fingers in his hair.

"I'm here. I'm home." My heart races, and I close my eyes, nuzzling my face into his hair.

I pull back, desperate to kiss him. He glances at my lips, about to lean in when the ground trembles and a roar rumbles through the Underworld. Hades and I tense, knowing exactly who that is.

"Let's fucking end this," I growl, my eyes hardening.

"Call the troops. It's time," Hades says, nuzzling his nose with mine. I stand and offer him my hand. He takes it, and I pull him to his feet, looking up at him.

The King and Queen of the Underworld united at last. As if on cue, a battle cry rings out over the Underworld.

I KNOW THAT SHOUT. NO... HE'S NOT THAT IN-
SANE. He wouldn't dare unleash him. It is just as
likely that he will turn on Kronos than fight for him.
My armor forms over my body. Shadows turn to scale metal
over my arms and legs, hardened leather covering the metal
on my chest.

Persephone's black vines turn to steel, covering her body
in her own unique armor. She stands at my side as we look
out the window of the palace. My hand squeezes hers tight,
horror coursing through me and twining around my stomach.

He is that insane.

Two hands have broken through the gates of Tartarus.
Larger than the gates themselves, they grip and shred the
adamantium easily. He wasn't in the cells but under them.
He'd reached up through them to break the gates, shattering
the cells in the process, killing some of the Titans imprisoned there with a single clench of his fist. The powers left
behind swirled where their bodies once stood, unable to be
absorbed by the creature. He isn't a god. He is a monster. A
god killer. *Typhon.*

Cerberus joins us, growling at the sight of the creature,
sensing the threat. His body changes, becoming even bigger, snakes appearing along his spine.

I wince as the hundreds of snakes on Typhon's shoulders
let out a monstrous cacophony. I cover Persephone's ears as
the sound echoes through the Underworld, shattering the
windows and one of my eardrums. She claps her hands over

264

my ears, both of us struggling to stand as the noise continues, shaking the walls and making the air vibrate.

The art on the walls shakes and falls as Typhon's battle cry slowly tapers off. I lower my hands slowly from her ears. My healing is slow, my ears still ringing. The Underworld is injured and struggling to heal amidst Typhon's destruction. Anything that happens to Persephone and me during this time will take a while to heal.

I rub at the blood from beneath my ringing ear, locking eyes with Persephone. "You need to go to Thanatos and tell him to get Zeus. I'll hold him off until you get back."

"I'm not leaving you," she snarls,

I grab her arms. "It has to be you. I'm sorry. I have to conserve my power as much as possible. Even summoning him takes something from me." I glance at my phone to confirm. "And Typhon fried all electronics with that scream." We need another plan. This is another thing I wasn't prepared for. "Go, get Thanatos, and come back."

She opens her mouth to argue, but I pull back and order, "Go!"

Her eyes narrow on me before she vanishes. She's going to make me pay for that later. Hopefully, we'll have the chance at least.

I put my hand onto Cerberus's flank, his fur hardening under my fingers. Preparing for battle. "We have to stay safe, all right?" I glance at him. "For her." Cerberus huffs at me, nodding his three heads. I swing up onto his back, my shadows forming a cloak around my shoulders. The bident hums as it appears in my hand. I lean down, whispering to him, "Let's go, *Berry*." He growls, his body humming as he lunges out the broken window. Cerberus's paws pound against the earth, eating up the distance between the terrifying Typhon and us.

I need to conserve my energy, especially as the wounds to the Underworld remain, leaving screaming pockets of Void. The essences of the Titans who were killed during Typhon's release were sucked into the Void, returning to Khaos. There will be no healing from that, no regeneration. If we fall in this battle, it is the end.

My fingers tighten on the bident, the hum resonating up my arm. I will not die here. I am not *fucking* done. The bident flies from my hand, soaring through the sky to hit Typhon in the shoulder. The monstrous giant turns toward me, smiling slowly, showing the rotting teeth and decaying flesh around his mouth. He is truly the Father of Horrors.

My legs tighten protectively around Cerberus. Typhon may be the three-headed dog's biological father, but he is not his dad.

Typhon keeps his eyes on me as he yanks the bident from his shoulder and flings his blood off the tip. It flies through the sky and hits the ground. A moment later, monstrous creatures sprout from the spilled blood and lunge for me. The first sends me flying off Cerberus. I bounce across the ground, each hit making me lose the breath in my lungs. When the fuck did he get that power?

I punch my jaw back into place. The monstrous creatures made of Typhon's blood keep coming for me, their movements disjointed. The screech they make is nearly as powerful as their creator's but not enough to debilitate me. I throw my hand out, hitting them with my shadows. They go flying, tumbling close to one of those gaping holes, and are swallowed whole by the Void.

I look up at Typhon, roaring to be heard. "Typhon! You are in violation of your imprisonment. Return to your cell or face my wrath!"

Typhon towers over me, looking down at me before throwing back his head and laughing. I cover a flinch at the sound, but I don't break my glare up at him.

"You think to order me, puny king?" he mocks.

My bident returns to my hand, the power ringing through the metal and up my arm. Cerberus is snarling, following my example, and tossing the monsters into the Void.

"I will give one more warning!" I continue, ignoring the giant's blustering. "You are in violation of your imprisonment. Return to your cell or face my wrath!"

He blinks, his yellow eyes scanning me. The size of a single eye is larger than my entire body. He moves slowly as he winds up his kick. So be it.

266

I use the new ability I acquired when I finally let my darkness free and move through the shadows, becoming one of them, swirling with them. I hurl the bident into his Achilles tendon, burying it deep. He screeches, stumbling with the injury and slamming into the mountain that marks the Gate of Dawn.

Souls scream at the intrusion, the walls that kept them regulated to their deserved afterlife coming down with the force of the giant's impact. They flood toward me, hitting me and hurling me back into the ruins of Tartarus. Fuck. Souls can still touch me even when I am in full shadow form. I did not expect that.

A familiar laugh echoes through the prison, and I freeze. "To think you were put in charge of maintaining my prison. Pathetic," my father croons, stepping from the rubble of the prison. I stumble to my feet and try to hide my gasps of pain. The landing fractured a rib, maybe more than one. I don't even try to heal them, needing to preserve my strength.

Kronos steps forward, and I recoil at seeing how he's dressed. He's wearing a bloody head as a crown, the face contorted with the horror of its death. It takes a second for me to identify the god.

Demeter.

The Titans that survived Typhon's release flank him on either side, ragged but ready to fight. I don't take my eyes off my father. I know who the most dangerous is.

"My sons," Kronos calls to his Titans, "are mine to kill."

My brow furrows. I was not expecting that. His need for retribution is clearly much more deeply rooted than I realized.

"The rest... make them scream," he orders. "Especially that pathetic little flower goddess who plays at being queen."

My darkness explodes from me. They will *never* touch Persephone. Light pierces through my shadows, my power faltering with the immensity. I shield my eyes as it breaks my concentration. I blink through it and see Hyperion, Titan of Light, and Helios's father. Fuck, does this mean Zeus was right, and Helios is not on our side?

A fist slams through my chest, creating a hole. I grab

267

Kronos's arm, trying to stop the blow even as his fist pierces my back. My eyes connect with my father's, the maniacal green searing me. He could have stolen time and put me out for the entire battle, but he didn't. Instead, he decided to kill me.

Blood pools in my mouth, and my vision goes hazy. "You... won't... win."

He laughs, but the sound is muted. He hurls me into a pocket of the Void. I grab onto the edge of the Underworld, fighting to keep myself from being swallowed whole. Kronos comes closer, hunching over, his eyes level with mine.

"Goodbye, Son," he says before he pushes me into the Void.

Chapter Fifty-Six

Hades

KRONOS IS A BOY TO US, NOTHING. THERE IS MORE COMING.

The voices of the Gods of Fates whirl around me as I fall into the Void. Is this death for gods? Is this where we go? My body jerks to a stop, my stomach lurching at the sudden change in pace.

My eyes attempt to take in my surroundings and understand what I'm seeing. The Titans consumed by the Void are nowhere to be found. There is only emptiness, the unanchored abyss. No. Not again. I open my mouth to scream, to beg, but there's no sound. There is nothing. Only Void.

Persephone. I have to get back to Persephone.

I tilt my head back, trying to find the hole that Kronos threw me into, but it's gone.

"I don't know about this, my love," a voice says, and my gaze snaps to the direction of the voice. It's disembodied, completely detached, but so familiar. I can't turn my body to find the source, so I try to shout for attention, but I am still unable to produce sound.

"We are not interfering. This is still neutral," another voice responds to the first. This time, I recognize the speaker as Nyx.

What are they talking about? Can they see me?

I struggle to move, but the Void holds me tight. Without firm hands or even the sensation of power wrapped around me, it holds me in the vacant abyss. Light sparks and intrudes on my vision. My eyes struggle to remain open against the brightness. It's so different from the rest of the

269

Void and the Chaos from which the Primordials are cut.

"You know the consequences if we do this," the first voice answers. *Erebus.*

"I know," Nyx whispers back. "We can't fight. The treaty binds our hands, but we can do this."

What are they talking about? My eyes dart around, trying to find them, but there's still nothing. Why can I hear the Primordials but not see them?

I struggle again, shouting even though no sound comes out. *Nyx! Erebus!*

Invisible fingers dig into my face. I try to tug away, but the phantom fingers dig in even more. "Don't struggle, boy. This is a gift."

I growl, but there is only silence. Unfamiliar power surrounds me, darkness but not my darkness. It is something infinitely more powerful. These are the shadows from which all shadows spring from, even mine. This is Primordial power. I try to pull back, unable to handle this power. I'm not a Primordial, and I am already powerful enough. If I take on Erebus's power, I will die.

"You're already dead, idiot," Erebus snaps, and I stop struggling. "This comes at a great cost to us, so do act a bit grateful."

"Erebus!" Nyx admonishes him.

More of Erebus's ability floods into me, drowning me in darkness. I have never experienced anything like this. Even when Persephone was gone, and I lost myself, it wasn't this overwhelming.

I whirl upwards through the Void, finally able to move. Light filters in, and I soar out of the pocket of Void, the hole in my chest healed. When I land in the Underworld, I inhale deeply. The Primordial power is coursing through me but no longer overwhelming me. Erebus must not have given me more than I could handle, but I wonder at what cost.

Typhon's screech shakes the Underworld, followed by the sounds of thunder. Shadows flicker and wrap around me. For the first time, I understand what Nyx meant when she told me not all darkness is evil. This darkness binding to mine feels *pure.*

270

A Titan shouts in surprise at my reappearance and charges at me. I throw my hand up, prepared to hurl him back with my shadows as I've done to many Titans before. But the shadows don't obey, or rather, they have a mind of their own. They wrap around the Titan, lifting him from the ground and trapping him in darkness. They hold him perfectly still, like in the Void.

I blink in surprise when I stretch my fingers slightly, and the Void *consumes* the Titan. I lower my hand carefully. What did those crazy Primordials do? I touch my chest. The hole my father left is gone. It must have taken considerable power to repair, and he gave me back not only my abilities but some of his own.

Erebus mentioned a price... Fuck, it must be astronomical.

Typhon has made his way to Elysium, crafting destruction in his wake. I snap my wings out and jump to take off. I soar closer to the giant, snapping my wings wide to hover at eye level with him.

"Typhon!" I order.

This time, the giant pauses and looks at me. For the first time, there's a flicker of fear in his eyes. Does he sense the change in me?

Shadows curl around him, forming chains and wrapping tight around his limbs, slowing him down. The monstrous chains turn to adamantium, controlling Typhon and stopping him from moving further.

My vision flickers. Binding him is draining me of my energy. Unconsciousness teases at the edges of my mind, and I plummet to the ground. I flare out my wings, barely managing to slow my descent enough to keep myself from becoming nothing but a splattered memory of a god. Even so, I hit the ground hard enough to force the air from my lungs and make every bone in my body ache.

Fuck, I may have Erebus' abilities, but I do not have his stamina. I can't use this new power unless I am ready to pay the price to my energy.

Typhon struggles, breaking the chains. I can't hold him. Fuck, I can't use this ability like this. Typhon looks down

271

at me and moves forward, his giant foot hovering over me, about to stomp down.

I struggle to my knees, still gasping for air as I wait for my body to heal. The shadows around me flicker but don't obey me. I'm too weak to command them.

Weak, pathetic boy.

I am all alone.

Chapter Fifty-Seven

Persephone

I **ZERO IN ON HADES IMMEDIATELY.** Hades is flat on the ground, Typhon's enormous foot hovering over him and a smile on his ugly, rotten face.

Not today, asshole.

A huge spike pushes from the ground right beside Hades. I swoop down, flying at Hades and tackling him, a whoosh of air leaving him as I crash against him. I hold him tight and roll, moving us out of danger just as Typhon drops his foot. The sharp golden spike pierces his sole, and his wail of pain reverberates throughout the Underworld. I pant, looking over my shoulder at Typhon, covering Hades' body with my own. Hades simply looks up at me in wonder, and after a moment, I meet his gaze.

"Don't get crushed." I kiss him hard and wink at him before rolling off him and launching myself back into the air.

Within five minutes, Zeus and Poseidon appear almost simultaneously, and I send a silent thank you to Thanatos for retrieving them. I know how hard it is for him to go topside for anything other than work.

This may be the only time I've ever been grateful to see Zeus's stupid face, but the way he rushes to Hades' side and starts throwing lightning bolts at Typhon makes me wonder if I should be nicer to him. Maybe that's a stretch, but

273

I'll send him a basket of mini muffins or something.

I hover nearby and see that the three brothers are slowly getting a handle on Typhon, or at least, they have more of a handle on him than when Hades was battling the beast solo. I turn my attention to the direction of the cells. There are Titans fucking everywhere.

I look back at Hades and his brothers. They are consumed with their current battle, and I steel myself, ready to take on as many Titans as I can alone. I land heavily into a crouch and look up, my gaze hard.

"Bring it on, fuckers," I growl, and though I'm about fifty feet away, many of them snap their heads in my direction and snarl. With a sharp whistle, I summon Cerberus, who has grown in size, his red eyes glowing menacingly. He stands at my side and snarls, his claws extending and sinking into the mud beneath us.

"Ready, boy?" I ask him, summoning my sword.

He barks in answer, his paws kicking at the mud, ready for me to say the word, ready to maul some Titan ass.

"Let's fucking do this. Charge!" I exclaim and launch into the air, flying alongside him. We meet the line of Titans at the same time. They're brandishing whatever they could find, some holding bits of their cell, some holding bricks, a few holding bones of fellow perished Titans. I snarl the first time my blade pierces flesh, and I have to work not to react, feeling a shiver travel over my skin. I'm not sure the feeling of steel piercing flesh will ever be something I grow used to or enjoy, but it is necessary.

Cerberus throws a Titan into the air, catching it again in his mouth and shaking him before ripping him into multiple pieces. I smile at my boy. He looks like he's having the best time, doing what he was made to do. Cerberus was born to protect the realm. Fuck, he really is something to behold.

My distraction costs me, and I'm caught around the ankle and thrown hard against a tree. I groan as I sag to the ground, but the pain only fuels my anger. My power flares inside me, and I send vines back at the Titan. They wrap him up and drag him into the ground. He screams as he

274

is stabbed with thousands of spikes, and I use my vines to wrap around his mouth and eyes, piercing them, too.

My head snaps up when I hear Cerberus snarl. A Titan has climbed onto his back and plunged a knife into him. I launch myself toward him and cut the Titan's head clean off. I yank the blade free for Cerberus and cover the wound with one of my golden leaves to protect it.

I look around. There is one kill that is the most important on this day. Kronos must know his time is coming, and as much as I understand that Zeus is desperate for the kill, it probably belongs to Hades. If I get the chance, I am ending this now. I can feel his presence in the Underworld, and I know he's watching, but I'd be willing to bet his attention will be on his three sons. I will be the farthest thing from his mind.

A bone-brandishing Titan swings at me, and I quickly dodge it. Cerberus comes out of nowhere, slicing him with his claws and splitting him into three equal pieces. I glance at him and wink, lifting my sword at the last possible moment to parry an attack. My sword slams against a dark brown brick, and it turns to dust in the Titan's hand. I smirk as he looks at his now empty hand, confused.

"Any last words?" I ask, tilting my head. I don't give him a chance to answer before I stab him through the abdomen. My vines wrap around him, and I throw him into what looks like a black hole. I watch it gulp him down and decide to stay far away from that fucking thing.

"Berry, go check on Daddy and come back," I call to Cerberus, who has the large intestine of a Titan hanging from his mouth. He tilts his head and then turns, barrelling toward Hades.

I look around. There is some fighting going on between the Titans, which is helping a little, but I'm scarily outnumbered.

Fuck.

I worry my lower lip, trying to think of a plan. While I consider, I'm stuck in the most frustrating melee with a female Titan. She'd managed to find some sort of sword and is actually fairly proficient. She slashes unexpectedly, and I snarl as the rusted steel embeds in my arm. I growl at her, sending a large spike up from the ground to pierce and hold her there.

"Whatever happened to women supporting women, hm?" I ask her uselessly as she stands there, barely conscious.

I push off the ground again, killing as many of them as I can, but more appear, and these are bigger and stronger. We need help. Fast.[18]

Chapter Fifty-Eight

Persephone

I'M SLAMMED INTO THE GROUND BY A TITAN I **DIDN'T SEE COMING.** Fuck. They're getting faster. How are they getting faster? I groan, pushing up from the ground to face my assailant. But all the air whooshes out of my lungs as I'm kicked in the stomach. I roll away, trying to escape the danger. A sharpened rusty pipe pierces the ground next to my head, almost stabbing me and slicing my cheek. I hiss and sit up, grabbing the pipe and launching it. It spears the Titan between the eyes, and he falls to his knees, confused.

"Fucking asshole," I snarl.

I take a quick glance around and notice that the number of Titans has increased tenfold. I look toward Typhon, hoping to see that Hades and his brothers have made headway, but alas, Typhon is swiping his large hand and clearing the ground of his attackers.

I curse again, looking at the Titans who are charging at me. No longer do they seem distracted by each other. They all have their eye on the prize, and that prize is my head on a silver platter. I shift into a battle stance, readying myself. I whisper to Hades, needing him to know I love him, and if this is the end, I have no regrets about our time together. He is the great love of my life and always will be.

I prepare for the onslaught, weighing my odds and ac-

277

cepting that they are anything but in my favor. Suddenly, the Titans seem to hit an invisible force field around ten feet away from me. My brows draw in confusion, and I look around, trying to find the one responsible, but there's no one here. Titans surround me completely, and I hear them snarl as they try to pierce the barrier, but they can't.

"What the fuck?" I look around, waiting for an answer. The Underworld shifts, and Mellie appears beside me in the bubble. Her hair is in two French braids, and she's wearing similar battle leathers to me, except hers are already stained with old blood. I blink at her, confused.

"What? You thought you'd be taking on these cretins without me?" She smirks wickedly.

I blink again, searching her eyes for even a scrap of insanity, but they seem clear.

"It doesn't make sense to clean the leathers. The blood makes me look even more terrifying."

I lift my eyebrows and then pull her into a hug. "I missed you, Mel."

Mellie hugs me and then pulls back. "I brought reinforcements."

I watch as other gods and goddesses appear, all ready for battle. They are here and ready to fight to the death to protect this realm. My realm. Mellie nods to Athena, who prepares to lower the force fields. At the signal, her blonde hair blows loose in the winds of chaos.

Ares' voice booms from across the battlefield, "Push them back with everything you've got!"

Athena winks at me, and the barrier drops. There is the briefest moment of the eeriest silence I've ever experienced before Ares' voice sounds again. His roar sounds like he's merely a hundred yards away, not half a mile. "Charge!"

Chaos. That's the only way to describe what happens next. The whole line collides in a kaleidoscope of gore and disarray as the gods and goddesses plunge themself into the fray. I look on for only a moment before I charge with them, Mellie at my side, her laugh maniacal and chilling.

Is Helios here?

The thought comes and goes as an attack from my left

278

side pulls my attention. I swing my sword, slicing the Titan's arm clean off. Blood spurts against my face, and if I didn't have another attacker in the next moment, I'd be horrified. I try to keep one eye on Mellie, knowing she can take care of herself but worried about her descending into depths she may not be able to return from. She swings up onto a large Titan's shoulders, her hands cupping his chin. She swiftly yanks his head around at a worrying angle. There is a sickening crunch before his eyes go dull. He falls heavily, and Mellie gracefully leaps off him as he falls and moves on to her next victim.

"Watch out!"

I'm yanked away, and a sword -brandishing hand surges forward, piercing an oncoming Titan who was about to end me. I look at my savior, happy to see Dionysus.

"Even the Queen of the Underworld needs to pay attention." He smirks.

I dust myself off, preparing to fight again. "I was checking on Mellie."

He laughs, swinging his blade. "I know, but she's doing fine. Hades will end us all if you get hurt."

I laugh, slamming my sword into another Titan. "How are you doing, Dion? It's been a while."

"Yes, well, you got taken and shit." He laughs, fighting a particularly deft Titan. "Things are… complicated in the human realm."

I lift an eyebrow, looking at him as I relieve a Titan of his head.

Dion merely shakes his head. "A story for another time."

I laugh and push deeper into the melee, taking whatever chance I can to look for Hades, Cerberus, or Mellie.[19]

Chapter Fifty Nine
Hades

ZEUS SLAMS TYPHON BACK WITH BOLTS, **HURLING THEM** repeatedly, his arms close to a blur. Gods are flooding the field, clashing against each other. Athena, in full armor, lets out a brutal war cry as she launches into the fray. Ares is already drenched in Titan blood, his eyes glowing with battle frenzy and very much in his element.

A blinding flash of light overwhelms the battlefield, making me shield my eyes. My breath catches as my eyes adjust, seeing the newest arrival on the battlefield.

Helios.

My eyes lock on the Titan, waiting to see what he does next. In the last battle, he rode at my father's side, but he has never declared which side he is on. Melinoë is on the field somewhere. I saw her earlier, but now Helios is alone.

He waves his hand, and flashes of sunlight illuminate the field. Titans appear, his two sisters, Selene and Eos. My eyes focus on him, even as he flashes more Titans to the field. I realize he is using the invitation I gave him to ferry his kind here.

Mellie appears at my side, a strangled sound of distress coming from her throat. Her eyes are locked on Helios as she struggles to understand. The Titan doesn't look regretful or even ashamed. Instead, he has the fucking gall to look at me and *wink*. Prick. He dares to make Melinoë fall for him and then betray her like—

The Titan of the Sun turns his back on us, as do the Titans he brought with him. He lets out a loud shout and rushes to-

280

ward the opposing Titans, turning against his own kind. He clashes with Hyperion, facing off with his own father. The conflicting light blinds those near them. Helios is a glowing yellow sun, and Hyperion is a pure white light.

Yet, even as he clashes with his father, more sunlight filters into the Underworld, delivering gods using Helios's invitation. These are gods I never expected to see.

I freeze when I see a goddess with midnight hair cascading down her back. She looks back at me over her shoulder, her golden eyes molten even at this distance. The smile that curls her red lips makes me tense, and my apprehension increases when I recognize the being beside her. They take in the battle, their cropped black hair shining in the flashes of sunlight. They throw back their head and laugh, the sound seeming to amp up the chaos on the field.

I can't believe he brought these two specifically here. Not them. They are tricksters, wildcards, and horribly unpredictable. They cut a swath of devastation and mayhem wherever they land.

Atë, Goddess of Ruin.
Eris, Goddess of Discord.

There was a time when I once called Atë a friend. Eris, though, supported Typhon once upon a time. Even now, Eris stands in their non-binary form. They shift along the spectrum from male to female to non-binary whenever it pleases them, a natural form of chaos.

Eris lets out a whoop of delight before launching at the Titans. Atë touches the ground beneath her feet. It erodes, and more Titans and Olympians fall into the Void, disappearing into the abyss.

"Atë!" I shout.

She laughs. "Oops?"

I glare at her. "Keep it to the Titans."

She winks and waves her hand negligently before diving into the fray, following her mother. Well, the Titans are handled, at least for the moment. Even the hundred -handed Hecatoncheires seem momentarily occupied. Persephone is barking orders like a seasoned general, keeping the gods organized and her eye on the big picture.

281

I return my attention to Typhon. Zeus and Poseidon are both fighting the monstrous giant, and it is time I rejoin the fray. Using my shadows, I slam my bident into his neck. I cling to it as he shakes, trying to throw me off.

"Zeus!" I scream. "Aim for his neck!"

Zeus nods and spins his hands, building up the strike of lighting. Poseidon embeds his trident into the giant's opposite shoulder. My shadows turn to shackles around Typhon's left wrist, and at Poseidon's command, water encases his right. He tosses his head back, the snakes that form a halo around his head striking out. I growl when one sinks its fangs into my shoulder, its head as big as one of Cerberus's. Another snake sinks its fangs into Poseidon's torso, poison leeching into both of us.

"Hurry the fuck up!" Poseidon screams down to Zeus.

Typhon roars, shaking the realm, trying to break free from us before Zeus can smite him. His roar breaks off suddenly. Everything goes unusually quiet, and unease slides down my spine. The snakes release us, but the poison is coursing through me, and my grip on my bident slips, my vision wavering. The Underworld is trying to heal me and give me strength, but it's so broken that there's only so much it can do.

The snakes all lift toward the sky, letting out a screech. The sound is quickly followed by a broken shout from Typhon.

I look at Zeus. He is still gathering his power, but he hasn't released it yet. What is Typhon reacting to? His massive body ripples, and a green, ominous glow emits from his skin. Too late, I realize why.

Kronos.

I shout a warning to Poseidon, snapping my wings out as Typhon begins to decay beneath us. Kronos is stealing time from him, leaching it until he is nothing, not even dust remaining.

Poseidon's eyes connect with mine as we land hard on the ground where Typhon, the Father of Giants, had stood only a moment before. There's only one reason Kronos would take that much time from Typhon, someone who

282

was his ally or at least his pawn.

The world fractures around me a moment later, confirming my theory. He's ripping through the timelines. We must be winning if he's resorted to this. His ultimate goal is the destruction of Poseidon, Zeus, and me in every single timeline. He was never going to be satisfied with just this one. No, Kronos has to have all of them.

As the timelines around us tear, there are glimpses into the other realities and worlds where little choices have resulted in different futures. My mind struggles to process what I'm seeing. A boy, no older than fourteen, soars above our heads, the arches of his wings black before fading to white at the ends. My eyes track his flight, watching him. I jolt when he locks eyes with me. They are Persephone's eyes. A moment later, he vanishes.

I spin at the sound of a bell tolling, another timeline ringing out. A man stands at the timeline rip. He is taller than even me, with molten silver eyes and a scar bisecting his left eyebrow. He waves his hand, and a spell circle appears filled with ancient Greek runes. He slams it against the tear in his reality, snapping it shut. In another, a red -haired witch with lilac eyes grumbles with annoyance, waving her hand to seal the rift.

I shake myself, forcing myself to focus.

"Poseidon!" I shout, seeing him equally overwhelmed by the various realities.

His eyes snap to mine, even as I close the distance between us, darting between the tears littering the air. Wordlessly, we fall back easily on years of experience. We head for our father, guided by his maniacal laughter. His eyes are glowing green as time devolves.

I throw the first hit and Poseidon the second, breaking his concentration enough to let some timelines fade. He grabs my fist before I can land a third punch, breaking bones with a single squeeze. Pain shoots through my hand, but Poseidon kicks out, landing a hit to Kronos's knee, throwing him off balance. It is enough for me to wrench free.

We don't falter. This is our chance. Our revenge for the childhood we never got to have. The life we never got to

283

live. Each hit we land is for the mother we never knew, the warriors we were forced to become, for crimes too numerous to list, and for the lives that would be lost today. We lay it all at our sire's doorstep.

I take another hit, and I know he broke another bone, but I barely feel it. The release of finally giving my father the beating he deserves is euphoric. As his blood splatters, a part of the child I never got to be heals.

Electricity makes the hair on my arms rise, and it is the only warning we get. I shove Poseidon out of the way and throw myself to the ground, leaving Kronos open for Zeus.

Zeus unleashes the killing strike he had built for Typhon on the former King of the Titans, the bolt of lightning hitting our father in the chest. I cover my mouth and nose as the smell of burning flesh overwhelms me, the black smoke curling over the ground. I shield my eyes as I look back, aware of how easily the lightning could sear my corneas. But I need to see his end with my own eyes.

Kronos stretches his arms out on either side, and I curse when I see him tear open a timeline at his feet.

"No!" I shout, trying to reach out and stop him.

My father vanishes through the rift in time, and the remains of Zeus's lightning soar across the battlefield, hitting a mountain and exploding.

He escaped. *Again.* Fuck.

Poseidon stands, the poison slowly weeping from his wounds, being ferried out of his blood by his control over water.

"We'll find him," my brother assures me. "But we need to finish the battle here first."

I nod, struggling to stand and preparing to fight. Yet when I look out to the rest of the battlefield, shock suffuses me.

Persephone rides Cerberus, her armor stained with Titan blood, and the remaining Titans, who didn't side with us, are down for the count. She's wrapped them in her black vines and is riding around the battlefield, sending them one by one to the cells.

I lean down, touching the soaked ground, tugging on

284

my bond to the Underworld and my new bond to the Void. While Persephone sends Titans to their cells, I focus on closing those pockets to the abyss, knitting the wounds of the worlds closed.

As if she feels my gaze, Persephone looks at me, her eyes clear even from a distance.

We survived. [20]

Chapter Sixty

Persephone

I **LAND IN THE PALACE GARDENS, GROANING A LITTLE AS MY FEET** collide with the solid ground of the Underworld. Mud and blood coat my skin, and my chest heaves as I pant, but I can feel myself healing along with the Underworld.

A moment later, Hades lands beside me, and my gaze immediately goes to his. He cups my cheeks in his hands, and his eyes roam over my filthy face, checking me for injuries. I lean into him, understanding. I feel the same need to know that he's okay, that he's safe. My hands rest on his chest, and even through the metal of his armor, I feel his heartbeat. It centers me.

"Are you all right?" Hades asks breathlessly.

I nod, and my gaze falls to his lips. How have we not kissed since I returned home?

"Kiss me." I don't wait for his reply before standing on my tiptoes and slamming my lips to his. The instant euphoria makes my head spin. Hades slides his fingers into my hair, holding me to him and deepening the kiss. It is fucking perfect.

I pull back before I get too lost in him for any coherent thought. "Your father…" I silently curse that the slimy bastard slid through our defenses.

Hades looks less than bothered, his dark eyes fixed on my face. "We'll find him." He presses his lips to mine again, captivating me with the most incredible kiss. Every kiss is better than the last.

I moan into the kiss, letting him taste my pleasure. His tongue flicks against mine, and I move my hands to his arms, digging my nails into his armor.

Hades pulls back too soon, and his eyes stray to the palace doors. "My brothers are summoning me to the throne room." He looks back at me, carefully brushing his thumb along my cheek. "They will want to start the hunt again. I'll meet up with you."

Part of me longs to stay with him, to glue myself to him, and never be separated. Part of me feels like I should go, if not to keep stupid Zeus in line, but also to stay in the loop of their plans. A louder part of me longs to be clean. More than anything, I want to go back to our room, feel the plush rug beneath my feet, luxuriate in my own shower, and then change into my own clothes. I want to slip into the most form-fitting, shortest nightdress I own, just because I fucking can.

I slide my hand into his and walk through the palace with him until we get to the grand staircase that leads up to the bedrooms. We stop at the bottom of the stairs, and I can tell Hades is as reluctant to leave me as I am to stay. I can still see a glimmer of fear in his eyes that I'm not truly here. I lean up and brush my lips over his softly.

"I'll be in *our* room," I murmur into his lips before pulling back. Hades' eyes darken, and he looks more comfortable.

I feel him watching me as I walk up the stairs, his gaze a warm caress until I turn the corner and am out of sight.

I navigate the corridors expertly as I meander to our room, but when I reach the door, I hesitate, just standing and looking at it. What if it isn't as I remember?

I close my hand on the doorknob and take a deep breath before opening the door. Hades' scent hits me like a wall, and while it's potent, I can tell he's not been sleeping in here. The room looks untouched.

287

My eyes are drawn to the spot where I fell when my mother snapped our bond and ripped me from Hades' arms. The pain echoes within me, but I know that in time it will disappear. It only needs to be replaced with the new memories I will make with Hades.

I step across the threshold, and my weary body relaxes when I am fully immersed in the room. Part of me wishes Cerberus was here so that I am not alone. The other part is grateful for the time to decompress and reacquaint myself with my home, my room, my power, and myself. I kick my boots off and step onto the dark rug, letting my toes curl into its plush softness. My lips tug into a smile. I could spend all day here, just appreciating being here and whole again, but I am acutely aware of the mud and ichor coating my skin, and the shower beckons me. I have not felt this gross since I dreamed of Hades in the tree.

I walk into the adjoining bathroom before pulling off my armor and leggings. Shoving them in my sink, I take a moment to look at myself in the mirror. I've definitely looked better. Not only am I covered in grime and filth, but I have lost weight, and even through the gore, I can see the dark circles under my eyes. I lean in closer and smile, noticing my eyes are shimmering, filled with life and hope. No, I don't look bad. I just look fucking exhausted. The battle took its toll, but I still feel my power coursing through me. I look like a warrior queen.

I step into the shower, and I don't even attempt to hold back my moan as the hot water slides over my body. Everything aches, even muscles I didn't know I had, and the steaming water makes them shift deliciously, loosening the knots and strains.

I wash the dirt from my hair and smile as I rub in my familiar strawberry -scented shampoo. All of my toiletries at my mother's house were magnolia -scented, which is fine, but this is my preferred scent.

Following my shower, I pull on shorts and a cami top, feeling more like myself.

Hades hasn't returned to me yet, and I need to see him. I leave the comfort of our room to seek him out.

288

The doors to the throne room open as I approach, my outfit morphing into the familiar curve-hugging black dress the moment I step over the threshold. My heels elevate as four-inch pumps replace my comfortable slippers. I sigh and instinctively adjust my gait.

My annoyance at my outfit change is extinguished the second my eyes land on Hades in his exquisite suit. It seems his outfit also changed when he entered the throne room. He's sitting on his throne, his legs wide as he slouches. While he's wearing his suit, he's removed the jacket and rolled the sleeves of his shirt up to just below his elbows. His arms are resting on the arms of the throne, but I can tell he's been running his fingers through his hair by how tousled it is. He rubs one of his hands over his face before his gaze meets mine, and he sits up a little.

"Hi." I can hear the affection in his voice, but he sounds as exhausted as I feel.

My heels click as I take the steps up to the dais. "Hi."

Hades holds his hand out for mine, and I slide my hand into his. "They're hot on his trail," he says, almost growling. He yanks me closer, pulling me into his lap, and I wrap my arms around his neck.

"My demon," I say, cupping his cheeks as he slips his hand into the slit of my dress and squeezes my thigh firmly, sure of his welcome.

"My spring," he whispers back, squeezing my thigh again.

I brush my lips over his, whispering, "I told you I would find my way back to you."

"And you did." He kisses me deeper. "My dark spring."

I smile against his lips. "My mushy demon."

Hades bites my lip. "Mushy? I've never been called mushy before."

I moan. "My sexy demon."

Hades lifts me, shifting me so I straddle him. The slit in my skirt that already tracks high up my leg rips slightly to accommodate the spread of my thighs.

Hades groans at the sound, his eyes straying to the ripped fabric at my thigh.

I grin and ask, "Sexy?"

289

"Extremely," he says, trailing his fingers along the silk of my dress and following the split fabric, careful not to touch my skin. "My queen," Hades growls, and my whole body hums in awareness.

"My king," I reply, glancing at his lips.

Hades' maddening exploration continues, his fingers teasing, only ever touching the silk of my dress. "You know. It's a tragedy no one has ever fucked on these thrones," he says.

His eyes have gone black with desire, and I know mine reflect the same hunger. "We should rectify that," I say, nipping sharply at his lower lip in retaliation for his teasing.

"I agree, Queen Persephone," Hades growls.

I slam my lips to his, unable to take it any longer, unable to resist him for another moment. Hades moves his hands back to my hips and digs his fingers into my flesh, grinding my pussy against his already hard length. His claws come through for the briefest of moments, but in that time, he completely shreds the dress, leaving me naked on top of him. There is something so fucking erotic about being on top of him naked while he is fully clothed beneath me. It's definitely a vulnerable thing, but I trust him completely. I pull back, feeling my crown appear on my head, the weight pressing down softly, fitting me perfectly.

Hades looks up at me in wonder, his eyes going from my body to my face to the crown, hungrily taking it all in. "If I could have you like this every fucking day, I would," he groans, rocking me against him again. His cock throbs beneath me, and I'm cursing those fucking trousers separating us.

I slowly unbutton his shirt, keeping my gaze locked on his. "You can."

"Dance for me," Hades growls, his voice so low and commanding that I can't help but follow his instruction.

I move off his lap and step back on the dais. Music fills the room, but not the usual music that plays in here. This melody is slow, tantalizing, and sensual. I sway, and my black vines shoot from the ground. They twist around one of my calves and track up my thigh. I watch Hades as I dance

290

for him, his cock a hard bulge beneath his zipper. It takes less than a minute for Hades to get his shadows involved. They brush against my vines, following and caressing them as they curl around my hips, stomach, and chest.

His shadow hands roll my nipples between strong fingers and tangle in my hair, yanking my head back. My eyelids flutter closed, but I continue to dance for him.

Every inch of my skin feels like he is touching it, but I want his hands. I want his actual touch. My skin tingles from the sensation and the desperate desire I'm feeling for him. His sinful shadows slip between my thighs and start rubbing against my clit, in perfect rhythm with the music, and I rock my hips.

"My king," I moan, and it sounds like I'm worshiping him. He is my husband, my fated, my king, and my god.

My body trembles at the feeling of his shadows. There is not one part of my body he isn't touching. My eyes roll back and close in helpless pleasure.

I'm pulled from my stupor by his actual hand clasping my chin. "Eyes on me, Persephone." His low voice sends a shiver of pleasure through me, and I meet his gaze, panting. "You dance for me alone," Hades growls. "For your king."

Who else would I dance for?

He steps closer, his body pressed to mine. I continue to sway to the music, rubbing against him. "And you only watch me dance. Your queen."

Hades drags his thumb along my bottom lip. "Do you want your king's cock?"

"Desperately," I whisper, my whole body thrumming for him.

Hades releases me, his shadows disappearing and leaving my body aching for more.

"Bend over my throne, brace your hands on the arms," Hades growls. "I'll give you what you want. What you *need*."

I brush past him as I follow his instructions. I face his throne and bend over, placing my hands on the arms. My body trembles in anticipation, and I pant as I wait for him, straining to hear any movement. But there is no sound, only my heart racing in my chest.

291

After the longest moment I've ever experienced, I hear his steps echo in the silent room. He glides the very tips of his fingers over the swell of my ass, then lands his palm down on it hard. The crack of his hand against my ass cheek is ear-splitting in the room, but he gives me no time to recover before slamming his cock inside me. My soaking pussy is more than ready for him, yet his size always takes me off guard. There is a perfect bite of pain when he first slams into me, and my cunt slowly stretches to accommodate him.

My back arches, and I cry out. My body bathes his cock in a rush of heat, welcoming him home. Hades' moan from behind me almost completely undoes me, but I hold on, desperate for this to last for as long as possible.

Hades spanks me again. "You're dripping, Persephone. Making a mess on the floor." He growls, slamming into me again.

My hips lurch forward at the force, and I shove them back again, greedy for more of him, feeling my arousal sliding down my thighs.

"Hades!"

"Look," he growls.

I shift a little, glancing between my legs to see the mess I've made. The floor glows faintly as the evidence of my need puddled on the ground turns to diamonds embedded in the marble. Hades has forever memorialized that we fucked here, that the king took his queen against his throne.

I push my hips back, needing more, needing fucking everything. "Demon, please."

Hades snarls behind me, slamming into me harder, almost punishingly. I dig my nails into his throne, leaving scratch marks.

He spanks me again, harder this time, and the cool air stings my ass where his hand collided with my flesh.

Hades hisses, noticing the scratch marks on the throne. "Every time I sit here. I will see you like this."

I glance at him over my shoulder, moaning. "Let me ride you, my king? Then you can see me like that, too."

I shiver when he pulls out of me, but before I can mourn the loss of him, he lifts me easily and sits on his throne. He

292

arranges me on his lap, straddling him, and I eagerly drop my cunt down on his length. Even that brief pause of not being full of him was too much.

Hades digs his fingers into my hair, bringing my lips to his and kissing me desperately. Our crowns fall off, crashing to the floor, but I barely notice, too lost in my husband.

The bond within us hums happily, excited to be reunited and this close again. Our powers seem to dance with one another, complementing one another. My power stirs, and I sense one of my vines sprout. It wraps lovingly and possessively around one of his calves like he does to me with his tail. I slam my hips down on him harder, faster, my orgasm building, heat stoking low in my stomach.

Hades yanks my hair, pulling me closer and moaning against my lips, "Come for me, Persephone."

My hands tighten on his shoulders at the intimate command, and my body responds. I slam my pussy down on him one more time before pleasure overtakes my whole body. His name tears from my throat like a benediction as I come hard around his cock, my pussy contracting around him, demanding my due.

Hades roars in triumphant release, and our powers explode from us, finally joined once again. Shadows and flowers fill the space and litter the floor of the throne room.

I pant, pressing my forehead to his, still slowly rocking my hips, taking and giving every last ounce of pleasure I can.

"I love you," Hades pants, closing his eyes.

"I love you so much," I reply, tilting my head to press my lips to his. "Fuck, I missed you."

"I ached for you. Every single second," Hades whispers against my lips, cradling me close against his chest.

I pull back, looking into his eyes. "We will never be apart again. Ever."

"Never," Hades agrees, running his fingers through my hair. "Fate has to finally let us be. It owes us."

I exhale and smile at him, sending up a small prayer.

Fate, you put us together. Let us be.

293

Chapter Sixty-One

Hades

IWANT TO BELIEVE THAT FATE WILL LEAVE US **BE,** that we have bled enough, have given enough to have earned some peace. Careful to only draw on my power, I wrap the shadows around us and deposit us in our bed.

Our bed.

She smothers me in kisses, pressing her lips to every inch of my face. My cheeks hurt from smiling, from the love she has for me, the love I have for her, and for the love we share.

I pause for a moment, the emotions of the battle hitting me as the adrenaline finally dissipates. Rage, sorrow, pain, and regret slam into me all at once.

"My spring?" I whisper, stroking her hair back.

"Hm?" she asks, biting my jaw affectionately.

"It's all right to miss what she could have been."

She tenses against me, her eyes flickering with vulnerability. I know I am the only one she shows this side of herself.

"As we fought... I found myself wishing he was different, too," I admit. That was the thing. No matter how cruel or evil my father is, there will always be a part of me that wishes he was different. That small boy wishing for his father to love him would always wonder if I were different, would he have been too?

She nods and cuddles closer. "She apologized at the end. But I know she wouldn't have done anything differently when she was alive."

294

I stroke her hair as I listen, her breath gently brushing my chest as she speaks.

"Before Kronos took me, there was a moment that I thought she was reflecting." She draws on my chest with her fingers. "Yet, when I said I had my memory back, she admitted she would continue to have it erased over and over. Only after being killed did she finally see the error in her ways, and even then, I am not sure she regretted her actions."

A tear hits my chest, shed for the mother she despised and for the mother she should have had.

"I saw something when we were fighting." I keep stroking her hair. "This boy was soaring above us with white and black wings. He looked down at me with your eyes. Then I blinked, and he was gone."

She looks up at me, her brow furrowed.

"We haven't talked about it... about kids," I add, scanning her face, trying to read her. "About the future." She watches me, and my heart races. "What future do you dream of, my spring?"

She puts her chin on my chest, gazing at me. "An eternity of you."

My lips twitch. Fuck, I love her. "That I can certainly arrange."

"You?"

"You, me, and the dog," I cup her cheek softly. "Till the end."

She searches my eyes, looking for something, those eyes clear of any lingering marks of Gaia's power. "You don't want kids?"

I mull over the idea in my head. That boy I saw soaring above the battlefield was so clear. Was it one of the other timelines flashing through as my father tried to bring them to us? Or was it a vision of the future I wanted and the son we'd have one day?

"Do you want them?"

She shrugs. "I might. In the future."

I stroke her cheek with my thumb, watching her eyes and trying to read her thoughts. I know she's considering

295

the idea of children… children with me. Can she see him as clearly as I did? A boy with feathered wings, the arches black but fading to white at the primaries.

She shifts to look into my eyes, the serious nature of the conversation settling over us. Our future is hanging in the balance.

"So… you're not saying for sure you don't?" she asks, her voice hesitant.

I press my forehead to hers. "I haven't in the past," I admit. "But… I could in the future."

She presses her lips to mine. "Why not in the past?"

Where to start?

"I don't think I'll be a good father," I whisper, nuzzling her nose, saying the deep fear out loud. How could I be a good father? What example do I have?

"I think you're wrong," she says, her brow furrowing stubbornly, her voice full of the confidence and surety I lack. "You're an incredible husband and an incredible father to Berry." She makes it sound so simple.

"My brothers aren't good fathers." I stroke her cheek. If it were just Zeus, I could dismiss it as Zeus being who he is, but Poseidon is, at best, an absent parent. It's in my genes.

"They're not good husbands either," she scoffs, kissing me hard as if proving a point.

"I could be a bad husband. We haven't exactly had an easy time."

She laughs. "You couldn't be a bad husband, ever."

I tilt my head, raising a brow at her. "How do you know?"

She tunnels her fingers into my hair, forcing my eyes to hers. "Because I know you, Hades Plutus. Our very souls are joined."

My chest aches at the way she leaves no room for doubt. Her faith and confidence in me is humbling.

"For now, it's just you, me, and the dog," I whisper, pressing my lips to hers. "I love you."

She presses her body against me more insistently. "I missed you."

I groan, my cock already stirring. "And I missed you too."

296

Chapter Sixty-Two

Persephone

I **MISSED HIM SO MUCH, BUT IT'S ALMOST LIKE I COULDN'T** comprehend how much until this moment. If he weren't lying right beside me, I swear I would die from longing for him. My body is so aware of him, every single place it meets his. This has always been the case, but the ache has never been so keen as it feels now. I look at him, his sapphire eyes gazing back at me. I can't stop myself from touching him, kissing him. Gods. I'm obsessed.

I press my lips to his, my hand wandering down his body and wrapping around his already hard cock. I squeeze and nuzzle against his neck.

He groans and arches into my touch. "You need me again, my spring?"

"Well, it's just that we were apart for so long." I squeeze his cock again. "And now we're back in our bed, and I—"

Hades rolls on top of me, his hands grabbing my thighs and pulling them up. I bend my knees at his hips, opening myself for him. He shifts, positioning his cock so the underside is pressed against me, the tip rubbing against my clit with every slow thrust.

I slide my hands under his shirt and drag my nails down his back, meeting his rhythm and rocking my hips with him. I tilt them slightly, trying to position him, needing him to push inside me, but he continues to just rub against me.

297

I'm vaguely aware of the state of things outside the palace, of the work that needs to be done, but we deserve this reunion after everything we've been through.

"Fuck," I curse, moaning into his lips.

Hades bites my lip, and he moves his hands to grab my wrists, pinning them above my head. "You need to be fucked?"

I look up at him, panting. "Yes, please."

Hades moans, looking down at me. "I ached for you."

My pussy throbs, and I lift my hips again, needing him inside me. He finally gives me what I need, tilting his hips and thrusting inside me, slamming his cock in to the hilt.

"My fucking wife," he growls.

"Husband," I moan and arch beneath him. "Mine." I look up at him, my heart swelling at the sight of him above me. There is so much pleasure and love in his expression. "Marry me, Hades?" I ask.

He doesn't slow his thrusts, but something in his gaze changes, showing surprise and elation. He smiles and kisses me hard. "Yes. Officially."

I smile against his lips, moaning as I deepen the kiss.

"I need to be tied to you in every conceivable way. My wife. My queen." Hades growls into me, the words filling my body with such a deep sense of belonging and love.

Hades bucks his hips harder, faster. He needs more, just like I do. I need to feel him in my soul, and finally, I do.

Hades releases my wrists and grabs the headboard, the leverage allowing him to thrust into me harder. I dig my nails into his sides and lift my hips in time with his thrusts, taking him deeper inside me. My pussy drenches his cock as he slams into me over and over.

"Hades! I love you!"

Hades locks his gaze with mine, and we both come at the same time, our shouts of pleasure filling the room. I keep my nails embedded in his sides, moaning at the feeling of him filling me. He slows his thrusts, giving me every last drop of his cum. He looks down at me for a long moment before collapsing on top of me, his full weight crushing me, and fuck, I've never felt safer. I pant, kissing along his neck

298

and jaw, anywhere I can reach.

He groans. "Can't move. You killed me."

I laugh, nuzzling into him and biting his neck. Hades growls, the vibrations from his chest making me shiver. He rolls, pulling me with him so I'm sprawled on top of him.

"Fuck, being back in our bed is—"

Hades nuzzles the top of my head. "I haven't slept here since you were taken."

I press a soft kiss to his shoulder. "I know, baby."

He sighs contentedly beneath me. "I wonder what I will dream of tonight now that I don't have to dreamwalk."

"Probably still me. You're kinda obsessed with me." I smirk, pulling back to bite his earlobe.

He laughs, and it's such a joyful sound that I can't help but join in. "Are you saying it's not mutual?"

I nip playfully at his jaw. "That's definitely not what I'm saying."

"Then what are you saying, hm?" Hades pinches my ass hard, making me yelp. "Menace."

I brush my lips over his, teasing him. "That you'll definitely dream of me, and it'll probably be a dirty dream. But now, when you wake up tomorrow morning, hard and desperate for me, maybe we can reenact it."

His eyes darken. "Is that right?"

I nod and kiss him. "So better make it extra dirty."

"Oh, my spring, my menace. You have no idea how filthy my dreams of you get." He smirks wickedly, and my core pulses in response.

I slowly drag my nails down his chest. "Oh?"

"You'll have to wait to find out."

Fucker. I fucking love playful, flirty Hades. I kiss him deeply. When I pull back, his lips chase mine, but I don't allow him to catch them. Two can play at this game.

We shift, getting more comfortable, suddenly hit by a wall of exhaustion. I've been running on desire and adrenaline, but now that I'm sated and safe in my mate's arms, I feel sleep tugging at me, lulling me into it. I nuzzle into his neck, inhaling his scent, and my eyes droop closed.

"Love you, my Hades," I manage to get out before I drop

299

off into unconsciousness.

Chapter Sixty-Three
Hades

FALLING ASLEEP FEELS ALMOST ODD. I'm not drifting off to see her. I'm actually trying to rest. Fuck. When was the last time I actually rested? It feels like years, centuries even. I know there's still so much to do. My father is still at large, yet at the moment, with Persephone in my arms, I think things might just work out.

I smile and kiss her softly before finally closing my eyes and drifting off.

I expected to be in our meadow, to see Persephone again, our dreams linked because our bond has been renewed. What I did not expect was to once again be in front of the Fates of all the Pantheons.

I groan. "What now?"

"Wow, ungrateful," Atropos snaps, crossing her arms over her chest.

I glare at her and perform a mocking bow. "How might I serve the Fates?"

"You think to mock our summoning, boy?" Orunmila, the Orisha of Destiny from the Yoruba, hisses.

My jaw ticks. "I mock that you have anything to offer me other than cryptic warnings."

Orunmila's dark eyes narrow on me, and he steps closer as if to intimidate me, but I don't falter. If anything, I stand straighter. I am done bowing to Fate.

Skuld, the Norn of the Future from the Norse Pantheon, holds up her hand, stopping Orunmila. "This is not why we are here."

I cross my arms, glaring down the Gods of Fate. "Yes, do inform me. Why are you once again intruding on my dream?"

Orunmila growls but bites his tongue, gesturing to Atropos. She pauses as even more Gods of Destiny arrive, surrounding me in the dream. "The Destroyer of Worlds," Atropos whispers, watching my reaction.

The dream shakes as the Primordial power, the heart of darkness from which all shadows spring, awakens. The gods look at each other nervously. "Destiny. Fate. Future. I don't care," I warn. "Choose your next words carefully when you mention my wife."

Atropos shakes her head, holding up her hands in supplication. "You misunderstand. We are not threatening your queen."

The dream slowly steadies, though the gods don't look any more relaxed.

"Then why bring her up?"

"We need to discuss the role she will play in the upcoming conflict," Atropos answers.

Even inside the dream, I feel my body respond. It tenses, and every muscle locks down on bone.

"Let me make this perfectly clear. Any ideas or plans you're spinning around Persephone and me are done. We are not puppets to be strung along at your will. We have given enough, endured enough, and now we get the happiness and peace we deserve."

"You think to order us?" Hesmut asks, astonished. "The Gods of Fate?"

"Yes, I do," I snap, the dream around us flickering. The Primordial power rouses further, responding to my anger and frustration. "I am not a boy or a soldier. I am a king, and the only reason you would summon me here is because you need something from me."

A heavy silence falls, and I keep my eyes on Atropos. She may not be the oldest god present, but of all of them here, she has the most experience with me, and she will know to weigh my words

302

carefully.

I bow mockingly again. "Now, if you don't mind, I'll be returning to my dream."

The Anunnaki, the Mesopotamian Deities of Fate, watch me, their faces curled with annoyance. I know what they see. I'm a young god acting like I have control over my destiny, over my fate. All the gods older than my pantheon give me the same look before they vanish from my dream one by one, leaving only Atropos and me.

"You used to be so diplomatic." Atropos hums. "You've changed."

I laugh hoarsely. "You could say that."

"They will not be happy with your willfulness."

I nod. "I don't care, so long as they need me for whatever reason, they'll work on my terms."

Atropos scans the lines etched into my face, searching for something. She won't find whatever she's looking for. I've set fire to the person I used to be and rebuilt myself from the ashes.

"You've made enemies of them," Atropos adds. "They will lash out."

"I..." My voice trails off, and I touch my throat. "I..."

"What is it?" Atropos frowns and steps closer.

My eyes shoot open, and I summon a weapon to my hand, but it's too late. My father grabs me by the throat and squeezes, lifting me from the bed and off the ground. Persephone and Cerberus jolt awake. We were all too exhausted from the battle to be properly on guard, and he took advantage of that.

"Hades!" Persephone shouts.

I claw at my father's hand on my throat, unable to breathe enough to focus my shadows. I feel my life slipping from me. Cerberus lunges at my father, but Kronos sweeps his arm out, throwing him against the wall. The three-headed dog hits with a bone-shattering crack and lands in a heap on the ground.

Kronos squeezes tighter, crushing my voice box before pulling me closer to his face. The madness rages in his eyes. He's lost everything and has nothing left to lose.

He smirks maniacally before hurling me out the window. I sail over the balcony, careening to the stone patio

303

below.

Chapter Sixty-four

Persephone

IFEEL THROUGH MY BOND WITH HADES THAT **HE IS** unconscious but still alive. I watch as Kronos turns his back to me and walks toward the door.

Strike one was escaping his cell in the first place, and strike two was hurting Hades. Strike three is the utter disrespect of how openly he underestimates me. I narrow my eyes at his back, and my black vines shoot from the ground, wrapping around his ankles first, then his wrist. Sharp poisonous spikes penetrate his skin, holding him there.

"Where are you going, Kronos? You just got home," I croon. "Tartarus is only a few hundred miles away, and we are both so happy to see you again."

In the flash of a thought, I summon Thanatos to watch Hades. I briefly consider that I should conserve my power, but I have no other way of contacting him right now, and I don't want to leave him defenseless.

Kronos scoffs, twisting his hand to touch the vines, trying to wilt them as he did before, but things are different now. I am back in my home, and my bond has been restored. I am no longer weakened. My vines do not wither under his touch but grow stronger, tightening their hold on him. The spines grow inside his hands and ankles, more golden leaves growing as they absorb his power. He yanks on the vines angrily, losing patience with the silly little powers of the Goddess of Spring.

I slip from the bed and move around him to face him. My lips tilt into a smirk as I watch him struggle against my hold.

"You won't be able to stop it. When I get to him, I'm going to make him scream."

I slowly walk toward him, looking at his hate-filled face. My vines slither up his legs. "That wouldn't be you threatening my king, would it?"

A spike pierces his knee, and while he holds back his grunt of pain, he stumbles a little.

"I'm your king. I am the only fucking king!" he snarls through clenched teeth, practically spitting his words at me.

I twist my hands, the spikes curling inside him. "I have one king," I smile, moving closer, "and it's certainly not you."

"You can't kill me. You are too weak and pathetic to hold this power," Kronos hisses, his face contorted into an expression of rage and pain.

I laugh and tilt my head. "You got one thing wrong, Kronos." My laughter dies. "I am not simply the Goddess of Spring."

Kronos narrows his eyes at me, and my gaze hardens. I can practically feel my power flaring in my eyes.

"I am the Goddess of Dark Spring. I am Queen of the Underworld, and..." I pause, lifting my chin, looking down at him though he towers over me, "I am your end."

His eyes glow with fury, and I can feel his power swell around me, but no matter how much power he sinks into my vines, they don't budge.

"An inconsequential bitch like you is no threat to me," he roars.

My smirk deepens, and my hands shake as I delve into my power, my vision blurring. I instinctively feel myself pulling from the Underworld, though it takes so little effort. It's as if the Underworld is eager to give me whatever I need. I open my arms, allowing the power to fill me, basking in the feeling of it rushing through every cell. My feet leave the ground, my hair billowing around me in a mysterious wind. I close my eyes and raise my chin, reveling in it. This doesn't feel like when I was hosting Gaia's power. Every scrap of this power is mine, and I have never had control over so much. It belongs to me, and it moves through me, caressing me as it does. The power drawn from the Underworld dances with my power, ebbing and flowing in tandem.

I open my eyes and look at Kronos. My vines have turned solid gold, and he looks up at me, falling to his knees. The rage in his eyes has morphed into pure, untainted fear.

"N-no. You... It can't be you," Kronos stutters out. "You're a flower goddess, unimportant and inconsequential!"

The power swells within me, levitating me higher. The cyclone increases around us, thriving off his fear. He underestimated the wrong goddess.

"I am your queen. You bow to me, and you are mine to destroy." The words come from me, but my voice sounds foreign, lower, darker, and more threatening.

My vines are now tightly wrapped around his chest, piercing him there, too. They are climbing up his throat, leaching power from him and giving it back to the Underworld, giving it to me.

"Destroyer... of... Worlds," Kronos grinds out, struggling to breathe.

I smirk at him and lift my arms, my palms facing the ceiling. "This is for my husband and everything you ever put him through. This is for my realm and the power you stole from it. This is for me and believing I am merely a *flower goddess*."

I watch as he hyperventilates, struggling to pull in any air, but I don't let him. My vines squeeze him tighter, traveling up his cheeks, and I groan as more power floods me. I throw my head back and release it all.

His scream shatters the windows, sending shards of broken glass flying everywhere. I barely feel it as it slices my skin. Kronos shatters into oblivion, and I lift my head again, looking at the space he used to take up. My vines still stand there, an empty shell that once held Kronos. I smile weakly, and then... everything goes black.

307

Something warm and wet drags along my face, and my brows furrow at the feeling. It happens again, and then something cold and wet nudges against my cheek, whimpering. My eyes fly open, and I blink to see two of Cerberus's heads panting down at me, his hot breath fanning over my face. I groan, pushing him back slightly as I sit up, my head pounding a little.

"Berry, Mama is okay."

He whines, nudging me with his nose again and then looking down at his front left paw. It is hanging awkwardly and at a strange angle. My eyes go wide, and I look up at him, slowly reaching for the paw.

"What happened?"

Berry barks loudly, and I can hear the pain in it. He whines, nuzzling into me, needing comfort. I kiss his nose and try to reach for the paw again. Berry turns, wanting me to follow him, but he's limping.

"Cerberus." I make my voice stern. "We are not going anywhere until I fix that leg."

Cerberus sighs and limps back to me, holding it out. He turns his head and closes his eyes as if he doesn't want to see what's about to happen. He is such a big baby.

I brush my fingers over his paw, and using some of the residual power from the Underworld, I heal it. There's a nasty snap, and then it's instantly better. Berry glances at his paw and then at me. He licks my face again, his large tongue almost spanning my full face.

I laugh and push him away. He spins happily, the ground shaking beneath his enthusiasm. I laugh again, moving a little out of his way. I turn toward the door and meet the stunned sapphire blue eyes of my mate.

Chapter Sixty-Five
Hades

I **GROAN AS I COME TO ON THE COLD STONE BE-NEATH THE BALCONY.** My skull cracked when I landed, remnants of my brain staining the ground around me in a macabre halo. I touch the side of my skull, my regeneration knitting me back together.

Persephone!

I stumble to my feet, my mind still too scrambled to shadow up the stairs. I support myself on the wall, struggling up each step. Kronos must be desperate to attack us like this. This is a last-resort kind of interaction, not a carefully executed plan. Which just makes him all the more dangerous. I slam my shoulder against the door, breaking it open, ready to fight.

Instead, my breath catches. Persephone is hovering about two feet off the ground. Her hair has turned black and is floating around her head. Her lips are blood-red, and even her eyes have turned black. The script that usually decorates her body in this form, moving over it in a hypnotic symphony, has changed. Now, the words are warnings of crossing the person they mark and what happens when the power is awakened.

Destroyer of Worlds. This is the being the Fates whispered of. The one they hoped to use for their own purposes and plans. Darkness slithers through her veins as she feeds her power into Kronos, summoning the Primordial power contained within the Underworld. It's not just the power that springs from the remains of Tartarus. She summons all

309

Primordial power within our realm, including mine.

I drop to one knee as she drains me, funneling the power into my father. She rips open the Underworld beneath him and sends Kronos into the depths of the Void. The Underworld fluctuates as it absorbs my father's power. It doesn't send it to Persephone or me, obeying its queen. Persephone is the physical manifestation of Primordial power. She *is* the Underworld, not merely ruling over it, and that is all her own ability.

Destroyer of Worlds. The Gods of Fates' words ring in my head.

Persephone didn't just imprison Kronos. She decimated him. The Void opened and consumed him. He is gone, truly and completely gone.

I struggle to remain conscious as Persephone collapses, much less summon the strength to go to her. Her body changes back to her glamoured version, and Cerberus limps to her side, licking her face and waking her up. I am frozen there, unable to move the entire time, feeling completely helpless.

Cerberus starts toward me, but Persephone calls him back when she sees the limp. I struggle to sit up, pushing myself to my feet as she heals him, and he dances around her in relief and happiness.

Persephone laughs, and her eyes flicker toward the door, a look of uncertainty lingering there. Her body is still glowing with remnants of her power. "Hades?"

I limp over to her, cupping her cheeks. "Are you all right?"

She gazes up at me, and I watch as any lingering remnants of that absolutely awesome power inside her fades.

Dark Spring. Iron Queen.

I press my forehead to hers. "How? You don't have Gaia's powers anymore."

Does she realize the truth? Does she see what I see? Does she understand the implications of everything she just did? I had scoffed at the Gods of Destiny, insisting that they would have nothing from us and that we were in control of our own fate. *Fuck.*

"I... the Underworld..." she whispers.

I shake my head. "You are connected to the Underworld, yes, but that was not... You *became* the Underworld."

She became a physical manifestation of the Underworld, like Helios being the physical manifestation of the Sun, but Persephone is the manifestation of a mystical realm of the dead. A realm that contains the decaying corpse of a Primordial, and now Persephone has the ability to harness that Primordial's power for her own purposes.

Fuck.

"I've been connected to it since I came down here," she whispers, trying to understand and adjust, rationalize what just happened.

"But you've never transformed like that before."

She pulls back, studying my eyes. "I drew from the realm, but it was like... I was drawing from a well of my own power, just a part I've never delved into before."

"Destroyer of Worlds." I smile softly at her. "That's what the Fates called you. Destroyer of Worlds."

She smiles back at me, her eyes shining. "Why are you not kissing me?"

What a fucking good question. I press my lips to hers and put my hands on her hips, lifting her and spinning with her. She can destroy any world, any life, so long as it ends like this. With her and me, together.

Chapter Sixty-Six

Persephone

IT'S BEEN TWO DAYS SINCE THE BATTLE, SINCE I **ENDED KRONOS**, and the night I ended Kronos. To say they've been complete bliss would be the biggest understatement ever. Hades and I have spent the days repairing the Underworld, reassuring the dwelling souls, and reinforcing the prison again. We've spent the nights reacquainting with each other. I'm not sure I've ever slept less or been happier, and while it's been a chaotic few days, the next few are reserved for planning our wedding. We decided we didn't want to wait any longer.

I wait in the library for Mellie to arrive, excited to see my best friend again after so long. I understand why Helios is keeping her away, wanting to keep her safe, and I bet she made his life hell for it. Truthfully, I'm glad she was safe. I hope in time, she comes to be comfortable in the Underworld. Hades explained that he offered them both safety here, to live in peace, but I know Mellie doesn't want that, not yet anyway.

There is a subtle shift in the Underworld, informing me of her arrival a fraction of a second before her ear-splitting howl. Her screams and the pounding of her footsteps echo down the corridor. I barely have time to consider how long I have before her attack when she tackles me, taking me to the ground.

"You're here!" she screeches, hugging me tightly.

I laugh, hugging her back. "Ow! Mellie!"

She pulls back, grinning. Her scars are still present, but there's something about how she glows that makes them less visible. "Oh, my gods! I have missed you so fucking much! Hades is so boring, and he gives the *worst* advice," she says, standing and yanking me up with her.

"Oh, he's not that bad." I laugh and sit on the couch.

Mellie rolls her eyes. "It's his fault that Helios and I keep fucking."

I bite my lip to stop my smile. "Right."

Mellie crosses her arms, pouting a little. "It is."

"Mel..." I give her a knowing look. "You may be able to get away with that shit with Hades, but you know I can read you like a book."

She glares at me. "Maybe I didn't miss you after all." But her lips twitch as she gives me her death stare.

"Listen, I get it." I hold my hands up. "You remember how it was at the start of Hades and me?"

Mellie thinks for a moment. "This isn't like that. Helios is just the worst. You don't even know."

I lift an eyebrow.

"I mean, Hades is also the worst, but Helios is like—"

"He loves you," I interrupt. Mellie's face turns mutinous, but after a moment, it falters into something more vulnerable.

"How do you know?" she asks me, her eyes searching mine.

"That Helios loves you? He told me."

Mellie shakes her head. "How do you know Hades loves you exactly as you are and won't try to change you down the line? And that Helios..." she trails off.

I take her hand. "Truthfully, it's extremely hard, but it is something I can thank my mother for. I've experienced love where the person loves the *idea* of me, and I've experienced *true* love." I squeeze her hand, waiting for her to meet my gaze again. "Helios sees you, Mellie. It's obvious to everyone but you. The question you need to ask yourself is, does he *love* you, or does he love who you could be?"

"He always tells me not to go anywhere he can't follow." A tear slides down her cheek. "What a fucking idiot. Right?"

I shrug. "We're all idiots when we're in love, and that idiot would follow you into the depths of madness, just so you're not alone there."

Mellie looks away thoughtfully, another tear falling. She brushes it off after a moment and looks at me. I notice that while I can still see the inner madness behind her eyes, they've never looked so clear.

"I missed you," she admits.

"I missed you too." I squeeze her hand again. "And I have a very important question to ask you."

Mellie groans. "No, I won't be your third. Hades is gross, and he's also like my father."

I roll my eyes. "Not what I was going to ask."

Mellie brightens. "You need butt plug recommendations?"

I blink, then burst out laughing. "As fun as this guessing game is, why don't I just ask you?"

Mellie shrugs. "Boring, but whatever."

"Will you be my maid of honor?"

Mellie's eyes go wide, and then she narrows them. "Do I have to wear pastels?"

I shake my head, and she squeals, lunging at me again. "Yes! Of course, I will!"

I hug her, thrilled to have my best friend back. I know that while it may take some time, she and Helios are going to be okay.

Mellie and I set about planning the wedding, and at the end of it, I call Aphrodite to ask her if she will design the dresses for the event.

Chapter Sixty-Seven

Hades

I **FIDDLE WITH THE CUFFS OF MY SUIT,** cursing when I can't get them right. It slips again, and I am about to summon my shadows and let them do it for me when a slightly amused voice calls from the doorway.

"It almost looks like you're nervous."

I frown as I turn to catch sight of Eros. He is leaning against the doorframe, the arrow he is twirling through his fingers a golden blur.

My eyes narrow. "I don't recall you having an invitation to the Underworld."

Eros's lips twitch into a knowing smile. "Love finds a way."

I grind my teeth. Of course, Eros has a way to slip past any defenses. Anywhere there is love, there is Eros. He is such a fucking pain in my ass. I give up on the cuff for the moment and lower my hands, taking in the younger god. He is... *dirty.* I can't remember ever seeing the God of Love looking anything other than immaculate. From his hair to his clothes, he is always pristine, but now, his eyes are a little tired, the sky-blue tinged with exhaustion, and what looks like dirt is smeared on his neck.

Eros straightens, catching the arrow and tucking it back into his quiver. His golden bow is still slung on his back. That is the other thing about the God of Love that perplexes me. He is always armed. He turns away from me, and there's a tug in my chest. My eyes lock on the newest arrows in his quiver, midnight black ones with unique fletching. Something is calling to me. No, not to me, to my power.

My breath catches when I realize these are Void arrows. I reach out to take one from Eros's quiver, but he spins on his heel, catching my hand before I can touch it. His eyes are cold. Instead of the warm blue of the sky, they're the frigid cold of deep ice.

He stares at me, and the truth settles on my shoulders. Unease ripples through me, and I whisper, "You're the emissary. The one that the Gods of Destiny spoke of."

Eros's eyes flash before the irreverent mask settles over his face again. "You must be more nervous than I thought if you're inventing things like that."

I narrow my eyes on him. "Why are you here, Eros?"

Eros smiles, but it's forced. "To give my blessing, of course."

I blink, then blink again. "I… Thank you," I grit out, "for buying Persephone time. I am in your debt."

"The God of the Dead in my debt. How fortuitous," Eros hums, glancing around.

"Your mother gave her blessing," I say, watching him carefully. "You didn't have to come to give it yourself."

"Didn't I?"

A knock on the door draws my attention, and I look away for only a second. "One second!" I call out.

I turn back to face Eros, frowning when I see the God of Love has vanished, leaving a single white feather on the ground behind. I glare at the feather. Why did it feel like the conversation we just had was not the conversation we *truly* had? It's as if each word was laden with implication, a secret meaning I was unaware of, a code only Eros knew.

"Come in!" I shout to the door, unsurprised when the Titan of the Sun stands there. He is still glowing. He has been glowing since the end of the battle, and it gets brighter whenever Melinoë is within his reach. Sometimes, the glow of his skin becomes almost blinding.

Helios glides forward and fixes my cufflinks for me. "You're not ready yet?"

"I was getting ready," I growl.

Helios snickers. "You getting cold feet?"

I yank my cuffs away from him, summoning my shadows to fix the cufflinks. "Of course not. I was speaking with Eros."

Helios looks around the empty room, raising a skeptical brow. "You were?"

Fuck. I sound insane.

"I'm surprised you came to check on me. I expected you to be holed up somewhere with my adopted daughter, doing... whatever it is you two do."

Helios smiles slowly. "She wanted time to catch up with P, plus it gives me the opportunity to get you alone."

I pick up my suit coat and pull it on. "I miss the days you were scared to be in the same room as me."

Helios laughs and looks in the mirror, making sure his own suit is in line. "I'm going to marry her."

My brain stops functioning for a moment. He *cannot* be talking about Melinoë. Melinoë and marriage? The only thing the Goddess of Nightmares is married to is carnage.

"She'll say no," I say, not to be cruel, but honest.

"The first time, definitely," Helios says. "I think around the fiftieth time, I'll have worn her down, and by the ninety-fifth time, she'll say yes."

That kind of determination is teetering on insanity.

"You're confident that she truly cares for you?"

Helios pulls out his phone and clicks on a video. I hear Melinoë's voice come through the speakers.

Yes, I said I love you. Can you stop asking me to repeat it? she snaps.

Helios turns off the video. "See? Proof."

"Should I even ask how or why you have that on video?"

Helios laughs and starts toward the door. "Definitely not. Let me go make sure everything is set up. Can't keep the wedding postponed."

Postponed?

Helios leaves the guest room, and once again, I'm alone. I rub my arm, the Primordial power still present in my body. Erebus sacrificed all his power to resurrect me and give us a fighting chance in the battle. Yet, when I tried to contact the two Primordials, they ignored my calls. I didn't go see them or force their summoning. I didn't want to be away from

317

Persephone for that long.

How much longer do I have to wait to marry her?

Chapter Sixty-Eight

Hades

A KNOCK SOUNDS ON THE DOOR BEFORE IT CREAKS OPEN. "Yo, demon daddy, you ready?"

I take one last look in the mirror, rubbing my hand down my suit. The formal black is emblazoned with silver skulls and vines around the collar and wrists. I glance over at Mellie. "I am. She's... she's ready? Can I see her?"

This short separation has been awful. Being apart feels unnatural. We spent so much time in forced separation that even a minute more we don't need to endure is unbearable.

Melinoë leans against the door frame. "You're terrible at this, my dude. You're not allowed to see her until she's walking down the aisle."

Traditions? Fuck traditions. I cross my arms, frowning at her. "We're not traditional."

She rolls her eyes and holds out her hand to look at her manicure. "Obviously. But you both wanted a," Mellie grimaces, "proper wedding. Ugh. And this is part of that. Plus, we both know you spent the night with her last night."

Well. Wait, how did she know about that?

"Well... you spent the night with Helios!" I accuse.

She gives me a dry look. "We're not talking about that ball of hot, festering plasma."

Their relationship is odd.

"That's better than calling him a cancer, I suppose," I muse.

"Fucking carcinogenic fucker," she mutters.

Very odd.

I fiddle with my cuffs. "He's planning to propose."

319

Melinoë moves in between breaths and appears in front of me, her dual-colored eyes wild.

"And you told him to shove his engagement ring up his urethra?" she demands.

His *urethra?*

"No, I didn't," I answer because who would say such a thing to another person?

Melinoë recoils, her eyes turning feral. "You traitorous mother fucker. Just because you and Persephone are all gross and in love and need to basically conjoin yourselves, doesn't mean we all are!"

"You love him," I state plainly, watching her.

"You take that back, you demonic dickhead," she hisses.

My lips twitch. She is in such denial. Is this what I looked like when I once thought to resist the pull I felt toward Persephone? "He showed me a video of you saying it to him. How touchingly sweet you can be, Melinoë."

Her jaw clicks audibly. "Oh, that UV fucker is about to get disemboweled." She whirls on her heel and storms out of the room, no doubt to make good on her threat against the Titan of the Sun.

Without her standing guard, I stride toward the throne room, hoping to catch a glimpse of Persephone. I mask my disappointment at only seeing Hera standing at the dais. She is clad in a stark ivory sheath, and her blonde hair is pulled into a neat chignon. Her nails are painted the same red as her lips.

I step onto the dais, practically buzzing with excitement.

"Look how eager you are." Hera smirks.

I shoot her a droll look. "It must be odd for you to see a husband excited to see his wife."

Her eyes flash with anger. "It won't last."

Hera can try all she likes, but unlike her husband, she'll never get under my skin. I swear Zeus only has to breathe to do so. It is his special talent.

"I said the same thing about you and Z," I volley back at her. She bristles, and I know how much she hated Zeus's infidelity, but it was not jealousy, or at least not completely. Hera found his affairs and bastard children to be *unbecom-*

ing. She despised that he failed to take his reputation and image seriously. He is the King of Gods and refuses to act as such.

I look away as Helios approaches and makes his way up the dais to stand at my side. He is sporting a new black eye, but his skin is still glowing. The black eye doesn't do anything to diminish the happy smirk on his face. I suppose I should have asked Poseidon or Zeus to stand at my side for the ceremony, but there is something about Helios being there that simply makes sense. I can depend on his reactions. He wouldn't dare to upset Persephone and, by extension, Melinoë. I couldn't say the same with any certainty when it comes to my brothers.

Music swells, a haunting, beautiful melody in the throne room, and I straighten more, clasping my hands in front of me. It felt odd to have them just sitting at my side while I waited for Persephone.

The doors open, revealing Cerberus, adorned in black bow ties on each of his necks. He trots happily down the aisle, his injury already healed from the skirmish with my father. His middle head holds a black velvet pillow with two onyx rings tied to it.

"Good boy," I praise, as I take the rings from him and hand them to Helios to hold.

Melinoë comes next, wearing a deep purple dress with a slit to her thigh, her heavy black boots peeking from beneath the hem as she walks. Her scars are pale, yet she wears them confidently and without hesitation, comfortable in her own skin.

Helios whistles at Melinoë. She meets his eyes, fire sparking in the mismatched depths of hers. She keeps up the glare until she steps up to the other side of the dais and looks back down the aisle, waiting for the doors to open.

There's a long moment as I wait for Persephone. Where is she? She didn't change her mind, did she?

Her scent hits me first. That perfect rose within a dense fog. I close my eyes and inhale deeply.

My queen.

My spring.

My home.

Chapter Sixty-Nine

Persephone

APHRODITE COMPLETELY KILLED IT WITH MY **DRESS.** I had asked for something non-traditional, not wanting to be married in virginal white.

Nothing about Hades and I has been traditional, and it didn't seem right to be walking down the black marble aisle in a poofy cream wedding dress. Besides, being the Goddess of Spring, everyone would expect me to wear a pretty floral wedding dress, but I am not simply the Goddess of Spring. I am the Goddess of Dark Spring, and I am Queen of the Underworld. There is as much darkness in me as there is light. I've spent most of my life catering to one. It is time to embrace the other.

Aphrodite got back to me less than twenty-four hours later with a single design, and she had knocked it right out of the park.

I knew it was right the first time I laid eyes on the gown. It is pure onyx black. The corset top perfectly hugs my curves and is imbued with small diamonds and rubies. The silk skirt then bustles out a little from my hips, leading into the most ornate train I've ever seen. A delicate lace panel lays over the silk train. My favorite thing about the skirt is the small, perfectly embroidered skulls, roses, and vines. It is the perfect way to represent us both with the dress.

Mellie's dress is just as perfect as mine. The deep purple silk fits her perfectly, and the second she saw it, she was already considering what Dr. Martens to pair with it.

It's funny to think that was only last week. In the space of seven days, we have put together a wedding, something small, intimate, and romantic.

I look at myself in the mirror. My hair is half up, my black and gold vines holding it secure. I've kept my makeup simple save for my red lips and black kohl lining my eyes. I am every bit dark spring, every bit the Queen of the Underworld, every bit the rose with a bite.

I skim my fingers over the silk of my skirt, taking a moment to reflect and think about all the decisions that led me to this moment.

Everything has been an uphill battle. We have had to fight every step of the way, and I take a moment to curse myself for being one of the roadblocks. I let my fear overrule my instincts and pushed back against fate, thinking I would win. My only excuse is that I was young and new to autonomy. Now, here we are, and I wouldn't change a fucking moment.

There's a soft knock at my door, and I glance at it in the mirror. "Come in," I call, expecting Mellie.

Helios pops his head inside and smiles at me through my reflection. "She's gone to make sure Hades hasn't done a runner."

Helios looks slightly disappointed before stepping into the room. "You look stunning, petal."

I turn to face him, smiling so brightly that my cheeks ache. "Thank you, Helios."

He sighs and leans against the door, but his lips pull into a cocky smile. "You know, in exactly five years, three months, and two days, it'll be my hellcat in the wedding dress."

I lift an eyebrow. "Is that right?"

Helios's smirk deepens. "Absolutely."

"And do you plan to drug her to get her up there?"

He laughs. "Persephone, she'll practically be crawling up the aisle to bind herself to me."

I roll my eyes. "We'll see."

"She loves me, you know," he says, completely at ease.

324

I laugh. "I know." I tilt my head. "Has she said it yet?"

Helios grins. "Yes."

Shock makes my eyes go wide. "On purpose?"

Helios wiggles his eyebrows. "Sort of."

I walk to the door and place my hand on his arm. "You have the patience of a saint." I squeeze his arm. "Thank you for loving my best friend like she deserves."

Helios covers my hand. "She makes it easy."

I smile at him. "If you'll excuse me, I have a rather important appointment to get to."

He pushes off the wall. "I better get to the altar. I'm the best man!"

I roll my eyes. "The best man and the maid of honor is such a tired cliche."

Helios grins and opens the door.

"Helios?" He stops in his tracks, glancing at me over his shoulder. "There are unlimited bedrooms in this palace. If I find out that you and Mellie have had crazy, weird, stabby sex in mine, I'll sic Berry on you."

He laughs and winks at me before he continues on his way.

I check my makeup and hair in the mirror once more before heading toward the throne room. The walk barely takes any time at all, and before I know it, I see Mellie standing outside the throne room, wearing her deep purple gown. She's pacing nervously, no doubt anxious about seeing Helios in such an intimate setting.

"Mel. Are you good?"

She stops pacing and looks at me, her eyes wide as she takes in my gown. She's seen it before, but not when I'm all dressed up and ready to marry the love of my life.

"P, you look..." She thinks for a moment before her lips twitch, "like a rose with a bite."

I grin and pull her into a hug. "Love you, Mel."

"Love you too, P." She pulls back, bracing her hands on my upper arms and looking at me gravely. "Okay, I have to ask you this as your best friend."

"No, I don't want butt plug recommendations."

Mellie gives me a look. "Are you sure you want to marry Hades? He's like super boring, and I've been told he doesn't even stab you."

My lips twitch. "I'm more than sure."

Mellie grins. "Then let's get you hitched to demon daddy, spring mommy."

"Okay, let's nip that in the bud." I laugh.

The music swells from within the room, and Mellie winks at me. "That's my cue!"

The doors open as if by magic, and Mellie walks down the aisle. Even from here, I can see Helios's eyes darken as he watches her move toward him.

My heart flutters, and I close my eyes, taking a breath. It's my turn.

I step into the doorway and start walking down the aisle. My gaze locks on Hades, and I am so captivated by his eyes that I can't even appreciate how he looks in his suit. I'm not even halfway down the aisle when Hades starts to descend the steps, trying to get to me. I watch as a silent conversation takes place between Mellie and Helios. He steps forward and grabs the back of Hades' jacket, holding him on the dais.

I glance at Mellie, who is mouthing, "I will kill you," to Helios, and my lips twitch. My eyes only stray from Hades for the briefest of moments before I need to look at him again, drawn to him like a moth to a flame.

Hades holds out his hand to me when I'm closer, and my skin tingles, already anticipating his touch. I've not seen him since early this morning, and honestly, it's been awful. I place my hand in his, and my stomach warms with rightness.

Hades yanks me to him, wrapping his arm around my back and looking down at me with such intensity my cheeks heat. "You look beautiful," he croons, stroking my back with his thumb.

I slide my hands up his powerful arms. "And you look so handsome."

Hades smiles so genuinely that my body throbs for him. He leans in to kiss me, and I push to my tiptoes, hungry for him. Our lips are just a breath apart when Mellie groans loudly.

"You are both terrible at this," she says, her voice filled with irritated despair.

I smile, biting my lips together to stop my laugh.

Hades reluctantly pulls back and looks at Hera, who I only just noticed. Her face is pulled into a bitter scowl.

"Let's make this official," Hades says with a nod, ushering Hera on.

She bristles, and I look back at Hades, smiling brightly. I can practically feel myself glowing.

"Face one another and place your left hand in Hades'.'" Hera's voice is full of spite.

It must suck to be the Goddess of Marriage when your husband is such a massive dickhead.

I look up at Hades and slip my hand into his. Hera hovers her hand over ours, and a gold rope binds our joined hands.

"Speak your vows. You first, Hades," Hera practically spits at him.

Hades doesn't seem to notice. His gaze is locked on mine, and while Hera might be venomous towards our union, this ceremony is full of love.

"For a long time, I've been utterly alone. I thought I preferred it that way until you burst into my life, filling it with so much laughter and love that my heart felt like it was overflowing. Fate may have matched us, but the choice is still ours, and I will pick you every morning, every evening, every spring, and every winter to be my wife and queen." He holds my gaze with such intensity, honesty, and devotion that my eyes sting with tears. "From now until the end."

The rope begins to glow.

"Persephone." Hera sighs.

A tear slides down my cheek as I look up at him. "Hades. Before you, I was lost in so many ways, constantly searching for something that I couldn't identify. From the time I was a little girl, there was something pulling at me. I thought it was a draw to the mortal world, and I was supposed to make it my home. I was half right. The connection wasn't to the mortal realm, but it was to my home. It was my bond to you." My voice breaks a little. "My love. My home. My husband and my king. I choose you, Hades. Yesterday, today, and tomorrow. From now until eternity."

The glow on the rope grows brighter before it dissolves into our bound hands, cementing our bond. It doesn't feel a whole lot different. The bond we already have completely obliterates me every day in the best way.

Hades wipes a stray tear from my cheek. "Hera, say I can kiss my bride now."

"You still need to do the rings, losers," Mellie chimes in, but there's emotion in her voice that I've never heard from her before.

Hades hands me the ring to put on his finger before he takes my hand again, sliding my wedding ring on. The ruby rose sparkles softly on top, and once again, my finger is bound by the comforting weight of our union.

I look down at Hades' ring. It is the same one I gave him all those weeks ago when I officially chose him. I slide it onto his finger and meet his misty-eyed gaze.

"You better kiss me now, Husband."

"You may now kiss the bride," Hera says with all the joy and enthusiasm of a funeral.

Before Hera has even finished speaking, Hades' lips are against mine in the most heartbreaking kiss I've ever experienced. I wrap my arms around his neck and press my body to his, deepening the kiss.

Husband. Mine.

He dips me over his arm, and I smile against his lips before he straightens, lifting me off the ground.

There is the slightest of shifts as Hera leaves, but I barely notice, just like I barely noticed her presence.

Hades places me down on my feet and pulls back. He looks down at me with such love, such lust.

"Mellie, Helios, don't burn the palace down, and take care of Berry," Hades says, and without waiting for a response, he wraps us in his shadows, taking us on our honeymoon.[21]

Chapter Seventy

Hades

THAT MOMENT SHE WALKED DOWN THE AISLE
TO ME will be something I'll remember with
perfect clarity no matter the millennia that pass.
I'll recall the slight blush in her cheeks, the way her gown
hugged her curves, and the design marking the duality of
her—the Goddess of Spring and Queen of the Dead. She's
both life and death, light and darkness. As am I.

For so long, I thought my abilities and my calling de-
fined me. I thought my darkness was something to be hidden away, but as Persephone vowed herself to me, I saw
myself through her eyes. Darkness might be my ability, but
it is not who I am, just as she is not solely the Goddess of
Spring. We are more than our gifts, more than what we can
give to others.

I carry her to the cliffside cabin I created, not breaking the kiss for a moment. Luckily, the cliffs of the Isle of
the Blessed are untouched by the battle that consumed the
Underworld. She moans into my mouth, keeping us fused
together.

I kick the door open, ripping the back of her gown open.
I should be careful with it. It is beautiful, and I'm sure she's
attached to the garment, but at the moment, it's between
my wife and my touch. She grabs my bow tie, yanking at it
insistently, even though we don't break the kiss.

I grunt in annoyance when her gown doesn't slide off,
appearing attached by more than just a couple of strings.
My claws shred the gown, and I growl against her lips, "This

gown... I couldn't think of anything but how it would look in tatters on the floor."

She smirks and pulls back, ripping open my shirt. "Funny... that's what I was thinking about your suit."

We fall toward the bed, even as we struggle to remove each other's clothes. Neither of us is willing to stop kissing long enough to remove our clothes completely. There's an unspoken hesitation, a sensation of doubt in our reality, and a fear that, at any moment, this peace might shatter. We couldn't bear being torn apart again.

She shoves my shirt off my shoulders and scrapes her nails against my arms. That small bit of connection is enough to reassure me, enough to remind me not to waste precious moments worrying about what might be.

I push the tattered remains of her gown off her body. "I missed you so much."

It wasn't just the time apart before the wedding or that we didn't even have a moment to truly reconnect before the battle began. It was the weeks we spent apart, only connecting in dreams, the time I spent being devoured, and when we were at odds. We wasted so much time.

She fumbles with my belt in frustration, throwing it aside once she gets it off. "Those hours were unbearable."

I help her tear my pants open, freeing my cock for her. "Every second," I agree. Every breath I took without her was torturous. From this moment on, nothing will tear me from her side. I will wind our souls around each other so tightly that there will be no separating. Not again. Never again.

"Torture," she moans against my lips.

I should take my time enjoying her body, bury my face into her cunt and suck her orgasm from her—multiple orgasms. But right now, I need to fuck her and make our bodies one. I press my lips to hers and thrust inside her without warning.

I taste the way she gasps, losing her breath as I fill her with my cock.

She arches into me, her nipples brushing against my chest. "Hades!"

I buck my hips, moving almost frantically, needing to

seal our bond permanently. If only I could fuck her in such a way that we can never be parted again. She wraps her legs around me, spurring me on with her heels, pulling me closer. She feels it, too.

Her fingers tunnel into my hair, holding me to her, sealing our lips together as her pussy pulses on me. The sounds of our labored breaths and our skin meeting as I thrust fill the bedroom, echoing off the stone walls.

I need her to take more of me. I yank her legs apart and put them on my shoulders so I can thrust deeper, making her take more until she knows nothing but how we're connected and bonded in the flesh.

Her eyes are glazed with pleasure, her nails dragging down my arms as she cries out, "Fuck!"

I pull out completely before slamming back in, making her teeth clatter and the bed shake with the force.

Persephone grabs my face, locking her eyes on mine. "My king. My husband…"

The words soothe me and keep me grounded. She's offering a light in a sea of darkness.

"My queen. My wife," I growl back to her.

She soaks my cock as I continue, never breaking eye contact with her, sharing this bond of our hearts and very souls.

"You want to come for me? For your husband?" I pant, even as I pull out completely, only to provide another brutal thrust.

Her eyes darken, and her vines tickle my calves as they grow around me.

"Please…"

"Come for me."

She screams, squeezing my cock with her orgasm. I shout as I fall into my own release almost immediately, unable to hold back when her pussy tightens like that.

This is a bond deeper than soul level, more profound than fate. It is a bond I will kill to keep in place.

Chapter Seventy-One

Persephone

I *LAY ON TOP OF HADES, MY HANDS BRACED ON HIS CHEST.* As I look up at him, he runs his fingers through my hair lovingly.

Peace.

I haven't had a chance to really look around the little cabin situated in this remote part of our realm, but I can tell it's cozy, warm, and a place that he built from his love for me.

"We're married," I whisper, my cheeks hurting from my wide smile.

Hades kisses me and then presses kisses all over my face. "Married." His voice is soft and filled with awe like he can't quite believe it either.

My heart feels like it's about to explode just looking at him. "Fuck, I love you."

Hades nuzzles his nose with mine and closes his eyes. "You're here. You're safe. You're mine."

I pull back for a moment, looking into his shimmering sapphire eyes. "Hades?"

"Yes, Persephone?" His gaze penetrates me.

"I need you to know," I cup his cheek, "I wouldn't change a thing."

His brows knit a little. "But we had so much time stolen."

I nod. "But we have an eternity. All we've been through has only deepened my love and appreciation for you."

"I will spend all of eternity proving that you made the right choice." His eyes mist with emotion.

"Oh, my Hades. You already have." I lean in, kissing him deeply, needing him to feel how much I love him. How desperately I need him.

He smiles against my lips, and I pull back, burying my face into his neck and inhaling him.

"What do you want to do on our honeymoon?" he asks, running his fingers through my hair.

"I want to do this. All day. Every day." I kiss his neck softly.

"I could definitely be amenable to that idea." Hades growls, and I lift my head, kissing him once more before we lose ourselves in each other's bodies all over again.

I wake in his arms, wrapped in his warmth and scent, unable to imagine anything more perfect than this moment. I stretch and unwrap myself from him before climbing out of bed carefully, not wanting to wake him.

In the bathroom, I wash my face and brush my teeth before pulling on Hades' shirt to explore the cabin a little. It's quaint, rustic, and sweet. Though I know Hades has only recently built it, there's something old about it. It feels lived in.

I lean against the bedroom door, watching Hades. His sleeping form has moved only slightly, his face buried in my pillow, cuddling it close. His dark hair is stark against the white linens. The sheet is draped low on his hips, just covering him. I bite my lip, noticing that he's half -hard in his sleep. My heart speeds up a little, looking at him. He's so fucking beautiful, and he's all fucking mine.

Leaving him to sleep, I head downstairs and turn on the coffee machine. The kitchen follows the design of the rest of the cabin. All the gleaming wood gives it a rustic feel, but the state-of-the-art appliances add a modern flair. The smell of brewing coffee permeates the open plan of the downstairs. Large patio windows look out over the cliff, and I can't help but go out to look out at the edge of our realm. The wind blows my hair, and I wrap my arms around myself, trying to protect myself from the bracing cold. I stand at the edge, watching the waves crashing below me. Birds soar overhead, gliding on the air currents, and I cannot wait to join them out there.

Freedom. At last.

Finally, I will have the true freedom I have always longed for. But as I think about it, I realize something at this moment. Before, I only felt free when I was flying because it was my only escape. Now, I don't need to escape. Flying will always represent freedom to me, but I will no longer be flying away. I will be flying toward my life, toward my friends, toward my husband.

Strong, perfect arms wrap around me, and I instinctively lean back into them, knowing exactly who it is. I know the feel of his embrace better than I know anything else.

"Hello, my spring." His deep voice reverberates down my spine, and heat coils low in my stomach.

"Hello, demon." I place my hands on his forearms, leaning my head back against his shoulder.

He kisses my temple, and I can feel his smile against my skin.

I will always make you happy, Hades.

I now know true peace. I now know freedom. I now know love.

I am Persephone Prosperina Plutus. Wife of Hades. Goddess of Dark Spring. Queen of the Underworld. *Destroyer of Worlds.*

Hades and I are inevitable, and we are forever.